Praise for the Novels of
#1 *New York Times* Bestselling Author

NICHOLAS SPARKS

SEE ME

"Sparks takes readers on a roller-coaster ride of emotion, from the soft tone of a love story to the adrenaline rush of a thriller."

—Associated Press

"See Me is not only a tender, engaging, and heartwarming story, but it displays the meshing of two different and opposite lives that come together to prove that love conquers all. Gripping and riveting suspense adds another layer of depth and interest."

—*New York Journal of Books*

"Powerful proof that Nicholas Sparks is a masterful storyteller who remains at the top of his game."   —Bookreporter.com

"This deeply emotional book once again proves that Sparks understands human nature and relationships as well as anyone writing today."   —BarnesandNoble.com

THE LONGEST RIDE

"Sparks is a poet...a master."   —*Philadelphia Inquirer*

"THE LONGEST RIDE is epic Sparks...It showcases the author's most accomplished work to date...There are moments of perfection...Reaching not only young and old, the novel is commingled with enough cowboy action, literary flavor, and a maturing gift for dialogue to reach across the sexes."

—*Mountain Times* (NC)

THE BEST OF ME

"A creative genius...his book is great for any love story enthusiast."
—HubPages.com

"Unforgettable...Makes you settle in for another romantic date with this well-respected and talented storyteller."
—*Fredericksburg Free Lance-Star* (VA)

"I could not put it down...a classic Nicholas Sparks tragedy but with a twist of hope...If I can pick my favorites from him, *The Best of Me* will rank with *Message in a Bottle* and *The Notebook*— it was *that* good."
—BookReporter.com

SAFE HAVEN

"A compelling love story...a gripping tale of love and survival... a riveting 'read all night' page-turner."
—BookReporter.com

"Sparks has written another wonderful love story that makes you see true love in its simplest form and believe in it...a fantastic book about relationships, love, trust, and friendships."
—BestsellersWorld.com

THE LAST SONG

"Romance, betrayal, and youthful discovery...Fans of *The Notebook, Message in a Bottle*, etc., will gobble it up."
—*Entertainment Weekly*

"A very enjoyable read...a plot that allows his characters to learn and grow from their experiences...Sparks is at his best."
—*Greensboro News-Record* (NC)

"Raw emotion, young love, family angst, and—ultimately—sweet resolution."
                                                                —*BookPage*

THE LUCKY ONE

"A tale of redemption...holds readers in suspense until the final chapter...it will test readers' beliefs in the power of destiny and fate, and how they relate to choices one makes in life."
                                        —*Chattanooga Times Free Press*

"In true Nicholas Sparks fashion, the reader is engaged from the first to last page. The characters are authentic and the plot is engrossing and emotionally charged."   —BookLoons.com

THE CHOICE

"A tender and moving love story."   —*Publishers Weekly*

"A heartrending love story...will have you entranced. And if *The Notebook* left you teary-eyed, his latest will have the same effect."   —*Myrtle Beach Sun News*

DEAR JOHN

"Beautifully moving...Has tremendous emotional depth, revealing the true meaning of unconditional love."
                                                —*RT Book Reviews*

"For Sparks, weighty matters of the day remain set pieces, furniture upon which to hang timeless tales of chaste longing and harsh fate."   —*Washington Post Book World*

"Sparks lives up to his reputation...a tribute to courageous and self-sacrificing soldiers."   —*Booklist*

"Nicholas Sparks is a top-notch writer. He has created a truly spine-tingling thriller exploring love and obsession with a kind of suspense never before experienced in his novels."

—RedBank.com

NIGHTS IN RODANTHE

"Bittersweet... romance blooms... You'll cry in spite of yourself."
—*People*

"Passionate and memorable... smooth, sensitive writing... This is a novel that can hold its own."   —Associated Press

"Extremely hard to put down... a love story, and a good love story at that."   —*Boston Herald*

A BEND IN THE ROAD

"Sweet, accessible, uplifting."   —*Publishers Weekly*

"A powerful tale of true love."   —*Booklist*

THE RESCUE

"A romantic page-turner... Sparks's fans won't be disappointed."
—*Glamour*

"All of Sparks's trademark elements—love, loss, and small-town life—are present in this terrific read."   —*Booklist*

A WALK TO REMEMBER

"An extraordinary book... touching, at times riveting... a book you won't soon forget."   —*New York Post*

"A sweet tale of young but everlasting love."

—*Chicago Sun-Times*

"Bittersweet...a tragic yet spiritual love story." —*Variety*

MESSAGE IN A BOTTLE

"The novel's unabashed emotion—and an unexpected turn—will put tears in your eyes." —*People*

"Glows with moments of tenderness...delve[s] deeply into the mysteries of eternal love." —*Cleveland Plain Dealer*

"Deeply moving, beautifully written, and extremely romantic."

—*Booklist*

THE NOTEBOOK

"Nicholas Sparks...will not let you go. His novel shines."

—*Dallas Morning News*

"Proves that good things come in small packages...a classic tale of love." —*Christian Science Monitor*

"The lyrical beauty of this touching love story...will captivate the heart of every reader and establish Nicholas Sparks as a gifted novelist." —*Denver Rocky Mountain News*

SEE ME

NICHOLAS SPARKS

SEE ME

GCP

GRAND CENTRAL
PUBLISHING

NEW YORK   BOSTON

Copyright © 2015 by Willow Holdings, Inc.

Cover design by Claire Brown

Cover photograph of beach by kc.bangkhew/ Shutterstock

Cover photograph of roses by Herman Estevez

Cover copyright © 2016 by Hachette Book Group, Inc.

Grand Central Publishing
Hachette Book Group
1290 Avenue of the Americas
New York, NY 10104
grandcentralpublishing.com
twitter.com/grandcentralpub

Originally published in hardcover and ebook by Grand Central Publishing in October 2015.
First Trade Paperback Edition: August 2016

Grand Central Publishing is a division of Hachette Book Group, Inc.
The Grand Central Publishing name and logo is a trademark of Hachette Book Group, Inc.

The publisher is not responsible for websites (or their content) that are not owned by the publisher.

The Hachette Speakers Bureau provides a wide range of authors for speaking events. To find out more, go to www.hachettespeakersbureau.com or call (866) 376-6591.

ISBNs: 978-1-4555-2062-6 (trade paperback), 978-1-4555-4365-6 (Target exclusive trade paperback), 978-1-4555-7055-3 (Walmart exclusive trade paperback)

Printed in the United States of America

RRD-C

10 9 8 7 6 5 4 3 2 1

For Jeannie Armentrout

SEE ME

PROLOGUE

He hadn't been in Wilmington for more than a day before he knew it was the kind of city he'd never settle in for good. It was too touristy, and the whole place seemed as though it had grown willy-nilly, without any planning. While the historic district had the kind of porch-fronted homes he'd anticipated, with columns and detailed wainscoting and sprawling magnolia trees in the yards, those lovely neighborhoods gradually gave way to a commercial area of strip malls, convenience stores, chain restaurants, and car dealerships. Endless traffic snaked through the district, growing even more unbearable in the summers.

But the grounds of UNC Wilmington had been a pleasant surprise. Somehow, he'd imagined a campus heavy on the ugly architecture of the sixties and seventies. There were a few of those buildings, especially at the fringes of the university, but the central quads had proved to be an oasis of sorts—shaded walkways and manicured lawns, the Georgian columns and brick façades of Hoggard and Kenan Halls gleaming in the late-afternoon sunlight.

He admired the commons as well. There was a clock tower there and when he'd first arrived, he'd stared at the image reflected in the pond behind it, time itself mirrored and unreadable at a glance. As long as he had an open textbook in his lap, he could sit and watch the activities, almost invisible to the students who wandered around in their self-absorbed trances.

It was warm for late September, students lounging in shorts and tank tops, skin evident everywhere. He wondered if they dressed the same way for class. Like them, he'd come to the campus to learn.

He'd visited three times in three days, but there were still too many people around; too many possible memories, and he didn't want to be remembered. He debated whether to move to another area before finally deciding there was no reason. As far as he could tell, no one cared that he was here.

He was close, so very close, but for now it was important to remain patient. He drew a long breath, holding it in before finally releasing it. On the walkways, he saw a pair of students walking to their classes, backpacks slung over their shoulders, but at this time of day, they were outnumbered by those classmates who were getting an early start to the weekend. Here and there, students were clustered in groups of three or four, talking and sipping from water bottles he suspected were filled with alcohol, while a couple of Abercrombie-model lookalikes were tossing a Frisbee back and forth, their girlfriends chatting off to the side. He spotted a young man and woman arguing, the woman's face flushed. He watched as she pushed at her boyfriend, creating space between them. He smiled at that, respecting her anger and the fact that unlike him, she wasn't compelled to hide the way she was feeling. Beyond the couple, another group of students played a game of touch football with the carefree abandon of those without real responsibility.

He figured that many of the students he saw were planning to go out tonight and tomorrow night. Fraternity houses. Sorority houses. Bars. Clubs. For many of them, the weekend would start tonight, since many classes didn't even meet on Fridays. He'd been surprised when he'd first learned that; with the cost of a college education so high, he would have thought that students would have been demanding more time in class with their professors, not three-day weekends. Then again, he supposed the schedule suited both the students and the professors. Didn't everyone want things to be easy these days? To expend the least effort possible? To take shortcuts?

Yes, he thought. That's exactly what students were learning here. They were learning that hard decisions weren't necessary, that making the right choice was unimportant, especially if it entailed extra work. Why study or try to change the world on a Friday afternoon when you could be out enjoying the sun?

Shifting his eyes from left to right, he wondered how many of these students even gave much thought to the lives they were going to lead. Cassie used to, he remembered. She thought about the future all the time. She had plans. She'd mapped out her future by seventeen, but he could remember thinking that there was something tentative about the way she'd talked about it, and he'd had the sense that she didn't quite believe in herself or the face she showed to the world. Why else would she have made the decisions that she had?

He'd tried to help her. He'd done the right thing, followed the law, filed reports with the police, even talked to the assistant district attorney. And up until that point, he'd believed in society's rules. He'd held the naïve view that good would triumph over evil, that danger could be corralled, that events could be controlled. Rules would keep a person safe from harm. Cassie had believed that, too—after all, wasn't that what kids were taught when they were young? Why else would parents say the things they did? Look both ways before you cross the road. Don't get into a car with a stranger. Brush your teeth. Eat your vegetables. Put on your seat belt. The list went on and on, rules to protect and save us.

But rules could be dangerous, too, he'd learned. Rules were about averages, not specifics, and since people were conditioned since childhood to accept rules, it was easy to follow them blindly. To trust in the system. It was easier not to worry about random possibilities. It meant that people didn't have to think about potential consequences, and when the sun was shining on Friday afternoons, they could play Frisbee without a care in the world.

Experience was the most painful of teachers. For nearly two years, the lessons he'd learned had been all he could think about. They had nearly consumed him, but slowly a clarity had begun to emerge. She had known about the danger. He had warned her what would happen. And in the end, she'd cared only about following the rules, because it was convenient.

Checking his watch, he saw it was finally time to go. He closed the textbook and rose from his spot, pausing to see if his movement had caused others to notice him. It hadn't. He set off then, crossing the commons, textbook beneath his arm. In his pocket was a letter he'd written, and he veered toward the mailbox just outside the science building. He dropped the envelope through the slot and waited; a few minutes later, he spotted Serena emerging from the doors, precisely on time.

He already knew much about her. These days, it seemed that every young person had Facebook and Twitter and Instagram and Snapchat, their lives on display for anyone who cared to put the pieces together. What they liked, who their friends were, where they spent their time. He already knew from a Facebook post that she'd be having brunch at her parents' house with her sister this Sunday, and as he watched her walking ahead of him, her dark brown hair tumbling past her shoulders, he noted again how beautiful she was. There was a natural grace about her, and she drew appreciative smiles from the guys she passed, though lost in conversation, she didn't seem to notice. She was walking with a short, heavy blonde, a friend from class. They'd been in an education seminar together; he knew she wanted to become an elementary school teacher. Making plans, just like Cassie used to do.

He kept his distance, energized by the power he felt in her presence. The power he'd been husbanding for the last two years. She had no idea how close he was or what he could do. She never so much as glanced over her shoulder, but why should she? He was no one to her, just another face in the crowd...

He wondered whether she was telling the blonde about her weekend plans, rattling off places to go or the people she intended to see. For his part, he planned to join the family for brunch on Sunday, though not as a guest. Instead, he would watch them from a nearby house, located in a neighborhood that was solidly middle class. The house had been empty for a month, the owners having lost it to foreclosure, but it was not yet up for sale. Though the locks on the doors were solid, he'd been able to gain entry through a window along the side of the house without much trouble. He already knew that from the master bedroom, he could see onto their back porch and into the kitchen. On Sunday, he'd watch the close-knit family laugh and joke at the table on the porch.

He knew something about each of them. Felix Sanchez was the classic immigrant success story; the newspaper article that was proudly laminated and on display at their restaurant chronicled how he'd arrived in the country illegally as a teenager without speaking a word of English and begun working as a dishwasher in a local restaurant. Fifteen years later, after becoming an American citizen, he'd saved enough money to open his own place in a strip mall—La Cocina de la Familia—serving his wife Carmen's recipes. While she cooked, he did everything else, especially in the early years of the business. Little by little, their restaurant had expanded, and it was now regarded as one of the best Mexican restaurants in the city. Though there were more than fifteen employees, many were relatives, retaining the restaurant's family character. Both parents still worked there, and Serena waited tables three times a week, just as her older sister, Maria, once had. Felix was a member of both the Chamber of Commerce and the Rotary Club, and he and his wife attended the seven a.m. mass at St. Mary's every Sunday, where he also served as a deacon. Carmen was a bit more of a mystery; he knew only that she was still more comfortable speaking Spanish than English and, like her husband, was proud of the fact that Maria had become the first college graduate in the family.

As for Maria . . .

He hadn't yet seen her in Wilmington. She'd been out of town for the last few days at a legal conference, but he knew her best of all. In the past, when she'd lived in Charlotte, he'd seen her many times. He'd talked to her. He'd tried to convince her she was wrong. And in the end, she'd made him suffer as no one should ever suffer, and he hated her for what she'd done.

When Serena waved good-bye to her friend and headed toward

the parking lot, he continued walking straight. There was no reason to follow her, and he was content knowing that he'd see the small but happy family on Sunday. Especially Maria. Maria was arguably even more beautiful than her sister, though frankly, both had been winners in the genetic lottery, with their dark eyes and nearly perfect bone structure. He tried to imagine them sitting close together at the table; despite the seven-year age difference, many people might assume they were twins. And yet they were different. Where Serena was outgoing to a fault, Maria had always been quieter and driven, the more serious and studious of the two. Even so, they were close, best friends as well as sisters. He speculated that perhaps Serena saw traits in her sister that she wanted to emulate, and vice versa. He felt a frisson of excitement at the thought of the weekend, knowing it might be one of the last times the family would all be together with any semblance of normalcy. He wanted to see how they would act before tension began to infect their sweet happy family . . . before the fear took hold. Before their lives were slowly—and then furiously—brought to ruin.

He'd come here, after all, for a purpose, and that purpose had a name.

Its name was vengeance.

CHAPTER I

——— ❦ ———

Colin

Colin Hancock stood over the sink in the bathroom at the diner, his shirt raised to better examine the bruise on his ribs. He guessed that it would deepen to a dark purple by the time he woke tomorrow. Even grazing the bruise made him wince, and while he knew from experience that the pain could be overridden for a while, he wondered whether it would hurt to breathe in the morning.

His face, though...

That might end up being a problem—not for him, but for others. Certainly his college classmates would stare at him with wide, frightened eyes and whisper about him behind his back, though he doubted that any of them would actually ask him what had happened. During the first few weeks at the university, most of his classmates had seemed nice enough, but it had been clear that none of them knew what to make of him, nor had any tried to speak to him. Not that it bothered him. For one thing, virtually all of them were six or seven years younger than he was, all were female, and he suspected that as far as recent life experiences went, they had little in common with him. In time, like everyone else, they'd end up drawing their own conclusions about him. Frankly, it wasn't worth worrying about.

Still, he had to admit that he was particularly ghoulish right now. His left eye was swollen and the white of his right eye was a bloody red. There was a gash in the center of his forehead that had been glued back together, and the lead-colored bruise on his right cheekbone resembled a birthmark. His split, swollen lips completed the picture. What he really needed was to put an ice pack on his face as soon as possible if he wanted the girls in his classes to be able to concentrate at all. But first things first; right now, he was starved and he needed fuel. He hadn't eaten much in the last two days, and he'd wanted something fast, convenient, and—if possible—not entirely unhealthy. Unfortunately, at this time of night most places were already closed, so he'd ended up at a run-down diner just off the highway with bars on the windows, water stains on the walls, peeling linoleum on the floor, and booths held together with duct tape. But if the place had one saving grace, it was that none of the other customers cared how he looked when he made his way to the table. People who came to dives like this late at night were good at minding their own business. As far as he could tell, half the people here were trying to sober up after a night of hard drinking, while the other half—designated drivers, no doubt—were sobering up, too, only marginally less intoxicated.

It was the kind of place where it would have been easy to get in trouble, and after he'd turned into the gravel lot with Evan following in his Prius, he'd half expected Evan to keep going. But Evan must have suspected the same thing about possible trouble. It was the only reason he'd ever set foot in an establishment like this, especially at this time of night. Evan didn't exactly blend in with the late-evening crowd here, what with his pink shirt, argyle socks, leather loafers, and neatly parted sandy blond hair. In fact, his Prius might as well have been a neon sign announcing that his goal was to get beaten up by the good old boys in pickup trucks who'd just spent most of the night getting wasted.

Colin turned on the faucet and wet his hands before bringing them to his face. The water was cold, exactly what he wanted.

His skin felt like it was on fire. The marine he'd fought had hit a lot harder than he'd expected—and that didn't count the illegal blows—but who would have known by looking at him? Tall and thin, jarhead haircut, goofy eyebrows...He shouldn't have underestimated the guy, and he told himself he wouldn't let it happen again. Either that, or he'd end up scaring his classmates all year long, which just might ruin the whole college experience for them. *There's this super scary guy in my class with bruises all over his face and these crazy tattoos, Mom!*, he could imagine them saying on the phone. *And I have to sit right next to him!*

He shook the water from his hands. Leaving the restroom, he spotted Evan in the corner booth. Unlike him, Evan would have fit right in at the college. He still had a baby face, and as he approached, Colin wondered how many times a week he even had to shave.

"That took you long enough," Evan said as Colin slid into the booth. "I was wondering if you got lost."

Colin slouched against the vinyl cushion. "I hope you weren't too nervous all alone out here."

"Ha, ha."

"I have a question for you."

"Go ahead."

"How many times a week do you shave?"

Evan blinked. "You were in the bathroom for ten minutes and that's what you were thinking about?"

"I wondered about it while I was walking to the table."

Evan stared at him. "I shave every morning."

"Why?"

"What do you mean, why? For the same reason you do."

"I don't shave every morning."

"Why are we even talking about this?"

"Because I was curious and I asked and then you answered," Colin said. Ignoring Evan's expression, he nodded toward the menus. "Did you change your mind and decide to order?"

Evan shook his head. "Not a chance."

"You're not going to eat anything?"

"No."

"Acid reflux?"

"Actually, it has more to do with my suspicion that the last time the kitchen was inspected, Reagan was president."

"It's not that bad."

"Have you seen the cook?"

Colin glanced toward the grill behind the counter; the cook was right out of central casting, with a greasy apron straining to cover his ample gut, a long ponytail, and tattoos covering most of his lower arms.

"I like his tats."

"Gee, there's a surprise."

"It's the truth."

"I know. You always tell the truth. That's part of your problem."

"Why is it a problem?"

"Because people don't always want the truth. Like when your girlfriend asks if a particular outfit makes her look fat, you should tell her she looks beautiful."

"I don't have a girlfriend."

"That's probably because you told the last one she looked fat without adding the beautiful part."

"That's not what happened."

"You get my point, though. Sometimes, you need to . . . stretch the truth to get along with people."

"Why?"

"Because that's what normal people do. That's the way society works. You can't just tell people whatever pops into your mind. It makes them uncomfortable or hurts their feelings. And just so you know, employers hate it."

"Okay."

"You don't believe me?"

"I believe you."

"But you don't care."

"No."

"Because you'd rather tell the truth."

"Yes."

"Why?"

"It's what I've learned works for me."

Evan stayed silent for a moment. "Sometimes I wish I could be more like that. Just tell my boss what I really think of him without caring about the consequences."

"You can. You choose not to."

"I need the paycheck."

"That's an excuse."

"Maybe." Evan shrugged. "But it's what I've learned works for me. Sometimes lying is necessary. For instance, if I told you that I saw a couple of roaches under the table while you were in the bathroom, you might feel the same way about eating here that I do."

"You know you don't have to stay, right? I'll be okay."

"So you say."

"You need to worry about yourself, not me. And besides, it's getting late. Aren't you heading to Raleigh with Lily tomorrow?"

"First thing in the morning. We'll go to service at eleven with my parents, and have brunch right afterwards. But unlike you, I won't have any trouble getting out of bed tomorrow morning. You look terrible, by the way."

"Thanks."

"Your eye, especially."

"It won't be as swollen tomorrow."

"Your other one. I think you popped a few blood vessels. Either that, or you're actually a vampire."

"I noticed that."

Evan leaned back, spreading his arms slightly. "Do me a favor, okay? Keep yourself hidden from the neighbors tomorrow. I'd hate for them to think I had to get rough on you for being late on the rent or whatever. I don't want to get a bad reputation as a landlord."

Colin smiled. He outweighed Evan by at least thirty pounds, and he liked to joke that if Evan had ever set foot in a gym, it was probably to conduct an audit.

"I promise to stay out of sight," Colin offered.

"Good. Considering my reputation and all."

Just then, the waitress came by, dropping off a plate loaded with scrambled egg whites and ham, along with a gelatinous bowl of oatmeal. As Colin pulled the bowl closer, he glanced at Evan's mug.

"What are you drinking?"

"Hot water with lemon."

"Seriously?"

"It's past midnight. If I had coffee, I'd be up all night."

Colin scooped a bit of oatmeal into his mouth before swallowing. "Okay."

"What? No snide comment?"

"I'm just surprised they have lemon here."

"And I'm surprised they do scrambled egg whites. You're probably the first person in history who's ever even attempted to eat a healthy meal here." He reached for his water. "By the way, what *are* you planning to do tomorrow?"

"I have to change the ignition switch in my car. It's not starting the way it should. After that, I'll do the lawn and then hit the gym."

"Do you want to come with us?"

"Brunch isn't really my thing."

"I wasn't inviting you to brunch. I doubt they'd even let you in the country club looking the way you do. But you could see your parents in Raleigh. Or your sisters. It's on the way to Chapel Hill."

"No."

"I just thought I'd ask."

Colin scooped a spoonful of oatmeal. "Don't."

Evan leaned back in his seat. "There were a few great fights tonight, by the way. The one after yours was awesome."

"Yeah?"

"A guy named Johnny Reese had a submission in the first round. Took the guy down like a stud, maneuvered him into a choke hold, and it was lights out. The dude moves like a cat."

"Your point is?"

"He's way better than you."

"Okay."

Evan drummed his fingers on the table. "So...are you okay with how your fight went tonight?"

"It's over."

Evan waited. "And?"

"That's it."

"Do you still think that what you're doing is a good idea? I mean...you know."

Colin scooped a bite of eggs onto his fork. "I'm still here with you, aren't I?"

Half an hour later, Colin was back on the highway. The clouds that had been threatening a storm for the last few hours finally obliged, releasing a torrent of wind and rain punctuated by lightning and thunder. Evan had left a few minutes before Colin did, and as Colin settled in behind the wheel of the Camaro he'd been restoring over the last few years, he found his thoughts drifting to his friend.

He'd known Evan as long as he could remember. When Colin was young, his family used to spend summers at a beach cottage in Wrightsville Beach, and Evan's family lived right next door. They'd passed long, sun-drenched days walking the beach, playing catch, fishing, and either surfing or riding boogie boards. More often than not, they'd spent the night at each other's houses, until Evan's family moved to Chapel Hill and Colin's life went completely in the toilet.

The facts were fairly straightforward: He was the third child and only son of wealthy parents with a fondness for nannies and absolutely no desire for a third child. He was a colicky baby and then a high-energy child with a raging case of ADHD, the kind of kid who threw regular temper tantrums, couldn't focus, and found it impossible to sit still. He drove his parents crazy at home, ran off one nanny after another, and struggled endlessly in school. He had a great teacher in third grade who made things better for a while, but in fourth grade, he started going downhill again. He got in one fight after another on the playground and was nearly held back. It was around that time that he came to be regarded as having *serious issues*, and in the end, not knowing what else to do, his parents shipped him off to military school, hoping the structure would do him good. His experience that first year was horrific, and he was expelled halfway through the spring semester.

From there, he was sent to another military school in a different state, and over the next few years, he expended his energies in combat sports—wrestling, boxing, and judo. He took his aggression out on others, sometimes with too much enthusiasm, often just because he wanted to. He cared nothing about grades or discipline. Five more expulsions and five different military schools later, he graduated, just barely, as an angry and violent young man with no plans for his life and no interest in finding any. He moved back in with his parents and seven bad years followed. He watched his mother cry and listened to his father plead with him to change, but he ignored them. He worked with a therapist at his parents' insistence, but he continued his downward spiral, subconscious self-destruction his primary goal. The therapists' words, not his, though he now agreed with them. Whenever his parents kicked him out of the main house in Raleigh, he'd crash at the family's beach cottage, biding his time before returning home, the cycle beginning anew. When Colin was twenty-five, he was given one final chance to make changes in his life. Unexpectedly, he did just that. And now here he was, in college with plans to spend the next few decades in the classroom, hoping to be a mentor to children, which would make no sense at all to most people.

Colin knew there was an irony to his wanting to spend the rest of his life in school—a place he'd always hated—but that's the way it was. He didn't dwell on the irony and he generally didn't dwell on the past. He wouldn't have been thinking of any of these things at all if it hadn't been for Evan's comment about visiting his parents tomorrow. What Evan still didn't grasp was that simply being in the same room as them was stressful for both Colin and his parents—especially if the visit wasn't planned well in advance. Had he shown up unexpectedly, he knew they'd sit uncomfortably in the living room trying to make small talk while memories of the past filled the air between them like a poisonous gas. He'd feel waves of disappointment and judgment radiating out from them, apparent in the things they said or didn't say, and who needed that? He didn't, and neither did they. In the last three years, he'd tried to keep his infrequent visits to about an hour, almost always on the holidays, an arrangement that seemed to suit them all.

His older sisters, Rebecca and Andrea, had tried to talk to him about making amends to his parents, but he'd shut down those conversations the same way he'd done with Evan. Their lives with their parents, after all, had been different from his. They'd both been *wanted*, while he'd been a big fat *whoops* seven years later. He knew they meant well, but he didn't have a lot in common with them. Both of them were college graduates and married with kids. They lived in the same upscale neighborhood as their parents and played tennis on the weekends. The older he'd gotten, the more he'd come to acknowledge that the choices they'd made in their own lives had been a lot smarter than his own. Then again, they didn't have *serious issues*.

He knew that his parents, like his sisters, were essentially good people. It had taken him years in therapy to accept the fact that he'd been the one with the problems, not them. He no longer blamed his mother and father for the things that had happened to him or for what they had or hadn't done; if anything, he considered himself a lucky son of two incredibly patient people. So what if he'd been raised by nannies? So what if his folks had finally thrown in the towel and shipped him off to military school? When he'd really needed them, when other parents probably would have given up, they'd never lost hope that he could turn his life around.

And they'd put up with his crap for *years*. Serious crap. They'd ignored the drinking and the pot smoking and the music cranked way too loud at all hours; they'd put up with the parties he threw whenever they went out of town that left the house in shambles. They'd overlooked the bar fights and multiple arrests. They never contacted the authorities when he broke into the beach cottage, even though he did serious damage to that place as well. They'd bailed him out more times than he could remember and paid his legal bills, and three years ago—when Colin was facing a long prison sentence after a bar fight in Wilmington—his dad had pulled some strings to strike a deal that would clear his criminal record entirely. If, of course, Colin didn't screw it up. As part of his probation, Colin had been required to spend four months at an anger-management treatment facility in Arizona. Upon his return and because his parents wouldn't let him stay at their home, he'd crashed again at the beach cottage, which by then was for sale. He'd also been ordered to meet regularly with Detective Pete Margolis from the Wilmington police department. The man whom Colin had beaten in the bar was a longtime confidential informant of Margolis's, and as a result of the fight, a high-profile case Margolis was working on had gone suddenly south. Consequently, Margolis hated Colin with a passion. Having argued strongly against the deal in the first place, he then insisted on monitoring Colin regularly and at random, like a makeshift probation officer. Finally, the deal stipulated that if Colin was arrested again, for *anything*, the entirety of his original record would be reinstated and he'd automatically be sentenced to prison for nearly a decade.

Despite the requirements, despite having to deal with Margolis, who plainly itched to place him in handcuffs, it was a great deal. An *unbelievable* deal, and it was all thanks to his father... even if he and Colin had trouble speaking these days. Colin was technically banned from ever setting foot in the house again, though his dad had softened on that particular stance lately. Being permanently kicked out of the house after he'd returned from Arizona and then watching from the street as new owners took possession of the beach cottage had forced Colin to reevaluate his life. He'd ended up sleeping at friends' places back in Raleigh, drifting from one couch to the next. Little by little, he'd come to the conclusion that if he didn't change his life, he'd self-destruct entirely. The environment there wasn't good for him, and his circle of friends was as out of control as he was. With nowhere else to go, he'd driven back to Wilmington and surprised himself by showing up at Evan's door. Evan had been living there after graduating from North Carolina State and had been equally surprised to see his old friend. Cautious and a bit nervous, too, but Evan was Evan, and he had no problem with Colin staying at his place for a while.

It took some time to earn Evan's trust again. By that point, their lives had diverged. Evan was a lot more like Rebecca and Andrea, a responsible citizen whose only experience with jail was what he'd seen on television. He worked as an accountant and financial planner, and in keeping with the fiscally prudent ideals of his profession, he'd also purchased a house with a first-floor apartment and separate entrance to help lower his mortgage payments, an apartment that happened to be vacant when Colin had shown up. Colin hadn't intended to stay long, but one thing led to another and when he'd gotten a job tending bar, he'd moved in downstairs for good. Three years later, he was still paying rent to the best friend he had in the world.

So far, it was working out well. He mowed the lawn and trimmed the bushes and paid a reasonable rent in return. He had his own space with his own entrance, but Evan was right there, too, and Evan was exactly what Colin needed in his life right now. Evan wore a suit and tie to work, he kept his tastefully decorated house spotless, and he never drank more than two beers when he went out. He was also just about the nicest guy in the world, and he accepted Colin, faults and all. And—for God knows what reason—he believed in him, even when Colin knew he didn't always deserve it.

Lily, Evan's fiancée, was pretty much cut from the same cloth. Though she worked in advertising and had her own condo at the beach—her parents had bought it for her—she spent enough time at Evan's to have become an important part of Colin's life. It had taken her a while to warm up to him—when they'd first met, Colin had been sporting a blond Mohawk and had piercings in both ears, and their initial conversation had centered around a bar fight in Raleigh where the other guy had ended up in the hospital. For a while, she simply couldn't comprehend how Evan could ever be friends with him. A Charleston debutante who'd attended college at Meredith, Lily was prim and polite, and the phrases she used were a throwback to an earlier era. She was also just about the most drop-dead gorgeous girl Colin had ever seen, and it was no wonder that Evan was putty in her hands. With her blond hair and blue eyes and an accent that sounded like honey even when she was angry, she seemed like the last person in the world who would give Colin a chance. And yet, she had. And like Evan, she had eventually come to believe in him. It had been Lily who'd suggested that he start taking classes at the junior college two years ago, and it had been Lily who'd tutored him in the evenings. And on two separate occasions, it had been Lily and Evan who had kept Colin from making the kind of impulsive mistake that might have landed him in prison. He loved her for those things, just as he loved the relationship between her and Evan. He'd long since decided that if anyone ever threatened the two of them in any way, he would handle it, no matter what the consequences, even if it meant he'd have to spend the rest of his life behind bars.

But all good things come to an end. Isn't that what people said? The life he'd lived for the last three years was going to change, if only because Evan and Lily were engaged, with plans for a spring wedding already in the works. While they'd both insisted that Colin could continue to live in the downstairs apartment after they were married, he also knew they'd spent the previous weekend walking through model homes in a subdivision closer to Wrightsville Beach, with homes that featured the kind of double porches common in Charleston. They both wanted kids, they both wanted the whole white-picket-fence thing, and Colin had no doubt that within a year, Evan's current house would be for sale. After that, Colin would be on his own again, and while he knew it wasn't fair to expect Evan and Lily to be responsible for him, he sometimes wondered whether they were aware of how important they'd become to him in the last few years.

Like tonight, for instance. He hadn't asked Evan to come to the fight; that had been Evan's idea. Nor had he asked Evan to sit with him while he ate. But Evan probably suspected that had he not done those things, Colin might have ended up at a bar instead of the diner, unwinding with shots instead of midnight breakfast. And though Colin worked as a bartender, being on the other side of the bar didn't exactly work for him these days.

Finally exiting the highway, Colin steered onto a winding county road, loblolly pine and red oak mingling on either side, kudzu playing no favorites between the two. It was less a shortcut than an attempt to avoid an endless series of stoplights. Lightning continued to strike, turning the clouds silver and illuminating the surroundings in otherworldly strobes. The rain and wind intensified, the wipers barely keeping the windshield clear, but he knew this road well. He eased into one of its many blind curves before instinctively stomping on the brakes.

Up ahead, a car with storage racks across the roof was halfway off the road at a cockeyed angle, its hazards flashing. The trunk stood propped open to the elements. As the Camaro slowed, Colin felt the rear fishtail slightly before the tires caught again. He merged into the oncoming lane to give the car a wide berth, thinking that the guy couldn't have picked a worse time and place to break down. Not only was the storm limiting visibility, but drunks like the ones back at the diner would be setting out for home right about now, and he could imagine one of them taking the corner too fast and plowing into the back of the car.

Not good, he thought. It was definitely an accident waiting to happen, but at the same time, it wasn't his business. It wasn't his job to rescue strangers, and he probably wouldn't be much help anyway. He understood the engine in his car, but only because the Camaro was older than he was; modern engines had more in common with computers. Besides, the driver had no doubt already called for help.

As he rolled slowly past the stopped car, however, he noticed the rear tire was flat and behind the trunk, a woman—soaked to the bone in jeans and a short-sleeved blouse—was struggling to remove the spare tire from its compartment. Lightning flashed, a long series of flickering camera strobes that captured her mascara-streaked distress. In that instant, he realized that her dark hair and wide-set eyes reminded him of one of the girls in his classes, and his shoulders slumped.

A girl? Why did it have to be a girl in trouble out here? For all he knew, it *was* the girl in his class, and he couldn't very well pretend he hadn't noticed that she needed help. He really didn't need this right now, but what choice did he have?

With a sigh, he pulled over to the side of the road, leaving some distance between her car and his. He turned on his hazards and grabbed his jacket from the backseat. By then the rain was coming down in sheets, instantly soaking him as he exited, like the diagonal spray of an outdoor shower. Running a hand through his hair, he took a deep breath and then started toward her car, calculating how quickly he could change the tire and be on the road again.

"Need a hand?" he called.

Surprising him, she didn't say anything. Instead, staring at him with stricken eyes, she let go of the tire and began slowly backing away.

CHAPTER 2

❧

Maria

In the past, when she'd worked in the Mecklenburg County district attorney's office, Maria Sanchez had been in the courtroom with any number of criminals, some of whom had been charged with the kinds of violent crimes that kept her awake at night. She'd had nightmares about various cases and had been threatened by a sociopath, but the simple fact was that she'd never been quite as frightened back then as she felt right now on this deserted stretch as *that* car, driven by *that* guy, suddenly pulled to the side of the road.

It didn't matter that she was twenty-eight, or that she'd graduated summa cum laude from UNC Chapel Hill, or that she'd gone to law school at Duke. It didn't matter that she'd been a rising star in the district attorney's office before finding other work at one of the best legal firms in Wilmington, or that until that moment, she'd always had a pretty good handle on her emotions. As soon as he stepped out of the car, all those truths went out the window and the only thing she could think was that she was a young woman all alone in the middle of nowhere. When he began to walk toward her, panic flooded through her. *I'm going to die out here*, she suddenly realized, *and no one's ever going to find my body.*

Moments earlier, when his car had slowly drifted past hers,

she'd seen him staring at her—almost leering, like he was sizing her up—and her first thought was that he'd been wearing a mask, which was terrifying enough, but way less scary than the sudden realization that she'd actually seen his *face*. It was bruised on both sides; one eye was swollen shut, the other one bright red and bloody. She was pretty sure that even more blood was dripping down his forehead, and it had been all she could do not to start screaming. But for whatever reason, not a sound escaped her. *For the love of God*, she remembered thinking as soon as he'd passed, *please keep going. Whatever you do, please don't stop.*

But obviously God hadn't been listening. Why would God intervene to keep her from ending up dead in a ditch out in the middle of nowhere? He wouldn't. Instead, He'd decided to have the guy pull over, and now a man with a mangled face was gliding toward her like something out of a low-budget horror film. Or prison, from which he'd just escaped, because the guy was positively ripped, and wasn't that what prisoners did? Lift weights all the time? His haircut was severe, almost military style—the signature of one of the gangs in prison she'd heard about? The ratty black concert T-shirt didn't help, nor did the torn-up jeans, and the way he was holding his jacket freaked her out. In this storm, why wasn't he wearing it? Maybe he was using it to hide...

A *knife*.

Or, God forbid, a *gun*...

A squeak escaped her throat and her mind began racing through options as she tried to figure out what to do. Toss the tire at him? She couldn't even get the thing out of the trunk. Scream for help? There was no one nearby, not a single car had passed in the last ten minutes, and she'd left her cell phone God knows where or she wouldn't have been trying to change the tire in the first place. Run? Maybe, but the liquid ease with which he moved suggested he'd easily catch her. The only thing she could do was get back into the car and lock the doors, but he was already *right there*, and there was no way to get past him...

"Need a hand?"

It was the sound of his voice that jolted her out of her trance. Letting go of the tire, she began backing away, focusing only on creating distance between the two of them. Lightning flashed again and she noticed a blankness in his expression, almost like something elemental was missing in his personality, the piece that signaled that it wasn't okay to rape and kill women.

"What do you want with me?" she finally choked out.

"I don't want anything," he answered.

"Then what are you doing here?"

"I thought you might need some help changing your tire."

"I'm fine," she said. "I can handle it myself."

He looked from her to the flat tire, then back to her again. "Okay. Good night," he said. Wheeling around, he started back toward his car, his figure suddenly receding. His reaction was so unexpected that for a second she felt paralyzed. He was leaving? Why was he leaving? She was glad about that—actually, she was *thrilled* about that—and yet, and yet...

"I'm having trouble getting the tire out of the trunk!" she said, hearing the panic in her own voice.

He turned on his heel as he reached his car. "Seems like it." He reached for his door and pulled it open, ready to climb in—

"Wait!" she suddenly cried.

He squinted at her through the downpour. "Why?" he called back.

Why? She wasn't sure she'd heard him right. But then again, she'd told him she didn't need any help. And she didn't, except that she did, but it wasn't as though she could call anyone, and with her thoughts racing and jumbled, the next words spilled out involuntarily.

"Do you have a phone?" she shouted.

He closed some of the gap between, stopping when he could be heard without shouting, but not getting too close. Thank God. "Yes," he answered.

She shifted from one foot to the other, thinking *Now what?* "I lost my phone," she said. "I mean, I didn't *lose* lose it." She knew she was rambling, but the way he kept staring at her made the words impossible to stop. "It's either at the office or I left it at my parents', but I won't know for sure until I get to my MacBook."

"Okay." He added nothing else; instead, he stood unmoving, his eyes steady on hers.

"I use that Find My iPhone thing. The app, I mean. I can track my phone because it's synced with the computer."

"Okay."

"Well?"

"Well what?"

"Can I borrow yours for a minute? I want to call my sister."

"Sure," he answered. He tucked the phone into the folds of his jacket and as he began to approach, she reflexively took another step backward. He placed the jacket on the hood of her car and gestured at it.

She hesitated. He was definitely odd, but she appreciated the fact that he'd stepped away. She hurried to the bundle and found his iPhone tucked inside, the same model as hers. When she pressed the button, the screen lit up and sure enough, he was getting service. But it wouldn't do any good unless...

"Five-six-eight-one," he offered.

"You're giving me your code?"

"You can't access the phone without it," he noted.

"Aren't you worried about giving it to a stranger?"

"Are you going to steal my phone?"

She blinked. "No. Of course not."

"Then I'm not worried."

She wasn't sure what to say to that, but whatever. She typed in the code with trembling fingers and dialed her sister. By the third ring, she knew she'd get Serena's voice mail. Maria did her best to keep her frustration in check as she left a message, explaining what had happened to the car and asking her sister to come pick her up. She tucked the phone back into the jacket on the hood and then stepped away, watching him.

"No answer?" he asked.

"She's coming."

"Okay." When the lightning flashed again, he motioned toward the rear of her car. "While you're waiting for her, do you want me to change your tire?"

She opened her mouth to again decline his offer, but who knew when—or if—Serena would get her message? And then there was the fact that she'd never actually changed a tire in her life. Instead of answering, she let out a breath, trying to keep the tremor from her voice. "Can I ask you a question?"

"Yes."

"What . . . what happened to your face?"

"I was in a fight."

She waited a few beats before finally realizing he wasn't going to add anything else. *That's it? No further explanation?* His demeanor was so utterly foreign, she wasn't sure what to make of it. As he stood in place, obviously waiting for the answer to his earlier question, she glanced at the trunk, wishing she actually knew how to change a tire.

"Yes," she finally said. "If you wouldn't mind, I'd love some help changing the tire."

"Okay." He nodded. She watched as he reached for the bundle on the hood and tucked his phone back into his pocket before slipping his jacket on. "You're afraid of me," he said.

"What?"

"You're afraid I'm going to hurt you." When she said nothing, he went on. "I won't, but whether you believe that is up to you."

"Why are you telling me this?"

"Because if I'm going to change your tire, I'm going to have to approach the trunk. Which means I'll be approaching you, too."

"I'm not afraid of you," she lied.

"Okay."

"I'm not."

"Okay," he said again, then started toward her. She felt her heart squeeze as he passed within arm's reach of her, only to feel foolish when he walked right past without slowing. He unscrewed something, then lifted the spare tire out and set it aside before he disappeared behind the trunk again, no doubt to retrieve the jack.

"One of us needs to move your car onto the road," he said. "It needs to be level before I get the jack going, otherwise the car might slip."

"But I've got a flat tire."

He peeked around the side, jack in hand. "It won't hurt the car. Just go slow."

"But it will block most of the lane."

"It's blocking half the lane already."

He had a point there . . . but . . .

But what if that was all part of his plan? To distract her somehow? To get her to turn her back?

A plan that included letting me use his phone? And removing the tire from the trunk?

Rattled and self-conscious, she got into the car and started the engine, slowly but surely edging it back onto the road and setting the emergency brake. By the time she opened the door, he was rolling the spare toward the rear tire, lug wrench in hand.

"You can stay in the car if you want," he said. "This shouldn't take long."

She debated before closing the door, then spent several minutes watching in the side mirror as he continued to loosen the bolts before sliding the jack into place. A moment later, she could feel the car lifting slightly, bouncing its way slowly upward and then stopping. She watched as he finished unscrewing the bolts before sliding the tire off, just as the storm began to intensify, rain blowing in gusty sheets. The spare went on quickly, along with the bolts, and then all at once, the car was being lowered again. He placed the flat tire back in her trunk along with the jack and the lug wrench, and she felt him gently push the trunk closed. And just like that, it was over. Still, she startled a little when he tapped on her window. She lowered the glass and rain began to spit through the opening. With his face still shadowed, it was almost possible to see past the bruises and the swelling and the bloody eye. Almost, but not entirely.

"You're good to go," he shouted over the gale, "but you should probably get the tire fixed or replace it sooner rather than later. Your spare isn't meant to be used permanently."

She nodded, but before she could thank him, he had already turned and was jogging toward his car. He jerked his door open and slid behind the wheel. She heard the roar of his engine and then—before she knew it—she was alone on the road again, albeit now in a car that would get her home.

"I heard the phone ring, but I didn't recognize the number so I let it go to voice mail," Serena said in between sips of orange juice. Beside her at the table on the back porch, Maria nursed a cup of coffee, the morning sunlight already warming the air. "Sorry about that."

"Well, next time, just answer, okay?"

"Can't do that." Serena smiled. "What if it was some crazy person trying to reach me?"

"That was the problem! I was *with* a crazy person and I needed you to rescue me."

"It doesn't sound like it. He sounds like a nice guy."

Maria glared at her over the rim of her coffee mug. "You didn't see him. Trust me. I've seen scary people, and he was beyond scary."

"He told you he'd been in a fight..."

"And that's the point. He's obviously violent."

"But he wasn't the least bit violent toward you—you said he didn't even go near you at first. And then he let you borrow his phone. And after that, he changed your tire and then got back in his car and drove away."

"You're missing the point."

"What point? That you shouldn't judge a book by its cover?"

"I'm being serious here!"

Serena laughed. "Wow, someone's touchy. And you know I'm just teasing you. If it was me out there, I probably would have peed my pants. Broken car, deserted road, no phone, blood on some stranger's face . . . it's like every girl's worst nightmare."

"Exactly."

"Did you ever find your phone?"

"It's at the office. Probably still on my desk."

"You mean it's been there since Friday? And you didn't realize you didn't have it until Saturday night?"

"So?"

"I guess not too many people call you, huh?"

"Ha, ha."

Serena shook her head, then reached for her phone. "I can't live without mine, just so you know." She snapped a quick photo of Maria.

"What's that for?"

"Instagram."

"Seriously?"

Serena was already tapping away. "Don't worry. It'll be funny," she added before presenting the image and caption. "Maria, after surviving Nightmare on Dark Street."

"You're not going to post that, are you?"

"Already did." Serena winked.

"You've got to stop posting about me. I'm serious. What if one of my clients finds it?"

"Then blame me." She shrugged. "Where's Dad, by the way?"

"He's still walking Copo," she said. Copo was a female, nearly all-white shih tzu. After Serena had moved to the dorms, she and Maria had returned home one Christmas to find that their parents had purchased a dog. Now Copo went practically everywhere with them: to the restaurant—where she had her own bed in the office—to the supermarket, even to the accountant. Copo was far more spoiled than either of the girls had ever been.

"I still can't get over it," Serena muttered. "They *love* that dog."

"Ya think?"

"Did you notice the rhinestone collar Mom bought? I almost gagged."

"Be nice."

"I am being nice!" Serena said. "I just never pictured them owning a dog in the first place. We never had one growing up, and I begged them for one for years. I even promised to take care of it."

"That's because they knew you wouldn't."

"I might not have skipped a grade and gone to college when I was seventeen like you, but I'm pretty sure I could have handled a dog. And I'll have you know that I'm in the running for the Charles Alexander Scholarship next year."

"Mmm, right." Maria raised a skeptical eyebrow.

"I'm serious. It's for bilingual education majors. I filled out the application, wrote an essay, got recommendations from two of my professors and everything. It's sponsored by a private foundation, and I have an interview with the chairman next Saturday. So there." She crossed her arms.

"Wow. That's great."

"Don't tell Dad, though. I want to surprise him."

"He'd be thrilled if you won."

"I know, right? Just think how many more collars they'd be able to buy Copo if he didn't have to pay tuition."

Maria laughed. Inside, they could hear their mother humming to herself in the kitchen, the smell of huevos rancheros drifting through the open window.

"But anyway," Serena went on, "back to last night. Why were you out so late? That's way past your normal bedtime."

Maria scowled at her sister before figuring that she might as well get it over with. "Actually, I was on a date."

"No way."

"What's the big deal?"

"Nothing. I just thought that you'd made the decision to be celibate."

"Why would you say that?"

"Hello? Did you forget who I was talking to?"

"I go out."

"You might paddleboard, but you don't go out at night. Instead, you work. You read. You watch bad TV. You don't even go dancing anymore, and you used to love that. And I tried to get you to come to that warehouse with me, remember? With the salsa dancing on Saturday nights?"

"As I recall, you said there were a lot of creepy guys there."

"But I also had a lot of fun. And unlike you, I'm terrible at dancing."

"Not all of us are in college, you know, with classes that start at noon and Fridays off. Some of us have responsibilities."

"Yeah, yeah, I've heard that before," Serena said, waving it off. "I take it you didn't get lucky?"

Maria peeked over her shoulder toward the partially open window, making sure her mother wasn't listening.

Serena rolled her eyes. "You're an adult, you know. You don't have to hide your social life from Mom and Dad anymore."

"Yeah, well, we've always been a little different in that way."

"What? You think I tell them everything?"

"I hope not."

Serena stifled a giggle. "Sorry your date didn't work out."

"How do you know? Maybe it did."

"I don't think so," Serena said, shaking her head. "Otherwise you wouldn't have been heading home alone."

Oops, Maria thought. Serena had always been quick-thinking, but more than that, she was endowed with a common sense that sometimes eluded Maria.

"Hello?" Serena added. "Anyone home? I was asking about your date."

"I don't think he'll be calling me."

Serena feigned compassion, though her amused cynicism was apparent. "Why? Did you bring your computer and work the whole time?"

"No. And it wasn't me. It was just...bad."

"Talk to me, big sister. Tell me all about it."

Maria surveyed the backyard, reflecting that Serena was the only person in the world she could really talk to. "There's really not that much to tell. For starters, I didn't plan on having a date in the first place—"

"No! You?"

"Do you want to hear this or not?"

"My mistake." Serena grinned. "Go on."

"You remember Jill, right? My friend from work?"

"Super smart, coming up on forty and dying to get married, funny as hell? The one who came over for brunch and scooped Copo up and almost gave Dad a heart attack?"

"Yes."

"No, I don't remember her."

"*Anyway*," Maria said, "we were having lunch a few days ago and she convinced me to join her and her boyfriend, Paul, for dinner, after I got back from the conference. But unbeknownst to me, it turns out that they had also invited one of Paul's friends from work to join us, and—"

"Wait, back up. Was the guy hot?"

"He was definitely handsome. But the problem was, he knew it. He was rude and arrogant and he flirted with the waitress all night long. I think he even got her phone number while I was sitting beside him."

"Classy."

"Jill was as mortified as I was, but the strange thing was, I'm not sure that Paul even noticed. Maybe it was the wine or whatever, but he kept saying that the four of us should head out to a club afterwards and that he was so glad we were getting along, that he just knew we'd be perfect for each other. Which is strange, because he's not normally like that. Usually he's quiet and Jill and I do all the talking."

"Maybe he just likes his friend. Or maybe he thought that you and his friend would make pretty babies and you might name one after him."

Despite herself, Maria laughed. "Maybe. But anyway, I don't think I'm his type. I'm pretty sure he'd be more comfortable with someone..."

When Maria trailed off, Serena finished. "Dumber?"

"I was thinking blonder, like the waitress."

"Yeah, well, just so you know, that's always been part of your problem when it comes to guys. You're too smart. And to guys, that's kind of intimidating."

"Not all guys. Luis and I were together for over two years."

"*Were* together," Serena said. "Those are the operative words. And just so you know? He may have been sexy as hell, but Luis was a total loser."

"He wasn't that bad."

"Don't start getting all nostalgic about the good things about him. It wasn't like you ever had a future with him and you know it."

Maria nodded, knowing Serena was right but indulging momentarily in a bit of nostalgia anyway before shutting it down. "Yeah, well, live and learn."

"I'm just glad you decided to start dating again."

"I didn't. Jill and Paul decided for me."

"Whatever. You need to be..."

While Serena searched for the right words, Maria suggested, "More like you?"

"Why not? Going out, enjoying life, making friends? It beats working all the time."

"How would you know? You only work a couple of shifts a week."

"Good point. I'm just making an assumption based on your lack of a social life."

"Believe it or not, I actually like working."

"I'll make sure to put that on your tombstone," Serena said. "How's work going, by the way?"

Maria shifted in her seat, wondering how much to say. "It's all right."

"You just said you liked it."

"I do, but…"

"Let me guess…the conference, right? The one you went to with your boss?" When Maria nodded, Serena went on. "Was it as awful as you thought it might be?"

"Not exactly awful, but…"

"Did he hit on you?"

"Sort of," Maria admitted. "But it wasn't anything I couldn't handle."

"This is the guy who's married? With three kids?"

"That's the one."

"You need to tell him to knock it off. Threaten him with sexual harassment, or whatever."

"It's more complicated than that. For now, it's probably better for me if I just try to ignore it." When a slight smirk began to play across Serena's lips, Maria went on. "What?"

"I was just thinking that you really have a way with men. Your old boyfriend cheated on you, your latest date flirts with other girls, and meanwhile, your boss won't stop hitting on you."

"Welcome to my world."

"Of course, it's not all bad. You met a nice guy last night. The kind of guy who helps a woman in her time of need, despite a raging storm…"

When Maria scowled, Serena laughed and went on. "I really wish I could have seen your face."

"It wasn't pretty."

"And yet here you are, safe and sound," Serena reminded her. "And I'm happy about that, if only so that you have continued access to my wisdom."

"You really need to work on your self-esteem issues," Maria said sourly.

"I know, right? But seriously, I'm glad you moved back to town. These brunches would be deadly if you weren't here. Having you around gives Mom and Dad someone else to worry about."

"I'm glad I can be of service to you."

"I appreciate it. And besides, we've had a chance to get to know each other better."

"We've always known each other."

"You went off to college when I was ten."

"And I came home almost every weekend, and spent every vacation here."

"That's true. You were kind of wimpy like that. For the first couple of years, you were so homesick, you'd cry all weekend."

"It was hard to be so far from home."

"Why do you think I go to college here? In that way, I'm almost as smart as you are."

"You're smart. You might get a scholarship, remember?"

"I'm not smart like you. But that's okay. It'll make it much easier to find a guy in the end—not that I'm interested in anything serious. But listen, if you want, I'd be happy to keep a lookout for you. I meet guys all the time."

"College guys?"

"Some of them might just like an older woman."

"You're insane."

"I don't know. I tend to have pretty good taste."

"Are you referring to Steve?"

"We're just going out. It's not serious yet. But he seems like a nice guy. He even volunteers at the Humane Society, doing pet adoptions on Sundays."

"Do you like him?"

"You mean...*like* like? Or just like?"

"What? Are we in middle school now?"

Serena laughed. "I'm not sure how I feel yet. But he's cute, which gives me more time to find out."

"When do I get to meet him?"

"Well...let's see where it goes. Because if you're going to meet him, then Mom and Dad will want to meet him, and then I lose control of the whole situation. No matter what happens after that, he'll think that I think it's serious, and unlike you, I'm too young to settle down."

"I don't want to settle down yet, either."

"Maybe. But you definitely need a date."

"Would you stop?"

"Okay, fine. You don't need a date. What you need is to get lucky."

When Maria didn't bother responding, Serena giggled. "Touched a nerve, huh?" she chirped. "Okay, never mind. What's on your agenda today? After we get out of here? Are you going paddle-boarding again?"

"I was thinking about it."

"Alone?"

"Unless you want to try it again."

"Not a chance. I still don't understand why you like it so much. It's not like dancing. It's boring."

"It's good exercise. And it's peaceful."

"Didn't I just say that?" Serena asked.

Maria smiled. "How about you? What are your plans?"

"I'm going to take a nice long nap. And then, after that, I'll play it by ear."

"I hope you find something to do. I'd hate for you to miss a wild Sunday night on Greek row."

"Now, now...jealousy's an ugly thing," Serena said. She hooked her thumb toward the windows. "Dad's finally back and I'm starved. Let's go eat."

Later that afternoon, while Serena was no doubt sound asleep, Maria was on her paddleboard in Masonboro Sound, a place that had long since become her favorite spot to spend a weekend afternoon. Masonboro Island was the largest barrier island along the southern coast of the state, and while she sometimes navigated to the Atlantic side of the island, most of the time she preferred the glassy waters of the marsh. As always, the wildlife was spectacular. In her first hour on the water, she'd seen ospreys, pelicans, and egrets and had taken what she thought were some pretty good photographs. In June, for her birthday, she'd treated herself to a high-quality waterproof camera, and though it had been a financial stretch and she was still paying off the credit card bill, she hadn't yet regretted it. While they wouldn't end up in *National Geographic*, a few of her photos *had* been good enough to hang on the walls of her condominium, which was a prudent decorating option since she could barely afford the condo, either.

But out here, it was easy to think about those things without necessarily worrying about them. Though she'd only taken up paddleboarding since she'd moved back to Wilmington, it had the same effect on her that dancing used to have. She'd reached the point where keeping her balance was effortless and the steady paddling rhythm melted the stress away. Usually, within a few minutes of being on the water she was left with the sensation that all was right with the world. It was a warm, relaxing glow that started in her neck and shoulders before spreading to the rest of her body, and by the time she was in the shower after returning home, she'd feel ready to face yet another week in the office. Serena was wrong about paddleboarding. It wasn't boring; it was necessary these days for her mental health, and she had to admit it wasn't half bad for her figure, either. In the last year, she'd become toned in places she didn't even know could be toned, and she'd had to have her suits altered because they'd grown too loose in the waist and butt.

Not that it would matter. Serena might have been wrong about paddleboarding, but she had been right about Maria's run of bad luck in her love life, starting with Luis. He was the first guy she'd ever been serious about, the first guy she'd ever really loved. They'd been friends for almost a year before they'd finally started going out, and on the surface, they had a lot in common. Like her, he was the child of Mexican immigrants and intended to become a lawyer; like her, he enjoyed dancing, and after they'd been dating for a couple of years, it had been easy for her to imagine a future with him. Luis, on the other hand, had made it clear that he was content to continue going out—and sleeping with her—as long as she never expected anything more than that. Even bringing up the subject of marriage had freaked him out, and while she'd initially tried to convince herself that it didn't really matter, she'd known deep down that it did.

Still, in the end, the breakup had been a surprise; he'd simply called one evening and told her it was over. She'd eventually tried to console herself with the facts that they wanted different things in life and Luis simply wasn't ready for the kind of commitment she knew she wanted. But then? Just a little over a year later, right after she'd taken the bar exam, she'd learned that he was engaged. She'd spent the next six weeks in a funk, trying to figure out why the other girl had been good enough to marry while he hadn't even been able to discuss the subject with her. Where had she gone wrong? Had she been too pushy? Too boring? Or too...something else? Looking back, she had no idea. Of course, the whole experience would have been easier if she'd met someone else after Luis, but with every passing year she found herself wondering more and more where all the good guys had gone. Or even if there really was such a thing anymore. Where were the guys who didn't expect you to sleep with them after only a date or two? Or guys who believed that picking up the check on a first date was a classy thing to do? Or even a guy with a somewhat decent job and plans for the future? God knows, after she and Luis had broken up, she'd put herself out there. Despite the long hours she spent studying in law school and then later, working in Charlotte, she'd gone out regularly with friends on the weekends, but had anyone halfway decent asked her out?

She momentarily broke off her paddling, allowing the board to glide as she straightened up, stretching her back. Well, actually, they probably had, she thought. But back then, she'd tended to focus first on their appearance, and she could remember saying no to a few guys who hadn't been quite cute enough. And maybe that had been the problem. Maybe she'd turned down Mr. Right because he hadn't been tall enough or whatever, and now—because he was Mr. Right—he was already off the market. These days, it seemed like Mr. Rights tended to fly off the shelves, perhaps because they were as rare as California condors.

Most of the time, it didn't bother her. She was different from her mom, who believed that a woman's relationship status defined her. She had her own life, she could come and go as she pleased, and while she didn't have anyone to take care of her, she didn't have to take care of anyone else, either. Yet in the past couple of years—as she began inching closer to thirty—there had been moments when she thought that it might be nice to have someone to go dancing with, or who would join her while she paddle-boarded, or even someone willing to listen to her complain after a bad day at work. Having a wide circle of friends, like Serena did, might have filled that void, but most of Maria's friends lived in either the Raleigh or Charlotte areas, and getting together with them almost always meant a road trip and sleeping on someone's couch. Aside from her immediate family, relatives, Jill, and a few other coworkers—and, yes, even Paul, despite the other night— the only people she knew here were those she'd gone to high school with, and because she'd been away for years, they'd drifted apart. She supposed that she could try to reestablish contact, but by the time she finished up at work, all she usually wanted to do was unwind in the bathtub with a glass of wine and a good book. Or, if she felt energetic, maybe hit the water on the paddleboard. Even friendships took energy, and lately she didn't have enough to go around. While that meant her life wasn't all that exciting, it was also the kind of low-key predictability she needed. Her last year in Charlotte had been traumatic, and...

She shook her head, forcing away the memory of that final year. Taking a calming breath, she told herself firmly to focus on the positive, as she'd trained herself to do. There were a lot of good things in her life. She had her family, her own place, and a job she enjoyed...

Are you sure about that?, the little voice inside her suddenly asked. *Because you know that's not quite true.*

It had started off well enough, but wasn't that always the case? Martenson, Hertzberg & Holdman was a midsize firm, and she worked principally for the primary litigator, Barney Holdman, doing insurance defense work. Barney was in his early sixties and a rainmaker for the firm, a legal genius who wore seersucker suits and spoke with a slow, heavy drawl straight from the mountains of North Carolina. To both clients and juries, he came across as the friendly grandfather type, but beneath the surface, he was hard-driving, prepared for everything, and demanding of associates. In working for him, she had the privilege of time, expertise, and money to prepare her cases, all of which was a far cry from her work as a prosecutor.

Jill was a bonus. As the only women in the office aside from secretaries and paralegals, who had their own cliques, Jill and Maria had hit it off right away, even though they worked in different departments. They had lunch together three or four times a week, and Jill often dropped by Maria's office just to visit for a few minutes. She was quick-witted and made Maria laugh, but had an incisive legal mind and was one of the firm's key assets. Why she hadn't been made partner yet was a mystery. Maria sometimes wondered whether Jill was long for the firm, though she'd said nothing directly about it.

The real problem was Ken Martenson, the managing partner of the firm, who seemed to hire paralegals based on their attractiveness as opposed to their qualifications and spent too much time hovering around their desks. That part didn't necessarily bother Maria, nor did it bother her to see Ken fraternizing with one paralegal or another in a manner that sometimes seemed less than entirely professional. Jill had filled her in on Ken's reputation during Maria's first week on the job, especially his interest in attractive paralegals, but Maria had shrugged it off. That is, until Ken began to set his sights on her. It wasn't a good development, and lately the situation was getting even more complicated. It was one thing to try to avoid Ken at the office, where there were always other people around, but the conference in Winston-Salem they'd attended last week had amplified her fears that things might get worse. Though Ken hadn't gone so far as to walk her to her hotel room door—thank God for small favors—he *had* pressured her into joining him for dinner both nights. And then? He'd given her the whole *my wife just doesn't appreciate me* spiel while continually asking whether she wanted another glass of wine, despite the fact that she'd barely touched the first one. He'd talked about his place at the beach and how quiet and relaxing it was and noted more than once that it was usually empty. If she ever wanted to use it, all she had to do was ask. And had he mentioned how rare it was to work with someone who was both intelligent *and* beautiful?

Could the man have been more obvious? Nevertheless, when he'd hinted at what he wanted, she'd played dumb and then steered the subject back to the issues discussed at the conference. And it had worked, for the most part, but she hadn't been lying to Serena when she'd said it was complicated. Sometimes she wished that someone would have told her before she applied to law school that being an attorney wasn't quite the job guarantee she'd always imagined it would be. In the past few years, firms of all sizes had been cutting back, salaries were dropping, and right now there were too many lawyers chasing too few positions. After she'd left the district attorney's office, it had taken her nearly five months to land this job, and as far as she knew, none of the other firms in town were hiring. If she even mumbled the words *sexual harassment* or vaguely hinted about filing a lawsuit, she probably wouldn't be able to find another job in the entire state. Lawyers hated no one more than other lawyers who might sue them.

For the time being, she was stuck. She'd made it through the conference but vowed not to put herself in that kind of situation again. She'd avoid the break room and be a bit more cautious about working late, especially when she knew Ken would be there. For now, that was all she could do, aside from pray that he turned his sights back on one of the paralegals.

It was yet another example of the ways in which life had turned out to be more difficult than she'd imagined it would. When she'd started her first real job, she'd been idealistic; life had seemed more like an adventure. She'd fully believed that she had a meaningful role to play in keeping the streets safe and in giving victims a way to seek justice and redress. But over time, she'd begun to grow jaded about the entire process. It had become evident that even dangerous criminals often went free, the clogged wheels of the system turned impossibly slowly, and her caseload was never-ending. Now she was living again in the city where she'd grown up and practicing a kind of law vastly different from what she'd known as an assistant DA. While she'd been certain that things would be better once she was settled in, she'd slowly come to realize that job stress simply came in different flavors, and this one wasn't much better tasting than the one before it.

She'd been surprised by that, but then, she'd been surprised by almost everything in the last seven years. The world might view her as a young, home-owning professional, but there were moments when she felt like she was faking the whole thing. Part of it was financial—after paying her bills at the end of the month, she had less spending money than she'd had as a teenager—but the other part was that most of her friends from college were already married, and some of them already had kids. When she talked to them, most came across as completely content, as though their lives were unfolding exactly as they'd planned, while she, on the other hand, had a sex-crazed boss, a condo she could barely afford, and a younger sister who seemed simultaneously wiser and more carefree than Maria was. If this was adulthood, she wondered now why she'd been in such a rush to grow up in the first place.

For the next hour, she pulled steadily at the paddle, the board gliding forward as she did her best to enjoy her surroundings. She noted the slowly shifting clouds and the trees reflected in the water. She concentrated on the salty fresh scent of the breeze and basked in the warmth of the sun on her arms and shoulders. Every now and then she snapped a photograph, including a good one of an osprey clasping a fish in its talons as it rose from the water. It was too shadowed in the viewfinder and a little too distant, but with enough work in Photoshop, it might be something worth keeping.

When she finally returned home, she showered and poured herself a glass of wine, then sat in a rocking chair she'd placed in the small confines of her rear porch. She watched people as they walked along Market Street, idly wondering what their lives were like. She liked to invent stories about them— *That one's probably visiting from New York*, or *I'll bet that mom is taking her kids out for ice cream*. It was a harmless, relaxing capstone to a weekend that had its share of both highs and lows.

Like the blown tire. Which reminded her that she'd have to run out tomorrow to get it replaced. But when? She knew that while she'd been out of the office at the conference, Barney had filled her inbox with work. They also had two important meetings in the afternoon, which wasn't going to make it easy. Nor did she have any idea what Ken's next move would be.

The sense of dread intensified the following morning, when she spotted Ken speaking with Barney in his office while she chatted with Lynn, the voluptuous, though less than efficient, paralegal assigned to Barney's team. Ken and Barney often met before the Monday morning meeting, but what was unusual was that after Ken left Barney's office, he'd simply nodded at her without smiling before striding down the hallway. Part of her was relieved by the brevity of the encounter, but at the same time, the sudden frosty professionalism left a bad feeling in her stomach, because it no doubt meant he was angry at her.

A few minutes later, Jill poked her head in to apologize for the blind date, clearly mortified. They talked for a few minutes—Jill was heading out of town for the rest of the week for depositions—and Maria repeated to Jill the story she'd told Serena about her flat tire and the stranger who had rescued her, which only made Jill feel even worse.

As soon as Jill left, Maria started calling garages, trying to find someplace close where she could get her tire changed after work, but soon discovered that all of them would be closed by the time she arrived. Her only option was to try to get it done over her lunch hour. It took six attempts before she was finally able to snag an appointment at half past noon—cutting it close for the initial client meeting at one thirty. She warned Barney that she might be a few minutes late getting back. He frowned but told her to do her best, emphasizing that her presence was important. She left the office at a quarter to twelve, hoping that the mechanics would be able to start early.

But they didn't start early. Nor did they even start on time. In the end, she spent the next hour waiting, alternating between panic and slowly mounting fury, making calls to Barney's secretary and the paralegal, as well as to Barney's cell phone. It wasn't until after two that she was finally able to reclaim her car and speed back to the office. By the time she reached the conference room, the meeting had been in progress for nearly forty-five minutes. An icy stare from Barney signaled his displeasure, belying his slow, easy drawl as he welcomed her into the conference room.

After the meeting, she apologized profusely to Barney. He was clearly irate; gone was any trace of the friendly grandfather that clients were accustomed to. Things remained tense between them for the rest of the afternoon. It was no better the following day, and pouring herself into the various tasks at hand, Maria caught up on the matters she'd ignored while at the conference, in addition to preparing the documents she knew Barney needed for a trial the following week. She labored past midnight on both Monday and Tuesday, and with Jill out of the office, she worked through her lunch hours all week, eating takeout at her desk while toiling on various briefs. Barney apparently didn't notice or care, and it wasn't until Thursday that his icy demeanor began to thaw.

Later that afternoon, however—as she was finishing up a conversation with Barney in his office concerning an insurance claim that they both strongly suspected was fraudulent—she heard a voice behind her. Looking up, she saw Ken standing in the doorway.

"Excuse me," he said, addressing them both but mainly focusing on Barney. "Would you mind if I spoke to Maria for a moment?"

"Not at all," Barney drawled. He nodded at Maria. "Give them a ring and let them know that we'll need to set a conference call for tomorrow."

"Absolutely. I'll let you know what they say," Maria responded. She could feel Ken staring at her, could feel the tightness in her chest as she turned to face him. By then, Ken had already turned to leave, and without a word, she followed him down the hallway and through the reception area. Her feet dragged when she realized he was heading toward his office. As they approached, his secretary averted her gaze.

Ken held the door open for her, then closed it behind him. All business now, he moved behind his desk and gestured for her to sit in the chair opposite. He gazed out the window before finally turning to face her.

"Barney mentioned to me that you missed an important client meeting on Monday."

"I didn't miss it. I was late—"

"I didn't call you here to quibble over the details," he said, cutting her off. "Would you care to explain what happened?"

Caught off guard, Maria stammered out an admittedly pathetic account of her attempts to find a suitable garage and the events that had followed.

When she was finished, he said nothing for a moment. "You do understand what we do here, right? And why you were hired? Our clients expect a certain level of professionalism."

"Yes, of course I do. And I know our clients are important."

"Did you know that Barney was thinking of allowing you the opportunity to act as lead counsel on this matter? And that you took this opportunity off the table because you felt the suddenly urgent, desperate need to change your tire during business hours?"

Maria flushed, her thoughts spinning at this new revelation. "No, he didn't mention that," she sputtered. "And like I said, I wanted to get it done after work, but every place would have already been closed. I honestly thought I could get back in time. I knew there was a risk, but—"

"A risk you were clearly more than willing to take," he observed, again cutting her off.

She opened her mouth to respond, but by then, she knew already that there was nothing she could say to appease him. In the silence, Maria felt a knot form in her stomach as Ken finally took a seat at his desk.

"I must say that I'm very disappointed in your decision," he said, sounding in control. "We took the risk of hiring you because I, among others, went to bat for you. Your work at the DA's office was hardly relevant to our practice here, as you know. But I thought you had potential. Now, I'm not sure what to think or whether I made the wrong decision."

"I'm really sorry. It won't happen again."

"I hope not. For your sake, not mine."

The knot in her stomach grew even larger. "What can I do to make things right?"

"For now, nothing. I'll talk to Barney and find out what he thinks and then we'll let you know what we decide."

"Should I call the clients? Perhaps try to apologize?"

"I think you should do nothing for now. I said that Barney and I will discuss it. But if something like this ever happens again…" He leaned forward, turning on his desk lamp.

"It won't," she whispered, still trying to get her bearings. Barney was thinking about making her lead counsel? Why hadn't he mentioned that to her? In that instant, the phone on the desk rang and Ken picked it up. After announcing his name, he nodded before covering the mouthpiece.

"I've got to take this call. We'll finish our talk at another time."

The way he said it left no doubt that *they'd talk again* and Maria rose from her seat, humiliated and panicked. Her thoughts in disarray, she stumbled out of Ken's office. Passing his secretary, she was grateful that the woman ignored her. When she reached her office, she shut the door and ran through the conversation again. Despite herself, she wondered just how long she would be able to continue working there. Or whether she'd even be given a choice.

CHAPTER 3

———— ❦ ————

Colin

On the Monday after his fight, Colin stepped out of his apartment and was ambling toward the old Camaro when he suddenly spotted Detective Pete Margolis. The cop had parked in the street out front and was leaning against the hood of his sedan, holding a to-go cup of coffee, a toothpick in his mouth. Unlike most of the officers Colin had dealt with in the past, Margolis spent almost as much time in the gym as Colin did. His sleeves were rolled up, the fabric straining against his biceps. He was in his late thirties, his dark hair swept back and greased in place with God knows what. Once, sometimes twice a month, he would show up unannounced to check on Colin as part of Colin's court-ordered deal. Margolis clearly enjoyed the power he had over his charge.

"You look like hell, Hancock," he said as Colin drew near. "You do anything I should know about?"

"No," Colin answered.

"You sure about that?"

Colin watched Margolis instead of answering. He knew the guy would eventually get around to whatever he wanted to say.

Margolis moved his toothpick from one side of his mouth to the other. "There was a brawl in the parking lot at Crazy Horse a little after midnight. A bunch of guys swinging bottles at each other; a few cars in the lot got dented up and there was a man knocked unconscious. Witnesses said he'd been kicked in the head after he was on the ground. Right now, he's in the hospital with a cracked skull. That's assault with a deadly weapon, you know, and as soon as I heard about it, I thought to myself how familiar that sounded. Didn't I arrest you for something like that right here in Wilmington? Just a few years ago? And haven't you been in a couple of scrapes since then?"

Margolis already knew the answers, but Colin answered anyway. "Yes to the first. No to the second."

"Oh, that's right. Because your friends intervened. The goofy guy and the hot blond chick, right?"

Colin said nothing. Margolis stared. Colin continued to wait until Margolis finally went on.

"That's why I'm here, by the way."

"Okay."

"Just okay?"

Colin said nothing. He had learned to say as little as possible in the presence of the police.

"Put yourself in my shoes," Margolis finally went on. "The thing is, pretty much everyone scattered as soon as the sirens started closing in. A couple of witnesses stuck around and I talked to them, but I figured I was just wasting my time. It's a lot easier to go straight to the source, don't you think?"

Colin hitched his backpack a little higher on his shoulder. "Are we done here?"

"Not quite. I don't think you understand what's going on."

"I understand. But none of this concerns me. I wasn't there."

"Can you prove that?"

"Can you prove otherwise?"

Margolis took a sip of his coffee, then fished a fresh toothpick from his pocket. He took his time placing it in his mouth. "That almost sounds like you're trying to hide something."

"It was just a question," Colin said.

"All right, then. Let's get to the questions. Where were you Saturday night?"

"In Jacksonville."

"Oh yeah," he said. "The fight. MMA stuff, right? You told me about that. Did you win?"

Margolis didn't care and Colin knew it. He watched Margolis take another sip of coffee.

"The point is, we were able to get a couple of descriptions from the witnesses, and it turns out that the guy who did the kicking was in his midtwenties, muscular with tattoos on his arms and short brown hair, almost a buzz cut. And wouldn't you know it, it turns out that the guy was pretty bruised up even *before* the fight started. People had seen him inside. And because I knew you'd just been fighting in Jacksonville . . . well, it doesn't take a genius to figure out what happened."

Colin wondered how much, if any, of Margolis's story was true. "Do you have any other questions for me?"

Margolis shifted the toothpick again while setting his coffee on the hood. "Were you at the Crazy Horse on Saturday night?"

"No."

"You didn't even stop by? For a few minutes?"

"No."

"And if I have a witness that says he saw you there?"

"Then he's lying."

"But you're not."

Again, Colin didn't answer. There was no reason to. And part of him suspected that even Margolis knew it, because after a long moment, he crossed his arms, his muscles flexing almost—but not entirely—involuntarily. If the detective really had something, Colin knew he would have already been arrested.

"All right," Margolis said. "Then answer this: Where were you between midnight and one a.m. on Sunday?"

Colin sorted through his memory. "I wasn't watching the clock. But I was either about to leave Trey's Diner on Highway 17, or driving home, or changing some lady's tire during the storm. I was home right around one thirty."

"Trey's Diner? Why the hell would you eat there?"

"I was hungry."

"What time did you leave Jacksonville?"

"It was after midnight. Maybe five or ten minutes after, but I don't know for sure."

"Witnesses?"

"Dozens."

"And I assume you ate alone at Trey's?"

"I was with my landlord."

Margolis snorted. "Evan? One half of the dynamic duo? That's convenient."

Colin flexed his jaw, ignoring the barb. "I'm sure the waitress will remember the two of us."

"Because you look like you had your face run through a meat grinder?"

"No. Because Evan stood out in a place like that."

Margolis smirked, but business was business. "So you left the diner."

"Yes."

"Alone?"

"Yes. Evan left a few minutes before I did. He drove his own car."

"So there's no one who can say where you went afterwards?"

"I already told you what happened after that."

"Oh, that's right. You changed a lady's tire."

"Yes."

"In the storm?"

"Yes."

"Did you know her?"

"No."

"Then why did you stop?"

"Because I thought she might need my help."

Margolis considered Colin's answer, no doubt thinking that

Colin had been caught in a mistake. "How could you know she might need help unless you'd already stopped?"

"I saw she needed a hand getting the tire out. I stopped and got out of the car. I offered to help. She said no at first. She asked if she could borrow my phone and call her sister. I let her use my phone and she called her sister. And then she asked for my help in changing her tire. I changed it. Then I got in my car and drove straight home."

"What time was this?"

"I don't know. But a call was made from my phone from the woman to her sister. If you'd like, I'll show you my call log."

"By all means."

Colin reached into his back pocket and pulled out his phone; a few taps and the call log was on display, confirming his alibi. He showed it to Margolis.

Margolis took out his pad and made a point to slowly jot the number down. No doubt it was right around the time of the brawl, because his biceps flexed again. "How do I know that's the number for the lady's sister?"

"You don't."

"But you're fine if I call and check."

"Do what you want. It's your time that you'll be wasting."

Margolis's eyes narrowed slightly. "You think you're pretty smart, don't you?"

"No."

"Oh yeah you do. But you know what? You're not."

Colin didn't answer, and for a long moment, they continued to stare at each other. Margolis grabbed his coffee again and circled back to the driver's-side door. "I'm going to check this out, you know. Because you and I both know that you don't belong on the streets. A guy like you? How many people have you sent to the hospital over the years? You're violent, and while you think you can control it forever, you can't. And when that happens, I'm going to be there. And I'll be the first one to say, 'I told you so.'"

A moment later, the sedan was pulling away, Colin watching until it finally vanished around the corner.

❧

"What was that about?"

Colin turned around and spotted Evan on the porch. Already dressed for work, his friend stepped down and started up the walk.

"The usual."

"What was it this time?"

"Fight at the Crazy Horse."

"When?"

"When I was with you. Or driving or changing a tire."

"I might be your alibi this time?"

"I doubt it. He knows it wasn't me or he would have brought me in and questioned me at the station."

"Then why the big show?"

Colin shrugged. It was a rhetorical question, since they both already knew the answer. Colin motioned toward his friend.

"Isn't that the tie Lily bought for your birthday?"

Evan looked down to examine it. It was paisley, a kaleidoscope of color. "Yes it is, as a matter of fact. Good memory. What do you think? Too much?"

"It doesn't matter what I think."

"But you don't like it."

"I think that if you want to wear it, you should wear it."

Evan seemed momentarily undecided. "Why do you do that?"

"Do what?"

"Refuse to answer a simple question."

"Because my opinion is irrelevant. You should wear what you want."

"Just tell me, okay?"

"I don't like your tie."

"Really? Why not?"

"Because it's ugly."

"It's not ugly."

Colin nodded. "Okay."

"You don't know what you're talking about."

"Probably."

"You don't even wear ties."

"You're right."

"So why do I care what you think?"

"I don't know."

Evan scowled. "Talking to you can be infuriating, you know."

"I know. You've said that before."

"Of course I've said it before! Because it's true! Didn't we just talk about this the other night? You don't have to say whatever pops into your head."

"But you asked."

"Just...Oh, forget it." He turned and started back toward the house. "I'll talk to you later, okay?"

"Where are you going?"

Evan walked a couple of steps before answering without turning around. "To change my damn tie. And by the way, Margolis was right. Your face still looks like it was run through a meat grinder."

Colin smiled. "Hey, Evan!"

Evan stopped and turned. "What?"

"Thanks."

"For what?"

"For everything."

"Yeah, yeah. You're just lucky I won't tell Lily what you said."

"You can if you'd like. I already told her."

Evan stared. "Of course you did."

In class, Colin sat in the third row, taking notes and trying to concentrate on what the teacher was saying. The class focused on language and literacy development, and in the first few weeks of school, he'd been of two minds about it: first, thinking that most of what the professor was saying struck him as common sense, which made him wonder what he'd gain from being there; and second, that there might be some as-yet unknown advantage to quantifying common sense into some sort of cohesive classroom strategy so he'd be able to put together formal lesson plans. The only problem was that the professor—a neurotic middle-aged woman with a singsong voice—tended to wander from one subject to the next, which made paying attention somewhat difficult.

He was in his third year of college, but it was his first semester at UNC Wilmington. His first two years had been spent at Cape Fear Community College, where he'd finished with a perfect GPA. So far, he couldn't tell whether the classes were harder here or there; in the end, that would come down to the difficulty of the exams and the quality expected of his papers. He wasn't too concerned: He made a point to read ahead whenever possible, and he knew Lily would help him study, quizzing him when he needed it in addition to helping him edit his papers. As a rule, he liked to put in at least twenty-five hours a week of studying, in addition to time in class; whenever he had a break on campus, he wandered to the library, and so far, it seemed to be paying off. Unlike many of the students who were here for both an education *and* a social life, he was here only to learn as much as he could and get the best grades possible. He'd already done the *sow your wild oats* thing; in fact, it had been all he could do to escape it.

Still, he felt pretty good about having made it to this point. He had Evan and Lily; he had his MMA training and a place he called his own. He wasn't too fond of his job—the restaurant where he bartended was too touristy for his own tastes—but it wasn't the kind of place that led to him getting into any kind of trouble. Most people came there to eat, including lots of families with kids, and those who sat at the bar were usually waiting for a table or having dinner. It was certainly a far cry from the kind of bar he used to frequent. During his wild years, he'd favored pro bars—for professional alcoholics—those dark and dingy out-of-the-way dives with or without blaring music in the background. He'd expected problems almost as soon as he walked in the door, and the world had obliged him. These days, he avoided places like that at all costs. He knew his triggers and his limits, and though he'd come a long way in keeping his anger in check, there was always the possibility that he'd find himself in a situation that quickly spiraled out of control. And there was no doubt in his mind that even if he was involved in an incident in another state, Margolis would find out and he'd live in a cage for the next decade, surrounded by people who had the same kind of anger problems as he did.

Realizing that he was drifting, he forced himself to focus on the lecture again. The professor was telling them that some teachers found it beneficial to read passages from books that were age appropriate, as opposed to books that were geared toward older or younger students. He wondered whether to jot that down in his notes—did he really need to remind himself of that in the future?—before deciding, *Oh, what the hell.* If she thought it important enough to say, he'd make note of it.

It was around that point, however, that he noticed a dark-haired girl peeking at him over her shoulder. While he'd drawn the expected stares when he'd entered the classroom—even the professor had done a double take and broken off in midsentence—by now the stares had been redirected toward the front of the room.

Except for this girl. Definitely watching him, almost scrutinizing. He didn't get the sense that she was flirting; rather, it was almost like she was trying to figure him out. Not that it mattered to him one way or the other. Stare or not; it was her choice.

When class finished a few minutes later, Colin closed his notebook and stuffed it into his backpack. Flinging his backpack over his shoulder, he winced when it thumped against his bruised ribs.

After classes, he planned to head to the gym to work out, but he wasn't up for contact just yet. No sparring or grappling; just weights, core work, and a half hour of jumping rope. He'd take a break for a bit, then pop in his earbuds and run five miles while listening to the kind of music his parents had always hated, and after that, he'd shower and get ready for work. He wondered how his boss was going to react when she saw him; he suspected she wouldn't be pleased. His face wouldn't exactly blend in with the touristy atmosphere, but what could he do?

With an hour until his next class, he began walking toward the library. He had a paper to write, and though he'd gotten a start on it last week, he wanted to finish the first draft in the next couple of days, which wasn't going to be easy. Between training and work, he had to utilize his limited free time efficiently.

Still sore from the fight, he walked slowly, noting the reactions of the girls who passed him. They were nearly uniform: They'd spot him and do a quick double take, revealing expressions of shock and fear, and then pretend not to have even noticed him at all. The thought amused him—a single *Boo!* would likely send them fleeing in the opposite direction.

As he turned onto a different walkway, a voice called out from behind him. "Hey, wait up! You, up there!" Certain it wasn't directed at him, he ignored it.

"Hey you, with the hurt face! I said wait up!"

It took Colin a second to make sure he had heard right, but when he stopped and turned, he spotted the dark-haired girl from class, waving. He glanced over his shoulder; no one else was paying attention. As she finally closed in, he recognized her as the girl who'd been watching him in class.

"Are you talking to me?"

"Ya think?" she said, stopping a few feet away. "Who else has a hurt face around here?"

He wasn't sure whether to be offended or laugh, but she said it in a way that made it impossible to take umbrage.

"Do I know you?"

"We're in class together."

"I know. I saw you staring at me. But I still don't know you."

"You're right," she said. "We're strangers. But may I ask you a question?"

He knew exactly what was coming—the whole hurt-face thing was the tip-off—and he hitched up his backpack.

"I was in a fight."

"Obviously," she said. "But that's not what I wanted to ask you. I wanted to know how old you are."

He blinked in surprise. "I'm twenty-eight. Why?"

"That's perfect," she said, not answering his question. "Where are you going?"

"To the library."

"Good. Me too. May I join you? I think we should talk."

"Why?"

She smiled, vaguely reminding him of someone else. "If we talk, you can find out."

CHAPTER 4

Maria

W here are we going again?" Maria asked from the driver's seat. She'd picked up Serena half an hour earlier on South Front Street, which ran parallel to the Cape Fear River. Serena had been standing at an intersection in an area dotted with older office buildings and occasional clusters of shacks and boathouses at the river's edge, oblivious to the construction workers across the street who were clearly ogling her. Slowly but surely, the area was being revitalized, like the rest of the waterfront along the river, but for now it was a work in progress. "And why did I have to pick you up?"

"I've already told you. We're going to a *restaurant*," Serena answered. "And you picked me up because I don't plan on driving tonight, since I might have a couple of drinks." She tossed a lock of hair over her shoulder. "The interview went well, by the way. Charles said he found my answers very *thoughtful*. Thanks for asking."

Maria rolled her eyes. "How did you get there?"

"Steve dropped me off. I think he likes me. He's meeting me here later."

"He has to like you if he's willing to put up with this traffic." Though the first half of September had passed, the heat was more reminiscent of early August and the shore was packed. Maria had already circled the block twice searching for a place to park.

"Who cares? We're at the beach."

"There are better places to eat downtown."

"How would you know? Have you even been to Wrightsville Beach since you moved back?"

"No."

"My point exactly. You live in Wilmington. You need to get to the beach every now and then."

"I paddleboard, remember? I see the beach a lot more than you do."

"I mean someplace with actual people around, not just birds and turtles and the occasional jumping fish. You need to go someplace fun with a great view and a lot of atmosphere."

"Crabby Pete's?"

"It's a local institution."

"It's a tourist trap."

"So what? I've never been there and I want to find out what the big deal is."

Maria brought her lips together. "Why am I getting the sense that there's more to this than you're saying?"

"Because you're a lawyer. You're suspicious of everything."

"Maybe. Or it could simply be that you've got something planned."

"What makes you say that?"

"Because it's Saturday night. We *never* go out on Saturday night. You've never *wanted* to go out with me on Saturday night."

"That's why we're having an early dinner," Serena answered. "There are a bunch of bands playing in the bars down here this weekend, and Steve and I and a few friends are going to listen to some music before we hit the parties. They don't get going until ten or eleven anyway, so there's plenty of time."

Maria knew that Serena had something up her sleeve but couldn't quite put her finger on it. "I hope you don't expect me to tag along."

"Not a chance," Serena huffed. "You're way too old for that. It would be like going out with our parents."

"Gee, thanks."

"Don't blame me. You're the one who said you were too old for guys my age. Why? Are you changing your mind?"

"No."

"That's why we're just having dinner."

Maria suddenly spotted another car vacating a spot and she turned, closing in on it. It was still a block or two from the restaurant, but she doubted she'd be able to get any closer. As she parked, she couldn't shake the feeling that Serena was being way too coy, and Serena seemed to realize it.

"Stop worrying so much. You're killing the mood. What's wrong with spending a little time with your sister?"

Maria hesitated. "Fine, but just so we're clear . . . if you're planning to have some other guy join us at the table or something crazy like that, I'm not going to be happy."

"I'm not Jill and Paul, okay? I wouldn't set you up on some awful blind date without even asking you. But if it makes you feel any better, I can guarantee that no guy will sit with us. In fact, we'll just eat at the bar. The view is supposed to be better anyway. Deal?"

Maria debated before finally shutting off the engine. "Deal."

Located next to one of the piers at Wrightsville Beach, Crabby Pete's had been around for nearly forty years. Having barely survived one hurricane after the next, the structure might have been condemned had not numerous repairs of varying quality been undertaken over the years. The building sported peeling paint, a listing rooftop, and more than a few missing or broken shutters.

Despite its appearance, the restaurant was bustling and Maria and Serena had to squeeze through the crowd waiting for tables as they made for the stairs leading to the rooftop bar. Following her sister, Maria noticed the wooden tables, mismatched chairs, and personalized graffiti on the walls. From the ceiling hung items that the original Pete—who'd passed away years ago—had supposedly found in his nets while fishing: hubcaps and tennis shoes, deflated basketballs, a woman's bra, toys, and scores of license plates from more than ten states.

"Pretty cool, huh?" Serena called over her shoulder.

"It's certainly crowded."

"It's an experience. Come on!"

They climbed the creaking steps to the rooftop. Emerging into the sun, Maria squinted under a cloudless sky. Unlike in the restaurant downstairs, the tables up here were occupied by adults unwinding with open bottles of beer or mixed drinks in front of them. Three waitresses in shorts and black tank tops scurried among the customers, efficiently picking up empties and dropping off drinks. Half the tables had tin pails filled with crab legs, and she watched as diners cracked the shells to get to the meat.

"We're in luck," Serena said. "There are two seats at the bar."

The bar was on the far side, partially covered with a rusting tin awning and fronted by ten stools. Maria followed Serena, winding between the tables in the fierce sun. It was cooler in the shade of the bar's awning, though, and as they took their seats, she could feel the salt-tinged breeze lifting the long hair off her neck. Over Serena's shoulder, Maria could see the waves breaking on the shore, blue changing suddenly to white and back again. Even though it was almost dinnertime, hundreds of beachgoers still frolicked in the water or sprawled on towels. The pier was jammed with people leaning over the railing with their fishing poles, waiting for something to strike. Serena took in the scene before swiveling back to Maria.

"Admit it," Serena challenged. "This is exactly what you needed. Say that I was right."

"Fine. You were right."

"I love it when you say that," she crowed. "Now let's get something to drink. What are you in the mood for?"

"Just a glass of wine."

"No, no, no," Serena declared, suddenly shaking her head. "You're not having a glass of wine here. This isn't a glass-of-wine kind of place. We need to do something... beachy, like we're on vacation. A piña colada or margarita or something like that."

"Seriously?"

"You really have to learn to live a little." Serena leaned over the bar. "Hey, Colin! Can we get a couple of drinks?"

Maria hadn't noticed the bartender and her eyes followed Serena's. Dressed in faded jeans and a white collared shirt rolled to the elbows, he was finishing up an order for a waitress on the far side. Maria noticed automatically that he was exceptionally fit, with well-defined shoulders tapering down to narrow hips. He wore his hair very short, almost in a buzz cut that revealed an intricate tattooed ivy design wrapping around the back of his neck. Though his back was turned, Maria was impressed by how efficiently he moved as he readied the cocktails. She leaned toward her sister.

"I thought you said you've never been here before."

"I haven't."

"Then how do you know the bartender's name?"

"My friend works here."

At Serena's answer, the bartender turned. With his face partially shadowed, his features weren't immediately visible, and it wasn't until he stepped closer that Maria noticed the fading bruise on his cheek and all at once, it came together. The bartender froze for a second as well, no doubt mirroring her own thoughts: *You've got to be kidding.* In the awkward moment that followed, Maria had the impression that while he wasn't thrilled by Serena's surprise, he wasn't necessarily upset by it, either. He resumed his approach until he was standing right in front of them. Leaning forward, he rested his hand on the bar, revealing the sculpted, colorfully tattooed muscle of his forearm.

"Hey, Serena," he said. His unhurried, confident voice was exactly as Maria remembered. "You decided to come."

Serena seemed content to act as though she hadn't orchestrated the whole scenario. "I figured, why not? It's a gorgeous day!" She spread her arms wide. "What a great place! You were right about the view from up here. It's incredible. Has it been busy today?"

"I've been overrun."

"No wonder. Who wouldn't want to come on a day like today? Oh, by the way, this is my sister, Maria."

Colin's gaze met hers, unreadable except for a trace of amusement somewhere in its depths. Up close, his appearance was nothing like it had been on the night he'd changed her tire; with his high cheekbones, blue-gray eyes, and long lashes, it was easy to imagine him picking up almost any woman he wanted. "Hi, Maria," he said, extending his hand across the bar. "I'm Colin."

She took his hand in hers, feeling a restrained strength in his grip. Letting go, she watched as his gaze flickered from her to Serena and back again.

"What can I get you?" he asked.

Serena studied them both before finally propping her elbows on the bar. "How about a couple of piña coladas?"

"Coming right up," he said easily. Turning around, he grabbed the blender and bent over to reach into the refrigerator, his jeans growing tight around his thighs. Maria watched as he added the ingredients before turning her narrowed gaze on Serena.

"Really?" Maria said, more a statement than a question.

"What?" Serena asked, sounding pleased with herself.

"This is why we came? Because you wanted us to meet?"

"You're the one who said you never had a chance to thank him. Now's your chance."

Maria shook her head, amazed. "How did you . . . ?"

"Colin's in my class." She reached for a bucket of peanuts on the bar and snapped one of them open. "Actually, he's in two of my classes, but we really only met this week. While we were getting to know each other, he mentioned that he worked here and that he had a shift this afternoon. I thought it might be fun for us to drop in and say hello."

"Of course you did."

"What's the big deal? We'll be out of here soon and you can head back home and take up knitting mittens for cats or whatever. Don't make this into something that it isn't."

"Why should I? You've already done that."

"Talk to him, don't talk to him," Serena said, reaching for another peanut, "it doesn't matter to me. It's your life, not mine. And besides, we're already here, let's just enjoy it, okay?"

"I really hate that you—"

"In case you're interested," Serena interrupted, "Colin is actually a very nice guy. Smart, too. And you have to admit, he's kind of hot as far as bartenders go." She lowered her voice to a whisper. "I actually think his tattoos are sexy," she said, nodding toward him. "I'll bet he's got some more that aren't visible, too."

Maria struggled to find words. "I think…" she sputtered, trying to sort through it all and experiencing the same sort of confusion she had on the night she'd first met Colin. "Can we please just have our drinks and go?"

Serena made a face. "But I'm hungry."

Colin returned with their drinks and set the foamy glasses in front of them. "Anything else?" he asked.

Before Maria could decline, Serena raised her voice over the sound of the crowd. "Could we have a menu?"

Serena pointedly ignored Maria's obvious discomfort all through dinner.

Still, Maria had to admit that it wasn't as uncomfortable as she'd feared, mostly because Colin was too busy to treat them as anything other than ordinary customers. He mentioned nothing about changing Maria's tire or about his classes with Serena; because of the crowd at the bar, he had barely enough time to keep up with orders. He hustled continuously from one end of the bar to the other, taking orders and making drinks, closing out bills, and getting the waitresses what they needed. In the next hour, the rooftop only became more crowded, and despite the addition of a second bartender a few minutes after they'd arrived—a pretty blonde perhaps a year older than Serena—the wait for drinks continued to grow. If there was any indication that Colin knew Serena at all, it was that their dinner order was taken and delivered promptly, as was a second round of drinks. He cleared their plates moments after they finished and dropped off the bill, which he also closed out as soon as Maria laid down her credit card. Meanwhile, Serena kept up a steady flow of lively chatter.

There were even moments when Maria forgot about Colin entirely, though from time to time she found her gaze flickering his way. Serena hadn't said anything more about him, but Maria thought he seemed too old to be a college student. She supposed she could ask Serena about that, but she didn't want to give her the satisfaction, since she'd dragged Maria here under false pretenses.

Despite herself, Maria had to admit that Serena was right about the fact that Colin—when he wasn't bruised, bloody, and soaking wet on a deserted stretch of road—was seriously good-looking. Oddly clean-cut despite his tattoos and powerful build, he had a quick, almost wry grin, and as far as she could tell, all three of the waitresses had crushes on him. So did the group of women at the far end of the bar who'd shown up twenty minutes ago. She could tell by the way they smiled at him as he prepared their drinks and watched him after he'd turned away. Same thing with the other bartender; though she was as busy as Colin, she seemed to become noticeably distracted whenever he reached past her for a glass or a bottle of liquor.

Good-looking bartenders were common enough to be a cliché, as was the practice of flirting with them, but Colin's reaction to the subtle and not-so-subtle signals surprised her. Though he was pleasant with everyone, he otherwise seemed oblivious to his admirers' attention. Or, at least, he was *acting* oblivious. As she was trying to decode his motive, another, older male bartender moved behind the bar, partially blocking her view of Colin. Beside her, Serena had her phone out and was texting.

"I'm letting Steve and Melissa know that we're about done," Serena said, her fingers dancing.

"Are they here?"

"They're walking this way now," she said. When Maria just nodded, Serena went on. "He's twenty-eight, you know."

"Steve?"

"No," Serena answered. "Steve is my age. Colin is twenty-eight."

"And?"

"You're twenty-eight, too."

"Yes, I know."

Serena drained her drink. "I figured I might as well mention it, since you've been sneaking peeks at him all night."

"No, I haven't."

"You could have fooled me."

Maria reached for her own drink, feeling slightly buoyant from the alcohol. "Okay," she conceded, "maybe I did check him out once or twice. But twenty-eight is a little too old to still be in college, don't you think?"

"That depends."

"Depends on what?"

"On when he started. Colin didn't start until a couple of years ago, so he's right on schedule. He wants to be an elementary school teacher, just like me. And if you're curious, his grades are probably better than mine. He takes his classes very seriously. He sits at the front of the class and takes ridiculous notes."

"Why are you telling me this?"

"Because it's obvious that you're interested in him."

"I'm not interested in him."

"You've been making that clear all night," Serena agreed, feigning innocence. "He's definitely not the type you'd ever want to go dancing with. A guy that handsome? Please."

Maria opened her mouth to respond but closed it again, knowing that saying anything more would only encourage her sister further. In the silence, Serena's phone pinged and she peered down at it.

"Steve's downstairs. You ready to go? Or would you rather wait here for a bit?"

"Why? Because you want me to hit on Colin?"

"He's not here."

Maria looked up; sure enough, Colin was gone.

"He was working the afternoon shift, so he's probably off the clock," Serena added, sliding off her stool. She hitched her purse over her shoulder. "Thanks for dinner, by the way. Do you want to walk down with me?"

Maria reached for her purse. "I thought you said you didn't want me to meet Steve."

"I was kidding. He wants to be a lawyer, by the way. Maybe you can talk him out of it."

"Why would I do that?"

"Do you really need me to answer that question after all you've been through?"

Maria was silent. Serena, like their parents, knew how hard the last couple of years had been.

"Still," Serena said, "it's a shame."

"What's a shame?"

"I know Colin was busy tonight, but you never did thank him

for changing your tire. You might not want to talk to him, but it *was* a nice thing for him to do that night, and you could have told him so."

Again Maria said nothing, but as she followed Serena to the stairs, she found herself thinking that her sister was, as usual, right.

Steve was cute in a preppy kind of way, right down to the plaid shorts and light blue polo that matched his Topsiders. He came across as nice enough, though it was apparent within minutes that he was a lot more interested in Serena than she was in him, since she spent most of her time talking to Melissa. Though Maria chided herself for it as she started in the direction of her car, she found herself envying the ease with which her younger sister seemed to navigate every facet of her life.

Then again, how hard was life for a twenty-one-year-old student? College was a bubble that kept the rest of the world at bay. There was an abundance of free time, friends who lived either with you or right next door, and an overwhelming sense of optimism about the future, even if you had no idea as to the specifics of what that might mean. In college, everyone accepted the fact that their lives would turn out exactly as planned, buoying them from one good memory to the next in a cascade of carefree three-day weekends.

She hesitated, changing her mind. Well, for people like Serena, anyway. Maria's own experience had been different because she'd taken her education more seriously than most—she could remember being way too stressed way too often. In retrospect, she realized that she'd probably spent too much time studying and worrying about exams. She recalled working on papers until the wee hours of the morning, editing them over and over until every word was just right. At the time, it seemed like the most important thing in the world, but in the last few years, she'd begun to wonder why she'd taken it all so seriously. Bill Gates, Steve Jobs, Michael Dell, and Mark Zuckerberg had dropped out of college, and they'd done okay, right? They intuitively understood that the world didn't care about grades or even graduating, at least not in the long run, especially when compared to traits like creativity or persistence. Sure, her grades had likely helped her land her very first job with the district attorney's office, but had anyone cared since then? When she'd been hired at the firm, they'd been interested only in her work experience and seemed to regard the first twenty-four years of her life as inconsequential. These days, Barney's conversations were centered on her current work product, and Ken's interests were of a different nature entirely.

Thinking back, she regretted not taking a year off after graduation and going backpacking through Europe, or volunteering for Teach for America or whatever. Frankly, it didn't matter what she did as long as it was something interesting, but she'd been in such a headlong rush to grow up and become an adult that those thoughts had never even entered her mind. She didn't always feel like she was really *living*, though, and she sometimes found herself regretting the choices she'd made. And on that subject, wasn't she too young to have these kinds of regrets, anyway? Weren't those supposed to start in middle age? Lord knows, her mom and dad didn't seem to have any and they *were* middle-aged. Meanwhile, Serena acted as though she didn't have a care in the world, either—so where had Maria gone wrong?

She blamed her melancholy thoughts on the piña coladas, whose effects she was still feeling a bit. Deciding to give herself a little more time before she got behind the wheel, she squinted at the pier and decided, *Why not?* Dusk was coming on, but she still had another hour or so before it was dark.

Turning around, she started that way, watching the chaotic activity as families began to depart the beach en masse. Sun-burned kids, overtired and whining, trailed their equally sun-burned and overtired parents, who were hauling boogie boards, coolers, umbrellas, and towels.

At the beach, she stopped to slip off her sandals, wondering if she'd recognize anyone from high school or whether they'd recognize her, but she spotted no one familiar. She trudged through the sand and when she reached the pier, she made her way up the steps just as the sun was beginning its slow descent. Through the slats beneath her feet, she watched as sand gave way to shallow water, then finally to waves cascading toward the shore. In either direction, surfers were still catching swells. Admiring their graceful movements, she passed people fishing; men and women, young and old, all of them lost in their own worlds. She remembered that when she had been a teenager, a boy she'd liked had once talked her into giving it a try. It was a blazing-hot day and casting was more difficult than she thought it would be. They eventually left the pier empty-handed, and she later realized that she liked the boy a lot more than she'd ever like fishing.

The crowds grew sparser the farther out she got, and by the time she reached the end of the pier she noticed only a lone fisherman, his back toward her. He was dressed in faded jeans and a baseball cap, but from her cursory glance she could tell that he was put together just right. Shrugging off the thought, she turned her gaze to the horizon, catching sight of the moon rising from the sea. In the distance, a catamaran glided over the surface, and she idly wondered whether Serena might be persuaded to join her on a sailing trip one weekend.

"Are you following me?" The voice came from the corner of the pier.

When she turned, it took a few seconds for her to register that it was Colin. The fisherman in the baseball cap, she suddenly realized. She felt heat rise in her cheeks. Had Serena set this up, too? No, coming out here had been her idea. Hadn't it? Serena hadn't talked about Colin or the pier...which meant this had to be a coincidence, like the night he'd pulled over and changed her tire. What were the odds of meeting him here? Too low to be plausible, and yet...he was here and she was here, and she could tell he was waiting for an answer.

"No," she stammered. "I'm not following you. I just came out here to enjoy the view."

He seemed to weigh her answer. "And?"

"And what?"

"The view. How is it?"

Flustered, she had to process his question before she could answer. "It's beautiful," she finally said.

"Better than from the restaurant?"

"Different. More peaceful."

"I think so, too. That's why I'm here."

"But you're fishing...?"

"Not really," he said. "Like you, I'm mainly here to appreciate the scenery." He smiled before leaning over the railing. "I didn't mean to bother you," he assured her. "Enjoy the sunset, Maria."

Somehow, hearing him say her name out here felt more intimate than it had in the bar, and she absently watched as he began reeling in his line. He cast again, the line unspooling into the distance, and she wondered whether she should stay or go. He seemed content to give her space, just as he'd done the night they'd first met. Which reminded her...

"Hey, Colin?"

He turned his head. "Yes?"

"I should have thanked you for changing my tire the other night. You really saved me."

"You're welcome. I was glad to help." He smiled. "And I'm glad you came to the restaurant tonight, too."

"That was Serena's idea."

"I could tell. You didn't seem all that happy to see me."

"It wasn't that. I was just...surprised."

"Me too."

Maria could feel his gaze lingering on her before he finally turned away. She wasn't quite sure how to respond, and for a while, the two of them simply stood there in silence. Colin seemed perfectly relaxed and self-contained, while Maria tried to immerse herself in the view once again. A shrimp boat trawled the darker waters in the distance, and over her shoulder, the lights flickered on at Crabby Pete's. The faint strains of classic rock began to drift out of one of the restaurants, signaling the beginning of the evening festivities.

She studied Colin from the corner of her eye, trying to figure out why he seemed so different than other men. In her experience, men her age generally fell into one of five categories: arrogant types who believed themselves to be one of God's favorite creations; friendly guys who might become keepers except for the fact that they often weren't interested in relationships; shy guys who could barely speak; men who weren't interested in her at all for one reason or another; and really good ones—genuine keepers—who were almost always taken, in her experience. Colin didn't seem like the first kind, and based on what she'd observed at the bar, he didn't seem like the second or third kinds, either. Which meant, obviously, that he was either the fourth or fifth kind. He wasn't interested in her...and yet, deep down, she suspected that she might be wrong about that, though she wasn't sure why. Which left the possibility that he was in the fifth category, but unfortunately, she'd pretty much ended the conversation earlier, so maybe his silence was a reaction to her perceived standoffishness.

After he'd changed her tire. After his friendly efficiency at the bar. After Serena had assured her that he was a nice guy. And after he'd initiated a conversation just a few moments earlier. She felt her shoulders slump. No wonder she spent her weekends alone.

"Hey, Colin?" she tried again.

He was still leanin̶ ̶ ̶ ̶ ̶ ̶ailing, and when he turned after a moment, she de̶ ̶ ̶ ̶ ̶same trace of amusement she'd noticed in the bar. "Yes?̶"

"May I ask you a questio̶̶."

"Yes." His blue-gray eyes glowed like sea glass.

"Why do you like fishing?"

He reached up, tilting his hat back slightly. "I guess I don't, really. And I'm not very good at it, either. I hardly ever catch anything."

She registered the soft precision of his speech. "Then why do you do it?"

"It's a good way to unwind after work, especially when it's busy…It's just nice to have a few minutes to myself, you know? I come out here and it's quiet and the world slows down for a while. I started bringing a pole because it gave me something to do, instead of just standing out here and staring at the horizon."

"Like I was doing?"

"Exactly. Would you like to borrow my pole?" When she laughed under her breath, he went on. "Besides, I think it made people nervous when I just stood out here brooding, like I was up to no good. And earlier this week, with the bruises, I probably would have scared them, too."

"I'd like to think you came off as contemplative."

"I doubt it. You, on the other hand, come across as the type who frequently contemplates things. Life. Goals. Dreams."

She flushed, feeling too tongue-tied to answer. Despite herself, she couldn't help agreeing with Serena: Colin was seriously… *hot.* She shook the thought away, not wanting to go there.

"Do you mind?" he said, motioning toward her before leaning over and grabbing his tackle box. "I'm not having a lot of luck over here."

His suggestion caught her off guard. "Uh, yeah…sure. But if you're not very good at fishing, I can't promise this spot will be any better."

"It probably won't be," he admitted, drawing near. He set the tackle box beside him on the pier, leaving a comfortable distance between them. "But I won't have to talk so loud."

Unlike her, he seemed perfectly relaxed, and she watched as he reeled in his line and recast in a new location. He leaned forward, jerking the pole slightly.

"Your sister has quite a personality," he said after a moment.

"Why do you say that?"

"Her introduction to me included the words, 'Hey you, with the hurt face.'"

Maria grinned, thinking that sounded exactly like Serena. "She's one of a kind, that's for sure."

"But she's more like a friend than a sister, right?"

"Did she tell you that?"

"No," he said. "I noticed it while I waited on the two of you. It's easy to tell you're pretty close."

"We are," Maria agreed. "Do you have siblings?"

"Two older sisters."

"Are you close?"

"Not like you and Serena," he admitted as he adjusted the fishing line. "I love them and I care about them, but we kind of ended up taking different paths in life."

"Which means?"

"We don't really talk that often. Maybe once every couple of months or so. It's been improving lately, but it's a gradual process."

"That's too bad."

"It is what it is," he said.

His answer suggested he didn't really want to discuss it further. "Serena said that you and she are in class together?" she asked, venturing on to safer ground.

He nodded. "She caught up with me on the way to the library. I guess you must have told her how I looked that night and she put it all together. Which wasn't too hard, what with the hurt face and all."

"It wasn't so bad. I didn't really think much about it." When he raised an eyebrow, she shrugged. "All right. So maybe I was a *little* scared when you walked up."

"Makes sense. It was late and you were in the middle of nowhere. That's one of the reasons I stopped."

"What was the other reason?"

"You were a girl."

"And you think all girls need help changing a tire?"

"Not all girls. But my sisters and my mom would have needed help. And I didn't get the sense that you were having a lot of fun."

She nodded. "Thank you again."

"You already said that."

"I know. But it deserved to be said a second time."

"Okay."

"Just 'okay'?" The corners of her mouth turned up.

"It's my go-to phrase when someone makes a statement instead of asking a question."

She wrinkled her forehead. "I suppose that makes sense."

"Okay," he said, and despite herself, she laughed, finally beginning to relax.

"Do you like bartending?" she asked.

"It's all right," he answered. "It pays the bills while I'm in school, I can pretty much pick my schedule, and the tips are good. But I hope I'm not forced to make it a career. There's more I want to do with my life."

"Serena said you want to be a teacher."

"I do," he agreed. "Where did she go, by the way?"

"She met up with some friends. They'll troll the bars for a while and listen to music, then probably head off to a party or whatever."

"Why didn't you join them?"

"I'm a little old for college parties, don't you think?"

"I don't know. How old are you?"

"Twenty-eight."

"I'm twenty-eight and I'm still in college."

Yeah, she thought, *I know*. "And you go to college parties?"

"No," he conceded, "but it's not because I think I'm too old. I just don't go to parties. Bars, either."

"But you work at a bar."

"That's different."

"Why?"

"Because I work there. And even if I didn't, it's not the kind of bar where I'd end up getting in trouble, since it's really more of a restaurant."

"You get in trouble at bars?"

"I used to," he said. "Not anymore."

"But you just said you don't go."

"That's why I don't get into trouble."

"How about clubs?"

He shrugged. "Depends on the club and who I'm with. Usually, no. Every now and then, yes."

"Because you get into trouble there, too?"

"I have in the past."

She puzzled over his answer before finally turning toward the horizon again. The moon glowed against the backdrop of a sky that was beginning its slow progression from gray to black. Colin followed her gaze, neither of them speaking for a moment.

"What kind of trouble?" she finally asked.

He lifted the tip of his reel, jerking the line, before answering. "Fights," he said.

For a moment, she wasn't sure she'd heard him right. "You used to fight in bars?"

"Up until a few years ago, I used to fight in bars all the time."

"Why would you get into fights?"

"Guys usually go to bars for four reasons: to get drunk, to hang with friends, to pick up girls, or to fight. I would show up for all four."

"You wanted to fight?"

"Usually."

"How many times?"

"I'm not sure I understand the question."

"How many times did you get into fights?"

"I can't remember exactly. Probably over a hundred."

She blinked. "You were in over a hundred bar fights?"

"Yes."

She wasn't sure what to say. "Why are you telling me this?"

"Because you asked."

"And you answer everything that people ask you?"

"Not everything."

"But you think telling me about something like this is okay?"

"Yes."

"Why?"

"I'm guessing you're a lawyer, right?"

She inhaled, thrown by the sudden change in subject. "Did Serena tell you that?"

"No."

"Then how did you know I was a lawyer?"

"I didn't know. I thought it was a possibility because you ask a lot of questions. Most lawyers do."

"And given all those bar fights, you've probably had a lot of experience with lawyers?"

"Yes."

"I still can't believe you're telling me this."

"Why wouldn't I tell you?"

"Because admitting that you used to get in bar fights isn't something that people usually do when first getting to know each other."

"Okay," he said. "But like I said, I don't do that anymore."

"What about the other night?"

"That was an MMA match. Mixed martial arts. It's entirely different from what I used to do in the past."

"It's still fighting, isn't it?"

"It's a sport—like boxing or tae kwon do."

She squinted at him. "Is MMA the one in the cage? Where anything goes?"

"Yes to the first, and no to the second," he said. "There are rules. Actually, there are a lot of rules, even if it can be violent."

"And you enjoy the violence?"

"It's good for me."

"Why? Because it helps to keep you out of trouble?"

"Among other things." He smiled, and for the first time in a long, long while, she found herself utterly at a loss for words.

CHAPTER 5

———— ✾ ————

Colin

Colin had witnessed reactions like Maria's before, and he knew she was debating whether she should stick around. People generally had negative reactions to hearing about his past. While he no longer beat himself up for his mistakes, he wasn't proud of them, either. He was who he was, warts and all, and he accepted that. Now it was her turn to make a decision.

He knew that Evan would have shaken his head at the way Colin had answered her questions, but aside from Colin's desire to be honest, what Evan didn't understand was that trying to hide the truth about his past was futile, even if he wanted to keep it hidden. People were both curious and cautious, and he knew that a quick Internet search using his name would yield a handful of newspaper articles about him, none of them good. And if he hadn't laid it out there from the beginning? Either Maria or Serena may have Googled him the same way Victoria had.

He'd met Victoria at the gym a couple of years ago, and after chatting off and on for a few months, they'd fallen into occasionally working out together. He'd thought they were getting along well and considered her a good training partner until she'd suddenly begun to avoid him. She'd stopped returning his texts or calls and started working out in the mornings instead of the evenings. When he was finally able to talk to her about it, she'd revealed what she'd learned about him and insisted that he stop trying to contact her. She hadn't been interested in excuses and Colin hadn't offered any, but he did wonder why she'd conducted her Internet research in the first place. It wasn't as though they'd been dating; he wasn't sure they'd even reached the friendship stage yet. A month later, she'd stopped coming to the gym at all, and that was the last he'd seen of her.

She hadn't been the only one who'd shied away after learning the truth about Colin, and while Evan might joke that Colin immediately volunteered his full history to anyone who asked, it wasn't like that. It generally wasn't anyone else's business, and he kept it that way, unless someone was—or might become—part of his life somehow. Though it was way too early to tell whether Maria fell into that category, Serena was a classmate, and if she'd talked to him once, she just might talk to him again. He admitted that there was something about Maria that interested him, however. Part of it was the way she looked, of course—she was a more mature, more striking version of Serena, with the same dark hair and eyes—but at the bar, he'd noted her lack of vanity. Though she'd drawn stares from any number of men on the rooftop, she hadn't been aware of it, which was extremely rare. But his initial impressions ran deeper than that. Unlike Serena—who was bubbly and chatty and not really his type—Maria was quieter, more contemplative, and obviously intelligent.

And now? He observed Maria as she tried to figure out whether she wanted to stay or go, continue the conversation or say goodbye. He said nothing, giving her room to make her own decision. Instead, he concentrated on the feel of the breeze and the sound of the waves. Staring down the pier, he noticed that most of the people who'd been fishing had cleared out; those who still remained were packing up their gear or cleaning their catch.

Maria leaned a little farther over the railing. The darkening sky cast her face in shadow, making her appear mysterious, unknowable. He watched as she drew a long breath.

"What other things?" she finally asked. Colin smiled inwardly.

"As much as I enjoy working out, there are times when I'm just not in the mood. But knowing that I have a match coming up, and knowing I have to train for it, gets me off the couch and into the gym."

"Every day?"

He nodded. "Usually two or three different sessions. It takes a lot of time."

"What do you do?"

"Almost anything," he said with a shrug. "A big chunk of my training is centered around striking and grappling, but after that, I try to mix it up as much as I can. I do Olympic and heavy lifting, but I'll also do spin classes, yoga, kayaking, circuit work, running, rope climbs, stairs, plyometrics, body-weight exercises, whatever. As long as I can break a sweat, I'm happy."

"You do yoga?"

"It's not only good for flexibility and balance, but it's great for me mentally. It's like meditating." He nodded at the water, burnished red-gold in the last rays of the sun. "Kind of like being out here after a shift."

She squinted at him. "You don't look like a guy who does yoga. Guys who do yoga are..."

He finished for her. "Skinny? Bearded? Into things like incense and beads?"

She laughed. "I was going to say they're usually not into violence."

"Neither am I. Not anymore. Obviously, injuries can happen during one of my fights, but I don't necessarily want to hurt anyone. I just want to win."

"Don't the two go together?"

"Sometimes, but not always. If you get your opponents in the right submission hold, they'll tap out and walk away good as new."

She twirled the bracelet on her wrist. "Is it scary? Walking into that cage?"

"If you're scared, you probably shouldn't be getting into the ring in the first place. For me, it's more of a rush that gets the adrenaline flowing. The key is to keep the adrenaline under control."

He began reeling in his line.

"I take it you're pretty good."

"I'm all right for an amateur, but I'd struggle in the pros. Some of those guys were NCAA-level wrestlers or Olympic boxers, and they're out of my league. But I'm fine with that. It's not my dream to go pro—it's just something to do until I graduate. When the time comes, I'll be ready to walk away."

Instead of casting again, he fastened the hook and lure to the pole, then tightened the line. "And besides, teaching and cage fighting don't exactly mesh. I'd probably scare the little kids like I scared you."

"Little kids?"

"I want to teach third grade," he said. He bent over, reaching for his tackle box. "It's getting dark," he added. "You ready to head back? Or would you like to stay out here a bit longer?"

"We can go," she said. As Colin set the pole on his shoulder, she noted the restaurants lit from within, lines of people already forming at the doors, the faint strains of music filling the air. "It's starting to get crowded down here."

"That's why I asked to work the day shift. It'll be a zoo on the rooftop tonight."

"Good for tips, no?"

"Not worth the aggravation. Too many college kids."

She laughed, the sound warm and melodic. They began to retrace the steps they'd taken earlier, neither feeling the need to rush. In the dimming light, she was alluring, her slight smile making him wonder what she was thinking. "Have you always lived here?" he asked, breaking the peaceful lull.

"I grew up here and moved back last December," she answered. "Between college, law school, and working in Charlotte, I was gone for about ten years. You're not from here, though, right?"

"I'm from Raleigh," he said. "Spent summers here when I was a kid, lived here on and off for a month or two for a few years after high school. I've been living here permanently the last three years."

"We've probably been neighbors at times and didn't even know it. I went to UNC and Duke."

"Neighbors or not, I doubt we traveled in the same social circles."

She smiled. "So...you came here to go to college?"

"Not at first. College came a little after that. I came here because my parents kicked me out of the house and I wasn't sure where else to go. My friend Evan was living here and I ended up renting a room from him."

"Your parents kicked you out?"

He nodded. "I needed a wakeup call. They gave me one."

"Oh." She tried to keep her voice neutral.

"I don't blame them," he said. "I deserved it. I would have kicked me out, too."

"Because of the fights?"

"There's more to it than just that, but the fights were part of it. I was kind of a problem child. And then, after high school, I was a problem adult for a while." He glanced over at her. "What about you? Do you live with your parents?"

She shook her head. "I have a condo down on Market Street. As much as I love them, there's no way I could live with my parents."

"What do they do?"

"They own La Cocina de la Familia. It's a restaurant here in town."

"I've heard of it, but I haven't been there."

"You should go. The food is really authentic—my mom still cooks a lot of it herself—and the place is always packed."

"If I mention your name, will I get a discount?"

"Do you need a discount?"

"Not really. I'm just wondering how far we've progressed."

"I'll see what I can do. I'm sure I'd be able to pull some strings."

By then, they were over the sand and headed for the stairs. He followed as she bounded gracefully down the steps.

"Do you want me to walk you to your car?" he asked, meeting her gaze.

"I'll be okay," she demurred. "It's not far."

He moved the rod from one shoulder to the other, reluctant for the evening to end.

"If Serena's going out with her friends, what were your plans for the rest of the night?"

"Nothing, really. Why?"

"Do you want to listen to some music? Since we're already here? It's not that late yet."

His question seemed to take her by surprise, and for a moment, he thought she might say no. She adjusted her purse strap, fidgeting with the buckle. While he waited, he thought again that she was beautiful, her long, dark lashes shrouding her thoughts.

"I thought you didn't go to bars."

"I don't. But we could walk the beach for a bit, listen for something good, and enjoy it where we are."

"Are any of the bands any good?"

"I have no idea."

Uncertainty was written on her face before he saw something finally give way. "All right. But I don't want to stay long. Maybe just a walk on the beach, okay? I don't want to be down here when the crowds descend."

He smiled, feeling something unwind within him, and raised the tackle box. "Let me just drop this off, all right? I'd rather not carry it the whole time."

They backtracked to the restaurant, and once he stowed his things in the employee area, they wandered back down to the sand. The stars were beginning to emerge, brilliant pinpricks in the velvety sky. The waves continued their steady roll and the warm breeze was like a quiet exhale. As they strolled, he was conscious of the fact that she was close enough to touch, but he pushed the realization away.

"What kind of law do you practice?"

"Mainly insurance defense work. Research and depositions, negotiation, and as a final resort, litigation."

"And you defend insurance companies?"

"For the most part. Every now and then, we're on the plaintiff's side, but it's not that common."

"Does it keep you busy?"

"Very." She nodded. "There's a policy for everything, and as much as the policy tries to anticipate every possibility, there are always gray areas. Let's say someone slips in your store and he sues, or an employee sues after getting fired, or maybe you're throwing a birthday party for your son and one of his friends gets hurt in your swimming pool. The insurance company is responsible for paying the claim, but sometimes they decide to fight the claim. That's where we step in. Because the other side always has lawyers."

"Do you ever go to court?"

"I haven't yet. Not for this job, anyway. I'm still learning. The partner I do most of my work for goes to court quite a bit, but truthfully most of our cases are settled before they go to trial. In the end, it's cheaper and less hassle for everyone involved."

"I'll bet you hear a lot of lawyer jokes."

"Not too many," she said. "Why? Do you have one?"

He took a couple of steps. "How does a lawyer sleep?" At her shrug, he said, "First he lies on one side, then he lies on the other."

"Ha, ha."

"I'm kidding. I'm the first to appreciate good lawyers. I had some brilliant ones."

"And you needed them?"

"Yes," he answered. He knew that would trigger even more questions, but he continued on, nodding toward the ocean. "I love walking the beach at night."

"Why?"

"It's different than it is during the day, especially when the moon is out...I like the mystery of thinking that anything could be out there, swimming just beneath the surface."

"That's a scary thought."

"That's why we're here and not out there."

She smiled at his words, surprisingly at ease as they meandered down the beach. Neither of them felt the need to speak. Colin focused on the sensation of his feet sinking into the sand and the warm breeze on his face. Watching Maria's hair ripple in the wind, he realized that he was enjoying the walk more than he'd anticipated. He reminded himself that they were strangers, but for some reason, it didn't quite feel that way.

"I have a question, but I don't know if it's too personal," she finally said.

"Go ahead," he replied, already knowing what was coming.

"You said you were a problem adult and that you got in a lot of bar fights. And that you had some great lawyers."

"Yes."

"Was that because you were arrested?"

He adjusted his cap. "Yes."

"More than once?"

"A number of times," he admitted. "For a while there, I was pretty much on a first-name basis with any number of cops in Raleigh and Wilmington."

"Were you ever convicted?"

"A few times," he said.

"And you went to prison?"

"No. I probably spent a total of a year in county lockup. Not all at once, more like a month here, two months there. I never made it as far as prison. I would have—the last fight was pretty bad—but I caught a serious break and here I am."

She lowered her chin slightly, no doubt questioning her decision to walk with him.

"When you say you caught a serious break..."

He took a few steps before answering. "I've been on probation for the last three years, with two more to go. It's part of the five-year deal I received. Basically, if I don't get into any more trouble for the next two years, they'll clear my record entirely. Which means I'll be able to teach in the classroom, and that's important to me. People don't want felons teaching their children. On the other hand, if I mess up, the deal goes out the window and I go straight to prison."

"How is that possible? To completely clear your record?"

"I was diagnosed with an anger disorder and PTSD, which affected my mens rea. You know what that is, right?"

"In other words, you're saying you couldn't help it," she said.

He shrugged. "Not me. That's what my psychiatrists said, and fortunately, I had the records to prove it. I'd been in therapy for almost fifteen years, I've been on medication periodically, and as part of my deal, I had to spend a few months at a psychiatric hospital in Arizona that specialized in anger disorders."

"And...when you got back to Raleigh, your parents kicked you out of the house?"

"Yes," he said. "But all that together—the fight and potential prison sentence, the deal, my time at the hospital, and suddenly being forced to be on my own—led me to do some serious soul searching, and I realized that I was tired of the life I'd been living. I was tired of being me. I didn't want to be the guy who was known for stomping on someone's head after they were already on the ground, I wanted to be known as...a friend, a guy you could count on. Or at the very least, a guy with some kind of future ahead of him. So I stopped partying and I channeled all my energy into training and going to school and working instead."

"Just like that?"

"It wasn't quite as easy as it sounds, but yeah...just like that."

"People don't usually change."

"I didn't have a choice."

"Still..."

"Don't get the wrong idea. I'm not trying to make excuses for what I did. Regardless of what the doctors said about whether or not I could actually control my behavior, I knew I was messed up, and I didn't give a damn about getting better. Instead, I smoked pot and drank and trashed my parents' house and wrecked cars and I got arrested over and over for fighting. For a long time, I just didn't care about anything other than partying the way I wanted to."

"And now you care?"

"I care a lot. And I don't have any intention of going back to my old life."

He felt her eyes on him, and sensed her trying to reconcile the past he'd described with the man before her. "I can understand the anger disorder, but PTSD?"

"Yes."

"What happened?"

"Do you really want to hear this? It's kind of a long story." When she nodded, he went on. "Like I told you, I was a bit of a problem child, and by the time I was eleven, I was pretty much uncontrollable. In the end, my parents shipped me off to military school, and the first one I attended was just a bad place. There was this weird *Lord of the Flies* mentality among the upperclassmen, especially when someone new arrived. At first, it was little things—typical hazing kind of stuff, like taking my milk or dessert in the cafeteria, or making me shine their shoes or make their beds while another guy went over and trashed my room, which I'd have to clean before inspection. No big deal—every newbie goes through that kind of stuff. But some of these guys were different...just sadistic. They'd whip me with wet towels after I showered, or they'd sneak up behind me while I was studying and throw a blanket over me, and just start beating the crap out of me. After a while, they started to do that at night, when I was sleeping. Back then, I was kind of small for my age, and I made the mistake of crying a lot, which only amped them up even more. It's like I became their special project. They'd come for me two or three nights a week, always with the blanket, always with the punches, just beating the crap out of me while telling me that I'd be dead before the year was up. I was pretty freaked out, on edge all the time. I would try to stay awake and flinch at the slightest noise, but it's not like I could avoid sleeping. They'd bide their time and wait until I was out. That kind of crap went on for months. I still have nightmares about it."

"Did you tell anyone?"

"Of course I did. I told everyone I could. I told the commander, my teachers, the counselor, even my parents. None of them believed me. They kept telling me to stop lying and whining and just toughen up."

"That's awful—"

"No question. I was just a little kid, but after a while, I figured I had to get out of there, or they'd take it too far one day, so I ended up taking matters into my own hands. I smuggled in some spray paint and went to town in the administration building. I ended up getting kicked out, which was exactly what I wanted." He drew a long breath. "Anyway, they ended up closing the school a couple of years later, after the local paper did an exposé on the place. A kid died there. A little kid, my age. I wasn't one of the students mentioned in the exposé, but it was national news for a while. Criminal and civil charges, the whole works. Some people ended up in prison over it. And my parents felt terrible after that, because they hadn't believed me. I think that's why they put up with me for so long after I graduated. Because they still felt guilty."

"So after you were expelled…"

"I went to another military school and swore to myself that I'd never let myself get beaten up again. In the future, I'd be the one throwing the first punch. So I learned to fight. I studied it, practiced it. And after that, if someone ever grabbed me, I'd just…

lose it. It was like I was a little kid again. I got expelled over and over, barely made it through, and after I graduated, it sort of snowballed from there. Like I said, I used to be pretty messed up." He took a few steps in silence. "Anyway, all that came into play during the court proceedings."

"How do you get along with your parents right now?"

"Like my sisters, it's a work in progress. Right now, they have a restraining order against me."

A stunned expression crossed her face and he went on.

"I was arguing with my parents the night before I went to Arizona and I ended up pinning my dad against the wall. I wasn't going to hurt him and I kept telling him that—I just wanted them to listen to me—but it scared the hell out of my parents. They didn't press charges—or I wouldn't be here—but they did get a court order that prohibits me from being at their house. They don't necessarily enforce it now, but it's still in place, probably to keep me from ever thinking about moving back in."

She studied him. "I still don't understand how you can just . . . change. I mean, what if you get angry again?"

"I still get angry. Everyone does. But I've learned different ways to cope with it. Like not going to bars or doing drugs, and I never have more than a couple of beers when I'm with my friends. And being really physical every day—training hard, pushing myself— helps keep my moods in check. I also learned a lot of helpful things at the hospital, different ways to cope. The whole experience ended up being one of the better things I've ever done."

"What did you learn there?"

"Deep breathing, walking away, letting thoughts bounce off, or trying to accurately name the emotion when it strikes in the hopes of diminishing its power . . . it's not easy, but it becomes a habit after a while. It takes a lot of effort and a lot of conscious thought, but if I wasn't doing all of these things, I'd probably have to go back on lithium, and I hate that crap. It's a good drug for a lot of people and it works, but I just didn't feel like myself when

I used to take it. It was like part of me wasn't quite alive. And I was always starving, no matter how much I ate. I ended up gaining weight, getting fat. I'd rather train a few hours a day, do yoga, meditate, and avoid places where I might get into trouble."

"Is it working?"

"So far," he answered. "I just take it one day at a time."

As they walked farther down the beach, the music gradually faded beneath the sound of waves rolling up the shore. Beyond the dunes, businesses had given way to houses, lights glowing through the windows. The moon had risen higher, bathing the world in an ethereal glow. Ghost crabs scuttled from one spot to the next, scurrying at their slow approach.

"You're very open about all of this," Maria observed.

"I'm just answering your questions."

"Aren't you worried what I might think?"

"Not really."

"You don't care what other people think about you?"

"To a certain extent I do. Everyone does. But if you're going to make a judgment about me, then you need to know who I really am, not just the part I decide to tell you. I'd rather be honest about all of it and let you make the call as to whether you want to keep talking to me or not."

"Have you always been like this?" She peered up at him with genuine curiosity.

"What do you mean?"

"Honest? About . . . everything?"

"No," he said. "That came about after I got back from the hospital. Along with all the other changes I decided to make in my life."

"How do people react to it?"

"Most don't know what to make of it. Especially at first. Evan still doesn't. And I don't think you do, either. But it's still important to me to be truthful. Especially with friends, or someone I think I might see again."

"Is that why you told me? Because you think you might see me again?"

"Yes," he answered.

For a few seconds, she wasn't sure what to make of that.

"You're an interesting man, Colin," she said.

"It's been an interesting life," he admitted. "But you're interesting, too."

"Trust me, compared to you, I'm the furthest thing from interesting."

"Maybe. Maybe not. But you haven't run away yet."

"I still might. You're kind of scary."

"No, I'm not."

"For a girl like me? Believe me, you're a little scary. This is probably the first time I've ever spent an evening with a guy who talks about stomping on people's heads in bar fights or pinning his father against the wall."

"Or has been arrested. Or went to a psychiatric facility..."

"Those things, too."

"And?"

She brushed at a few windblown strands of hair. "I'm still deciding. Right now, I have no idea what to think about everything you've said. But if I suddenly take off running, don't try to catch me, okay?"

"Fair enough."

"Did you tell any of this to Serena?"

"No," he said. "Unlike you, she didn't ask."

"But would you have?"

"Probably."

"Of course you would."

"How about we talk about you instead? Would that make you feel better?"

She cracked a wry smile. "There's not much to tell. I told you a little about my family; you know I grew up here and went to

UNC and Duke Law School, and that I work as a lawyer. My past isn't quite as . . . colorful as yours."

"That's a good thing," he said. Somehow already on the same wavelength, they turned simultaneously and started back.

"Okay," she said, and when he laughed, she stopped for a moment, suddenly wincing. Reaching for his arm to steady herself, she lifted one foot from the sand. "Give me a second here. My sandals are killing me."

He watched as she slipped them off. When she finally let go of his arm, he felt the lingering afterglow of her touch. "Better," she said. "Thanks."

They began walking again, more slowly this time. On the roof at Crabby Pete's, the crowd was growing, and he suspected that other bars were filling up as well. Above them, most of the stars had been washed away by moonlight. In the easy silence, he found himself admiring her features: her cheekbones and her full lips, the sweep of her lashes against her flawless skin.

"You're very quiet," he observed.

"I'm just trying to digest everything you told me. It's a lot."

"No question," he agreed.

"I will say that you're different."

"In what way?"

"Before I took a job here, I was an assistant district attorney in Charlotte."

"No kidding?"

"A little over three years. It was my first job after I passed the bar."

"So you were more used to prosecuting guys like me than dating them?"

She half nodded in agreement, but went on. "It's more than that. Most people pick and choose the way they tell their stories. There's always a positive bias involved, and they frame the stories that way, but you . . . You're so objective, it's almost like you're describing someone else."

"Sometimes it feels that way to me, too."

"I don't know if I could do that." Frowning, she went on. "Actually, I don't know if I want to do that, at least to the extent that you do."

"You sound like Evan." He smiled. "How did you like working in the DA's office?"

"In the beginning it was all right. And the whole thing was a great learning experience. But after a while, I realized it wasn't what I thought it would be."

"Like taking a walk with me?"

"Kind of..." she said. "When I was in law school, I thought that being in a courtroom would be more like the stuff you watch on TV. I mean, I knew it would be different, but I wasn't prepared for just how different it actually was. To me, it seemed like I was going after the same person, with the same background, over and over. The DA would take the higher-profile cases, but the suspects I dealt with were like walking clichés; they were usually poor and unemployed with limited education, and drugs and alcohol were usually involved. And it was just...relentless. There were so many cases. I used to dread coming in on Monday mornings because I knew what would be waiting for me on my desk. The sheer volume put me in the position of having to prioritize the cases and continually negotiate plea bargains. We all know that murder and attempted murder or crimes with guns are serious, but how do you prioritize the rest of it? Is a guy who steals a car worse than a guy who broke into someone's house and stole jewelry? And how do either of those compare to a secretary who embezzles from her company? But there's only so much room on the court docket; there's only so much space available in prison. Even when the rare case did go to trial, it's not what you know happened, it's what you can prove beyond a reasonable doubt, and that's where it gets even trickier. The public believes we have unlimited resources to prosecute, with advanced forensic capabilities and expert witnesses at the ready, but that's just not the way it is. Matching DNA can take months, unless it's a high-profile crime. Witnesses are notoriously inconsistent. Evidence is ambiguous. And again, there are just too many cases... even if I wanted to really delve into a particular crime, I'd have to neglect all those other files waiting on my desk. So more often than not, the pragmatic thing was to simply work something out with opposing counsel, where the subject pled to a lesser offense."

She kicked at the sand, her footsteps dragging. "I was constantly being put into situations where people expected results that I couldn't deliver, and I'd end up being the bad guy. In their minds, the suspects had committed a crime and they should be held accountable, which to the victims almost always meant prison time or restitution of some sort, but that just wasn't possible. Afterwards, the arresting officers weren't happy, the victims weren't happy, and I felt like I was letting them down. And in a way, I was. Eventually I realized that I was just a cog in the wheel of this giant, broken machine."

She slowed, pulling her sweater tighter around her. "There's just...evil out there. You wouldn't believe the cases that would reach our office. A mom prostituting her six-year-old daughter to buy drugs, or a man raping a ninety-year-old woman. It's enough to make you lose faith in humanity. And because there's this great burden on you to go hard after the really horrible suspects, that means that other perpetrators don't get the punishment they deserve and end up back on the streets. And sometimes..." She shook her head. "Anyway, by the end of my time there, I was barely sleeping and I started getting these weird panic attacks when I was at work. I walked in one morning and just knew I couldn't do it anymore. So I went to my boss's office and resigned. I didn't even have another job lined up."

"It sounds to me like your job was draining in a lot of different ways."

"It was." She smiled grimly, a spectrum of conflicting emotions playing across her face.

"And?"

"And what?"

"Want to talk about it?"

"Talk about what?"

"The real reason you quit? The part that led to you having panic attacks?"

Startled, she turned toward him. "How would you know about that?"

"I don't," he said. "But if you'd been there for a while, something specific must have happened. Something bad. And I'm guessing it concerned a case, right?"

She stopped walking, turning to face the water. The moonlit shadows accentuated her expression—a mixture of sadness and guilt that brought with it a fleeting ache he hadn't expected.

"You're very intuitive." She closed her eyes, holding them that way for a moment. "I can't believe I'm about to tell you this."

Colin said nothing. By then, they'd almost reached the spot where they'd entered the beach, a cacophony of music audible now above the sound of the waves. She gestured toward the dune. "Do you mind if we sit?"

"Not at all."

Slipping off her purse and setting her sandals aside, she lowered herself to the sand. Colin made himself comfortable beside her.

"Cassie Manning," Maria offered. "That was her name...I hardly ever talk about her. It's not something that I like reliving." Her voice was tight and controlled. "The case came to me maybe three or four months after I'd begun working at the DA's office. On paper, it struck me as a fairly typical case. Cassie is dating a guy and they get into an argument, it escalates, and the guy ends up getting violent. Cassie ends up in the hospital with a black eye and a split lip, bruising, a cracked cheekbone. In other words, it wasn't just one punch; it was a beating. His name was Gerald Laws."

"Laws?"

"I've tried to find the irony, but I've never found any. And nothing about the case ended up being typical in the slightest. It turns out that they'd been dating for six months or so, and in the beginning of the relationship, Cassie found Laws utterly charming. He listened well, opened doors for her—a gentleman—but after a while, she began to notice aspects of his personality that concerned her. The longer they dated, the more jealous and possessive he started to become. Cassie told me that he began to get angry if she didn't answer immediately when he called her; he started showing up at her office when she was getting off work—she was a nurse at a pediatric office—and once, when she was having lunch with her brother, she spotted Laws on the other side of the restaurant, all by himself, just watching her. She knew that he'd followed her there and it bothered her.

"The next time he called, Cassie told him that she wanted to take a break for a while. He agreed, but soon thereafter, she realized that he was stalking her. She'd see him at the post office or when she was leaving the doctor's office or when she was jogging, and she'd get these calls where no one would talk on the other end. Then, one night, Laws showed up at her door saying that he wanted to apologize, and against her better judgment, she let him in. Once inside, he tried to convince her to go out with him again. When she said no, he grabbed her arm and she began to fight back, and she ended up hitting him with a vase. After that, he threw her to the floor and just . . . went at it. It happened that there was a police officer the next street over, and after the 911 call came in—the neighbors had heard screaming—he was at the house in minutes. Laws had her pinned to the floor and was punching her and there was blood everywhere. It turned out later that it was his blood from a cut over his ear where she'd hit him with the vase. The officer had to use a Taser on him. When they searched his car, they found duct tape, rope, a couple of knives, and videotaping equipment. Scary stuff. When I talked to Cassie, she told me that the guy was crazy and that she was afraid for her life. Her family was, too. Her mom and dad and her younger brother were adamant that Laws be put away for as long as possible."

She burrowed her toes in the sand. "I thought so, too. In my mind, there was no question that the guy needed to be put away. It was also pretty open-and-shut as far as cases go. In North Carolina, Laws could have been charged with either a Class C felony, which means he had the intent to kill her, or a Class E felony, where he didn't have the intent to kill her. The family, especially the father, wanted him to be charged with a Class C felony, which could have put him behind bars for anywhere between three and seven years. The arresting officer, too, believed that Laws was dangerous. But unfortunately, the district attorney didn't think we could prove intent, since there was no proof that any of the things in the car had anything to do with her. Nor were her injuries truly life-threatening. Cassie also had a bit of a credibility problem...while most of what she'd said Laws had done in the past was true, she also said he'd done things that he clearly hadn't. Then there was Laws: He looked like Mister Rogers, worked as a loan officer at a bank, and had no criminal record. He would have been a prosecutor's nightmare on the stand. So we ended up allowing Laws to plead guilty to misdemeanor assault, with a year in prison, and that's where I went wrong. Because Laws was extremely dangerous."

She paused, willing herself to keep telling the story. "Laws ended up serving nine months, since he'd already served three months pending trial. He wrote Cassie letters every other day, apologizing for his actions and begging for another chance. She never answered them; after a while, she didn't even open them, but she saved them all because she was still afraid of him. Afterwards, when we examined them more closely, we noticed the shift in tone over time. Laws was becoming more and more angry that she wouldn't respond. Had she actually read them and brought them to the DA..."

She stared toward the sand. "As soon as he got out, Laws showed up at her door. She slammed the door on him and called the police. She had a restraining order filed against him, and when the police talked to him, he promised that he wouldn't go anywhere near her again. All that did was make him more careful. He sent her flowers anonymously. Her cat was poisoned. She'd find bouquets of dead roses on her doorstep. Even her tires were slashed."

Maria swallowed, visibly shaken. When she continued, her voice was hoarse. "And then, one night, while Cassie was heading to her boyfriend's place—by then, she was dating someone else—Laws was waiting for her. Her boyfriend saw Laws grab her right off the sidewalk and force her into the car, and he wasn't able to stop it. Two days later, the police found Cassie's body in an old lakefront cabin the bank had foreclosed on. Laws tied her up and beat her extensively, set the cabin on fire, and then shot himself, but they couldn't tell whether she'd been alive when the fire..." She closed her eyes. "They had to be identified through dental records."

Knowing that she was reliving the past and trying to work through it, Colin remained quiet.

"I went to her funeral," she said, finally going on. "I know I probably shouldn't have, but I felt like I needed to go. I came in after it started and sat in the back row. The church was full, but I could still see the family. The mom couldn't stop crying. She was almost hysterical, and the father and the brother were just... white. I was sick to my stomach and I wanted the whole thing to be over. But it wasn't."

She turned toward him. "It...destroyed the family. I mean, all of them were a little strange, but it turned into a catastrophe. A few months after the murder, Cassie's mom committed suicide, then the father had his medical license suspended. I always thought there was something a little weird about the brother... anyway, that's when these terrible notes started to arrive. They came to my apartment and the office, in different envelopes, usually just a sentence or two. They were awful...calling me names, demanding to know why I hated Cassie or why I wanted to hurt the family. The police talked to the brother and the notes stopped. For a while, anyway, but when they started arriving again, they were...different. More threatening. Way scarier. So the police talked to him again, and I guess he just...snapped. Denied that he was responsible and insisted that I was out to get him, that the police were in cahoots with me. He ended up in a psychiatric hospital. Meanwhile, the father's threatening to sue me. The police theorized that Cassie's boyfriend might be responsible for the notes. Of course, when the police talked to him, he denied sending them, too. That's when the panic attacks started. I had the sense that whoever was sending those notes would never leave me alone and that's when I knew I had to go home."

Colin said nothing. He knew there was nothing he could say that would make her view the events she had just described in a different light.

"I should have listened to the family. And the officer."

Colin stared out at the waves, their rhythm ceaseless and soothing. When he didn't respond, she turned toward him.

"Don't you think?"

He chose his words carefully. "It's hard to answer that question."

"What do you mean?"

"By the way you said it, it's clear that you already think the answer is yes, but if I agree with you, you'll probably feel worse. If I say no, you'll dismiss my answer because you've already decided that the answer should be yes."

She opened her mouth to protest, then closed it. "I'm not even sure what to say to that," she offered.

"You don't have to say anything."

She sighed, resting her chin on her knees. "I should have lobbied the DA and insisted that we charge Laws with a felony."

"Maybe. But even if you had—and even if Laws was in prison longer—the outcome might still have been the same. He was fixated on her. And if you're curious, if I'd been in your shoes, I probably would have done the same thing."

"I know, but..."

"Have you talked to anyone about this?"

"Like a therapist? No."

He nodded. "Okay."

"You're not going to tell me that I should?"

"I don't give advice," he said.

"Ever?"

He shook his head. "Then again, you don't need my advice. If you think therapy might help you, try it out. If you don't think so, don't. I can only say that in my own experience, it's been beneficial."

Maria was quiet, and he couldn't tell whether she liked his answer. "Thanks," she finally said.

"For what?"

"For listening," she said. "And not trying to give advice."

Colin nodded, studying the horizon. More stars were evident now, and Venus glowed in the southern sky, bright and constant. A handful of people had wandered to the beach, their laughter carrying into the night air. Sitting beside Maria, it seemed like he'd known her far longer than the hour or so they'd spent together. He felt a distinct stab of regret that the evening was about to end.

But he could sense it coming in the way she suddenly sat straighter. He watched as she drew a long breath before finally glancing toward the boardwalk.

"I should probably get going," she said.

"Me too," he agreed, trying to hide his reluctance. "I still have to make it to the gym tonight."

They rose from their spot and he watched as she brushed off the sand before slipping her sandals back on. They started back toward the dunes bordering the commercial strip, the music growing louder with every step. By the time they left the sand and were back on solid ground, the sidewalks were thronged, the crowds already enjoying their Saturday night.

He stayed at her side, weaving between pedestrians until they reached the street, where things were quieter. Surprising him, she stayed close, their shoulders occasionally brushing. The sensation of her touch continued to linger. "What are your plans for tomorrow?" he finally asked.

"On Sundays, I always have brunch with my parents. After that, I'll probably go paddleboarding."

"Yeah?"

"It's fun. Have you ever done it?"

"No," he said. "I've always wanted to try, but I just haven't gotten around to it yet."

"Too busy doing real workouts?"

"Too lazy," he admitted.

She smiled. "How about you? Are you working?"

"No," he said. "I'll run, do some yard work, change the alternator on my car. It's still not starting right."

"Maybe it's the battery."

"Don't you think I would have checked that first?"

"I don't know. Would you?" He heard the teasing in her tone. "So after the manly yard and car work, what's on the rest of your agenda?"

"I'll hit the gym. There's a class that meets on Sunday mornings, and I'll probably do some sparring and ground work, hit the bags, things like that. A guy named Todd Daly runs the gym, and he tends to work us pretty hard. He's a retired UFC fighter, coaches like a drill sergeant."

"But if you had to, you could probably take him, right?"

"Daly? Not a chance."

She liked the fact that he admitted it. "And after that?"

"Nothing, really. I'll probably do some studying."

By then, they'd turned onto another street, around the corner from Crabby Pete's. He recognized her car up ahead from the night he'd changed her tire, and when they finally reached it, neither seemed to know what to say. Instead, he felt her eyes zeroing in on him, almost like she was really seeing him for the first time.

"Thanks for walking me to my car."

"Thanks for the walk on the beach."

She lifted her chin slightly. "I have another question."

"Okay."

"Were you serious about wanting to try paddleboarding?"

"Yes."

She lowered her lashes, slipping him a sidelong glance. "Would you like to join me tomorrow?"

"Yes," he said, feeling a dart of unexpected pleasure. "I'd like that. What time?"

"How about two o'clock? And we'll check out Masonboro Island? It's kind of hard to get to, but it's worth it."

"Sounds great. Where should we meet?"

"The parking isn't ideal. The only way to get there is to head down Wrightsville Beach, right to the very end of the island. Just park on the street. Bring some quarters because you'll have to feed the meter, but I'll meet you there."

"Can I rent a board somewhere?"

"You don't have to. I have two of them. You can use my beginner board."

"Great."

"It's hot pink, though. With stickers of bunnies and flowers on it."

"Really?"

She giggled. "I was kidding." Then: "I had a strangely good time tonight."

"Me too," he said, meaning it. "And I'm looking forward to tomorrow."

After she unlocked the car, he opened the door, watching as

she slid in. A moment later, she was backing out and then pulling away as Colin stood in place. It might have ended there, but she suddenly stopped the car and rolled down the window, leaning out.

"Hey, Colin?" she called out.

"Yeah?"

"When you're in your sparring class tomorrow morning? Try not to get hit in the face."

He smiled, watching as her car sailed up the boulevard, wondering what he was getting himself into. He hadn't expected her invitation, and as he made his way back to his Camaro, he replayed the evening, trying to figure it out. Whatever her reason, he couldn't deny the fact that he'd been pleased.

He wanted to see her again.

No question about it.

CHAPTER 6

Maria

I knew you'd like him!" Serena crowed. "Was I right or what?"

It was Sunday morning, and as usual, Maria was with her sister on the back porch while their mom was finishing up breakfast. Their father was walking Copo, who was fluffed and clean, with a pink bow near her ear.

"I didn't say I liked him," Maria answered. "I said he was interesting."

"But you also said you're meeting him today. In your bikini."

"I'm not going to be wearing my bikini while I'm paddleboarding."

"Why not?"

"Because I'm not you, okay? It would make me uncomfortable."

"Well, you better show some skin, because believe me, you're going to want him to take his shirt off. The whole sneaking-a-peek thing needs to work both ways."

"I don't want him to get the wrong idea."

"You're right. You should probably wear some baggy sweats or something like that. And no matter how you're dressed, I'm just glad you're finally going on a date."

"Don't try to make this into something that it isn't. It's not a date. We're just going paddleboarding."

"Uh-huh." Serena nodded. "Whatever you say."

"I don't know why I even try to talk to you about these things."

"You talk to me because you know I'll tell you the truth. Which is why, of course, the two of you hit it off so well. Because Colin is just like me."

"Yes, of course. You're right. I'm essentially going out with my younger sister."

"Don't blame me. I'm not the one who followed him out to the pier."

"I didn't follow him out to the pier!"

Serena giggled. "You're so touchy these days. But if you want my advice, I'd wear a bikini under the baggy sweats, okay? Just in case it gets too hot out there. Because it's going to be warm today."

"Can we talk about you instead? Like how the rest of your evening went?"

"There's not much to tell. We hit the bars, went to a party. Just a typical Saturday night."

"How's it going with Steve?"

"He's a little clingy, and I'm not sure I'm ready for something like that. But back to Colin again. He's *seriously* hot."

"Yes, I noticed."

"Did he try to kiss you good-bye?"

"No. And I didn't want him to."

"That's good," she said, "keep playing hard to get. Guys like that." Maria made a face and Serena giggled again. "Okay, okay, I'll stop. I think it's great, though. You not only have a date—a real date, no matter how you describe it—but you're the one who asked him. You're the epitome of the modern woman. And just so you know, I'm totally jealous that you're going to get to see him with his shirt off. I don't think he has an ounce of fat on him."

"I really couldn't tell you. It was kind of dark and he was walking beside me."

"I want pictures today. You always bring that camera with you anyway. Just sneak a few of him."

"No."

"I would think that you could do at least this one little thing for your baby sister, who also happens to be the one to set you up with him."

She thought about it. "Okay, maybe."

"Awesome. Or better yet, take some with your phone and send them to me and I'll put them on Instagram."

"Not a chance."

"Are you sure? I'd hate to have to tell Dad you're going out with an ex-con who's currently on probation."

"Don't you dare!"

"I was kidding! I don't even want to be in the same state when you drop that little bombshell. So warn me in advance, okay?"

"Will do."

"Still, you should get a selfie with him at the very least. Before the announcement. That way, you'll know you actually went out with him, since it'll never happen again after that."

"Are you done?"

Serena giggled. "Yes. Now I'm done."

Maria noticed a hummingbird sipping from the feeder her mother had hung, hovering in a way that had mesmerized her since she was a young girl. From inside, she could hear her mother quietly singing to herself, and while the aroma of eggs and refried beans should have been making her hungry, she was already a little nervous about the upcoming afternoon. She wondered how much she'd actually be able to eat.

"I'm still kind of surprised at the way he just . . . told you everything," Serena finally offered.

"Had you been there, you would have been in shock. Trust me."

"It's weird, though. I don't think I've ever met anyone like that before."

"You're telling *me*."

Two hours later, Maria was at home, debating what to wear. Serena's advice sounded in her ear, making the decision a lot more difficult than it should have been. Normally she wouldn't think twice about it; she'd wear shorts and either a halter or a bikini top, and she certainly wouldn't have showered beforehand or put on makeup or felt the clawing pangs of nervousness in her belly, but there they were. Standing in front of her chest of drawers, she debated what kind of impression she wanted to make. Bold? Casual? Sexy?

It was a whole lot easier for men, she decided: Throw on a T-shirt, flip-flops, and shorts and head out the door. Meanwhile, she had to debate the *length* of her shorts, and decide how *tight* or *faded* she wanted them to be, or whether she should wear the ones with the sexy tears below the back pockets or go a bit more conservative. And that was just the bottoms; trying to decide on her top was even more difficult, especially since she hadn't decided whether to wear the bikini or a one-piece underneath. Despite what she'd said to Serena, it was a date, and aside from the fiasco last weekend with Jill and Paul, she hadn't been on a lot of dates recently. Add in the fact that her thoughts had been drifting to Colin all morning and last night, and the whole thing left her feeling more jittery than ever.

What did she want with him, anyway? Colin was the kind of guy she used to *prosecute*. Until yesterday, had anyone even suggested that she go out with a guy with his past, she would have laughed aloud or—more likely—been offended. She should have simply said good-bye after he'd walked her to her car last night. The very idea of the two of them going out today was absurd, and yet... *she* had asked *him*, and she had trouble remembering exactly how that had happened or what she'd been thinking.

And yet, Colin was... *magnetic*. It was the word that had popped into her head while she was taking a shower, and the more she'd thought about it, the more apt the description seemed. While his answers had left her spinning at times, she had to admit that his *here's the real me and you can either accept me or not* shtick was refreshing. More than that, she sensed that his regret had been real, underscoring how much he really had changed. She wasn't naïve enough to ignore the possibility that he may have been trying to play on her sympathies, but it was impossible to reconcile that notion with the guy who'd changed her tire, or walked the beach with her, or attended classes with her sister in the hopes of becoming a teacher. He certainly hadn't tried to hit on her, and had she not asked him to go paddleboarding, she had no doubt he would have left her at her car without further ado.

She had to admit that she appreciated the fact that he had been so open and honest about his past. If he'd waited until today to reveal those surprises, she would have felt manipulated and angry, maybe even frightened. The chemistry she'd initially felt with him would have been doused almost instantly, leaving her wondering what else he'd been lying about. No one likes a bait and switch.

Truthfully, she didn't know a lot of people who'd turned their lives in an entirely new direction, like Colin had. And though she had no idea where today might lead—or even whether it was a beginning of sorts—she finally thought, *Oh, what the hell?* and put on her black bikini, then chose the sexy tight jean shorts with the tears below the pockets. Last, she pulled on a formfitting shirt with a plunging neckline. Serena, after all, had been right about something else. If Colin took off *his* shirt—and that, she had to admit, wouldn't bother her in the slightest—then at the very least, she should have the option of doing the same.

Colin was leaning against the side of his car as she pulled in behind him, and when he waved, all she could do was stare. He wore a gray T-shirt that clung from his sculpted shoulders all the way down to his narrow waist. The sleeves could barely contain his well-defined arms, and even from a distance, the deep blue-gray color of his eyes was visible, set off by his sharp cheekbones.

As improbable as it seemed, her first thought was that he was getting more handsome by the day. When he pushed away from the car and smiled, she felt something jump inside her while a little voice whispered, *If I'm not careful, I could get in serious trouble with this guy.*

Forcing the thought away, she waved from inside the car, then took a deep breath as she shut the engine down. When she opened the door, the heat assailed her almost immediately. Thankfully, the humidity was minimal and a slight breeze stirred the air, making it a bit more bearable.

"Hey there," she called out. "You're right on time."

She saw that he had brought a backpack, a small cooler, and a pair of towels. He leaned over, picking up the backpack and flinging it over his shoulder. "I got here early," he said. "I wasn't sure that I was parking in the right place. There aren't any other cars around."

"It's always quieter on the tip of the island," she said. "People don't like to feed the meters, which is good, since it means we don't have so far to walk." She shaded her eyes. "How did sparring go?"

"It was a little more intense than usual, but no bruising or broken noses."

"I can tell," she said with a smile. "How about the other guys? You didn't hurt them, did you?"

"They're fine." He squinted into the glare. "Your turn. How was brunch with your family?"

"No broken noses or bruising, either," she teased, and when she heard him laugh, she tucked a strand of hair behind her ear, reminding herself not to get too carried away. "On a more serious note, though, I should probably warn you that I told Serena we were going out on the water today. In case she hunts you down after class and asks you for lots of personal details."

"Will she do that?"

For sure, Maria thought. "Probably."

"Why doesn't she ask you?"

"I'm sure she'll be calling me later. She considers it her duty to be heavily involved in my personal life."

"Okay." He grinned. "You look beautiful, by the way."

She felt a flash of heat in her cheeks. "Thank you," she said. Then, trying to keep things light, she added, "You ready for today?"

"I can't wait."

"We're lucky there isn't a lot of wind. The water should be perfect."

She began to unhook one of the straps that held the paddle-boards in place on the roof rack. Noting what she was doing, he stepped close to help her unhook the other straps. The muscles in his forearms moved like piano strings, making his tattoo ripple as the two of them worked side by side. He smelled like salt and wind, clean and fresh. He lifted the top board off, leaning it against the car before doing the same with the other, propping the two against each other.

"How's your balance on the board?" he asked.

"Pretty good. Why?"

"Because I packed a small cooler," he said, gesturing at it behind him. "I was wondering if you'd be able to put it on your board. I'm not sure my balance will be good enough at first."

"It's not that hard," she said. "You'll get the hang of it. But to answer your question, yes, I can put the cooler on my board, and actually, that's perfect, since it will give me a place to put the towels. I hate wet towels."

Opening her door, she reached for both her camera and the carrier straps for the boards, consciously trying not to stare at him. She laid out the carrier straps, then hooked them to the boards, knowing Colin was watching her and liking the way it made her feel. When she was finished, he grabbed his backpack and both boards. Maria picked up the towels and cooler as they started toward the point. "What's in the cooler, by the way?" she asked.

"Snacks, basically. Fruit, some nuts, a couple bottles of water."

"Healthy," she commented.

"I'm pretty strict about what I eat."

"And the backpack?"

"A Frisbee, a Hacky Sack, and sunscreen. If we hit the beach or whatever."

"I'm not very good at Frisbee. And just so you know, I've never touched a Hacky Sack in my life."

"Then we'll both be trying something new today."

On the beach, the sand glowed almost white in the sunlight. Aside from a man tossing a ball to his golden retriever in the waves, the beach at this end of the island was deserted. Maria raised the cooler in the direction of the inlet. "That's Masonboro Island," she said.

"Until you mentioned it last night, I'd never heard of it."

"It's rustic. There are no roads or picnic areas. In the summers, a lot of boaters go there, but lately, I've had the place to myself. It's quiet and beautiful, and it's a great way to kick off my week, especially one like this one. My partner has a trial later this week, and I'll probably be working late every night to make sure he has everything he needs. I'll head in earlier than usual, too."

"That's a lot of hours."

"Gotta get ahead, you know," she cracked.

"Why?"

"If I don't do my job, I'll get fired."

"I wasn't asking about doing your job well. I understand that. I was just wondering why it's important to you to get ahead."

Maria frowned, realizing that he was the first person who'd ever asked her the question and she was at a loss. "I don't know," she finally answered. "I guess I'm just wired that way. Either that, or it was all my parents' fault. Isn't that what people say in therapy?"

"Sometimes. And sometimes it's even true."

"Don't you want to get ahead?"

"I'm not sure what getting ahead even means," he said. "Bigger house? Better cars? More exotic vacations? My parents have all those things, but I don't get the sense that either of them is really happy. There's always something more out there, but where does it end? I don't want to live like that."

"How do you want to live?"

"I want balance. Work is important because I have to support myself, but so are friends, health, rest. Having the time to do things that I enjoy, and sometimes doing nothing at all."

The cooler thumped gently against her leg. "That's very... sensible."

"Okay."

She smiled. *I could have predicted he was going to say that.* "You're right, of course. Balance is important, but I've always liked the feeling of succeeding at something difficult, whether it was grades when I was a little girl or a well-written brief now. Setting goals and then reaching them makes me feel like I'm not just going through the motions of life. And in the end, if I do it well enough, other people notice, and I get rewarded. I like that, too."

"That makes sense."

"But not for you?"

"We're different."

"Don't you set goals, too? Like finishing college or winning a fight?"

"Yes."

"Then how are we different?"

"Because I don't care about getting ahead. And I generally don't give a lot of thought to the way other people define it."

"And you think I do?"

"Yes."

"Care to elaborate?"

He took a couple of steps before answering. "I think you care deeply about the way you come across to other people, but to me, that's a mistake. In the end, the only one you can ever really please is yourself. How others feel is up to them."

She pressed her lips together, knowing he was right but still a little taken aback that he'd simply...say it. Then again, he was forthright about everything else, so why should she be surprised?

"Did you learn that in therapy?"

"Yes. But it took a long time to embrace it."

"Maybe I should talk to your therapist."

"Maybe," he agreed, and she laughed.

"Well, just so you know, it's not all me. The fact that I need so much external validation *is* my parents' fault."

When he arched a skeptical eyebrow, she nudged his shoulder playfully, the gesture strangely natural. "I'm being serious about this. I might have been born with drive or ambition or whatever you want to call it, but they definitely nurtured it. Neither one of my parents went to school past the eighth grade, and they had to sacrifice for years before they could start the restaurant. They had to learn a new language and accounting and a thousand other things from scratch when they were adults, so to them, a good education was everything. I grew up speaking Spanish at home, so right from the start, I had to work harder than the other kids because I didn't understand anything the teacher was saying. Even though my parents were both working fifteen-hour days, they never missed a meeting with my teachers, and they made sure I always did my homework. When I started to bring home good grades, they were just so proud. They'd invite my aunts and uncles and cousins over on the weekend—I've got a ton of relatives in town—and they'd pass around my report card, going on and on about what a good student I was. I was the center of attention and I liked the way it made me feel, so I began to work even harder. I'd sit in the front row and raise my hand whenever the teacher asked a question, and I'd stay up until the middle of the night studying for tests. As a result, I was pretty much a total nerd all the way through high school."

"Yeah?" He wore that amused expression again.

"Uh...yeah," she said sheepishly. "I got glasses when I was eight, these brown-rimmed monstrosities, and I had braces for three years. I was shy and gawky and I actually *liked* to study. I didn't go to a prom until I was a senior, and even then, I went with a group of other girls who didn't have dates, either. I never kissed a boy until the month before I started college. Trust me, I know what a nerd is, and I was one of them."

"And now?"

"I'm still kind of a nerd. I work too much, I don't visit my friends as often as I should, and I don't really do anything on the weekends except paddleboard and spend time with my family. On Friday nights, you can usually find me reading in bed."

"That doesn't make you a nerd. I don't go out much anymore, either. If I'm not working out or competing, I'm usually listening to some tunes or studying or hanging with Evan and Lily at the house."

"Lily?"

"Evan's fiancée."

"What's she like?"

"Blond. About the same size as you. Terrific personality. And very, very Southern. She's from Charleston."

"How about Evan? Is he anything like you?"

"He's more like you, actually. He's got his act together."

"You think I have my act together?"

"Yes."

"Then why doesn't it feel that way?"

"I have no idea," he answered. "But I think most people would say the same thing about you as I did."

She squinted over at him, liking what he'd said. By then, they had reached the shoreline, and she slipped off her sandals, focusing on the water. "Okay, this is good," she declared. "The tide's going in, which makes it easier. If it were going out, we'd have to launch from down there," she said, pointing over his shoulder. "You ready?"

"Almost," he said. He put the boards down and shrugged off the backpack, storing his flip-flops and removing a bottle of sunscreen. He pulled off his shirt, tucking it away in the backpack as well, and her first thought was that he looked almost sculpted. His chest and stomach were a landscape of contours and ridges, every muscle sharply defined. On his chest, a colorful dragon tattoo wound its way over one shoulder, intertwining artfully with a Chinese character. He stared toward the water as he began to apply the lotion. "It's gorgeous out here," he observed.

"I agree," she said, trying not to ogle.

He squeezed some more sunscreen into his hand before offering her the bottle. "Do you want some?"

"Maybe later. I put some on earlier, but I don't generally burn. Latin skin, you know."

He nodded, slathering some on the fronts of his legs and then turning around. "Would you mind putting some on my back?"

She nodded, her mouth going slightly dry. "Sure."

Their fingers brushed as she took the lotion. She squeezed a dab into her hands and slowly ran her hands over his back, feeling the interplay of muscles and skin, trying to ignore the strange intimacy of what she was doing. Serena was going to love hearing about this.

"Will we see any dolphins or porpoises?" he asked, seemingly oblivious to her thoughts.

Running her hands over the cords in his back, it took her a moment to answer. "I doubt it. At this time of day, they're usually on the ocean side." Then, feeling a pang of disappointment, she finished and closed the cap. "All right, you're done."

"Thanks," he said, putting the sunscreen away. "What's next?"

"We're almost ready." She unhooked the carrier straps and handed them to Colin to store in his backpack as she grabbed the smaller of the two boards. "Can you follow me out with the cooler and towels? I'll show you how to get up."

She waded into the ocean with her board, and when she was a bit more than knee-deep, she lay down on it, pulling herself along its length until she was centered. She set the oar perpendicular to the board, then held it fast as she first went to her knees, and then finally stood. "Ta-da...And that's all there is to it. The key is to find your sweet spot, where neither the nose nor the tail is underwater. And then, keep your knees bent—it'll help keep you upright."

"Got it."

"You can put the cooler behind me, and then stack the towels on. And would you hand me my camera?"

He waded into the water, following her instructions. She draped the camera strap around her neck as he retrieved his own board and repeated her movements. When he was standing, he shifted his weight, the board wobbling slightly.

"It's more stable than I thought it would be," he remarked.

"Now when you turn, you can either paddle forward for a wide, slow turn, or you can paddle backward for a tighter turn." She demonstrated the first, then the second, rotating in place, moving a bit farther from shore in the process. "You ready?"

"Let's go," he said. Within a few strokes he'd caught up to her, and they began to paddle side by side until they reached the fertile, still waters of the marsh. Above them, the blue sky was limned with thin cirrus clouds. Discreetly, she watched Colin taking in everything, his gaze lingering on the brown pelicans and the snowy egrets, or an osprey that passed overhead. He didn't seem to feel the need to break the silence, and she thought again that she'd never met anyone like him.

As her thoughts continued to drift, she turned her attention to the island, noting the gnarled remnants of tree stumps, gray and salt-coated, their roots twisting like frayed yarn on a loosely twined ball. Curving pathways cut through the saw-grass-speckled dunes, shortcuts to the ocean side of the island, and driftwood, stained black from the marsh, collected at the water's edge.

"You're thinking about something," she heard him say. Without her noticing it, Colin had moved his board closer to hers.

"Just how much I love being out here."

"Do you come out every weekend?"

"Most weekends," she said, keeping her strokes steady. "Unless it's raining or the wind is gusting. Strong winds make it feel like you're not getting anywhere, and the water can get kind of choppy. I made that mistake once when I brought Serena out here. She lasted about twenty minutes before she insisted on heading back, and she hasn't come out ever since. When it comes to the ocean, she's more of the lay-out-in-the-sun or relax-in-the-back-of-the-boat type of girl. Even though we're close, we're not that much alike."

The curiosity in the way he watched and listened urged her on, and Maria drew her paddle through the water. "Serena has always been more outgoing and popular than I ever was. She's had one boyfriend after the next and has a zillion friends. Her phone never stops ringing, people always want to spend time with her. It wasn't like that for me. I was always quieter, shyer I guess, and I grew up feeling like I never really fit in."

"You don't seem shy to me."

"No?" she asked. "How do I seem to you?"

He cocked his head. "Thoughtful. Intelligent. Empathetic. Beautiful."

The certainty with which he spoke—like he'd reviewed the list beforehand—made her feel suddenly self-conscious. "Thank you," she murmured. "That was . . . sweet."

"I'm sure you've heard it before."

"Not really."

"Then you're hanging out with the wrong people."

She adjusted her feet on the board, trying to mask how flattered and flustered she felt. "So no girlfriend for you?"

"No," he answered. "I wasn't really boyfriend material for a while there, and lately I've been pretty busy. You?"

"Still single," she said. "I had a serious boyfriend when I was in college, but it didn't work out. And lately I've had a tendency to attract the wrong kind of men."

"Like me?"

She gave a sheepish grin. "I wasn't thinking of you when I said that. I was thinking about the managing partner at my firm. Who happens to be married and has a family. He's been hitting on me and it's been making work pretty stressful."

"I can imagine."

"But you don't have any advice for me, right? Since you don't give advice?"

"No."

"You do realize that having a conversation with you takes some getting used to, right? Serena, for instance, always has loads of advice."

"Is it helpful?"

"Not really."

His expression said she'd just proved his point. "What happened with your boyfriend?"

"There's not much to say. We'd been going out for a couple of years and it felt to me like we were moving toward something more serious."

"Marriage?"

She nodded. "I thought so. But then, he decided that I wasn't what he wanted. He wanted someone else."

"That had to be rough."

"At the time, it was devastating," she agreed.

"And no boyfriends since then?"

"Not really. I've dated a few guys, but nothing ever really materialized." She paused, remembering. "I'd go dancing with my girlfriends at this salsa club in Charlotte, but most of the guys I ended up meeting wanted only one thing. To me, sleeping with someone is an outgrowth of a commitment, and a lot of guys just want a fling or whatever."

"That's their problem."

"I know. But..." She tried to think of the best way to phrase it. "It's hard sometimes. Maybe it's because my parents are so happy and make it seem so easy, but I've always assumed that I'd be able to find the perfect guy without having to settle. And growing up, I had all these plans...I just knew that by now, at my age, I'd be married and we'd live in a restored Victorian and we'd be talking about kids. But those things seem further away now than they did when I was a little girl. They seem further away than they did even a couple of years ago."

When he didn't respond, she shook her head. "I can't believe I'm telling you all this."

"I'm interested."

"Sure you are," she said, dismissing his comment. "It sounds boring, even to me."

"It's not boring," he countered. "It's your story and I like hearing it." He let that sit before abruptly changing the subject. "Salsa dancing, huh?"

"That's what you heard? In everything I said?" When he shrugged, she went on, wondering why it seemed so easy to talk to him. "I used to go almost every weekend."

"But you don't go anymore?"

"Not since I've moved back. They don't have any clubs here. Not officially, anyway. Serena tried to drag me to this one place and I thought about it, but I begged off at the last minute."

"It sounds like it might have been fun."

"Maybe. But it's not even a real club. It's in this abandoned warehouse, and I'm pretty sure the whole setup is illegal."

"Sometimes those are the best places to go."

"I assume you're speaking from experience?"

"Yes."

She smiled. "Do you know anything about salsa dancing?"

"Is it like the tango?"

"Not really. The tango is kind of like ballroom dancing, where you move around the room. Salsa dancing is more of a party dance with lots of spinning and changing hands, and you stay in one place on the floor. It's a great way to spend a couple of hours with friends, especially if your partner is good. It was the only time I felt like I could really let go and be myself."

"Aren't you being yourself right now?"

"Of course," she answered. "But this is definitely the quieter version of me, the more typical one." She raised the oar overhead to stretch for a moment, then dipped the tip into the water again. "I have a question," she said. "And I've been wondering about it since you mentioned it." When he turned toward her, she went on. "Why do you want to teach the third grade? I'd think that most guys would want to teach at the high school level."

He pulled his oar through the water.

"Because at that age, kids are old enough to understand most everything an adult tells them, but still young enough to believe that adults tell the truth. It's also the year when behavior problems begin to really manifest. Taken together with all the testing the state requires, third grade is just a critical year."

They glided on water almost as still as glass. "And?" she asked.

"And what?"

"You said the same thing to me last night. When you thought I wasn't telling you the whole story. So I'll ask you again—what's the real reason you want to teach the third grade?"

"Because it was my last good year in school," he said. "Until a couple of years ago, in fact, it was my last good year, period. And it was all because of Mr. Morris. He was a retired army officer who got into teaching later in life, and he knew exactly what I needed. Not the mindless discipline I had later in military school, but a specific plan just for me. He didn't take any crap in class from the very beginning, and as soon as I began acting up, he told me that I'd have to stay after school. I thought I'd just sit in the classroom with a book or he'd have me clean up or whatever, but instead he had me run laps around the lower school and do push-ups every time I passed him. And the whole time, he kept telling me that I was doing great, that I was really fast or strong or whatever, so it didn't feel like punishment. He did the same thing at recess the next day, and then he asked if I could start showing up early every day because it was clear that I had a gift for running. That I was stronger than the other kids. *Better* than the other kids. Looking back, I know he was doing it because of my ADHD and other emotional crap, and that all he really wanted to do was burn off my excess energy so that I could sit still in class."

His voice grew softer as he went on. "But back then, it was the first time I could ever remember being praised, and after that, all I wanted to do was make him even more proud of me. I buckled down and school started to get easier for me. I caught up in reading and math, and I was better behaved at home, too. Fast forward a year to Mrs. Crandall's class, and all that went right out the window. She was mean and angry and she hated boys, and I went back to being the troubled kid I used to be. After that, my parents shipped me off, and you already know the rest of that story."

He let out a long breath before facing her. "That's why I want to teach the third grade. Because maybe, just maybe, I'll come across a kid like me and I'll know exactly what to do. And in the long run, I know how much that single year might mean to that kid. Because without Mr. Morris so long ago, I would never have considered going back to college now and becoming a teacher."

While Colin spoke, Maria kept her gaze fixed on him. "I know I shouldn't be surprised, considering everything else you've told me," she said. "But I am."

"Because?"

"It's inspiring. Why you want to become a teacher, I mean. I don't have any stories like that. Half the time, I'm not even sure why I became a lawyer in the first place. It just kind of happened."

"How so?"

"When I first got to college, I wasn't sure what I wanted to do. I thought about business school or getting a master's and I even debated whether or not to go to medical school. It was hard enough just to pick a major, and even in my junior year, I still had no idea what I wanted to do with my life. My roommate, on the other hand, was set on going to law school, and I sort of convinced myself that the idea was a lot more glamorous than it really is. The next thing I knew, I was applying to law school, and three years later, I had a job lined up with the DA and was studying for the bar. And now, here I am. Don't get me wrong—I'm good at what I do, but sometimes it's hard for me to imagine that I'll be doing it the rest of my life."

"Who says you have to?"

"I can't just throw my education away. Or the past four years. What would I do?"

He scratched at his jaw. "I think," he finally said, "you can do whatever you want. In the end, we all live the life we choose for ourselves."

"What do your parents think about you being back in school?"

"I think they're still wondering whether I've really changed, or whether I'll revert to being the guy I used to be."

She smiled, liking that he said what he thought without worrying what she might think.

"I don't know why, but it's hard for me to imagine the other Colin, the one you used to be."

"You wouldn't have liked him much."

"Probably not," she said. "And he probably wouldn't have stopped to change my tire, either."

"Definitely not," he agreed.

"What else should I know about the new Colin?" she asked,

and her question gradually gave way to a meandering conversation about growing up in Raleigh and a bit more about his friendship with Evan and Lily. He told her about his parents and his older sisters, and what it had been like to grow up under the care of various nannies. He talked about the early fights he'd been in, the schools he'd attended, and offered more details about the years following high school, although he admitted that they'd largely blurred together. He talked about MMA, and when pressed, he recounted a few of his fights, including the most recent one with the marine, which had left him bruised and bloody. While many of the stories he told her underscored the rough edges of his past, they were of a piece with what she already knew.

As they talked, the tide began to roll in, propelling them forward side by side. The sun gradually bowed toward the horizon, the water beginning to gleam like old pennies. The thin cloud cover softened the glare and began to change colors—pinks and oranges and magentas.

"Would you like to check out the beach?" she finally asked. He nodded, and as they began paddling toward shore, Maria spotted the sleek, dark backs of three porpoises slowly approaching. They arced through the water, and when she pointed them out, Colin broke into a boyish grin. In unspoken agreement, they stopped paddling, allowing their boards to drift. To her surprise, the porpoises altered their course, gliding directly toward them. On instinct, Maria reached for the camera and began to snap photos, adjusting the framing with every shot. By some miracle, she captured an image of all three of the porpoises breaching the surface before they paraded past in single file, close enough to touch, their blowholes spraying water. Maria turned, watching them retreat toward the inlet and the ocean beyond, wondering what had brought them to this place in this exact moment.

When they finally vanished from sight, she noticed that Colin had been staring at her. He smiled, and on instinct, she raised the camera and snapped his picture, suddenly recalling the flash of vulnerability he'd shown a few minutes earlier. Despite the outward confidence he exuded, she understood that like her, Colin simply wanted to be accepted; in his own way, he was just as lonely as she was. The realization made her ache, and it suddenly felt like they were the only two people in the world. In this silent, intimate moment, she knew that she wanted to spend more afternoons with him just like this one, an ordinary afternoon that somehow felt magical.

CHAPTER 7

Colin

On the beach, Colin sat on a towel with Maria beside him, trying to ignore the way she looked in the black bikini that had been hidden beneath her clothing. Yesterday he'd viewed her as an intriguing stranger; while paddleboarding today, he'd come to view her as a friend; but now, he wasn't sure what might come next. All he really knew was that the black bikini was making it difficult to keep his thoughts straight. Maria, he decided, was beyond pretty, planted firmly in the stunning range, and although Colin sensed that something had changed between them over the course of the day, he couldn't quite put a name to it.

He didn't have much experience with women like Maria. Instead of college degrees and close-knit families, the women he'd dated tended to have numerous piercings and tattoos, angry façades, and serious daddy issues. They expected to be treated poorly, and he'd generally obliged. The mutual lack of expectation made for something resembling comfort when they hung out together. Damaged comfort for sure, but misery loves company. Only a couple of them had lasted as long as three months, but unlike Evan, having one special person in his life had never held much interest for Colin. He wasn't wired that way. He liked the freedom that came with being single, without having to answer to someone else. It was hard enough to keep his own life straight, let alone trying to meet someone else's expectations.

Or at least that was what he'd always believed, but now, as he surreptitiously admired Maria, he wondered whether he'd simply been making excuses. Whether maybe, just maybe, he hadn't cared about being in a relationship because he'd never given it an honest shot, or because he hadn't met the right person. He knew he was getting ahead of himself, but he couldn't deny the fact that he wanted to spend more time with her. Why she was still single was beyond him. He reminded himself that there wasn't a chance she'd be interested in a guy like him.

And yet...

In the hospital, he'd spent a lot of time in group therapy, where trying to figure out what made others tick was part and parcel of the exercise itself. Understanding others meant understanding yourself—and vice versa—and he'd long ago become attuned to body language and vocal cues people displayed as they shared their fears and flaws and regrets. And while he couldn't precisely read Maria, he suspected she was just as confused about what was happening as he was. Which made sense. Although he was doing okay now, she had to realize that the old Colin would always be part of him. That would be a concern for anyone; hell, he was concerned about it, too. While his explosive anger was dormant at the present time, it was like a hibernating bear, and he knew he had to structure his life a certain way to keep spring from arriving so the bear would stay asleep. Train hard to keep his anger in check; indulge in the occasional MMA match to purge his aggression. Study hard and work long hours to fill his schedule and keep him from visiting the wrong places. Stay away from drugs and limit alcohol. Spend time with Evan and Lily, who not only were model citizens, but were always there to lend support and keep him out of harm's way.

There wasn't room in his life for Maria. There wasn't time. He didn't have the energy.

And yet...

They were alone together on an isolated stretch of sand, and he thought again that she was sexy as hell. Logically, Maria should have run for the hills by now, but she seemed to be taking his past in stride, and for the life of him, he couldn't stop thinking about her.

He watched as she leaned back in the glow of the late-afternoon sun, propping herself on her elbows. He thought again that she was as naturally beautiful as anyone he'd ever seen, and in an effort to distract himself, he rolled to the side and reached behind her, pulling the cooler toward him. He popped off the lid and retrieved two bottles of water, then handed one of them to her.

"Banana or orange?" he asked.

"Banana," she said. She sat up, languid and graceful. "Oranges get my hands all sticky."

He handed it over and pulled out a couple of baggies of mixed nuts.

"Do you want some of these, too?"

"Sure," she said. "Why not?"

She took the baggie and popped a couple of almonds into her mouth. "This is just what I needed," she said with a wink. "I can already feel my cholesterol dropping and my muscles getting bigger."

He smiled, beginning to peel his orange. She did the same with her banana and took a bite before leaning back again. "I never do this," she said. "Come to the beach when I'm here, I mean. I've paddled past it, but I've never actually come out here just to relax."

"Why not?"

"In the summer, there are always too many people around. I'd feel weird coming out here alone."

"Why? It wouldn't bother me."

"I have no doubt you'd do it. For you, it's no big deal. But it's different for women. Coming out here, all alone—some guys might think it's an invitation. And what if some crazy man sat next to me and started hitting on me? Like someone who'd done drugs and was on probation and had a history of going to bars so he could fight strangers and stomp on people's heads...Oh, wait!" She feigned horror as she suddenly turned toward him.

He laughed. "What if he said he'd changed?"

"At first, I probably wouldn't believe him."

"What if he was charming?"

"He'd have to be really, really charming, but even then, I'd probably rather be alone."

"Even if he changed your tire in the middle of a storm?"

"I'd definitely be grateful for the way he helped me out, but I don't know if it would make much difference. Even crazy people can do something nice once in a while."

"That's probably a wise decision. A guy like that might be dangerous and definitely not someone you'd want to be alone with."

"Obviously," she said. "Of course, there's always the possibility that he really *had* changed and that he happened to be a nice guy, which means I'd be out of luck. Since I never even gave him a chance, I mean."

"I can understand how that might be a problem."

"Anyway, that's why I don't come out to the beach alone. It just eliminates the whole issue."

"Makes sense. Still, I have to admit that I'm not quite sure how I feel about what you just said."

"Good," she answered, nudging him playfully with her shoulder. "Then we're even. I haven't known how to feel about a lot of what you've told me."

Though he wasn't sure if she was flirting, he liked how natural it felt when she touched him. "How about we change the subject to safer ground?"

"Like what?"

"Tell me about your family. You said you have a lot of relatives in town?"

"My grandparents on both sides still live in Mexico, but three aunts and four uncles live in Wilmington, along with over twenty cousins. And we throw some rocking family parties."

"Sounds fun."

"It is. A lot of them either work or used to work at La Cocina de la Familia, so the restaurant was like our second home. Growing up, I probably spent more time there than at the house."

"Yeah?"

She nodded. "When I was little, my parents had this play area set up in the back so my mom could watch me, and when I started school, I'd do my homework in the office. After Serena was born, I'd watch Serena in the play area until my mom's shift ended, and then when Serena was older, I started working there, too. But the strange thing is, I never remember feeling like I came in second to the restaurant, or even like it dominated my life. Not only because my whole family was there, but because my parents were always popping in to check on me and make sure I was okay. And when we were at home, it didn't feel much different. We always had relatives over. A lot of them lived with us until they saved enough money to get their own place. For a kid, there's nothing better. There was always something going on; people talking or playing or cooking or listening to music. It was always loud, but it was good energy. Happy energy."

He tried to match her account with the woman sitting beside him, finding it surprisingly easy.

"How old were you when you started working at the restaurant?"

"Fourteen," she said. "I worked there after school and every summer and Christmas break until I graduated from law school. My parents thought it would be good for me to earn my own spending money."

"You sound proud of them."

"Wouldn't you be? Though I must admit that I'm not quite sure what my parents would think if they knew I was with you today."

"I have a pretty good idea of what they might think."

She laughed, lighthearted and unrestrained.

"You want to try tossing the Frisbee around?"

"I'll try. Don't say I didn't warn you."

She hadn't been lying. She wasn't very good; nearly all of her tosses veered off course, some hitting the sand and others getting caught in the breeze. Colin zigzagged gamely, trying to rescue the Frisbee before it hit the ground while hearing her call out, "I'm sorry!" Whenever she succeeded in making an accurate throw or catching the Frisbee, she reveled with almost childlike glee.

Through it all, she kept up a steady chatter. She told him about her trips to Mexico to visit her grandparents and described the tiny cinder-block houses where both sets had lived their entire lives. She touched on her high school years, along with a few of her college and law school experiences, and shared a few stories about working at the DA's office. He was perplexed at how her first boyfriend could have let her go and why no one else had come along since. Could anyone be so blind? He didn't know and didn't care: All he really knew for sure was that he was unbelievably lucky that she'd wandered out to the pier.

Abandoning the Frisbee, he'd grabbed the Hacky Sack and heard her laugh aloud. "Not a chance," she said before collapsing on her towel. Colin sat beside her, feeling the weariness of an active day in the sun and noticing that Maria's skin had taken on a buttery glow. They finished the rest of their water, sipping slowly as they watched the waves.

"I think I'd like to watch you fight," she said, turning toward him.

"Okay," he said.

"When's the next one?"

"Not for a few weeks. It's at the House of Blues in North Myrtle Beach."

"Who are you fighting?"

"I don't know yet."

"How can you not know who you're fighting?"

He ran his fingers through the sand. "In amateur events, the ticket isn't always finished until the day before. It all depends on who wants to fight, who's ready to fight, who's available to fight. And, of course, who actually signs up to fight."

"Does that make you nervous? Not knowing?"

"Not really."

"What if he's like ... a giant or something?"

"There are weight classes, so that's not a concern. My main worry is if the guy panics and breaks the rules. Some of the guys who show up in these amateur events don't have a lot of experience in the cage, and it's easy to lose control. That's what happened when my last opponent head-butted me. They had to stop the fight so I could get the bleeding under control, but the ref didn't catch it. My coach was going nuts."

"And you actually *enjoy* that?"

"It comes with the territory," he said. "The good news is that I got the guy in a guillotine choke hold in the next round and he had to tap out. And I did enjoy that part."

"You do realize that's not normal, right?"

"Okay."

"And just so we're clear, I don't care whether you win or lose, but I don't want you to get all bloodied and bruised."

"I'll do my best."

She furrowed her brow. "Wait—the House of Blues? Isn't that a restaurant?"

"Among other things. But it has enough room. Amateur events don't usually draw much of a crowd."

"I'm shocked! Who wouldn't want to watch men trying to beat the hell out of each other? What is wrong with society these days?"

He grinned. She wrapped her arms around her knees as she'd

done the night before, but this time, he could feel her shoulder brushing against his own. "How did the photos turn out?" he asked. "The ones of the porpoises?"

Maria reached for her camera and clicked to the display before handing it to him. "I think this one's the best," she said. "But there are a few more. Just use the arrow button there to go through them."

He stared at the image of the three porpoises. "It's incredible," he said. "It's almost like they were posing."

"Sometimes I get lucky. The light was just right." She leaned toward him, her arm grazing his. "There are others that I've taken in the last month that I liked, too."

He used the back arrow, scanning a long series of photos: pelicans and ospreys, a close-up of a butterfly, a mullet caught in midjump. When she leaned further into him to follow along, he caught the scent of wildflowers in the heat.

At the end of the series, she finally pulled back. "You should frame some of these," he said, handing her the camera.

"I do," she said. "But just the better ones."

"Better than these?"

"You'd be the one to judge," she said. "Of course, you'd have to come over first, since they're hanging on my walls."

"I'd think I'd like that, Maria."

Maria turned toward the water again, a slight smile playing on her lips, and it seemed odd to think that it was only yesterday that he'd spotted her at the end of the pier. Or how well he'd come to know her in such a short period of time. And how much he wanted to know even more about her.

"We should probably get going," she said, a note of regret in her voice. "Before it starts getting too dark."

He nodded, feeling a stab of disappointment as they rose to gather up their things. They paddled back, reaching Wrightsville Beach just as the first stars were emerging. Colin helped Maria strap the boards and paddles to the top of her car before turning to face her. Watching her brush the hair from her eyes, he felt oddly nervous, something he could never remember happening with a woman before.

"I had a great time today."

"Paddleboarding is a lot of fun," she agreed.

"I wasn't talking about the paddleboarding," he said. He shifted from one foot to the other, and he had the impression that she was waiting for him to finish. "I was talking about spending time with you."

"Yeah?" she asked, her voice soft.

"Yeah." Colin was sure she was more beautiful than any woman he'd ever known.

"What are you doing next weekend?"

"Other than brunch on Sunday, I don't have anything planned."

"Do you want to go to that warehouse Serena told you about? On Saturday night?"

"Are you asking me to go dancing?"

"I'd like to get to know the less typical Maria, the one who can really be herself."

"Because the quieter version isn't your type?"

"No," he said. "Actually, it's just the opposite. And I already know how I feel about that Maria."

Crickets were calling from the dunes, serenading them like nature's orchestra. They were alone, and as she stared up at him, he stepped toward her, instinct taking over. He wondered if she'd turn away and break the spell, but she didn't. Instead, she stayed in place as he moved even nearer, one arm slowly going around her back. He pulled her close, their lips coming together, and at that moment, he suddenly knew that this was what he'd wanted all along. He'd wanted her, in his arms, just like this, forever.

Colin took his time getting home, driving through Wilmington's prettier back streets and basking in the warm afterglow of his day with Maria. His body felt surprisingly well used by the afternoon of paddleboarding, his mind still circling the mystery of Maria. Getting out of his car, he was just ambling across the newly cut lawn toward his apartment when he heard Lily calling from the porch, her cell phone in hand.

"There you are," she said, her drawl almost a singsong. As always, she was perfectly coiffed. Tonight, though, in something of a rarity, she was wearing jeans—albeit with pumps, a pearl necklace, tastefully sized diamond studs, and a gardenia artfully pinned in her hair.

"What are you doing out here?" he asked, veering toward her.

"I was speaking to my mother while I was waiting for you," she answered, skipping down the steps toward him. Lily was the only girl he knew who actually skipped when she was happy. She leaned in for a hug. "Evan told me you were going on a date today and I want to hear all about it before we go inside."

"Where's Evan?"

"He's on the computer researching some pharmaceutical company for his clients. You know how serious he is about his work, bless his heart. But don't try to change the subject. For now, we're going to sit on the steps while you tell me about this special young woman, and I won't take no for an answer. And don't leave anything out. I want to hear everything."

She took a seat on the steps, patting the spot beside her. Colin knew he had no choice but to do as he'd been told, and he gave her the basics. Lily interrupted frequently, pressing him for details. When he finished, she squinted at him, obviously disappointed.

"You really must work on your storytelling skills, Colin," she chided. "All you did was recite a list of activities and the topics you talked about."

"How else was I supposed to tell it?"

"That's a silly question. You were supposed to make *me* fall in love with her, too."

"Why would I want to do that?"

"Because even as poorly as you told the story, it's obvious that you're smitten with her."

He said nothing.

"Colin?" she said. "This is exactly what I mean. What you should have said was something like, 'When I'm with Maria... I just...I...' and then trail off and shake your head because words are inadequate to convey the intensity of what you're experiencing."

"That sounds more like you than me."

"I know," she said, sounding almost sorry for him. "That's what makes you such a poor storyteller, bless your heart."

Only Lily could insult him in a way that made it sound as though it was harder for her to say than for him to hear. "How do you know I'm smitten with her?" he asked.

She sighed. "If you didn't enjoy spending the day in her presence, you would have given me that blank look of yours and said, 'There's nothing to talk about,' when I asked you about her. And all that, of course, brings the primary question to mind: When will I have the chance to meet her?"

"I'd have to ask her."

"And do you have immediate plans to spend more time with your lady friend?"

Colin hesitated, wondering if anyone besides Lily still used the term *lady friend*. "We're supposed to go out next weekend."

"Not to a bar, I hope."

"No," he said. He told her about the warehouse.

"Do you think that's a wise decision? Considering what happened the last time you went to a club with Evan and me?"

"I just want to take her dancing."

"Dancing can be very romantic," she admitted. "And yet..."

"It'll be fine. I promise."

"Then I shall take you at your word. Of course, you should also swing by her office sometime this week and surprise her with flowers or candy. Women love to receive those sorts of thoughtful gifts, though I've always held the opinion that candy is better during the cool months. So maybe just flowers."

"That's not my style."

"Of course it isn't, which is why I made the suggestion. Trust me. She'll be thrilled."

"Okay."

At his answer, she reached over and patted his hand. "Haven't we talked about this? Saying 'okay' when people talk to you? It's a habit you really need to break. It's *very* unattractive."

"Okay."

"And so it goes." She sighed. "One day, you'll understand the wisdom of my words."

Behind them, Evan opened the door, catching sight of her hand on Colin's, but Evan understood the relationship between the three of them the same way Colin did.

"Let me guess. You're grilling him about his date?" he asked his fiancée.

"I was doing no such thing," Lily huffed. "Ladies do not *grill*. I simply inquired how he believed their date went, and though Colin—poor thing—nearly put me to sleep at first, I do think our friend here is smitten."

Evan laughed. "Colin? Smitten? Those two things just don't go together."

"Colin, would you please inform my fiancé as to the truth of this matter?"

Colin hooked a thumb toward her. "She thinks I'm smitten."

"As I said," Lily noted, sounding satisfied. "Now that we've gotten to the truth of the matter," she went on, "when do you plan on calling your new lady friend?"

"I haven't thought about it."

"Have you learned nothing from me?" She shook her head. "Before you even shower, you must—you absolutely must—give your lady friend a call. And you must also tell her how wonderful she made you feel, and that you were honored by the pleasure of her company."

"Don't you think that's a little much?"

Lily sounded almost sad. "Colin...I know you struggle when it comes to expressing your sensitive side, and that is a flaw in your character that I've always been willing to overlook, if only out of dear friendship. But you *will* call her this evening. As soon as you walk in the door. Because gentlemen—*real* gentlemen—always call, and I only associate with gentlemen."

Evan raised his eyebrows and Colin knew he had no choice.

"Okay."

CHAPTER 8

—— ❦ ——

Maria

On Monday, Maria thought it best to hide out in her office, where she could concentrate in peace. Barney's stress level about the upcoming trial was escalating, and she didn't want to become an unwitting target. Closing her door, she jotted notes in preparation for a midmorning meeting with clients, made some phone calls, and responded to e-mails, wanting to get a jump on the week. And yet, despite her desire for efficiency, every now and then she'd catch herself staring out the window, replaying images from the weekend.

Some of her distraction had to do with Colin's phone call on Sunday night. If friends and magazines spoke the truth, guys didn't call right away, and most of them never called at all. Then again, everything about Colin verged on the unexpected. After hanging up, she'd examined the photo that she'd taken of him and imagined that she saw in it both the Colin she knew and Colin the stranger. His expression was gentle, but his body was a map of scars and tattoos. Though she'd promised to show Serena, she decided then and there that the photo would be for her eyes only.

"Someone's in a good mood."

At the sound, Maria saw Jill in the doorway.

"Oh, hey, Jill. What's up?"

"I suppose I should be asking you," she said, entering. "You were definitely lost in your own dreamy little world when I peeked in, and no one does that on Mondays."

"I had a good weekend."

"Yeah?" she asked. "By the way you just said it, I'm assuming that it went way better than my depositions last week. This has to be the first time I ever found myself actually *praying* I could return to the office."

"That bad?"

"Awful."

"You want to talk about it?"

"Only if you want to die of boredom. And anyway, I have a conference call in a few minutes. I mainly dropped by to see if you're doing anything for lunch. I'm dying for some sushi and good company now that I'm back in the saddle."

"Sounds great."

Jill adjusted the sleeve of her blouse. "I may be reading this wrong, but I take it that you're not still mad at me."

"Why would I be mad at you?"

"Maybe because I ambushed you with the worst blind date in history?"

"Oh, yeah," Maria said, surprised that she'd nearly forgotten. "That."

"I'm so sorry," Jill said. "You can't imagine how bad I felt all week, especially since I didn't have the chance to talk to you about it."

"We talked, remember? And you apologized."

"Not enough."

"It's okay. And actually, it ended up turning out fine."

"I can't imagine how."

"I met someone."

A couple of beats passed before the answer came to her. "You're not talking about the guy who changed your tire? The one who was bruised and bleeding and scared you half to death?"

"That's the one."

"How's that even possible?"

"It's kind of hard to explain."

Jill smirked. "Uh-oh."

"What?"

"You're smiling again."

"Am I?"

"Yes, you are. And part of me wants to cancel the conference call and just pull up a chair."

"I can't. Barney and I are meeting a client in a few minutes."

"But we're definitely on for lunch, right? And you'll fill me in then?"

"Without a doubt."

Ten minutes later, Serena called on her cell phone. When Maria saw who was on the line, she felt a sudden jolt of concern. Serena never called before ten a.m. Half the time, she wasn't even awake by ten.

"Serena? Are you okay?"

"Where is it?"

"Where's what?"

"The photo of Colin. It wasn't in my e-mail or text."

Maria blinked. "You're calling me at work, during work hours, about a photo?"

"I wouldn't have had to if you'd already sent it. Did it go okay? Tell me you didn't already run him off."

"No. As a matter of fact, we're going out Saturday night."

"Okay," Serena said. "The post won't have as much impact without a photo, though. Of course, I guess I could just use one of you from when you were a kid or whatever if you're not going to send it..."

"Good-bye, Serena."

She hung up the phone, only to reach for her cell phone a few minutes later, more out of morbid curiosity than anything.

And there, on Instagram, was her photo. From when she was in middle school. Braces. Acne. Glasses. Gawky. The worst school photo in the history of school photos. *"Try not to be jealous, guys, but my sister Maria has a date this Saturday night!"*

Maria closed her eyes. She was going to have to kill her sister. No question about it.

But she had to admit, Serena was kind of funny.

Over a plate of assorted sushi and sashimi a couple of hours later, Maria filled Jill in on much of what had happened with Colin, the story sounding unbelievable even to her.

"Wow," Jill breathed.

"Do you think I'm crazy? Considering his past?"

"Who am I to judge? Look at the blind date we set up. On something as out of the box as this, your best bet is to just keep following your instincts."

"What if my instincts are wrong?"

"Then at the very least, you got your tire changed. And had a nice date, which I'm hoping will get me totally off the hook for that double-date fiasco."

Maria smiled. "So the depositions were boring?"

"They were enough to make a monk go crazy, since half the people are perfectly willing to lie under oath and the other half say they can't remember anything at all. And now that I wasted my time all week, we'll probably just end up settling. Par for the course, but I can't say I'm ever going to enjoy it." She snagged another piece of sushi. "How goes it with Barney?"

"Better," she said.

"What does that mean?"

"Oh, that's right—you weren't here," Maria started, and she

told Jill about getting her tire changed and how it led to being late for the meeting, along with all the work she felt compelled to do in the aftermath. She also recounted the dressing-down Barney gave her, though she omitted the confrontation with Ken.

"Barney will get over it. He's always tense before trial."

Yes, but . . . Maria shifted in her seat. "The thing is, I heard that Barney was going to let me be lead counsel on this case."

"Where did you hear that?" Jill held her chopsticks at half-mast. "Don't get me wrong, you're a brilliant associate—but you're a little short on experience for Barney to saddle you with that kind of responsibility."

"Rumors," Maria said.

"I wouldn't put much stock in rumors. Barney enjoys the limelight too much, and he has a hard time ceding control—not to mention credit—to even the most senior associates. That's one of the reasons I transferred to labor and employment. I figured I'd never be able to move up, or even get the courtroom experience I needed."

"I still can't believe you were able to transfer departments."

"Lucky timing. I told you I was in labor and employment for a few years before I started at the firm, right?" When Maria nodded, Jill went on. "At the time, though, I wasn't sure it was what I really wanted to do, so I took a chance and tried insurance litigation. I worked with Barney for nine months and practically killed myself before I realized it was a dead end. I would have left, but it just so happened that the firm was building up its labor and employment practice and needed me."

"Unfortunately, I'm kind of stuck if this doesn't work out. Unless we start doing criminal defense."

"You could always change firms."

"That's not as easy as you might think."

"You haven't been looking, have you?"

"Not really. But I've been beginning to wonder if I should start."

Jill scrutinized her as she reached for her glass. "You know you can talk to me, right? About any concerns you have. While I'm not a partner, I do run my own department, which gives me some clout around here."

"I've just got a lot on my mind right now."

"Hopefully, you're talking about Colin."

The mention of his name brought more memories from the weekend, and she changed the subject. "How's Paul doing?"

"He's fine. I had to give him the cold shoulder for a couple of days as punishment for the date, but he got over it. We went to Asheville over the weekend for some wine tasting."

"That sounds fun."

"It was. Except, of course, there's no ring yet and the biological clock is still ticking and time is growing short. Pretending that everything is okay hasn't worked yet, so maybe it's time to try a new strategy."

"Like what?"

"I have no idea. If you have any foolproof plans, be sure to let me know."

"Will do."

Jill had another piece of sushi. "What do you have lined up this afternoon?"

"Same stuff as usual. There's a lot of prep work to finish for the trial. While trying to keep up with everything else, of course."

"Like I said, Barney expects a lot from his associates."

And Ken expects something else. "It's a job," she said.

"Are you sure everything is okay? Even with our lecherous managing partner?"

"Why would you ask?"

"Because you went off to that conference with him, and I've known him longer than you have. And remember—I know exactly how he operates."

"The conference was fine."

Jill gave her the once-over before finally offering a shrug. "Fair enough," she said. "The point is, I'm sensing that something else is bothering you."

Maria cleared her throat, wondering why it suddenly felt as if she were being interrogated.

"There's really nothing to say," she answered. "I'm just doing the best job I can."

The days that followed were too busy for the luxury of daydreaming, with Barney storming into her office every half hour asking her to examine additional details or to make calls, notwithstanding her work on other client matters. She barely had time to leave her desk, and on Wednesday afternoon, while working on a draft of Barney's opening statement, she failed to notice the way the sunlight began slanting through her windows, or the departures, one by one, of her colleagues. She stared at her MacBook screen with singular concentration until a knock at her office door startled her. She saw the door slowly swing open.

Ken.

With a jolt of panic, she looked through the open doorway; across the hall, Lynn was no longer at her desk. Barney's office was dark, and she couldn't hear anyone else in the hallway.

"I noticed that your lights were still on," he said, stepping into her office. "Do you have a few minutes?"

"I was just finishing up," she improvised, hearing a trace of uncertainty in her tone. "I must have lost track of time."

"I'm glad I caught you then," he said, his voice smooth and controlled. "I wanted to finish the conversation we started last week."

Maria felt a thud in her chest and began collecting the pages on her desk before slipping them back into their folders. The last thing she wanted was to be alone with him. She swallowed. "Is there any way we could do this tomorrow? I'm already late and I'm supposed to have dinner with my parents tonight."

"It won't take long," he said, ignoring her excuse as he came around her desk. He stood near the window and she noted the sky had darkened beyond the glass. "It might be easier for you this way, since we're away from prying eyes. There's no reason for everyone to know what happened with Barney's clients."

Not knowing what to say, she stayed quiet.

He glanced out the window, seemingly focused on something in the distance. "How do you like working with Barney?" he finally asked.

"I'm learning a lot from him," Maria began, choosing her words carefully. "He has great strategic instincts, the clients trust him, and as a colleague, he's good at explaining his thinking."

"You respect him, then."

"Of course."

"It's important to work with people that you respect. It's important that the two of you can work together as a team." Ken adjusted the venetian blinds, closing them slightly, then returning them to their original position. "Would you consider yourself a team player?"

The question hung in the air before she was able to answer. "I try to be," she said.

Ken waited a beat before going on. "I spoke to Barney again on Friday about the situation, and I must say that I was a bit surprised at how angry he still was over what happened. That's why I asked you about being a team player. Because I went to bat for you in that meeting, and I think I've been able to defuse the situation. I wanted to make sure I was doing the right thing."

Maria swallowed, wondering why Barney hadn't talked to her himself if he was still so upset. "Thank you," she finally murmured.

He turned from the window and took a step toward her. "I did it because I want you to have a long and successful tenure at the firm. You're going to need someone who's able to advocate for you in these kinds of situations, and I'm here to help you when I can." By then, he was standing over her, and she felt him place a hand on her shoulder. *Kind of.* His fingertips skimmed the area below her collarbone. "You should consider me a friend, albeit a friend in a high place."

Recoiling from his touch, she suddenly knew that all of this—the Monday cold shoulder, the dressing-down on Thursday, and now this *you and me against the world* show—was simply part of his latest plan to get her in bed, and she wondered why she hadn't been able to see it coming.

"We should go to lunch tomorrow," he said, his fingertips still brushing the exposed skin above her scoop-necked shirt. "We can talk about other ways that I can help you navigate the ins and outs of the office, especially if you hope to become a partner one day. I think you and I will be able to work together really well. Don't you think so, Maria?"

It was the sound of her name that brought her back, his words finally registering. *Not in this lifetime,* she suddenly thought. "I can't go to lunch tomorrow," she said, trying to hold her voice steady. "I already have plans."

A flash of annoyance crossed his face. "With Jill?"

That was usually the case, and Ken of course knew that. No doubt he'd suggest that she change the plan. For her own good.

"Actually, I'm going to lunch with my boyfriend."

She felt his hand slowly slip off her shoulder. "You have a boyfriend?"

"I told you about Colin, didn't I? When we were at the conference?"

"No," he answered. "You didn't mention him."

Sensing her chance, Maria rose from her seat and stepped away, continuing to collect documents, stuffing them into files, not caring where they ended up. She could sort them out later. "That's strange," she remarked. "I thought I did."

She could tell by his plastic smile that he was trying to decide whether or not to believe her. "Tell me about him," he said.

"He's an MMA fighter," she answered. "You know those guys

in the cage? I think it's crazy, but he's really into it. He works out and trains for hours every day and he loves to fight, so I kind of feel like I have to support him."

She could imagine the wheels in his mind continuing to turn as she hoisted her bag over her shoulder. "While I can't meet for lunch, do you want to talk in your office tomorrow? I'm sure I can clear part of my morning or afternoon." *When there are others around*, she didn't bother adding.

"I'm not sure that's necessary."

"Maybe I should talk to Barney?"

He shook his head, the movement almost imperceptible. "It's probably best to let it go for now."

Of course you'd say that. Because this whole thing was a ruse and you never talked to Barney at all. "All right. I guess I'll say good night, then."

She reached the door, breathing a sigh of relief as she made her escape. The whole boyfriend thing had been inspired, but that card had now been played. It wouldn't surprise him again; he'd be ready for it. In the long run—or maybe even in the short run—she doubted it would stop Ken's advances, even if it had been true.

Or became true?

Still reeling from her encounter, she wondered if she wanted it to be true. All she knew for certain was that when Colin had kissed her, she'd felt something electric, and the realization was both exhilarating and frightening—at exactly the same time.

Though she'd been lying when she told Ken that she was having dinner with her parents, she wasn't in the mood to be alone and found herself driving the familiar roads to the place she'd grown up.

The neighborhood was more blue collar than white, with homes showing signs of deferred maintenance and a few sporting

FOR SALE signs. Older-model cars and trucks were parked in virtually every driveway. Their neighbors had always been plumbers
and carpenters, clerical workers and secretaries. It was the kind
of community where kids played in the front yards and young
couples pushed strollers, where people would collect the mail
for each other when they were out of town. Though her parents
never talked about it, Maria had heard rumors growing up that
when her dad had first bought the house, more than a few neighbors living at this end of the block had been upset. The Sanchezes were the first nonwhite family on the street, and people
had quietly speculated about declining property values and rising
crime, as though everyone who'd been born in Mexico was somehow connected to the drug cartels.

She supposed it was one of the reasons that her dad had always
kept the yard immaculate and the bushes trimmed; he repainted
the exterior in the same color every fifth year, always parked his
cars in the garage instead of the driveway, and kept an American flag mounted on a pole on the front porch. He decorated the
house for both Halloween and Christmas and in their first years
would hand out restaurant coupons to any neighbor who happened to be outside, allowing them to eat at half price. Her mom
regularly made trays of food on the weekend afternoons when
she wasn't at the restaurant—burritos and enchiladas, tacos or
carnitas—which she would serve to any of the kids who were out
playing kickball or soccer. Little by little, they'd been accepted in
the neighborhood. Since then, most of the surrounding homes
had been sold more than once, and in every instance, her parents
showed up to welcome the new owners with a housewarming gift
in the hopes of preventing future whispers.

Maria sometimes had trouble imagining how hard it had been,
though in school, there'd been more than a couple of years when
she'd been the only Mexican in her classroom. Because she'd
been a good student, albeit a quiet one, she couldn't remember
feeling the sting of discrimination in the same way her parents

had experienced it, but even if she had, her parents would have told her to do what they had done. They would have told her to be herself, to be kind and welcoming to everyone, and they would have warned her that she should never sink to others' level. And then, she thought with a smile, they would have told her to study.

Unlike Serena, who was still reveling in finally being out from under her parents' thumbs, Maria enjoyed coming home. She loved the old place: the green and orange walls; the wildly playful ceramic tile in the kitchen; the eclectic furniture her mother had collected over the years; a refrigerator door that was endlessly decorated with photos and information relating to the family, anything that had made Carmen particularly proud. She loved the way her mother hummed whenever she was happy and especially when she was cooking. Growing up, Maria had taken these things for granted, but beginning in college, she could remember a feeling of comfort whenever she pushed through the front door, even after just a few weeks away.

Knowing her parents would be offended if she knocked, she went straight in, moving through the living room and into the kitchen. She set her bag on the counter.

"Mom? Dad? Where are you?" she called out.

As always when at home, she spoke Spanish, the shift from English as simple as breathing and just as unconscious.

"Out here!" she heard her mom answer.

Maria turned toward the back porch, where she saw her mom and dad rising from the table. Happy she was here and leaning in for hugs, they both spoke at once.

"We didn't know you were coming . . ."

"What a nice surprise . . ."

"You look wonderful . . ."

"You're so skinny . . ."

"Are you hungry?"

Maria greeted her mom, then her dad, then her mom again, then her dad a second time. In her parents' minds, *Maria would* always be their little girl. And though there'd been a period for a few teenage years when the idea had mortified her—especially when apparent in public—these days she had to admit that she kind of liked it.

"I'm okay. I can grab something later."

"I'll make you something," her mom said decisively, moving toward the refrigerator. Her dad watched her go with obvious appreciation. He had always been a hopeless romantic.

In his midfifties, he was neither thin nor fat. He had little gray in his hair, but Maria noticed a lingering, almost constant weariness, the effect of too much work for too many years. Tonight he seemed even less energetic than usual.

"Making you dinner makes her feel like she's still important to you," he said.

"Of course she's still important to me. Why would she think otherwise?"

"Because you don't need her the way you once did."

"I'm not a child."

"But she'll always be your mother," he said firmly. He motioned toward the table on the porch. "Do you want to sit outside and enjoy some wine? Your mom and I were having a glass."

"I can get it," she said. "Let me talk to Mom for a bit and I'll meet you out there."

While her dad returned to the porch, she retrieved a glass from the cupboard and poured herself some wine before sidling up to her mother. By then, Carmen had loaded up a casserole dish with pot roast, mashed potatoes, green beans, and a biscuit—enough calories for a couple of days, Maria estimated—and was sliding the dish into the oven. For whatever reason—maybe because it was something they never served at the restaurant—her dad loved pot roast and mashed potatoes.

"I'm so glad you came by," her mom said. "What's wrong?"

"Nothing's wrong," Maria said. She leaned against the counter and took a sip of wine. "I just wanted to surprise you."

"So you say. But something must have happened," she said. "You never visit us during the week."

"That's why it's a surprise."

Carmen evaluated her before crossing over to the counter and retrieving her own wineglass. "Is it your sister?"

"Is what my sister?"

"She didn't get turned down for the scholarship, did she?"

"You know about that?"

Carmen motioned to a letter tacked up on the refrigerator. "It's exciting, isn't it? She told us about it last night. The director will be coming to dinner this Saturday."

"Really?"

"We wanted to meet him," she said. "The letter says that she's one of the semifinalists. But back to your sister. What happened? If it's not about that, then it must have something to do with a boy. She's not in trouble, is she?"

Her mom was talking so fast that even Maria had trouble keeping up. "Serena's fine, as far as I know."

"Ah." Her mother nodded. "Good. It's something at your work, then. You're the one having problems."

"Work is . . . work. Why would you think there's a problem?"

"Because you came straight here afterwards."

"So?"

"That's what you've always done whenever something was bothering you. Don't you remember? Even in college, if you thought you got a bad grade, or when you were having trouble with your roommate your freshman year, or whenever you fought with Luis, you always came here. Mothers remember those kinds of things."

Huh, she thought. *I never realized that.* She changed the subject. "I think you worry too much."

"And I think I know my daughter."

Maria smiled. "How's Dad?"

"He's been quiet since he got home. He had to fire two people this week."

"What did they do?"

"Same old stuff. One of the dishwashers skipped a couple of shifts, and one of the waiters was letting his friends eat for free. You know how it goes. But it's still hard on your father. He wants to trust everyone, and he's always disappointed when people let him down. It wears on him. When he got home today, he took a nap instead of taking Copo out for a walk."

"Maybe he needs to see a doctor."

"That's what we were talking about when you came in."

"What does he say?"

"He says he'll go. But you know him. Unless I make the appointment, he'll never get around to it."

"Do you want me to call for you?"

"Would you mind?"

"Of course not," Maria answered. Because of her mom's language skills, she'd been making appointments ever since she was a young girl. "It's still Dr. Clark, right?"

Her mom nodded. "And schedule him for a full physical if you can."

"He's not going to like that."

"No, but he needs one. It's been almost three years."

"He shouldn't wait that long. He's got high blood pressure. And last year, he had those chest pains and he couldn't work for a week."

"I know, and you know, but he's stubborn and he insists his heart is fine. Maybe you can talk some sense into him." Her mom reached over and opened the oven; satisfied, she put on an oven mitt and pulled out the casserole dish before beginning to load up a plate for Maria.

"That's plenty," she said, trying to limit the quantity.

"You need to eat," her mom insisted, continuing to pile food on the plate while Maria retrieved some utensils. "Let's go sit with your father."

Outside at the table, a citronella candle was burning to keep the mosquitoes at bay. The night was as perfect as her dad had promised, with only the slightest breeze and a sky embroidered with stars. Copo sat in her father's lap, snoring slightly while his hand moved rhythmically through her fur. Maria began to cut a hunk of the pot roast into smaller pieces.

"I heard what happened today," Maria started, initiating a stream of conversation encompassing the restaurant, local news, and the latest family gossip. In an extended family like theirs, there was always some kind of drama worth talking about and dissecting. By the time Maria had finished dinner—no more than a quarter of the plate—the crickets had begun their evening melody.

"You look like you got some sun last weekend."

"I went paddleboarding after we had brunch."

"With your new friend?" her mom inquired. "The one from the pier?"

At Maria's startled expression, her mom shrugged. "I heard you and Serena talking. Your sister can be kind of loud sometimes."

Serena strikes again, Maria thought. She hadn't wanted to bring it up, but she couldn't deny it now, could she? Even her father appeared to have a sudden heightened interest in the conversation.

"His name's Colin." Then, knowing her parents would press for more but not wanting them to delve too deeply, she went on. "Serena knows him from her classes, and when she and I had dinner on Saturday, Colin was tending bar there. We got to talking at the pier and decided to meet up on Sunday."

"He's in college? How old is he?"

"He's my age. He didn't start college until a couple of years ago. He wants to become a teacher."

"Serena said he was very handsome," her mother commented with a mischievous smile.

Thanks, Serena. Next time, lower your voice. "He is."

"And you had a good time?"

"It was a lot of fun."

"When can we meet him?"

"Don't you think it's a little early for that?" Maria said.

"It depends. Are you going out again?"

"Uh, yes...on Saturday."

"Then we should meet him. You should invite him to brunch on Sunday."

Maria opened her mouth and then closed it again. There was no way her parents were ready for Colin, especially when there'd be no chance at escape. The thought that Colin would answer whatever questions they asked with his usual directness was enough to give her heart palpitations. She smiled at her dad with a trace of desperation.

"Why did he wait so long to go to college?" he asked.

She considered the best way to answer while still telling the truth. "He didn't figure out that he wanted to be a teacher until a couple of years ago."

Of her parents, her dad had always been better at reading between the lines, and she suspected he would continue to press for more details about Colin's past. But he was interrupted by the faint but audible ringing of a cell phone in the kitchen.

"Oh, that's me," she said, thanking God for the reprieve. "Let me get that."

Rising from the table, she raced into the kitchen. Pulling her phone from her bag, she saw Colin's name. She felt like a teenager as she pressed the button and raised the phone to her ear.

"Hey there," she said, "I was just talking about you." She paced the living room as they talked, catching up on how each had spent their day. As in person, he was an attentive listener, and when he sensed something in her voice, she found herself telling him about the incident with Ken. He grew quiet then, and when she asked whether he'd be interested in meeting her for lunch, he said he'd love to and asked what time he should pick her up at the office. She smiled, knowing that it would give her story more credence with Ken, and was secretly thrilled at the idea of seeing Colin so soon. When she hung up the phone, she had the sense that despite what her parents would no doubt think, Colin might be just what she needed in her life right now.

She returned to the porch, where her parents were still waiting at the table.

"Sorry," she said, reaching for her wineglass. "That was Colin."

"And he called just to say hello?"

Maria nodded. "We're going to lunch tomorrow."

As soon as the words were out of her mouth, she regretted them. Her mother could never comprehend why anyone would consider going anywhere else besides the family restaurant.

"Wonderful," her mom said. "I'll make something special for the two of you."

CHAPTER 9

———— ❀ ————

Colin

Really?" Evan called out, leaning over the porch rail as Colin crossed the yard. "You went running *again*?"

Colin was still breathing hard as he veered toward the porch, finally slowing to a walk. He pulled up his shirt to wipe his face before peering up at his friend. "I didn't run earlier today."

"You worked out this afternoon. And this morning."

"That was at the gym."

"So?"

"It's not the same," he answered, knowing that Evan really didn't care one way or the other. Instead, he nodded toward the front door. "Why aren't you inside with Lily?"

"Because my house smells."

"What does this have to do with me?"

"How about the fact that I can smell the stench from your clothes wafting up through the vents like a green, putrid fog? Instead of heading out to run, you should have done a load of laundry. Or better yet, you should start burning your workout clothes on a daily basis. Lily actually thought there was a dead mouse in the pantry. Or that the sewage had backed up."

Colin smiled. "I'll get right to it."

"Hurry up. And then meet me back over here. Lily wants to talk to you."

"Why?"

"I have no idea. She wouldn't tell me. But if I was to guess, I'd say it's about your girlfriend."

"I don't have a girlfriend."

"Whatever. The point is, she wants to talk to you."

"Why?

"Because she's Lily," Evan said, sounding exasperated. "She probably wants to ask whether you've handwritten a card to Maria with fancy calligraphy. Or she'll offer to help you select the perfect silk scarf for Maria's birthday. Or she wants to make sure you use the right spoon for your soup if you take her to the country club. You know how she is. But she brought home an extra bag, and she won't tell me what's in it."

"Why not?"

"Stop asking questions that I can't answer!" Evan sighed. "All I know for sure is that every time I tried to make my move, she told me that I had to wait. Because of you. And just so you know? I'm not happy about it. I was really looking forward to tonight. I needed tonight. I've had a crappy day."

"Okay."

Evan scowled at Colin's answer. "Why was it crappy, you ask?" he said, mimicking Colin. "Gee, thanks for asking, Colin. I appreciate your empathy. You plainly care about my well-being." He stared down at his friend. "It turns out that there was a terrible jobs report this morning, and the market tanked. And though I have no control over those things, I was nonetheless on the phone all afternoon with upset clients. And then, I get home and my house smells like a locker room, and now I have to wait for *her* to talk to *you* before my night can really begin."

"Let me change first. I'll be over in a couple of minutes."

"I surely hope not," Lily said to Colin, suddenly appearing next to Evan on the porch, wearing a yellow sundress. She slid her hand into her fiancé's and smiled up at him sweetly. "You wouldn't think of letting him come over without a chance to shower, would you, Evan? The poor man is practically soaked through. We can surely wait a few more minutes. Merely allowing him to change his clothes wouldn't be proper."

When Evan didn't answer, Colin cleared his throat. "She does have a point, Evan. It wouldn't be proper."

Evan glared. "Fine. Go shower. And start your laundry. And then come over."

"Oh, don't be so hard on him," Lily scolded. "It's not his fault that you invested your clients' money in the wrong companies."

She secretly winked at Colin.

"I didn't invest in the wrong companies! It wasn't my fault! Everything was down today."

"I'm just teasing you, sugar," she drawled. "I know you had an awful day and that it wasn't your fault. That mean old Mr. Market just took advantage of you, didn't he?"

"You're not helping," Evan said.

Lily turned her attention to Colin again.

"Have you spoken to your lady friend today?" she asked.

"I talked to her before I went running."

"Did you bring flowers to her office like I recommended?"

"No."

"Candy?"

"No."

"Whatever am I going to do with you?"

"I don't know."

She smiled before tugging Evan's hand. "We'll see you in a few minutes, okay?"

Colin watched them head back inside before entering his apartment. He stripped on his way to the bathroom and added his clothes to the laundry pile, noting that Evan was right. The pile reeked. He started a load of laundry and hopped in the shower. Afterward, he threw on a pair of jeans and a T-shirt before making his way back to Evan's.

Evan and Lily were sitting beside each other on the couch. Of the two, it was clear that Lily was the only one who was happy Colin was there.

"Colin! I'm so pleased you could join us," Lily said, rising from her spot, obviously ignoring the fact that they'd just talked. "May we offer you something to drink?"

"Water, please."

"Evan? Will you please get Colin some water?"

"Why?" Evan asked, leaning back, his arm over the top of the couch. "He knows where it is. He can get his own water."

Lily turned toward him. "It's your home. And you're the host."

"I didn't ask him to come over. You did."

"Evan?"

The way she said his name made it plain that Evan had no choice in the matter. That and the way she looked, of course. She was not only far and away the most beautiful woman Evan had ever dated, but she was well versed in the ways of using her appearance to her advantage.

"Fine," he grumbled, rising from the couch. "I'll get him a glass of water."

Evan slouched off toward the kitchen.

"With ice, please," Colin called out.

Evan scowled over his shoulder before Colin took a seat in the easy chair across from Lily.

"How are you this evening?" she asked.

"Okay."

"And Maria?"

Earlier on the phone, Maria had told him what had happened with her boss Ken Martenson and as he'd listened, Colin had found his jaw beginning to clench. Though he'd kept his voice steady, he'd imagined having a little talk with Ken, the kind that made it clear that it was in Ken's best interest to stop bothering her. He hadn't said that to Maria, but when he found himself grinding his teeth after hanging up, he'd thrown on his workout gear and gone running. It wasn't until he'd nearly finished his run that he'd begun to feel normal again.

That wasn't, however, what Lily had asked him.

"I spoke to her just a little while ago."

"And she's doing well?"

He thought about her job situation, but it wasn't his place to share that information. It was her life, her story, not his.

"I think she was glad to hear from me," he said truthfully.

"You hadn't called her?"

"I called her Sunday night. After I talked to you and Evan."

"And you didn't call her on either Monday or Tuesday?"

"I was working."

"You could have called on the way to or from work. Or on your break. Or on your way to class or the gym."

"Yes."

"But you didn't."

"No. But we're going to lunch tomorrow."

"Really? Someplace special, I hope."

"I haven't really thought about it."

Lily didn't bother to hide her disappointment. Evan reentered the room with a large glass of ice water. He thrust it out for Colin.

"Thanks, Evan," Colin said. "You didn't have to do that. I could have gotten it."

"Ha, ha," Evan answered as he sat back down. Then, to Lily: "Now, what did you want to talk to him about?"

"We were discussing his lunch date tomorrow. Colin has informed me that he and Maria will be dining together."

"My advice? Make sure your car starts," Evan said.

Lily glanced with disapproval in his direction. "My primary concern has to do with his date this weekend, and I wanted to discuss the matter with him."

"Why?" Evan asked.

"Because the first true evening one spends with the other is a critical time in any relationship," she answered, as though it were obvious. "Had Colin simply invited Maria to dinner or perhaps to walk the promenade downtown, I would have no worries at all. Or had he suggested that the four of us go out together, I'm sure that the conversation would be so engaging that Maria would have a wonderful time as well. Alas, Colin is going to be on his own and he's bringing Maria to a *club*, though I am certain *that* issue has already been addressed."

Evan raised his eyebrow. Colin said nothing.

Lily focused her attention on Colin again. "I asked you to visit with us this evening because I was curious if you have any experience or even familiarity with salsa dancing."

"No."

"Then, most likely, what you also don't know is that salsa is a partner dance."

"That's what dancing is," Evan cut in.

Lily ignored her fiancé. "Salsa dancing can be very enjoyable if the couple practices together," she explained. "But since that's not possible in this situation, you will have to do the best you can, and there are things you have to know. Like the way to move your feet, or lead your partner in a spin, or offer her the chance to separate and perform a few moves on her own, all the while making it feel as though it is a natural part of the dance all along. If you don't do those things, it will be almost impossible to impress her."

Evan laughed. "Who says he wants to impress her? Colin doesn't care what anyone thinks—"

"Go on," Colin said, cutting him off.

Evan turned toward him in surprise while Lily sat up straighter. "I'm pleased you understand the dilemma you're in. What I'm trying to tell you is that you need to learn the basics."

For a moment, neither Colin nor Evan said anything.

"And just how is he supposed to learn the basics?" Evan finally asked. "We live in Wilmington. I highly doubt there are any salsa dance instructors who will clear their schedules in the next couple of days so my friend here won't embarrass himself."

Lily leaned over, reaching for the small bag that had been placed next to the couch and pulling out an assortment of CDs.

"These are salsa albums, and you'll need to listen to them. I called my old dance teacher and she was more than happy to send a few samples. Nothing is very recent, but that's not important. Salsa is more about speed and rhythm—the beat, so to speak—than melody. And as for the instructor, I will be more than happy to help Colin learn what he needs to know."

"You know how to salsa dance?" Evan asked.

"Of course," she answered. "I danced for almost twelve years, and at various times, we focused on alternative dancing."

"Alternative?" Evan asked.

"I grew up in Charleston. Anything other than the shag or the waltz is considered alternative," she said, as though this were the kind of thing any civilized Southerner would know. "But really, Evan. You need to let Colin ask the questions. He's barely been able to say a single word." She turned to Colin. "Would you allow me to be your instructor for the next couple of days?"

"How much time are we talking about?"

"I'll show you a few things tonight—the basic steps and movements, turns, and how to lead your partner through a spin—so you know what you'll be working on. After that, we'll need three hours tomorrow evening, and another three hours on Friday evening. After I finish work and change, so beginning around six. And obviously, you should practice in your spare time before you get here."

"Will that be enough?"

"It's not nearly time enough to be good. Or even average. To be truly proficient at any form of dancing can take years. But if you focus and do exactly what I tell you, it just might be enough for your date on Saturday."

Colin took a sip of water, not answering right away.

"Don't tell me you're actually considering this," Evan said to him.

"Of course he's considering it. He knows I'm right."

Colin lowered the glass to his lap. "Okay," he said. "But I'll have to get someone to cover my shift on Friday night."

"Wonderful." Lily smiled.

"Wait," Evan said, turning to Lily. "I thought we were going out on Friday."

"I'm very sorry, but I'm going to have to cancel. A friend needs my help, and I honestly can't decline. He's been so sweet about asking."

"Seriously? Don't I get any say in this?"

"Of course you do," Lily said. "You'll be here both nights, too. As well as tonight, obviously."

"Here?"

"Where else?"

"I don't know. A dance studio, maybe?"

"Don't be silly. There's no need for that. But I will need you to move the furniture in the living room. You're right about us needing space to work. And you'll be responsible for the music, too—skipping back or forward when I tell you, starting the song over, things like that. We really need to maximize the use of our time. You'll be my little helper."

"Little helper?"

She smiled at him. "Did I mention that salsa dancing can really make a woman feel...*sensual*? And that the feeling can last for hours afterwards?"

Evan swallowed, staring at her. "I'd be glad to help."

"You folded like a cheap suit," Colin said. He and Evan were moving the couch to one side of the room while Lily went to the bedroom to fetch the proper pair of shoes, with just the right heel height, and change her clothes. Lily never did anything halfway.

"Whatever it takes to help a friend."

Colin smiled. "Okay."

"And after we're done, you're going to help me put the furniture back."

"Okay."

"And you're not going to ask to stay longer to practice, either. You're out of here by nine o'clock."

"Okay."

They set the couch down. "I don't know how she talks me into things like this."

Colin shrugged. "I think I have a pretty good idea."

Once the furniture was out of the way and the area rug rolled up, Lily pulled Colin into the center of the room. Evan sat glumly on the couch, books and a lamp and assorted knickknacks on the cushion beside him. Lily had changed into tight white jeans, a red silk blouse, and a pair of shoes that probably cost more than Colin earned in a week. Though she was Evan's fiancée and Colin's friend, Colin was aware that she fairly oozed sex appeal.

"Don't get too close, Colin," Evan called out.

"Hush, now," Lily told him, all business. "You may be wondering why I changed," she said to Colin.

"Not really," Colin answered.

"I changed so you can watch what my feet are doing. As I mentioned, I'm going to show you the most basic step, upon which much of salsa dancing is based. It's one you can always fall back on, no matter what Maria is doing. Does that make sense?"

"Yes."

"Before we begin, I'm making the assumption that Maria knows how to salsa dance."

"She told me she used to dance all the time."

"Perfect." Lily moved beside him, both of them facing the window, allowing Evan a profile view. "That means she'll be able to follow your lead. Are you ready?"

"Yes."

"Then watch my feet and do exactly what I'm doing," she said. "Step out with your left foot—that's a one count—then shift your weight onto the toe of your right foot—that's two—now bring the left foot back to its starting position—that's three— and pause for a beat—that's four." She demonstrated and Colin did the same. "Now, step back with your right foot—that's five— shift your weight to the toe of your left foot—six—then bring your right foot forward again to its starting position—seven— and pause again for a beat. That's eight. And you're done." Again, Colin followed her lead.

"That's it?"

She nodded. "Let's do it again, okay?"

They did. Then did it again. And again and again, repeating the movement over and over as Lily counted from one to eight, and then a dozen more times, and then gradually speeding up, and then continuing without counting. They took a break, then started slowly from the beginning, gradually speeding up again. Once he felt he was getting the hang of it, Lily stopped and watched as Colin continued. "That's perfect," she said, nodding. "You have the steps now, but the real key to this is not to be so bouncy. Right now, you're moving like a ruffian marching through the swamp. You want to be smoother, like a blossom slowly beginning to open. Keep your shoulders at the same height throughout the steps."

"How do I do that?"

"Use more hips," she said. "Like this." As she showed him what she meant—gliding through the movements, her hips sashaying back and forth, her shoulders level throughout—Lily was right about the dance being sensual. From the corner of his eye, Colin noted that Evan was sitting up straighter and staring at

Lily, though she didn't seem to notice. "So now, let's do the exact same thing again, this time with some music, and concentrate on being smoother." She turned toward Evan. "Sugar? Would you mind starting the song over?"

Evan shook his head, like a man trying to wake up from a dream. "What? Did you say something?"

They danced for a little more than two hours. In addition to the basic step, Colin learned how to turn, and at that point, they began to dance together. Lily showed him where to place his right hand (on her upper back, just below her arm, he reminded himself), and she showed him how to lead her through three different spins by making tiny signals with his left hand, which required him to take slightly different steps before falling back into the basic footfalls again.

Through it all, she reminded him to glide and use his hips, maintain eye contact, keep in rhythm with the beat, stop counting out loud, and smile. It required more concentration than he'd imagined. Afterward, they put the furniture back in place and Colin made to leave. Lily held Evan's hand as Colin stepped onto the porch.

"You did very well tonight," Lily said. "You have a natural rhythm when it comes to dancing."

"It's a bit like boxing," he observed.

"I surely hope not," she said, sounding almost offended.

He smiled. "Tomorrow night, right?"

"Six o'clock sharp," she said. She handed him a CD. "This is for you. Tomorrow, whenever you have extra time during the day, I insist that you practice your steps and turns and pretend to lead your partner through a spin. Concentrate on your hand signals, and try to be smooth. It would be most unproductive if we had to start over."

"Okay," he said. "And Lily?"

"Yes?"

"Thank you," he said.

"You're welcome, Colin." She smiled. "I'd be remiss, however, if I didn't take the opportunity to address another issue that has recently come to mind."

Colin waited expectantly.

"Concerning your luncheon date tomorrow with Maria, I'm sure I don't have to remind you that you'll be meeting her in a professional setting, which requires a more formal manner of dress. Nor, I hope, do I have to remind you that as much as you love your car, there is nothing less inviting than a cluttered interior, or a car that won't start. Am I correct in my assumptions?"

I've tried to fix my car for reasons other than Maria, but now that you mention it . . . "Yes," he answered.

"I'm pleased," she said, nodding. "A woman, after all, has certain expectations when it comes to courting. Now, as far as the flowers go . . . have you decided what to bring? Knowing that different bouquets might carry with them various assumptions?"

Lily sounded so serious that it was hard for Colin not to smile. "What do you recommend?"

She raised a manicured hand to her chin. "Well, considering that the two of you are still getting to know each other, and that it's only a lunch date, a bouquet of roses is far too formal, and lilies—while lovely—are much more suited to the spring. Carnations, obviously, convey nothing at all other than being an inexpensive choice, so that simply won't do."

Colin nodded. "Makes sense to me."

"Perhaps a simple autumn bouquet, then? With a mixture of yellow spray roses, bronze daisies, and maybe just a stem of red hypericum?" She nodded thoughtfully. "Yes, that strikes me as perfect for this occasion. You'll need to ask to have the flowers arranged in a vase, obviously, so she can place it in her office, but it's clearly the right choice for this occasion, don't you think?"

"Without a doubt."

"And make sure to order them from Michael's Florist. He's really quite an artist when it comes to arrangements. Call him first thing in the morning and mention my name. He'll know what to do."

Evan smirked, clearly enjoying this and probably suspecting that Colin would be no different than he was when it came to Lily and her requests. And because Evan knew him better than anyone, Colin finally nodded.

"Okay."

In the morning, Colin rose early and was pleased to find that the old Camaro started on the first turn of the key. He put in a hard workout at the gym—plyometrics and barbell work, jumping rope, and long intervals on both the heavy and speed bags. On the way back to his apartment he stopped by a Dumpster and cleared the clutter from his car. At home, with his muscles still warm and loose, he popped in one of Lily's CDs and spent half an hour practicing his salsa steps, amazed that he hadn't forgotten anything. He was surprised again at how much concentration it required.

He downed a protein smoothie and showered, then dressed in dark slacks, loafers, and a button-down shirt, leftovers from his courtroom days. He'd put on serious muscle since then and the shirt was too tight in the chest and arms, but it was the best he could do. Standing in front of the mirror, he thought to himself that, aside from the top being a bit snug, Evan might as well have dressed him. The outfit was ridiculous, especially since he'd be on a campus where shorts and flip-flops were the norm. Though he knew that Lily wouldn't have approved, he rolled the cuffs, exposing a bit of his forearms. Better. More comfortable, too.

His classmates either didn't notice or didn't care about his dress, and he listened and took notes as always. No Serena afterward, as they only had classes together on Mondays and Wednesdays. With a few extra minutes, he called the florist and ordered an autumn bouquet, whatever the hell that was. From there he trudged off to a classroom-management class, aware that he hadn't stopped moving since the alarm had gone off, his regular routine in tatters.

His final class of the day ended at a quarter to noon. By then, the sun was high, and with Indian summer hanging on, he walked slowly to his car, trying not to sweat. He stopped at the florist on the way to the address Maria had given him, and as if fate was toying with him, it took two turns of the key and a bit of pedal pumping to get the engine going. All he could do was keep his fingers crossed.

Martenson, Hertzberg & Holdman occupied its own building, a relatively modern structure a couple of blocks from the Cape Fear River and smack-dab in the middle of the historic district, with parking on both sides of the building. On either side and across the street, the buildings ran together, one shade of brick giving way to another, storefronts dotted with awnings. He pulled into a spot only a few slots away from Maria's car, and next to a shiny red Corvette.

He grabbed the vase of flowers—remembering Lily and her phrase *certain expectations*—and then thought about Ken and the problems he was causing. He wondered if the guy would be around; he wanted to put a face to a name. As he locked his car, he suddenly saw the entire morning as a countdown to the time when he could finally see Maria again.

Surprising no one more than himself, he realized that he'd missed her.

CHAPTER 10

———— ❧ ————

Maria

With Barney holed up in his office, readying himself for trial, Maria was on double duty. She spent the morning touching base with clients, doing her best to ensure that each one felt their case was still a priority. Every half hour or so, their paralegal, Lynn, would enter with even more documents or forms to be filed, and though it was all Maria could do to keep up, staying busy had the benefit of keeping her from fretting about her lunch date. Or, more accurately, how her parents were going to react when they met Colin. For starters—and unlike Luis—Colin was a gringo, and while it wasn't that big of a deal for people in her generation, her parents were probably going to be surprised. Allowing them to meet Colin meant the relationship was getting serious, and they'd probably always assumed Maria would only seriously date someone who was Mexican. Everyone in her family—even relatives by marriage—was Mexican, and there were cultural differences. Her family celebrated every family get-together with a piñata for the kids, listened to mariachi music, watched telenovelas obsessively, and spoke only Spanish among themselves. Some of her aunts and uncles spoke no English at all. She knew it wouldn't necessarily be a problem for her parents, but they'd probably wonder why Maria hadn't mentioned Colin's background. The rest of her family's opinions about it would probably fall along generational lines, with the younger relatives more likely to shrug off the idea as inconsequential. Still, she had no doubt that it was going to be a topic of conversation among the family at the restaurant, one that would probably continue long after Maria and Colin said good-bye.

Those things she could deal with. What she wasn't sure she could handle was any discussion concerning Colin's past, which she knew was unavoidable. Ordinary conversation ensured it, and what was going to happen if either her mom or her dad started asking him questions today? She supposed she could head off the answers by stating that they were simply friends and steering the conversation in another direction, but how long could she keep that up? Unless their relationship petered out after Saturday— and Maria admitted that she hoped it wouldn't—Colin's past *was* going to come up. And what had Serena said about that? *I don't even want to be in the same state when you drop that little bombshell.* To her parents, it wouldn't matter that she was a grown woman; they'd make their displeasure known, assuring themselves that they were doing the right thing, since it was obvious that Maria had no idea what she was getting herself into.

And the crazy thing was, her parents were probably right.

"You have a visitor," Jill said.

Maria was hanging up with Gwen, the receptionist, who'd just shared the same information when Jill appeared in her doorway, a handbag already over her shoulder.

"I just heard," she answered, noting that it was a quarter past twelve. "I don't know where the morning went. It feels like I just got here."

Jill smiled. "I take it that you and Colin are going out?"

"Yeah, about that," Maria said. "I'm sorry I didn't have a chance to tell you earlier that I had plans, but I've been slammed all morning. I barely had a second to breathe."

"No worries," Jill said, waving it off. "I remember the whole work-till-you-drop drill when Barney's getting ready for trial. Actually, I was coming by to tell you that I was planning to surprise Paul at his office and make him take me out."

"Are you sure you don't mind?"

"Not about lunch. But I do wish you had warned me that Colin was coming by. I would have had Paul come by here, too, so he could see for himself what eating right and working out will do for a man."

"Paul's fine."

"Easy for you to say. Look at who's waiting for you in the lobby. Paul, on the other hand, is getting a little soft and he doesn't even care. And I know he doesn't care, because I've been dropping little self-improvement hints. As in, 'Put the cookie down and hop on the treadmill, for God's sake.'"

"You don't really say that."

"No, but I *think* it. It's the same thing."

Maria laughed as she gathered her things and stood. "Do you want to walk with me?"

"That's why I'm still waiting. I also want to see your face when you find out."

"Find out what?"

"You'll know soon enough."

"What are you talking about?"

"Come on," Jill said. "And make sure you introduce us. I want to tell Paul all about it, especially if your beau flirts with me."

"Colin's not really the flirting type."

"Who cares? The truth is, I just want to get a closer peek at him. To make sure he's good enough for you, of course."

"That's very kind of you."

"What are friends for?"

As they started down the hallway, Maria took a deep breath, feeling her worries reassert themselves. Thankfully, Jill didn't notice, her mind clearly elsewhere.

"Hold up a second," she said. Maria watched as Jill reached into her handbag. Pulling out her lipstick, she applied some before dropping it back into her bag.

"Okay," Jill said, "now we can go."

Maria stared at her. "Really?"

Jill winked. "What can I say? First impressions matter."

Up ahead, Maria watched as two paralegals suddenly rounded the corner from the lobby, whispering excitedly to each other like a couple of high schoolers. Jill nodded toward them.

"Now do you understand what I mean? You were definitely holding out on me. That is one gorgeous man."

"He's not *that* good-looking."

"Uh…yeah. He is. Now come on. You've got a date and you shouldn't be late."

As soon as Maria spotted Colin in the lobby, her stomach did a little flip-flop. He was facing the opposite direction—*waiting for her*, she realized—and from the back he could have passed for a young lawyer, albeit an exceptionally fit one with visible tattoos. When Maria glanced toward the receptionist, she noted that Gwen was trying hard not to stare at Colin while she worked the phone.

Colin must have sensed their presence, and when he turned, Maria caught sight of a lovely assortment of flowers; oranges and yellows, with a burst of red in the center. Her mouth dropped open slightly.

"Surprise," Jill whispered, but Maria was too shocked to hear it.

"Oh," she finally said. "Hi." Beginning to approach, she was only vaguely aware that Jill had remained behind. Up close, his clean scent mingled with that of the flowers. "New clothes?"

"Freedom clothes," he answered. "They probably kept me out of prison."

She smiled, amused. And in the next instant, she thought, *And I can't believe his answer doesn't worry me.* But she didn't want to think about that. Instead, she nodded at the flowers. "For me?"

"Yes," he said, handing them over. "It's an autumn bouquet."

"They're beautiful. Thank you."

"You're welcome."

"Let me put them in my office. I'll be right back and then we can go."

"Okay."

Behind her, she heard Jill clear her throat and she turned. "Oh, this is my friend Jill. She's an attorney here, too."

Jill approached and he offered his hand. "Hi, Jill."

"Hi, Colin." She took his hand, her demeanor friendly yet professional. "It's a pleasure to meet you."

Leaving them to chat, Maria hurried back to her office, noticing the two paralegals who eyed her with a touch of envy as she passed them. She tried to remember the last time someone had bought her flowers. Aside from a single rose that Luis had given her on Valentine's Day after they'd been dating for a year, she couldn't remember a single instance.

Setting the vase in a prominent place in her office, she returned to the lobby just in time to catch the tail end of Jill and Colin's conversation.

Jill turned. "I hear you're a much better photographer than you let on. Colin says you took an amazing shot of some porpoises?"

"He's being overly kind," Maria said. "I get lucky every now and then."

"I'd still like to see it."

"I'll e-mail it," she said. Then, to Colin: "Are you ready?"

Colin nodded, and after saying good-bye to Jill, they headed down to the parking lot.

"Your friend is nice," Colin remarked.

"She's great," Maria agreed. "If it wasn't for her, I would have eaten alone at my desk since I've been here."

"Until today," Colin said with a smile. "How are things at work?"

"I'm buried," she admitted. "But I'm hoping things will slow down. My boss is going to be out of the office this afternoon and tomorrow"

"If that's the case, I wouldn't recommend throwing a massive party and trashing the office in his absence. I've learned that it tends to irritate people."

"I'll keep that in mind," she said as he opened the car door for her.

She slid into the Camaro. Once Colin was behind the wheel, he leaned toward her, keys in hand. "I was thinking we could head over to one of the restaurants downtown? We'd probably be able to get a table outside with a great view."

Oh yeah, she thought. *About that.* Maria fiddled with the seat-belt, wondering how best to explain it.

"It sounds wonderful," she ventured, "and ordinarily, I'd love to go. But the thing is, I was over at my parents' house last night when you called, and I happened to mention that we were going to lunch, and..." She exhaled, deciding to simply come out with it. "They're expecting us to have lunch at the restaurant."

Colin tapped his car key on the seat. "You want me to meet your parents?"

Not really. Not yet, anyway. But... She wrinkled her nose, unsure how he would react, hoping he wouldn't be angry. "Kind of."

He slipped the keys into the ignition. "Okay," he said.

"Really? It doesn't bother you? Even though we just met?"

"No."

"Just so you know, it would bother a lot of guys."

"Okay."

"Well...good," she said.

He said nothing right away. Finally: "You're nervous."

"They don't know you like I do." She inhaled slowly, thinking, *Now for the hard part.* "When you meet them, you have to understand that they're old-fashioned. My dad has always been protective and my mom worries, and I'm afraid that if they start asking questions..."

When she trailed off, Colin finished for her.

"You're worried what I'll say to them. And how they'll react."

Though she didn't answer, she suspected that he already knew what she was thinking.

"I won't lie to them," he said.

"I know," she said. *That's the problem.* "And I won't ask you to lie. I don't want you to lie, but it still makes me nervous."

"Because of my past," he said.

"I wish I wouldn't have had to say anything to you, and I'm sorry. Logically, I know that I'm an adult and I should be able to date whomever I want and it shouldn't matter what they think. But it does. Because I still want their approval. And believe me, I know how awful that sounds."

"It doesn't sound awful. It sounds normal."

"You don't need approval."

"Evan would probably say that I'm not normal."

Despite the tension, she laughed before getting quiet again. "Are you mad at me?"

"No," he answered.

"But you're probably offended."

"No," he said again.

"What are you feeling, then?"

He didn't answer right away. "I feel...flattered," he finally offered.

She blinked. "Flattered? How on earth could you feel flattered?"

"It's complicated."

"I'd still like to hear it."

He shrugged. "Because you told me how you were feeling, even though you suspected it might hurt my feelings. And you told the truth. And you did both those things from a place of vulnerability and concern, because you want them to like me. Because you care about me. That's flattering."

She smiled, half from surprise and half because he was right. "I think I'm going to give up trying to predict anything about you ever again."

"Okay," he said. He twisted the key and the engine rumbled to life. Before he slipped it into gear, he turned toward her. "So what do you want to do?"

"Go to lunch? Hope for the best?"

"Sounds like a plan."

La Cocina de la Familia was located a few blocks off Market Street in an aging strip mall, but the parking spaces in front of the restaurant were full. As they approached the front door, Colin struck her as being as calm as ever, which only put Maria more on edge. He reached for her hand. She clasped his in return, like someone clutching a life preserver on a listing ship.

"I forgot to ask whether you even like Mexican food."

"I remember that I used to like it a lot."

"But you don't eat it anymore? Because it's not healthy, right?"

"I can always find something to order."

She squeezed his hand, liking the way it felt in hers. "My mom said she's going to make us something special. Which means you might not get the chance. That said, I did tell her that you liked healthy food."

"It'll be fine," he said.

"Do you ever worry about anything?"

"I try not to."

"Well, when we're done, you're going to start giving me lessons, all right? Because lately, that feels like the only thing I'm doing."

He pulled open the door and she led the way inside. Her uncle Tito immediately approached, obviously excited she was here, rambling in Spanish. After greeting her with a kiss, he shook Colin's hand and reached for the menus before leading them to a booth in the corner. It was the only open table in the place, which meant that her parents must have been saving it.

Once they were seated, her cousin Anna brought glasses of water and a basket of chips and salsa to the table. Maria chatted with her briefly and introduced Colin a second time. When Anna left, Maria leaned across the table.

"I'm sorry," she said. "I don't come in as much as I should. They're probably as excited as my parents."

"How many of your relatives work here?"

"Right now?" She made a quick scan of the place, spotting another uncle at the bar and a couple of aunts waiting on tables. "I'd guess there's probably six or so. But I'd have to ask my parents to be sure."

He surveyed the restaurant. "It's busy in here."

"It always is. Over the years, we've had to expand the restaurant three times. When it first started, there were only eight tables." As she answered, she saw her parents emerge from the kitchen and she sat up straighter. "Okay, they're coming. My parents, I mean."

When her parents reached the table, she kissed her mother, then her father, all the while hoping they wouldn't make a spectacle. "This is my friend Colin," she said. "These are my parents, Felix and Carmen."

"Hi," Felix and Carmen said, almost in unison, both of them plainly giving him the once-over.

"It's a pleasure to meet you both," he said.

"Maria says you're a student?" Felix said, jumping right in. "And that you work as a bartender?"

"Yes," Colin responded. "Serena's actually in a couple of my classes. I work at Crabby Pete's, down by the beach." Then, no doubt thinking of Maria's worries and not wanting to get drawn into a long conversation about his past, he motioned around the restaurant. "This is an incredible business you've built. How long has it been around?"

"Thirty-one years," Felix answered, a trace of pride in his voice.

"Maria said you've had to expand over the years. That's impressive."

"We've been blessed," Felix agreed. "Have you eaten here before?"

"No," Colin admitted. "But Maria says your wife is an amazing chef."

Felix stood a little straighter. "She is the best," he said, glancing over at Carmen. "Of course, because of that, she sometimes believes that she is the boss."

"I am the boss," Carmen said in somewhat broken English.

Colin smiled, and after more small talk, Maria watched as her dad reached for her mom's arm.

"Let's go. We should let them visit," Felix said.

After saying good-bye, Maria watched her parents start back toward the kitchen.

"You know they're in there talking about you right now with Tito and Anna and all the rest of them. Aside from Luis, you're the only guy I've ever brought here."

"I'm honored," he said, and she had a feeling he actually meant it.

"It wasn't as bad as I thought it would be," she added.

"They're gracious people."

"Yes, but I'm still their daughter. And they didn't ask any hard questions."

"Maybe they won't."

"Oh, they will eventually. Unless, of course, we never see each other again."

"Is that what you want?"

Maria dropped her eyes for a moment. "No," she said. "I'm glad we're here. And I'm happy we'll be spending some time together this weekend."

"Which means?"

"That the next time we're all together—assuming there will be a next time—I'm going to be even more nervous."

Minutes later, Carmen and two of Maria's cousins began ferrying food to the table: plates of tacos, burritos, mole poblano, and enchiladas; tamales, carne asada, chile relleno, tilapia Veracruz, and a bowl of salad. As her mom began placing the dishes on the table, Maria waved her hands.

"Mom—this is way too much," Maria protested. Even Colin appeared to be surprised as all the plates began to arrive.

"Eat what you want," Carmen answered in Spanish. "We'll bring the rest of it to the back and set it out. People will finish it."

"But..."

Carmen glanced at Colin, then back to Maria. "Your sister was right. He's very handsome."

"Mom!"

"What? He doesn't understand me."

"That's not the point!"

"It's just good to see you happy. Your dad and I have been worried. All you ever do is work." She smiled before her gaze returned to Colin. "Colin? Is that an Irish name?"

"I have no idea."

"Is he Catholic?"

"I haven't asked him."

"What do you talk about?"

You have no idea, Maria thought. *And you don't want to know.* "It's not polite to talk in front of him like this, you know."

"Of course," her mom said, squeezing the last plate between their water glasses. "You're absolutely right." Switching to English, she smiled at Colin. "Please... enjoy," she offered.

"Thank you. We will."

A moment later, they were alone, mountains of food spread before them.

"It smells delicious," Colin said.

"Are you kidding? This is ridiculous! Who on earth could eat this much food?"

"You sound upset."

"Of course I'm upset. We should have been able to order off the menu, but instead, my mom had to do her thing."

"What's her thing?"

"I'm still trying to figure it out. To impress you? To make sure you feel welcome?"

"Those are good things."

"I know, but she tends to overdo it."

She watched as Colin's gaze moved from one plate to the next, and she pointed at the tilapia. "I think my mom made this one special for you. It's just baked fish, with tomatoes, olives, and raisins. Go ahead and serve up."

He took a couple of filets and added some salad to his plate; she also took one of the filets and salad, but added half an enchilada. The rest remained untouched. When Colin tasted the fish, he tapped his fork against his plate.

"This is unbelievable," he said. "No wonder she's the boss."

"She is good."

"Can you cook like this?"

She shook her head. "I wish. I'm not nearly as good as my mom, but I started in the kitchen and I learned the basics on how to make everything. I enjoyed it, too, but after a while, my parents thought it would be better if I learned to wait tables. They thought that being forced to talk to strangers would help me overcome my shyness."

"Again with the shy?"

"Obviously, in your estimation, it worked. And if you're curious, I'm an excellent waitress."

He laughed, and for the next hour they bounced from one subject to another—their favorite movies and the places they one day wanted to visit; he told her a bit more about his family and she did the same. Whenever she spoke, he listened with quiet concentration, his eyes never leaving hers. The conversation was easy and unforced, but through it all, she couldn't help feeling that he actually cared about everything she was saying. Despite her family's presence and the conversations drifting from other tables, their lunch together felt strangely intimate. By the time her parents dropped by their table a second time—and despite her mother's disappointment at how little either of them had eaten—Maria felt strangely relaxed and content.

After a series of warm good-byes, they drove back to the office, the old Camaro playing along perfectly. There, Colin walked her to the entryway, and when he slipped his hand into hers a second time, all she could think was how utterly natural it felt. At the entrance, she felt him tug gently, willing her to stop.

"What time on Saturday?" she asked, turning to him.

"I have a training session at four that ends at six, so how about I pick you up at your place around seven thirty? We'll have dinner first, and then head out?"

"Sounds great," she said. "What kind of training session?"

"Striking and ground work," he said. "Ground work is like wrestling."

"Can anyone watch?"

"I guess so," he said. "I'm sure the gym owner wouldn't mind, but I'd have to ask."

"Would you?"

"Why? Do you want to come?"

"Since we're going dancing, I might as well watch you doing something you enjoy, too."

He didn't hide his surprise. "Okay," he said. "But I'll have to head home to clean up before we go out, so is it okay if you meet me at the gym?" When she nodded, he gave her the name of the gym, and she jotted her home address on the back of her business card.

He slipped her card into his pocket and before she even realized what was happening, he was leaning in, his lips meeting hers. The kiss was gentle, and though it wasn't as electrifying as their kiss of the previous Sunday, there was something warm and reassuring about it. Suddenly it didn't matter what her parents might think. Here and now, Colin was the only thing that mattered, and when he pulled back, she found herself wishing that it had lasted a little longer. In that instant, however, she saw movement in her peripheral vision, and when she focused on it, she registered that Ken had rounded the corner—no doubt after parking on the other side of the building—and was standing motionless, watching them from a distance. She felt herself stiffen and Colin followed her gaze.

"Is that him?" he asked, his voice low. "Ken?"

"Yes," she said, and she watched as his expression suddenly went hard. He didn't separate from her, but his attention zeroed in on Ken. Though he didn't squeeze her hand, she could feel the tension in it, a coiled, deep-seated violence held in check by a thread. She wasn't afraid, but she had the sudden certainty that up close, Ken definitely would be.

Ken continued to watch them. It was a standoff of sorts, and still Colin continued to stare, turning to face her again only after Ken turned away. He kissed her again, this time with a trace of possessiveness, before pulling back.

"Don't let him bother you. He's not worth it," she said.

"He's bothering you."

"I'll be fine."

"I still don't like him."

"Is that why you kissed me again?"

"No."

"Then why did you do it?"

"I like you," he answered.

His comment—so direct, so obviously *truthful*—made her stomach do that ridiculous flip-flop again, and it was all she could do not to grin like a fool.

"What are you doing tonight and Friday?"

"I have plans with Evan and Lily."

"Both nights?"

"Yes."

"What are you doing?"

"I don't want to tell you."

"Why?"

"I don't want to tell you that, either."

She squeezed his hand before letting go. "I know you're telling the truth, but you're not really saying anything. Should I be worried? Are you going out with someone else?"

"No," he said, shaking his head. "There's nothing to worry about. I had a great time at lunch today. I enjoyed meeting your parents."

She peered up at him. "I'm glad."

He smiled then before finally taking a step backward. "It's probably time for you to go back to work."

"I know."

"Is he still watching us?"

She peeked past him and shook her head. "I think he went around to the back entrance."

"Will he be bothered by what he saw?"

She thought about it. "Probably. But now he knows you actually exist, and that's a good thing. If he bothers me again, I'll just hint that you're the jealous type."

"I'm not," he said. His blue-gray eyes were intense, yet gentle. "But I still don't like him."

CHAPTER II

—— ❧ ——

Colin

On Saturday morning, Colin rose early and went for a bike ride just as the sun was coming up. His bike—a rusting beater that he'd picked up at a pawn shop for almost nothing—was at least a decade old, but it did the job, and he was able to work up a serious sweat before he even reached the gym. There, he spent an hour in a cross-training class slamming heavy ropes, pushing weighted sleds, throwing medicine balls, and doing a variety of other exercises, then staggered back to his bike for the ride home. He mowed the lawn and trimmed the bushes, reflecting that though he'd been preoccupied by thoughts of Maria since they'd first met, those thoughts didn't compare to the almost obsessive way he dwelled on her now. Even Evan had noticed; earlier, when he'd stepped out onto the porch, he'd been wearing a smirk that let Colin know he was fully aware of the effect that Maria was having on him. Evan himself had been ebullient on both Thursday and Friday nights, and Colin suspected that it might have had something to do with the whole *salsa dancing is sensual* thing, but it wasn't his place to ask.

Lily, too, had noticed that Colin had developed feelings for Maria, but remained focused on his dancing lessons. However, she'd recommended a restaurant downtown, reminding him twice to make reservations. She'd taught him more about dancing than he thought possible, but he still wasn't entirely confident in his abilities. He didn't want to imagine how unprepared he would have been had she not intervened.

After completing his chores, Colin sipped on his second protein drink of the day while he straightened up the apartment, then began working on a paper for his classroom-management class. It was only five pages, but he was too distracted to do much more than put together an outline before he finally called it quits.

Changing back into his workout clothes, he grabbed his gym bag and headed out the door. Though it had been performing like a champ recently, today the engine coughed and coughed, finally sputtering reluctantly to life, meaning that the problem was neither the ignition switch nor the alternator. He should have been preoccupied with finding a solution, but instead he found himself conjuring up Maria's image, strangely anxious that their date go smoothly. He'd called her after work on Thursday and Friday and they'd talked for more than an hour each night, which was a new experience for him. He couldn't remember talking to anyone on the phone that long—ever. Until Maria, he couldn't imagine how anyone sustained such a lengthy conversation. But Maria made it easy, and more than once, he found himself smiling at whatever it was she was saying. She mentioned that Ken had been keeping his distance, and when she recounted the blind date she'd been on the night he'd changed her tire, he'd laughed aloud. After he hung up the phone, he'd found it difficult to fall asleep. Ordinarily, he collapsed in bed at the end of the day, unable to keep his eyes open.

For the first time in a long while, he considered calling his parents. He wasn't sure why the urge struck him, but he assumed it had something to do with the way Maria talked about her parents and how well they got along. He wondered how different his life might have been had he been brought up in a family like hers. It might not have been any different, of course—he'd been a handful even before he could walk—but if family dynamics played even a small role, then his life had taken a direction that wasn't entirely of his making. And though he was satisfied with his current path, the road had until recently been littered with potholes and boulders. That Maria was able to look past those things, considering her own respectable history, was still something of a surprise, though a surprise of the very best kind.

Pulling up at the gym, he spotted Maria standing out front. She was dressed in shorts and a T-shirt, and he thought again that she was one of the most beautiful women he'd ever met.

"Hey there," she said as he approached. "You ready to beat some people up?"

"It's only practice."

"You're sure I can go inside to watch?"

He reached for the door, nodding. "I talked to the owner this morning and he was fine with it. And unless you decide to go in the cage, he promised he wouldn't even make you sign a waiver."

"You're quite the negotiator."

"I try," he said. He held the door open, eyeing her figure as she slid past him. He watched as she surveyed her surroundings. Unlike many commercial gyms, this place had more of a warehouse feel. They walked past assorted racks of weights and other cross-training equipment, toward the training room at the far end of the building. Passing through another door, he led the way into a roomy space with padded walls and large mats, equipment piled in every corner; over to the left was the cage. A few of Colin's training partners were stretching or otherwise warming up, and he nodded toward them as he set down his bag. Maria wrinkled her nose.

"It smells back here."

"It's only going to get worse," he promised.

"Where should I sit?"

Colin gestured at a bunch of equipment in the corner: crates of boxing gloves, assorted pads, various elastics, jump ropes, and plyometric boxes.

"You can sit over there on the boxes if you'd like," he said. "We don't normally use that part of the room."

"Where will you be?"

"All over, most likely," he said.

"How many guys will be here?"

"Eight or nine, maybe? Saturdays are always a little slow. During the week, there are fifteen or sixteen of us."

"In other words, only the supremely dedicated are here?"

"It's more like the workout nuts, or guys who are just starting out and trying to hit every workout they can. On Saturdays, a lot of the serious ones are out of town at events."

"That's good. Since we're going out, I mean. I'd hate for you to end up all cut and bruised like you were the first night I saw you."

"Are you ever going to let that go?"

"I don't think I can," she said, standing on tiptoe to kiss him on the cheek. "The image is burned into my brain forever."

Colin did a quick warm-up; arm rolls and leg swings, a few minutes of jumping rope. By then, Todd Daly, the main instructor and a retired UFC fighter, and Jared Moore, who was fighting professionally but not quite at UFC level, had arrived, and Daly led the entire group through more warm-ups.

While awaiting his turn in the cage, Colin worked on his ground skills: arm bars and leg locks, various submission holds. Most of the skills had their roots in the martial arts and wrestling, with speed, instinct, and balance being far more important than brute strength. As was usual during Saturday classes, Daly demonstrated the moves first—occasionally using Colin as a partner—before the group split in two. Each group was given a chance to practice the move, repeating it ten or twelve times before switching positions with their partners. They would then move on to a different set of skills. Within ten minutes, Colin was breathing hard; by the half-hour mark, his shirt was drenched. Through it all, Daly critiqued them—telling them where to place a foot for additional leverage, or how to wrap more effectively with the legs, the subtle variations endless.

One by one, people rotated through the cage, and after an hour, it was Colin's turn. He put on headgear and heavier gloves and worked with a partner while Moore—a former Golden Gloves champ from Orlando—shouted coaching tips. Colin went through seven two-minute rounds, bouncing and circling, taking advantage of openings to strike or kick while trying to avoid leaving any open shots. He dominated, but less because of his own skill than his opponent's lack therof: The guy he faced was out of shape and relatively new, with only a single fight behind him, which he'd lost.

From there, it was back to the mats again, where they worked on takedowns while their partner's back was against the wall; then, switching positions, they tried to prevent takedowns. By the end of class, Colin's muscles were twitching with exhaustion.

Throughout the afternoon, he found his eyes drifting toward Maria. He'd expected her to be bored, but her gaze followed him the entire time, making the session harder than usual. Ordinarily, focusing exclusively on his opponent was easy, but her presence made him self-conscious in a way he'd never experienced. In a match, this lack of focus would land him in trouble. By the end of class he felt like he'd taken two steps back mentally, and he knew he'd have to work hard to regain ground. It was, after all, a sport that was equal parts mental and physical, even if most people didn't realize it.

Afterward, he went straight to his bag and tossed in his gear before looping it over his shoulder. By then, Maria had walked up.

"What did you think?" he asked, adjusting the strap.

"It looked hard. And tiring. And sweaty."

"That's about it, when you get right down to it."

"How do you think it went?"

"Okay," he said. "I got distracted."

"By me?"

"Yes."

"I'm sorry."

"Don't be." He smiled before tugging at his shirt. "Could you give me a few minutes to rinse off and change? I need to get out of these things or my car seat will be soaked by the time I get home."

Maria wrinkled her nose. "That's...kind of gross to think about."

"Is that a yes or a no?"

"By all means," she said. "I'll wait out front for you."

When Colin finally exited the locker room, he spotted Maria just outside the doors, talking on the phone. In her sunglasses, she resembled a glamorous fifties-era movie star. She hung up just as he approached.

"That was Serena."

"Is she all right?"

"She's having dinner at the house tonight with the director of some scholarship thing, so she's a bit nervous, but other than that, she's okay." She shrugged. "Do you feel better?"

"I feel cleaner. Temporarily, anyway. I'm still sweating."

She touched his arm. "I'm glad I came. It was a lot more interesting than I thought it would be."

"Are we still on for seven thirty?"

"I hope so," she said. "And just to warn you, when we go dancing, I might be a little rusty."

"I wouldn't worry. It'll be my first time ever. And Maria?"

"Yes?"

"Thanks for coming today. It meant a lot to me."

As soon as Colin got out of his car, Evan stepped onto the porch holding a plastic shopping bag.

"Here," he said, holding the bag out. "This is for you. And you owe me some money."

Colin stopped in front of the porch. "For what?"

"Lily thought you might need something to wear tonight."

"I have clothes."

"Don't blame me. I said exactly the same thing to her. But she's Lily, and she dragged me through the stores anyway, and like I said, you owe me some money. The receipt is in the bag."

"What did she buy?"

"It's actually not as bad as it could have been. I had visions of her selecting something with tassels or bells or whatever, but she didn't. It's black slacks, a red button-down shirt, and black shoes."

"How did she know my size?"

"Because she bought you clothes last Christmas."

"And she remembered?"

"She's Lily. She remembers things like that. And would you take the bag, please? My arm is getting tired."

Colin reached up to take it. "What's going to happen if I don't wear them?"

"For starters, you still have to pay me. Then, you'll also hurt her feelings, which is the last thing you should do after all the dance lessons. And, of course, you'll have to explain to Lily why you're not wearing them."

"How will she know whether I wear them or not?"

"Because she's here. And she insists that you drop by before you go out. She wants to talk to you."

At a bit of a loss, Colin said nothing.

"Just wear the damn clothes, all right?"

When Colin still didn't respond, Evan squinted slightly. "You owe me."

Colin stood in front of the bathroom mirror, acknowledging that it could have been a lot worse. The shirt was actually more burgundy than red, and though it wasn't something he would have picked out for himself, it wasn't half bad, especially with the sleeves rolled up. He'd been planning all along to wear black slacks—more leftovers from his courtroom days—and the shoes were a lot like the ones he already owned, without the scuffs, which meant he'd probably needed a new pair anyway. How Lily had known was beyond him, but he'd long since given up being surprised by anything she did.

In the kitchen, he scribbled out a check to Evan, grabbed his keys, and turned off his lights on the way out the door. Rounding the house, he went up the steps, noting that the door had been left ajar. Pushing it open, he saw Lily and Evan in the kitchen, each holding a glass of wine. Lily set her glass on the counter with a smile.

"Well, aren't you handsome?" she declared as she approached. She leaned in and kissed him on the cheek. "The color is perfect on you, and I'm certain that Maria will find you quite dashing."

"Thank you," Colin said.

"It was my pleasure. And I'm hopeful that you remember everything we practiced. I assume you went through the steps today?"

"Not today."

"What on earth did you do?"

"I went to the gym."

"Of course you did," she said, not hiding her disappointment. "You really need to learn to prioritize, and I simply can't let you go until I know for certain that you retained everything you need to know."

"I'm sure I'll be fine. And I'm supposed to pick her up in a few minutes."

"Then we'll have to make it quick. Evan?" she called out. "Will you please put on some music?"

"Sure," he said. Grabbing his phone, he tapped a few buttons as he walked over. "I just happen to have a song right here."

Obviously, Lily had been planning this all along. She reached for Colin's hand. "Just run me through a bit of everything, okay? At full speed."

Colin complied before finally separating from Lily. "Good enough?"

"You're going to dazzle her." Lily winked. "Just like you did with the flowers."

"And you know what else will dazzle her?" Evan asked. When Colin turned toward him, he knew that Evan's thoughts had taken a serious turn. "First your car starts, and then you don't end up getting arrested."

Colin had barely finished knocking when Maria pulled the door open. For a long moment, all he could do was stare. Her blouse hugged her curves and her skirt reached only to midthigh; her strappy high heels made her nearly as tall as he was. With a touch of mascara and lipstick, she looked nothing like the professional he'd gone to lunch with only a couple of days earlier, nor did she resemble the sun-kissed woman on the paddleboard. As he stood before her, he wasn't sure which version of her he most preferred, though this one, he had to admit, was pretty stunning.

"You're right on time," she said, giving him a kiss on the cheek. "I'm impressed."

His hands automatically went to her hips. "You look beautiful," he murmured. Up close, he caught a whiff of perfume, something floral and understated. Perfect.

"Thank you," she said. She patted his chest. "I like the shirt."

"It's new."

"Yeah? For tonight?"

"You could say that."

"I feel special," she said. "And, I have to say, you clean up pretty well."

"Sometimes," he admitted. "Are you ready to go?"

"Just let me grab my purse, and then I'm ready. Where are we going?"

"The Pilot House."

"Wow . . . I love that place. The food is fabulous."

"So I've heard. Lily recommended it."

"Then she obviously has good taste."

The restaurant wasn't far, but Colin drove at a leisurely speed with the windows rolled down, both of them enjoying the flickering stars that spread to the horizon and a breeze just strong enough to erase the lingering heat of the day.

Near the river, Colin left Market Street, eventually pulling into the restaurant's lot. Walking around the car to open Maria's door, he reached for her hand and escorted her to the entrance. Once inside, he was surprised to note that it was less formal than he'd expected—a clean, unpretentious place with white tables and a million-dollar view. The restaurant was crowded, people clustering near the bar while they waited for indoor and outdoor tables. After checking in with the hostess, he followed her and Maria to a corner table with a breathtaking view of the Cape Fear River. Moonlight spilled over the slow-moving surface, forming a liquid vein of light between coal-dark banks. As Maria stared toward the water, Colin mentally traced the graceful outlines of her profile, watching her hair catch in the breeze. How had she come to mean so much to him so quickly?

As if sensing his thoughts, she met his gaze and smiled slightly before stretching her hands across the table. He took them in his, marveling at their softness and warmth.

"It's a gorgeous night, don't you think?" she asked.

"Gorgeous," he answered, but he knew that he was really referring to her. Sitting across from her, Colin had the strange feeling that he was living someone else's blessed life, someone more deserving than he. And by the end of dinner, after all the dishes had been cleared and the wineglasses emptied and the candles were flickering out, it dawned on him that he'd spent his entire life searching for Maria, and only recently been lucky enough to find her.

CHAPTER 12

―――― 🌸 ――――

Maria

The warehouse was located in a run-down neighborhood on the outskirts of town, and the only hint that it served a different purpose than any of the other abandoned warehouses nearby was the scores of cars parked haphazardly on the far side of the building, out of sight from the main road.

Not that its sketchy vibe seemed to matter. In addition to the crowd already inside, there was a long line of people—almost exclusively male—still waiting to get in. Many were dragging coolers, no doubt filled with alcohol; others drank beer or sipped from plastic cups as they slowly edged toward the entrance and the music blaring within. Unless they were with a date, girls didn't have to wait in line, and Maria watched as one group after the next cheerfully marched toward the door in tight tops, short skirts, and stiletto heels, ignoring the litter-strewn surroundings, whistles, and catcalls.

Colin appeared relaxed, taking it all in quietly. When they reached the door, they were met by a heavyset man in sunglasses who was collecting the cover charge. The bouncer studied Colin up and down—no doubt trying to decide whether he was with law enforcement—then did the same to Maria before reluctantly taking the bills Colin was offering and nodding toward the door.

Inside, they encountered a solid mass of swaying bodies, and with the booming music, the place shook with a vibrant, barely contained energy. No one seemed to care about the oil-stained concrete floor or the lack of décor or the industrial-grade lighting; guys were clustered around their coolers, drinking and shouting to be heard above the music, trying to get the attention of any girl who happened to pass by. Like at most nightclubs, men clearly outnumbered women, and most appeared to be in their twenties or thirties. Maria presumed that the vast majority were working people out for a fun Saturday night. There were, as Serena had noted, some pretty scary-looking guys here, too, with tattoos and bandannas representing various gangs and wearing baggy pants that could easily conceal a weapon. Ordinarily that would have made her nervous, but the atmosphere indicated that most people were simply focused on having a good time. All the same, she found herself scouting out possible exits in case trouble broke out.

Beside her, Colin was also taking in the scene. He leaned toward her ear. "Would you like to move closer to the music?"

She nodded, and Colin began leading her deeper into the warehouse. They squeezed through the crowd, careful not to bump too hard into anyone, and inched their way to the dance area on the far side of the building, the music pulsing ever louder. Along the way, guys tried to get Maria's attention—demanding her name or commenting on her beauty or even trying to pinch her butt—but afraid to give Colin any reason for confrontation, she merely scowled at them in silence.

The dance floor was separated from the rest of the warehouse by a makeshift barrier of two-by-fours nailed together and fastened across metal barrels. Directly opposite them, on pallets stacked against the back wall, was the DJ, his equipment arranged on a fold-out table. He was flanked by two speakers the size of refrigerators. The music was loud enough to make Maria's chest thump. On the floor, she watched couples move and spin, triggering in her a surge of memories from a time when life seemed more carefree.

Leaning closer to Colin, she could smell the cologne he must have put on earlier.

"Are you sure you're ready for this?"

"Yes," he said, moving past the barrier.

Before she knew it, they were surrounded by couples. She was about to tell Colin what to do when he suddenly took her right hand in his left and placed his right hand on her left shoulder blade. And with that, he began to lead her, his steps moving in unison with hers as the music surged around them. Her eyes widened, and when he led her through a perfectly executed spin, followed almost immediately by a second, she was too shocked to say anything at all. Colin merely raised his eyebrows in amusement, making her laugh aloud. And little by little, as one song rolled into the next, she felt herself beginning to let go, losing herself in the music, and in him.

It was past midnight when they finally left the jammed warehouse and drove back to her condo. Neither of them said much, both feeling warm and slightly flushed as they navigated the quiet streets. Like he had for much of the past few hours, Colin held her hand, his thumb moving against her skin and making it tingle. As they neared her place, she imagined what might happen if she invited Colin upstairs, and was both frightened and excited by her thoughts. They hadn't known each other long enough, and she wasn't sure she was quite ready...yet she had to admit that she wanted him to come up. She wanted their evening together to continue; she wanted him to kiss her again and take her in his arms. Despite her conflicting emotions, she directed him to the parking area behind her condo.

After locking the car, they walked up the steps beside each other, both of them quiet. When they reached the door, she fumbled with her keys, her hands trembling ever so slightly as she unlocked the door. Entering and passing through the living area, she turned on the lamp near the couch, but when she turned around, she realized that Colin had stopped at the threshold. He seemed to sense her confusion, offering her a chance to end the evening now, before it went too far. But something had taken hold of her, and tucking a loose strand of hair behind her ear, she smiled.

"Come on in," she said her voice sounding hoarse and foreign to her own ears. Colin quietly closed the door behind him as he took in the living area with its dark pine flooring and crown molding, and the French doors that opened to the small balcony. Though she suspected he probably wouldn't have cared one way or the other, she was suddenly glad she'd spent the morning straightening up, right down to fluffing the decorative pillows on the couch.

"You have a beautiful place."

"Thank you."

Moving closer to examine the framed photos above the couch, he asked, "Did you take these?"

She nodded. "Earlier this summer."

He studied them in silence—especially the close-up of the osprey clasping a fish in its talons and surrounded by droplets of water. "You're very good," he said, visibly impressed.

"You don't know how many bad shots it took to get these, but thank you." Standing close, she could feel the heat still radiating from his body. "Would you like something to drink? I have a bottle of wine in the fridge."

"Maybe half a glass. I've never been a big wine drinker. And if you have some water, that would be great, too."

Leaving him, she went to the kitchen and pulled a couple of wineglasses from the cabinets. In the refrigerator was a bottle she'd opened the night before. She poured two glasses and took a sip before retrieving another glass for his water.

"Would you like ice?"

"Sure, if it's not too much trouble."

"I think I can handle ice."

She handed him the water glass, and watched as Colin drained it. Taking the empty glass from him, she set it on the breakfast bar before gesturing toward the French doors.

"Shall we go out on the balcony? I'm in the mood for a little fresh air."

"Sounds good," he agreed, reaching for his wineglass. Opening the doors, they stepped onto the balcony. The air was cool against her skin, haze beginning to roll in with the breeze. Traffic was light and the sidewalks stood empty. Streetlights cast a yellow glow, and from the bar at the corner she could hear the faint strains of eighties pop music.

He motioned to the rocking chairs off to the side. "Do you ever sit out here?"

"Not enough. Which is kind of sad, since the balcony is one of the reasons I bought the condo in the first place. I think I had this idea that I'd unwind out here after work, but it usually doesn't turn out that way. Most nights, I'll have a quick dinner and either plant myself at the dining room table or at the desk in the spare bedroom with my MacBook." She shrugged. "The whole trying-to-get-ahead thing again, but we've already talked about that, haven't we?"

"We've talked about a lot of things."

"Does that mean you're getting bored with me already?"

He turned toward her, his eyes reflecting the evening light. "No."

"You know what I find interesting about you?" Colin waited, saying nothing. "You don't feel the need to always explain your reasoning when you answer questions. You get straight to the point. The only time you elaborate is when you're asked to do so. You're a man of very few words."

"Okay."

"That's exactly what I mean!" she teased. "But all right, you've made me curious. Why don't you elaborate unless you're specifically asked to do so?"

"Because it's easier. And it takes less time."

"Don't you think that including others in your thought process helps them understand you better?"

"That assumes they want to understand me better. And if they do, they'll ask me to explain and then I'll do it."

"And if they don't ask?"

"Then they probably don't care about my reasoning in the first place. They just want to know the answer. I know I do. If I ask someone what time it is, I don't need a history of clock-making and I don't care who gave them the watch, or how expensive it was, or whether it was a Christmas present. I just want the time."

"I'm not talking about that. I'm talking about trying to get to know someone. Making conversation."

"So am I. But not everyone needs—or even wants—to know why you feel the way you do about something. Some things are better left private."

"Excuse me? Weren't you the one who told me your life story that first night on the beach?"

"You asked questions and I answered them."

"And you think that works?"

"It has for us. We have no trouble talking."

"But that's because I ask a lot of questions."

"Yes."

"Well, it's a good thing I do. Or we'd end up like some of those older couples I see in coffee shops who don't say a word to each other while they eat breakfast. Of course, that's probably right up your alley. I can easily imagine you going an entire day without saying anything to anyone."

"Sometimes I do."

"That's not normal."

"Okay."

She took a sip of wine and waved a hand at him. "More detail, please."

"I don't know what 'normal' really means. I think everyone has his own definition, and it's shaped by culture, by family and friends, by character and experience, by events and a thousand other things. What's normal for one person isn't normal for another. For some people, jumping out of airplanes is crazy. For other people, life isn't worth living without it."

She nodded, conceding the point. Still...

"All right. Without me asking a question first, I want you to say how you really feel about something. Something unexpected and completely off topic. Something I wouldn't expect you to say. And then elaborate, without me having to ask a single question."

"Why?"

"Humor me," she said, nudging him. "Just for fun."

He rotated the wineglass with his fingers before raising his eyes to hers. "You're amazing. You're intelligent and beautiful and it should be easy for you to meet someone who doesn't have my past, who hasn't made the mistakes I have...Truthfully, it makes me wonder what I'm doing here, or why you even invited me. Part of me thinks that all of this is too good to be true and that it's going to come crashing down, but even if it does, it wouldn't change the fact that you've already added something to my life, something that I hadn't even realized was missing." Colin paused. When he spoke again, his voice was quiet. "You've come to mean more to me than I think you realize. Before you came along, I had Evan and Lily, and I thought that was enough. But it isn't. Not anymore. Not since last weekend. Being with you makes me feel vulnerable again, and I haven't felt vulnerable since I was a kid. I can't say that I always like it, but the alternative would be worse because it would mean not seeing you again."

Maria realized she'd been holding her breath; by the time he finished, she felt almost dizzy, overwhelmed by his response, and tried to steady herself.

Colin, on the other hand, continued to exude an easy confidence, and it was that, more than anything, which allowed her to regain her equilibrium.

"I'm not sure what to say," she admitted.

"You don't have to say anything. I didn't say it because I wanted a response. I said it because I wanted to."

She wrapped both hands around the stem of her glass. "May I ask you a question?" she asked shyly. "About something else?"

"Of course."

"Why did you act like you didn't know anything about salsa dancing?"

"When we talked about it, I didn't. Lily spent the week giving me lessons. That's what I was doing on Thursday and Friday nights."

"You learned how to dance for me?"

"Yes."

She turned away and took a sip of wine, trying to mask her amazement. "Thank you. And I guess I should thank Lily, too."

He flashed a quick smile. "Would you mind if I refill my water glass? I'm still a bit thirsty."

"Of course not."

Colin stepped away and Maria shook her head, wondering when, or even if, she would cease being surprised by him.

Luis had never spoken to her like Colin just had. As she leaned over the railing, she suddenly found it hard to remember what she'd really seen in him. On the surface, he was attractive and intelligent, but underneath he'd been arrogant and vain. She'd often made excuses for his behavior, and if anyone questioned her feelings, she'd reacted defensively. Thinking back, she admitted that she'd desperately wanted his approval and not only did he sense that, but he frequently took advantage of it. It wasn't a healthy relationship, she knew, and when she tried to imagine him behaving as Colin had—calling her, bringing flowers, learning to dance—she couldn't. And despite all that, she'd loved Luis with an intensity she could still sometimes feel.

Earlier, as she and Colin had been dancing, she'd caught herself thinking that the night couldn't possibly get any better. And then, all at once, it had. Listening to him express his feelings without fear or regret had left her speechless. She wondered whether she was capable of such a thing. Probably not, but then again, Colin wasn't like most people. He accepted himself, faults and all, and forgave himself for the mistakes he'd made. More than that, he seemed to live in the moment without regard for either the past or the future.

The greatest revelation was how deeply Colin was able to experience his emotions, perhaps even more deeply than she did. Watching him over dinner and on the dance floor, and hearing his words just now, she knew that if he wasn't in love with her yet, he was on the brink. Like her, he was willing to surrender to the inevitable, an idea that made her hands tremble. As Colin stepped back onto the balcony behind her, she took a long breath, savoring the wave of desire that flooded through her. He leaned over the railing next to her, and as their breaths fell into steady rhythm, she took another sip of wine, the warmth coursing down her throat into her stomach and limbs.

Studying his face in profile, she thought again about the way his external calm enveloped the coiled emotions within him, and she suddenly imagined the way Colin might look as he hovered naked above her, his lips gently brushing hers, as they gave themselves over to each other. Her stomach tightened and she felt her mouth curve into a faint smile.

"Did you mean what you said to me earlier?"

He didn't answer right away. Instead, he lowered his head before turning to face her.

"I meant every single word."

Feeling a cascade of sensations in her body, she moved closer and kissed him gently on the lips. They were soft and warm, and pulling back, she saw in his expression something akin to hope. She kissed him a second time then and felt her skin begin to come alive as he slid his arms around her. He tugged softly, bringing their bodies together, and in that instant, she began to lose herself in him. She could feel the strength of his chest and arms surrounding her and the warm urgency of his tongue, and she knew with fierce certainty that she needed Colin, all of him. They continued to kiss on the balcony beneath a foggy, star-filled sky until she finally reached for his hand. Their fingers intertwined as he kissed the hollow of her neck, the sensation tantalizing and erotic. She shivered, enjoying the sensation before wordlessly leading him to the bedroom.

Moments after she woke the next morning, Maria felt the soft glare of the early-autumn sun, and the night came rushing back. She rolled over and saw Colin lying on his side, only half covered by the sheet, already awake and alert. "Good morning," he whispered.

"Good morning," she said. "How long have you been up?"

"About an hour."

"Why didn't you go back to sleep?"

"I wasn't tired. And besides, I kind of enjoyed watching you."

"That has the potential to sound very creepy, you know."

"Okay."

She smiled. "Well, since you were watching me, I hope I didn't do anything embarrassing or make any strange noises."

"You didn't. You just lay there looking sexy as hell."

"My hair is messy and I need to brush my teeth."

"Right now?"

"Why? What did you have in mind?"

He reached toward her, using his finger to trace her collarbone, and after that, no words were necessary.

Later, they showered together and dressed. Maria dried her hair and put on makeup while Colin leaned against the bathroom counter beside her, nursing a cup of coffee.

"Are we going someplace?" he asked.

"Brunch. With my parents."

"Sounds good. I'm going to need to change first, though. What time?"

"Eleven."

"I take it that we won't be riding together."

"That's probably not a good idea. It's going to be hard enough to prepare them for your visit. Because this time, they're going to ask a lot of questions."

"Okay."

Maria put down her mascara wand and took his hand. "Does that bother you? Or scare you?"

"No."

"Well, it sure scares me," she admitted, returning to her makeup. "The whole thing is terrifying, in fact."

He took a sip of coffee. "What are you going to tell them about me?"

"Hopefully, as little as possible. Any details will just spur more questions that you should answer, not me."

"What are you hoping for today?"

"For my mom to get through it without tears, and my father not to demand that you leave the house."

"That's not a very high bar."

"Trust me," she said. "It's higher than you think."

CHAPTER 13

Colin

Colin pulled up to Maria's parents' house just before eleven. He had no idea how the conversation with her parents had gone, and as he stepped out of the car, he figured there was no use in speculating, since he'd find out soon enough anyway.

Had Lily been around, he would have asked her what he should bring to a family brunch, but she and Evan were already at church when he got home, and in the end, it probably wouldn't do much good anyway. Like everyone else, they were going to form their own opinions, and a basket of muffins wasn't going to alter them.

Still, as he walked to the door, he hoped that Maria was all right. Earlier, on his way home, he'd thought about her virtually nonstop, one series of images giving way to the next, each more ravishing than the one before. That was a first for him, *she* was a first, and he took a deep breath, reminding himself that even though he wouldn't shy away from any questions, his answers could be framed in a lot of different ways and still remain honest.

He knocked at the door and it swung open almost immediately, revealing Serena. He noticed again how much she resembled her older sister, though she seemed even more high-strung than usual, which probably wasn't a good sign.

"Hey, Colin," she said, stepping aside to let him in. "I saw you walking up. Come on in."

"Thank you. How did your dinner go last night?"

"Awesome," she answered. "But I should be the one asking you."

"We had a good time."

"I'm sure." Serena winked. "Maria's in the kitchen with Mom," she said, closing the door behind him. "And I'm amazed you were able to get her to go dancing."

"Why?"

"If you don't know yet, I think you need to spend even more time with her," she answered. "But here's a word to the wise—I wouldn't get too descriptive about last night, especially anything that might have happened after the dancing. It's already a little tense around here. I have a hunch that my parents think you're a terrorist."

"Okay."

"I might be exaggerating, but who really knows?" she babbled. "I didn't get here until the three of them were finished talking, and my parents barely said hello to me. All I really know for sure is that my dad wasn't smiling and my mom kept making the sign of the cross, despite how well last night's dinner with the director of the foundation went . . . not that my little challenges matter right now. Anyway, I decided it was best if I just waited for you in the living room."

By then, they'd reached the kitchen, where he saw Maria standing over a sizzling frying pan while her mom pulled a small baking pan from the oven. The air smelled of bacon and cinnamon.

"Colin's here," Serena called out.

Maria turned and he noticed she was wearing an apron. "Hi, Colin," she said tightly. "You remember my mom, right?"

Carmen forced on a plastic smile, and though Colin might have been imagining it, she seemed paler than she'd been just a couple of days earlier. "Good morning, Mrs. Sanchez," he said, figuring a bit of formality was probably a good bet.

"Good morning." She nodded and, obviously uncomfortable,

turned her attention back to the pan as she placed it on an iron rack on the counter.

Serena leaned toward him. "My mom decided to do an American breakfast just for you," she whispered. "Bacon and eggs, French toast, cinnamon rolls. Of course, that was before Maria told her about you."

Maria pulled a couple of strips of bacon from the pan and set them on a napkin-covered plate off to the side of the stove. "Hey, Serena? Can you take over for a second?"

"Be glad to," Serena chirped. "But only if I get to wear the cool apron."

Maria started toward them, slipping off the apron as she walked and passing it to Serena like trading places was normal. In this kitchen, Colin assumed it was. Serena started chatting away with her mother in Spanish as she donned the apron.

Up close, Colin noticed tension in the way Maria was moving. She gave him a quick peck on the cheek, careful to keep a bit of distance between them. "Any trouble finding the place?"

"Google," he answered. Glancing over his shoulder, it was hard not to notice the way Carmen frowned slightly. He knew enough not to ask how it had gone earlier; instead, he defaulted to silence. Maria lowered her voice, concern etched on her face.

"Would you mind talking to my dad before we eat?"

"Okay."

"And, um . . ." She trailed off.

"It's your father," he said. "I won't forget."

She nodded, the movement almost imperceptible. "I'm going to stay in here and help my mom in the kitchen," she said. "My dad's at the table on the back porch. Do you want any coffee?"

"I'm fine," Colin replied.

"Water?"

"I'm fine," he said again.

"Okay . . ." She took a step backward. "I guess I better get back to the kitchen, then."

Colin watched as she backed away, past a refrigerator deco-rated with dozens of photos, letters, and other keepsakes, before she turned around. He moved toward the slider and as soon as he opened the door, Felix turned his way. There was less anger than he'd anticipated, though the shock and disappointment were evi-dent, as was his obvious antagonism. In his lap, a small white dog was sleeping.

Colin closed the door behind him and walked toward Felix, his eyes steady. Nearing the table, he offered his hand.

"Good morning, Mr. Sanchez. Maria said you wanted to speak with me."

Felix looked toward the hand before he reluctantly offered his own. Colin stood, waiting for Felix to invite him to sit at the table. Eventually Felix nodded toward a chair, and Colin sat. He clasped his hands and rested them in front of him, remaining quiet. There was no point in trying to make small talk or pre-tending that he didn't know what Felix wanted to discuss.

Felix was in no rush to speak and took his time scrutinizing him. "Maria said that you were in trouble with the law," he finally began. "Is that true?"

"Yes," Colin answered. Over the next half hour, the full story came out in bits and pieces, much as it had with Maria that first night on the beach. He didn't sugarcoat his past or attempt to mislead Felix; he was who he was. Like with Maria, Felix's shock was pronounced at times and he pressed for further clarification; when Colin eventually recounted what happened at the first military school he'd attended, Colin thought he saw a flash of sudden understanding. By the time he finished, Felix was less on edge than he had been when Colin had first joined him on the porch, but it was also clear that he needed time to think about all that he'd learned. No surprise there. Felix was a father and Maria was his daughter, and there was only so far he would go.

"You claim that you've changed and I would like to believe you, but I'm not sure that I do."

"Okay." Colin nodded.

"What if you get arrested again?"

"I don't plan on it."

"That's the problem. People seldom plan on it."

Colin said nothing. There was really nothing to say.

Felix continued to pet the little white dog. "If you do get arrested, what will happen?"

"I won't see her. I'll end it. The worst thing would be for her to think she should wait."

After a moment, Felix offered a slight nod, satisfied but still unsure as to whether he believed it. "If you ever hurt my daughter or put my daughter in danger..."

He didn't finish, but he didn't need to. Colin knew what Felix wanted to hear, and because it was true, he had no trouble saying it.

"It won't happen."

"I have your word."

"Yes."

Just then, Maria popped her head out, clearly nervous but also relieved that she hadn't heard any shouting. "Are you two about finished? Brunch is ready."

Felix exhaled. "We're done," he said. "Let's eat."

After they'd finished eating, Serena and her parents began to clean up while Maria lingered behind with Colin. "What did you say to him?" Maria asked.

"The truth," Colin answered.

"All of it?"

"Yes."

Maria appeared flummoxed. "Then it went a lot better than I thought it would."

Maria was right—the brunch had been relatively pleasant, with Serena chattering on about the scholarship, Steve, and the escapades of her numerous friends. Felix and Carmen had occasionally asked questions, even lobbing a few queries toward Colin, though all were about work or school. When he'd mentioned MMA, he thought that Carmen had paled just a bit.

"Still…" Maria said. "I guess you were right. It was best to get it all out there in the beginning."

Sometimes, Colin thought. *Not always*. Felix had been cordial, but there wasn't any fondness or trust evident, both of which would take time to achieve, if that was possible at all. He didn't say that, though. Instead, he reached for the door.

"Do you want to do some paddleboarding later?" he asked.

"How about we do something different instead. Like…Jet Skiing. We can rent them at the beach. Does that sound fun?"

He recalled the sight of her in a bikini again. "Actually, that sounds great."

They met at Wrightsville Beach later that afternoon and spent a couple of hours on Jet Skis before Colin returned home to squeeze in a quick workout. They cooked dinner at Maria's and then, like the night before, spent the next few hours wrapped in each other's arms.

Monday morning came too soon, but that week they spent as much time together as they could. Colin met Maria for lunch twice, and on Wednesday, she spent the evening at Crabby Pete's, nursing a Diet Pepsi and working on a legal brief for Barney with her MacBook propped on the bar in front of her. Aside from his shifts and classes, a few hours for working out, and family brunch, they were together almost every minute, and went to both the farmers' market and the aquarium, neither of which Colin had ever contemplated visiting before.

Through it all, he simply tried to embrace the way he felt about her. He didn't think about it, didn't worry about it, didn't try to understand it. Instead, he enjoyed the way he felt whenever she laughed, and how sexy she was when she knit her eyebrows in concentration; he savored the feel of her hand in his as they walked and talked, their conversations drifting from the serious to the silly.

On Sunday night, in bed after making love, Maria was lying on her stomach, her knees bent and feet up as she nibbled on some grapes. Colin found it impossible to take his eyes from her, ogling her until she playfully tossed a grape at him.

"Stop staring. You're making me feel self-conscious."

He reached for the grape and popped it in his mouth. "Why?"

"Because I'm Catholic and we're not married, maybe?"

He chuckled. "Your mother asked if I was Catholic, didn't she? When we were at lunch the first time?"

"You understand Spanish?"

"Not really. I took it in high school and barely passed, but I heard my name and the word *católico* when she was at the table. It wasn't that hard to translate. But yes," he continued. "I was raised Catholic. I was baptized and confirmed, the whole nine yards. But I pretty much stopped going to church after I got sent off to school, so I'm not sure what that makes me now."

"She'll still be happy."

"Good."

"How did they get you confirmed if you stopped going to church?"

"Donations, I guess. Probably a big one, because the priest let me do a cram course one summer and even though I didn't do any of the work, the next year, they let me get confirmed anyway."

"That's kind of cheating."

"It's not kind of cheating. It *is* cheating. On the plus side, I got a go-kart out of it, so that was kind of nice."

"A go-kart?"

"It was either that or I wouldn't do it. For all the good it did me. I totaled it within a couple of weeks and refused to talk to my parents the rest of the summer because they wouldn't buy me a new one."

"Nice," she said sarcastically.

"I've never hidden the fact that I have issues."

"I'm aware." She smiled. "But sometimes, I wish you'd surprise me in a good way when you talk about your younger years."

He thought about it. "I beat up my older sister's ex-boyfriend once. Does that count? Since he was a total jerk?"

"No," she said, "that doesn't count."

He smiled. "Do you want to have lunch tomorrow?"

"I'd love to, but I already promised Jill. She texted me earlier and I forgot to mention it. I'm open to a late dinner, though."

"I can't," he said. "I have to work."

"You mean we might not see each other tomorrow? Whatever am I going to do?"

It might have been the playfulness in her tone or the fact that a long and wonderful weekend was finally coming to an end, but he didn't respond. Instead, he just stared at her, noting the sensual curves of her body, perfect in nearly every way. "You are incredibly beautiful," he whispered.

A light smile played across her lips, seductive and lovely. "Yeah?"

"Yeah," he echoed, and as he continued to gaze at her, he couldn't shake the feeling that a long journey was finally coming to an end. He knew what that meant, and while the feeling had been unimaginable even a month ago, there was no reason to deny it. He reached toward her, gently running his fingers through her hair, the sensation luxurious, and he let out a long breath. "I love you, Maria," he finally murmured. He watched as her surprise gave way to comprehension.

With his hand still in her hair, she wrapped it in hers.

"Oh, Colin," she whispered, "I love you, too."

CHAPTER 14

---- 🌹 ----

Maria

They made love early the following morning; afterward, Colin told her he wanted to get a workout in before class, and though the sun had not yet risen when he left, Maria tossed and turned, unable to fall back to sleep. She finally got out of bed, resolved to catch up on some long-neglected work.

She brewed coffee, showered, and dressed, and with the best of intentions opened up her MacBook to get some work done in the hour and a half before she left for the office. And yet, as she settled in, she couldn't escape a growing, though inchoate, sense that something was wrong. Even as she sifted through her feelings, she couldn't pinpoint the cause. The timing made her suspect that it had something to do with Colin; the relationship *had* been a bit of a whirlwind, although she certainly didn't regret it. They'd fallen in love, and there was nothing wrong with that. It was normal. It happened to other people every day. And considering all the time they'd spent getting to know each other, it wasn't even all that unexpected.

So what on earth was bothering her?

Refilling her cup, she abandoned the table and wandered to the balcony, watching as the port city slowly came to life. A light mist lingered just above the sidewalk, making it appear almost out of focus. As she sipped her coffee, she remembered standing in the same spot the night they had first made love, and though it brought a smile to her face, the memory was accompanied by a definite pang of anxiety.

Okay, so maybe her feelings about Colin weren't as simple and straightforward as she wanted to pretend. But what, exactly, was throwing her off? That they were sleeping together? The words they'd spoken to each other last night? The fact that her parents didn't approve of him? Or that a month ago, she couldn't have even imagined falling for someone like him?

That pretty much sums it up, she admitted. But why this anxiety *this* morning? It was ridiculous to think that simply saying *I love you* could upset her equilibrium this way. Logically, it made no sense. She finished her coffee and decided to head in to work early, sure that she was blowing the whole thing out of proportion.

And yet, throughout the morning, the feeling didn't dissipate; if anything, it only grew more pronounced. By ten, even her stomach had grown slightly upset. The more she tried to convince herself that worrying about Colin didn't make sense, the more difficult she found it to concentrate. As the clock clicked toward the lunch hour, all she could think was that she needed to talk to Jill.

Maria went through all of it, including the way she was feeling, as she watched Jill pull several pieces of sushi from the platter onto her plate and begin wolfing them down. For her part, Maria put a single piece on her plate before realizing there wasn't a chance she could force it down. By the time she finished speaking, Jill was nodding.

"So let me get this straight," Jill said. "You met a guy, the two of you slept together after not dating all that long, you introduced him to your parents and they didn't run for the hills, and he told you that he loved you. And then, this morning, you suddenly began questioning everything. Have I summed that up correctly?"

"Pretty much."

"And you're not sure why?"

Maria made a face. "Humor me."

"It's simple. You're just going through a grown-up version of the walk of shame."

"Excuse me?"

"The walk of shame? From college? After you had too much to drink at a party and you hooked up with a guy that you thought was perfect and then, when morning came around, you couldn't believe what had just happened? And then walked back across the campus to your place wondering what the hell you were doing, still dressed in what you'd been wearing the night before?"

"I know what the walk of shame is. And it's not anything like that."

Jill used her chopsticks to pick up the last remaining maki roll. "Maybe not specifically, but I'd be surprised if your emotions weren't seesawing from one extreme to the other, which is what most girls go through during the walk of shame. As in, 'Did that really happen? Was it as good as I remember? What did I do?' Falling in love is terrifying. That's why they say 'falling in love' and not something like 'floating toward love.' Falling is scary. Floating is kind of dreamy." She shook her head sorrowfully at Maria's plate. "I just ate all of our food and I'm going to blame you when I get on the scale."

"In other words, you think that what I'm going through is normal?"

"I'd be way more worried if you weren't questioning everything. Because then, it would mean you're crazy."

"Did this happen with Paul? When you first fell in love with him?"

"Of course. One day, he'd be all I could think about, and the next, I'd wonder whether I was making the biggest mistake of

my life. And here's a little secret—sometimes it still happens.
I know I love him, but I'm not sure I love him enough to date
him forever. I want to get married and have children. Or at least
one. And by the way? His parents don't like me that much, and I
struggle with that, too."

"Why don't they like you?"

"They think I talk too much. And that I'm too opinionated."

"You're kidding."

"I know, right?"

Maria laughed before growing serious again. "I think it's hard
because everything about Colin and me just seems so...foreign.
With Luis, it all made sense. We were friends first, and even after
we were dating, it must have been six months before I told him
that I loved him. My parents liked him, and he came from a good
family, and there was nothing about his past to even question."

"If memory serves, I believe you also told me that Serena didn't
like Luis at all. And in the end, he turned out to be a selfish jerk."

Oh yeah. That. "But..."

"Luis was your first love. You can't compare what happened
then with what's happening now."

"That's what I just said."

"You're missing my point. My point is that first loves *always*
make sense because you don't know any better. Everything is a
first and any warning bells are drowned out by the sheer novelty
of it all. In the beginning, anyway. Now you're older and wiser,
and you need someone in your life who's older and wiser, too. You
want someone who doesn't play games, and with Colin, what you
see is what you get. You trust him and you enjoy spending time
with him. Or at least, that's what you've been telling me."

"And you don't think it's moving too fast?"

"Compared to what? It's your life. My advice is to go with the
flow and take it one day at a time. And again, what you're feeling
today is perfectly normal."

"I'd rather not feel this way at all."

"Who would? But I have a hunch that you'll feel better as soon as you talk to him again. That's the way it usually works."

Maria pushed her lonely piece of sushi around, finally beginning to feel the first pangs of hunger. "I hope you're right."

"Of course I'm right. Love makes everything complicated, and emotions always go wild in the beginning. But when it's real, you should hold on tight, because we're both old enough to know that true love doesn't come along all that often."

After lunch with Jill, Maria did feel better. Maybe not entirely normal, but at the very least somewhat *centered* again. The more she thought about it, the more she recognized that Jill had been right about pretty much everything. Falling in love *was* a little frightening and enough to make anyone a bit screwy in the beginning. It had been so long that she'd forgotten what it was supposed to feel like.

Jill had also been spot-on when she'd assured Maria that talking to Colin would help settle her doubts. He called a little after four while he was on his way to work. Although they didn't chat for long, simply hearing his voice seemed to diminish the tension in her neck and shoulders. And when he asked if she was free the following evening and whether they could spend time together, she realized how much she wanted exactly that.

The thought of spending time with Colin after work made the following day pass more quickly than usual. Even Barney—who either dropped by her office or called a dozen times to get the latest updates on various matters—couldn't shake her good spirits. When the phone rang halfway through the afternoon, she answered automatically, expecting to hear Barney's voice, only to hear Jill on the other end.

"Now he's just showing off," her friend announced.

It took a second to identify the voice. "Jill?"

"So either the two of you got into a fight last night and he's hoping for forgiveness, or he's trying to make other men look bad."

"What are you talking about?"

"Colin. And the bouquet of roses he just sent you."

"He sent roses?"

"What did you think I was talking about? The delivery guy is waiting for you."

Maria glanced at her phone, noting the extension. "Why are you calling from Gwen's phone in the lobby?"

"Because I happened to be talking to Gwen when the delivery guy walked in, and I insisted that I be allowed to call you because this is getting ridiculous. Do you know how often Paul has sent me roses at work? Try never. And if you don't get out here soon, I might take the bouquet and stomp on it because it's making me question my entire relationship again. And believe me—you don't want *that* on your conscience."

Maria laughed. "No stomping, okay? I'll be right there."

When she entered the lobby, she spotted Jill standing beside a deliveryman in a baseball cap who was, sure enough, holding a bouquet of pink roses. Before she could thank him, the delivery guy handed the bouquet to her and abruptly turned away. A moment later, the lobby door was closing behind him, almost like he'd never been there at all.

"Charming fellow," Jill commented. "He couldn't even make small talk. He just kept saying your name whenever I asked a question. But you have to admit the bouquet is gorgeous."

Maria had to agree. The buds, enveloped in sprigs of baby's breath, were either closed or just barely beginning to wink open, and as she bent to smell them, she realized that the florist had been thoughtful enough to trim the thorns. "I can't believe he would do this," she remarked, inhaling the bouquet's delicate scent.

"It's almost sad," Jill said, shaking her head. "He must have serious self-esteem issues. Since he's always seeking your approval, I mean."

"I don't think Colin has self-esteem issues."

"Then he must be needy. You should probably break up with

him before it gets any worse. You need someone like Paul, a guy who thinks first and foremost about himself."

Maria peered up at her friend. "Are you finished?"

"Did you get the sense that I'm envious?"

"Yes."

"Then yes. I'm finished. And I take it that the two of you talked and all is well again?"

"We made plans for tonight, in fact." She held out the bouquet toward Jill. "Would you mind holding this while I open the card?"

"Why not? It's not like you're trying to rub it in."

Maria rolled her eyes as she slid the card out and read it. She blinked before reading it a second time, her brow beginning to crease.

"What is it?" Jill asked.

"I wonder if they attached the wrong card. This one doesn't make sense."

"What does it say?"

Maria held it open to show Jill. "It says," she read, *"You will know how it feels."*

Jill wrinkled her nose. "Is that a private joke or something?"

"No."

"Then what is it supposed to mean?"

"I have no idea," Maria answered, growing more puzzled by the minute.

Jill handed back the bouquet. "It's a strange thing to write, don't you think?"

"Definitely strange," Maria conceded.

"Maybe you should call him and ask about what he meant."

Maybe, Maria thought. "He's probably at the gym."

"So what? I'll bet he has his phone with him. Or you know what it could be? Maybe the florist made a mistake. He either attached the wrong card or wrote it down wrong."

"I guess that's possible," Maria agreed, and though she tried to convince herself it was true, she wondered whether either of them really believed it.

After putting the roses in the vase from the first bouquet of flowers, Maria continued to examine the card until finally deciding, *Oh, what the hell?* Pulling her cell phone from her purse, she rang Colin.

"Hey there," he said. "You're not calling to cancel on me tonight, are you?" He was breathing hard, and in the background, Maria could hear music and the sound of people running on the treadmill.

"No. I'm looking forward to it. Did I catch you at a bad time?"

"Not at all. What's up?"

"Just a quick question. I wanted to ask you about your message."

"What message?"

"On the card that came with the roses today. The card said, 'You will know how it feels,' and I'm not sure what you meant by that."

She could hear him breathing on the other end. "It wasn't me. I didn't send you roses today. Or a card."

Maria felt a sudden prickle on the back of her neck. *You will know how it feels?* It was weird enough if Colin had written it, but if it wasn't from him, that made the note . . .

Strange. Even creepy.

"What's it supposed to mean?" Colin said into the silence.

"I don't know. I'm still trying to figure it out."

"And you don't know who they came from?"

"There was no name on the card."

Colin said nothing to that, and trying to hide her own feeling of unease, she changed the subject. "I know you've got to get back to your workout—and I should get back to work—but what time will you be coming by tonight?"

"How about six thirty? I was thinking that we head down to

the Riverwalk and play it by ear. I'm kind of in the mood to move, not just sit. And we can grab a bite while we're there."

"Sounds perfect. I've been planted in my chair the last couple of days, and a walk is just what I need."

As they hung up, she was picturing the way he looked in the gym...but then she caught sight of the roses again, as well as the card. The card with no name.

You will know how it feels.

She examined the card again, wondering if she'd be able to call the florist and find out who ordered them, only to realize that neither the envelope nor the card bore any markings whatsoever.

"You're distracted," Colin said as they walked hand in hand on the Riverwalk, the popular promenade along the Cape Fear River. Because it was midweek, the streets weren't crowded, and though it was still warm, the northerly breeze hinted at the possibility of cooler temperatures in the weeks ahead. For the first time in months, she was glad she was wearing jeans.

She shook her head. "I'm just trying to figure out who would have sent me the roses."

"Maybe you have a secret admirer."

"Aside from you, I haven't met anyone new lately. It's not as though I go out much, either. I'm either visiting my parents, paddleboarding, or at my place."

"Except when you're at work."

"No one at work would have sent them," she responded, but even as she said the words, Ken's image popped into her head. He wouldn't do that, would he? "Besides, the message doesn't really reflect someone's attempt to make me feel special. It does just the opposite, in fact."

"What about a client?"

"I guess it's possible," she conceded, but she had trouble believing it.

Colin squeezed her hand. "One way or the other, you'll find out who he is."

"You think it's a he?"

"Don't you?"

She nodded, absolutely sure of it, though there was no real indication. "The message...bothers me."

She hoped that he'd say something to make her feel better. Instead, he took a few steps before glancing at her.

"It bothers me, too."

Spending time with Colin somehow lessened her unease. Or at least it prevented her from dwelling on who might have sent the flowers and written the note. She didn't have the faintest clue who it might be, other than Ken, and while there was much to dislike about the man, she couldn't imagine him doing something like that.

As she and Colin walked, the conversation drifted from one topic to another. Eventually they stopped for ice cream cones, Colin surprising her by ordering one as well. They ate them as they stood at the railing that offered a view of the USS *North Carolina*, a battleship that had engaged in extensive action in World War II and had been formally retired, now docked on the other side of the Cape Fear River. She remembered touring it once on a field trip, recalling how cramped it was belowdecks, the claustrophobic feeling of the narrow corridors and tiny rooms. She wondered how sailors had managed to stay on board for months at a time without losing their minds.

They traversed the length of the Riverwalk while the setting sun slowly turned the river to gold, then leisurely browsed through whatever shops caught their interest. By the time the moon had begun to glow over the horizon, they finally stopped for dinner, and as she sat across the table from Colin, she found herself hoping that her parents would get to know this side of him, the one that made her feel comfortable and at ease. She wanted them to witness how happy she was when she was with him. On their way back to her condo, she invited Colin to brunch again, even if she wasn't sure her parents were ready for another visit.

When they made love that night, it was slow and tender, a deliberate dance as he moved above her, whispering her name and how much she meant to him. She gave herself over to him completely, lost in the moment and lost in him. In the afterglow, she fell asleep with her head on his chest, lulled by the steady rhythm of his heartbeat. She woke up twice—once a little after midnight and the second time an hour before dawn—and in the stillness of those moments she stared at him, still amazed that they'd become a couple and more certain than ever that each of them was exactly what the other needed.

When she entered her office Wednesday morning, her first thought was that she needed to get rid of the card. She tore it into pieces and dropped them into the wastebasket, then pulled up to her office computer. Reviewing her messages, she checked whether any of her clients had mentioned sending the flowers, but found nothing.

Meanwhile, Barney was waiting for her in the conference room, and it wasn't until nearly noon that she finally got back to her office. In her inbox she found yet another file that Barney had e-mailed, accompanied by a message suggesting she get a jump-start on it since he needed a summary by tomorrow. Which meant takeout lunch at her desk *again*. Glancing over at the roses, she realized she didn't want them in her office. Grabbing the bouquet and her purse, she left the building, rounding the corner toward the garbage bins.

She heaved the bouquet into the Dumpster, and was starting toward her car when she had the sudden sense that someone was watching her. Spotting no one in her vicinity, she dismissed the feeling at first. But it grew stronger, and as she began fishing through her purse for her car keys, she glanced toward the building.

There, standing at his office window, was Ken.

She dropped her gaze toward her purse again, pretending she hadn't noticed him. What was he doing and how long had he been standing there? For all she knew, there was someone else in his office and he was standing near the window with his back to them, but if he had been at the window when she'd walked out, he'd no doubt seen her throwing away the roses. And that wasn't good. If he'd sent them, he was probably going to be angry; if he hadn't, he might assume that she and Colin were on the outs. Either way, she worried that Ken just might feel the urge to drop by her office again for further discussions on whether she was really a *team player.*

Pulling open her car door, she was hit by a blast of heat from the sun-cooked interior, and as soon as she turned on the engine, she turned on the air conditioner. She decided to drive to the organic market, which had an amazing salad bar, and as she exited the parking lot, she checked her rearview mirror, assuming Ken would be gone.

But he hadn't left the window. And though he was too far away for her to know for sure, she couldn't escape the feeling that he'd been watching her all along.

❦

Returning from the store, she parked in the same spot she'd vacated, deciding to leave the windows cracked to cool the interior. Ken's car was already gone, and if history was any indication, he wouldn't be back until one thirty or so. Relieved, she tried to settle into work. Between the roses, the message, and now Ken, she felt ready to collect her things and go home. Maybe she could feign a migraine and leave early...but what was the point? Barney would still expect her to complete the work, and even at home, she knew she'd continue to obsess over the day's events.

You will know how it feels.

How what feels?

Because she'd rejected Ken's advances, was he planning to make her work life even more miserable?

If so, what would that mean?

She tried to force the questions away while putting together a time line relating to a customer who'd been injured in a fall and was suing a department store. It would take most of the afternoon, and as she began to jot down notes, she observed that her entire profession was part of a giant *game* in which the *object* was to amass billable hours, making attorneys the only guaranteed winners.

It was a cynical view, but how else could she explain how she was always so busy despite the fact that justice was anything but swift? She was still working on cases that had been initially filed years ago, and the case Barney had just assigned her had no chance of reaching the courtroom for at least eighteen months. And that's if things went smoothly, which was virtually impossible, since things never went smoothly. So why did Barney need the time line by tomorrow? What was so urgent?

At the back of her mind, she kept picturing Ken as he'd watched her. She wasn't going to let him blindside her again if he dropped by to supposedly discuss her *career*. She decided to keep her office door wide open even though the ambient office noise tended to distract her. That way, if Ken did decide to pay her a visit, she'd have a few extra seconds to prepare.

From her window, it was possible to see Ken's parking spot. Predictably, the man drove a red Corvette, and at one thirty on the dot, he pulled in. She half expected him to drop by as soon as he entered the building, but to her relief, he didn't appear. Nor did he swing by later, even to visit the paralegals. When he remained a no-show at five, she reminded herself not to stay late. She closed down her MacBook and gathered paper copies of her files, loading it all into her bag. Peeking out the window, she did a quick double take when she realized that Ken's car was already gone for the day.

Whatever. Tomorrow would likely bring more surprises.

Leaving her office, she said good-bye to Jill and headed for her car. As always, she went around to the passenger-side door first so she could put her bag on the seat, but as soon as she pulled it open, she let out an inadvertent cry.

The bouquet of roses, already shriveling in the heat, was fanned neatly across the seat, as if trying to taunt her.

Colin sat across from her in her living room, his elbows on his knees. Maria had called him right after throwing the roses back into the Dumpster, and he'd been waiting at her door when she got home.

"I don't get it," she said, still feeling flushed and panicky. "What does Ken want?"

"You know what he wants."

"And he thinks this is the best way to get it? By sending me flowers and a weird unsigned note? And by stuffing the roses back in my car and freaking me out?"

"I can't answer that," Colin said. "I think the real question is what you're going to do about it." He continued to hold her gaze, unmoving, but the tensing of his jaw made it clear that he was as disturbed by the whole thing as she was.

"I don't know that there's anything I can do. The note was unsigned and I didn't actually watch him put the roses in my car. I can't prove any of it."

"And you're positive it was Ken?"

"Who else could it be? There was no one else around."

"Are you sure?"

She opened her mouth to reply but quickly closed it because she hadn't even considered the alternative. Just because she hadn't seen anyone else didn't mean there actually had been no one else, but the idea was too frightening to contemplate.

"It's him," she said. "It has to be him." But even to her own ears, it almost sounded like she was trying to convince herself.

CHAPTER 15

Colin

Colin spent the night with Maria. Though she hadn't asked him to stay, he'd known that she hadn't wanted him to leave. She'd been on edge most of the evening, unable to eat, and he could sense her mind drifting off. After she'd finally fallen asleep, he lay awake staring at the ceiling, trying to put the pieces together. She'd told him enough about Ken to give Colin a pretty good picture, and he'd been fighting the urge ever since to pay the man a visit. The sexual harassment was bad enough, but Ken was a bully as well, and Colin knew from his own experience that people like that didn't stop abusing their power unless someone made them. Or put the fear of God into them.

However, Maria had made it clear that she didn't want Colin to talk to Ken or even go anywhere near him, if only for Colin's own good. Colin understood that: The man *was* a well-known lawyer, and even a credible threat might be enough to put Colin behind bars. He had no doubt that Margolis and the local judges would make sure of that.

Still, the situation had felt more confusing the more they'd talked about it. The note, combined with the fact that the roses had been placed in her car, felt like a *threat*. It felt *personal*, and while Ken had trouble controlling his libido and *had* been standing at the window, the rest of it didn't add up. What was the point of the note? How had Ken known Maria would decide to throw the roses away at that moment? Or if Ken had planned to put them in the car, why had he continued to stand in the window, knowing that Maria would no doubt assume he was guilty? He had to know that scaring Maria would make it more likely that she'd report his harassment. And what if another employee in the office had noticed him retrieving the roses from the garbage and placing them in Maria's car? Would he have been willing to take that kind of risk? Most of the offices had windows.

All of which meant...*what*? If Ken had done it, he'd slipped off the mental building ledge and was plummeting toward the ground, obviously unable to think clearly. And if it *wasn't* Ken?

That was the question that bothered him most.

When Maria woke in the morning, Colin offered to follow her in to work, but she told him that she'd be fine. It wasn't until he was driving back to Evan's that he realized he was as edgy about the whole thing as she'd been the night before. Angry, even, and as soon as he got home, he tossed on his workout gear and was out the door.

He went for a run and put the music volume on high, picking up his pace until his breathing grew labored. When he finally felt drained of his anger, he experienced a slowly emerging clarity.

He'd do what Maria asked and stay away from Ken, but that didn't mean that he was willing to sit back and do nothing.

No one was going to frighten Maria and get away with it.

"Have either of you considered calling the police?" Evan asked.

They were at the table in Evan's kitchen, a few minutes after Colin had offered Evan the CliffsNotes version of all that had happened, including what he planned to do.

Colin shook his head. "The police won't do anything."

"But someone broke into her car."

"Her car was unlocked, the windows were open, nothing was taken, and there was no damage. The first thing they'll ask is, what's the crime? And then they'll ask who did it, and all she'll be able to offer is her opinions."

"What about the message? Aren't there stalking laws?"

"The note is weird, but there's no clear threat. And there's no proof that the person who sent the flowers was the same person who put them in her car."

"I sometimes forget that you've had a lot of experience in this area. But I'm still not sure why you think you need to take care of it."

"I don't need to do it. I want to."

"And what if Maria doesn't like your plan?" When Colin didn't answer, Evan waved a hand. "Because you plan on telling her, right? Since you're all about honesty?"

"It's not that big of a deal."

"You didn't answer my question."

"Yes, I'll tell her."

"When?"

"Today."

"And if she asks you not to?"

When Colin didn't answer, Evan sat up straighter.

"You'll do it anyway. Because you've already made your decision, am I correct?"

"I want to know what's going on."

"You do know that this is what you've done in the past, right? Do whatever the hell you want, your future be damned?"

"I'm making phone calls. I'll talk to people." Colin shrugged. "It's not illegal."

"No argument there. But I'm talking about what you might decide to do afterwards."

"I know what I'm doing."

"Do you?"

When Colin didn't respond right away, Evan leaned back in

his seat. "Did I tell you that Lily wants the four of us to go out together this weekend?"

"No."

"She was thinking Saturday night. She wants to meet Maria."

"Okay."

"Shouldn't you check with Maria first?"

"I'll talk to her, but I'm sure she'll be fine with it. What are you thinking about doing?"

"Dinner. And then afterwards, we'll find someplace fun. I think all those lessons put her in the mood to go dancing."

"Salsa dancing?"

"She says I don't have the rhythm for it. It'll be some other kind of dancing."

"At a club?"

"Since you obviously escaped without trouble last time, Lily's of the opinion that you can do it again."

"Okay."

"I have another question, though." Colin waited as Evan stared across the table at him. "What happens if you do find the guy?"

"I'll talk to him."

"Even if it's her boss?" When Colin didn't answer, Evan shook his head. "I knew I was right."

"Right about what?"

"You don't have the slightest idea what you're getting into."

While Colin understood that Evan was worried, he didn't think his concern was justified. How hard could it be to figure out whether Ken sent the roses? All it would take was a few phone calls, some pointed questions, and a photo...Lord knows he'd been on the receiving end of countless interrogations, and he knew that getting answers was often about presence and expectation and sounding official. Most people wanted to talk; most people couldn't shut up, even when it was in their best interest. He figured that if he was lucky, he'd have his answer by midafternoon.

In the kitchen back at his place, he opened his computer and did a quick search for Ken Martenson. Not hard to find—the guy was even more connected than Colin expected—but there were fewer photos than he'd thought there would be, and none were what he really wanted; too far away, too blurry. Even the photo on the firm website had to be at least ten years old—at the time, Ken had a goatee, which altered his appearance to a significant degree. Colin would have to take his own photo, he decided. Except he didn't have a high-quality camera with a telephoto lens. He doubted whether Evan had a decent camera, either; Evan wouldn't have spent the money. The guy was tighter than a tick.

But Maria had one.

He called her cell and left a message asking if she was free for lunch. By the time she texted him back to see whether he could meet at half past noon, he was in class. But as he read her text, the professor droning on in the background, he realized that he'd been holding more tension in his neck than he'd noticed.

He forced himself to take deep, steady breaths.

"You want to borrow my camera?"

They were seated on the outdoor patio of a small café, waiting for their food to arrive. Though Colin hadn't eaten since the night before, he wasn't hungry.

"Yes." Colin nodded.

"Why?"

"I need a photo of Ken."

She blinked. "Excuse me?"

"The only way to know for sure who ordered the flowers is to find the florist. I can then show the florist the photo and ask if he's the one who bought them."

"What if he ordered by phone?"

"If he paid with a credit card, I'll get the name."

"They won't give it to you."

"Maybe. Maybe not. I'd still like to borrow your camera."

Maria debated before shaking her head. "No."

"Why not?"

"For starters, he's my boss. He also knows what you look like, and if he sees you, it's only going to get worse for me around there. Besides, I saw Ken this morning and I have the sense it's already over."

"You saw him?"

"He came to talk to Barney and me about one of our cases first thing in the morning. To let us know he'd heard that it was finally on the docket."

"You didn't mention that when I called..."

"I didn't know I had to."

He caught the first hint of frustration creeping into her tone. "How did he act?"

"It was fine," she stated. "He was normal."

"And you weren't bothered when he showed up?"

"Of course I was. My heart practically jumped out of my chest, but what could I do? Barney was right there. But Ken didn't try to talk to me alone, and he didn't spend any time with the paralegals, either. He was all business."

Colin clasped his hands together beneath the table. "With or without your camera, I'm going to find out who sent you the flowers."

"I don't need you to solve my problems, Colin."

"I know."

"Then why are we still talking about this?"

Colin kept his expression steady. "Because you still don't know with any certainty that Ken was the one who did it. You're making an assumption."

"It's not an assumption."

"Would it be so wrong to make sure?"

There was a time, Colin knew, when he wouldn't have given a damn about any of this. There was no reason to get involved. She was right, after all. It was her problem, and frankly, he had enough problems of his own.

However, Colin considered himself an expert in anger. And at its heart, that's what this was all about. At the hospital, he'd learned the differences between overt and covert anger; in his own life, he'd been well versed in both. At the bars, when he was in the mood to fight, his anger had been overt. His agenda was clear, with no hidden meanings, no shame, and no regret. In the first couple of weeks at the hospital, though, he hadn't been able to act out in any way if he became angry. The doctors had made it clear that if he became violent—if he so much as raised his voice—he'd end up in the acute care ward, which meant being stuck in a communal room with a dozen other people, and mandatory lithium in doses that made him feel dull, while doctors and nurses watched his every move. That was the last thing he wanted. Instead, he'd pushed his anger down, trying to keep it hidden, but after a while he realized that the anger didn't go away. Instead, it simply transformed from overt to covert. Subconsciously, he began to manipulate people; he sensed exactly what buttons needed to be pressed to piss someone off, and he jabbed at those buttons until they finally blew. One by one, others were sent to the acute care ward while he played innocent, until his doctor finally called him on what he'd been doing. Countless hours of therapy later, Colin finally understood that anger was anger, whether overt or covert, and equally destructive either way.

That's what someone was acting out here, he thought. Anger with the intent to manipulate. Whoever it was wanted Maria's emotions to start going haywire, and while it was covert for now, he sensed this was only the beginning.

To Colin's mind, that made Ken even less likely as a suspect, but then it was the only name he had. No choice but to start there. After Maria reluctantly handed him the key to her condo at the end of lunch, he drove to her place and retrieved the camera. He turned it on, making sure the batteries had enough juice, and ran through the various settings. Checked the zoom and took some shots off her balcony before realizing that he really needed to shoot faces to know how close he'd have to be.

After tucking the key into a planter pot near the door as instructed, he drove to the beach, where no one would think twice about a man with a camera. It wasn't crowded, but there were enough people around for him to get what he needed, and he spent an hour photographing people from various distances. In the end, he calculated that he could be no more than fifty yards away. Good, but not great. Ken might still be able to recognize him. He'd need a vantage point where he wouldn't be spotted.

Most of the historical buildings on either side of the block where Maria's office stood were two or three stories tall, with flat roofs. Cars lined both sides of the street, and though there were a few trees, none was big enough to hide behind. The foot traffic was not heavy but steady; remaining inconspicuous while hunkering down for an hour or more with a camera in hand was pretty much out of the question.

Raising his gaze, he focused on the buildings he'd just walked past, the ones opposite the office entrance. The distance was good and the angle was perfect, but it raised the question of how—or even if—he could get up there.

He recrossed the street, hoping to find a fire escape. Modern two- to three-story buildings didn't have them, and as soon as he reached the narrow alley that ran behind the block, he realized he was half-lucky. The buildings directly opposite the law office had no roof access, but the three-story building next to those had an old-fashioned drop-down ladder ten or eleven feet up that led to a metal landing on the second floor. Tough but not impossible to reach, and though the angle the building offered wasn't ideal, it was his best and only bet. Heading down the alley, he put the strap around his neck and tucked the camera beneath his shirt. He took a couple of explosive steps toward the wall, hoping to use it as a springboard to launch himself even higher and gain the last few inches he knew he'd need.

He did it just right, grabbing on to the bottom rung with both hands. With a hard jerk upward, he got one hand on the next rung up, repeating the process until he reached the landing. Thankfully, the ladder was attached to the building above that, and a few moments later, he was on the roof. Down on the street, no one appeared to have noticed him.

So far, so good.

He made his way to the corner closest to Maria's office. The lip of the roof was low—no more than six inches—but some cover was better than none. Thankfully the gravel was smooth here; there were no big pebbles, though these were scattered everywhere else. There were a bunch of gum wrappers though, and as he got into position on his stomach, he brushed those away. He aimed the camera and settled in to wait. To his surprise, he could actually see Maria as she worked at her desk in her office; he could also make out her car and, beyond that, the garbage bins. Her car was parked in her usual spot, and a few spots down he saw Ken's Corvette.

A bit more than an hour later, the first people in the office began to stream out, usually one at a time, but sometimes in pairs. Paralegals—and yes, as Maria had mentioned, all of them were attractive—a couple of guys in their forties, Maria's friend Jill. Several other people, followed a few minutes later by Maria. He followed her with the lens, thinking that she was moving more slowly than usual. When she reached the corner of the building, she glanced around, no doubt trying to find him. He watched her forehead form a frown before she finally headed to her car.

Focusing on the entrance again, he still saw no sign of Ken. Just when he began to wonder whether the onset of dusk would blur the detail he wanted, Ken finally pushed through the door. Colin held his breath, snapped off a dozen photos before Ken turned into the parking lot, then rolled to his side to examine the images, hoping that one or two would be good enough.

They were.

He waited until Ken pulled away before getting up and making his way down from the roof the same way he'd gone up. Again, no one appeared to notice him, and by the time he reached his car, dusk was settling in. He stopped at a drugstore on the way home and selected two of the photos for processing before heading back to Maria's.

He'd promised to bring her camera back.

"No wonder I couldn't find you," she said to him later, the photos on her kitchen table. "So tomorrow..."

"I'll start calling florists. And hopefully find out the truth."

"And if it was a phone order?"

"I'll tell them the truth. That you were wondering whether the wrong card was attached to the delivery. And that you're wondering who they're from."

"They might not tell you."

"I'm just asking for a name, not the number. I'd bet that most people would be willing to help."

"And when you find out that it was Ken?"

It was the same question that Evan had asked him earlier, and he'd pondered it on and off since then. "The decision as to what to do next would be yours."

She nodded, tight-lipped, before finally standing from the table and moving to the balcony doors. She stood before them, saying nothing for a long moment. Colin rose from his seat. When he was close, he put a hand on her lower back and felt something collapse beneath his touch.

"I'm just so tired of talking about it. I'm tired of even thinking about it."

"Let's get out of here and go do something that will take your mind off it."

"Like what?"

"How about I surprise you?"

Staring out the window of the Camaro as it sat between a couple of minivans, she made no move to get out of the car. "This is your surprise?"

"I thought it might be fun."

"Mini golf? Seriously?"

Maria eyed with obvious skepticism the cheery lights that surrounded the entrance. Beyond the glass doors she could make out an arcade; off to the left was the miniature golf course, complete with rotating windmills as part of what Colin guessed was a Scandinavian theme.

"Not just mini golf. It's glow-in-the-dark mini golf."

"And . . . I take it that you've mistaken me for a twelve-year-old?"

"It's a good distraction. And when was the last time you played?"

"I just told you. When I was twelve. Kevin Ross had his birthday party here. But he pretty much invited the entire sixth grade and my mom came, too, so it wasn't exactly a date."

"But it was memorable. Afterwards, if you want, we can try the laser maze."

"Laser maze?"

"I saw the banner a couple of months back when I was driving by. I think it's like that scene in *Get Smart* with Steve Carell, where you have to try crossing a room without breaking the beams." When she didn't answer, he went on. "I'd hate to think you're just afraid I might win and that's what this is all about."

"I'm not afraid of losing to you. If memory serves, I think I was the best in my class."

"Is that a yes?"

"You're on."

Friday morning, Colin woke early and was out the door before dawn. He put in a quick six miles and visited the gym before going online and gathering the phone numbers he needed. He'd been surprised to learn that Wilmington had more than forty florists, in addition to grocery stores that also sold flowers, which meant he'd be busy.

He felt good about the night before. Though it took Maria a few holes and a couple of lucky putts before she began to relax, by the time they'd finished, she was laughing and even dancing on the green after she sank a hole in one on the sixteenth hole to pull ahead for good. Hungry, they skipped the laser maze and he brought her to a roadside stand near the beach that specialized in fish tacos, which they washed down with ice-cold beer. He asked if she'd be willing to go out with Evan and Lily—she told him *of course*—and when she kissed him good night, he could tell that the evening had been just what she needed.

At the breakfast bar, he began making the first of his calls, hoping he'd be able to knock out the list in a couple of hours, only to realize that the person he needed to talk to wasn't always immediately available, which meant a second or even third call to the same number. Still, he ran through the explanation and questions he thought might work best: that the wrong card might have been attached; had a delivery been sent to the office; had a bouquet of pink roses even been assembled; and fortunately, most of the people he spoke with had been more than willing to help. By the time he had called all but a handful of shops, it was early afternoon and he'd begun to suspect that the last ones would say the same thing the others had said: that they hadn't been the florist who assembled or delivered the bouquet.

He was right. Wondering what to do next, he decided to try some out-of-town florists; the only question was which direction to choose. He chose north. He called both florists in Hampstead, then found another eighteen in Jacksonville.

On his sixth call, at a place named Floral Heaven near the gates of Camp Lejeune, he hit the jackpot. Yes, the owner told him, he remembered the man who'd ordered the bouquet. It had been a cash order, he added. Yes, the store would be open tomorrow, and he'd be there as well.

Later that night, as he was tending bar, Colin found his thoughts returning to the fact that someone had gone to an awful lot of trouble to try to hide his identity.

A thunderstorm rolled through on Friday night, bringing with it cooler temperatures. After finishing his run and doing some yard work on Saturday morning, Colin made the drive to Floral Heaven in Jacksonville, a little over an hour away. At the shop, Colin pulled out the photo of Ken and showed it to the man.

"This wouldn't happen to be the guy, would it?"

The owner, a portly man in his sixties with spectacles, took only a second before shaking his head. "The man in the photo is a lot older. The guy who bought them was maybe in his late twenties, not that I had that great a look at him."

"No?"

"He was kind of a strange guy, which is why I remember him at all. He wore a baseball hat and stared at the counter when he talked. Sort of mumbled. Just told me what he wanted and walked out the door. He came back an hour later, paid cash, and left."

"Did you happen to notice if he was alone?"

"I wasn't paying attention," he answered. "What's this all about again?"

"As I mentioned on the phone, there was a strange message written on the card."

"He didn't ask for a card. I remember that, too, because everyone always wants to write something. Like I said, he was a strange guy."

Colin's afternoon workout at the gym focused heavily on defensive work and grappling. Surprising him, Daly worked almost exclusively with him, pushing him harder than usual. In his day, Daly had been a beast when it came to ground work, and more than once, Colin found himself out of position, feeling like he was fighting for his life. By the time the workout ended, he realized that he hadn't thought about the guy in the baseball hat even once.

Whoever he was.

The preoccupation returned, however, as soon as he stepped out of the ring. Before he reached the locker room, Daly jogged over and pulled him aside.

"Can I talk to you for a couple of minutes?"

Colin used his still soaking shirt to wipe the sweat from his face.

"How would you feel about fighting next weekend? In Havelock." Before Colin could respond, Daly went on. "I know you're three weeks out, but I got a call earlier from Bill Jensen. You know Bill, right?"

"The promoter," Colin said.

"You know how much he's done for our fighters over the years... including you—and he's in a bind. Anyway, Johnny Reese is headlining the event, and the guy he was supposed to fight broke his hand a few days ago and had to scratch. Reese needs a new opponent."

As soon as Daly said the name, Colin remembered the conversation with Evan from the diner. *The dude moves like a cat.* Daly continued. "Jensen's been trying to find someone, and it turns out that you're the only guy in the weight class who actually might make it interesting. This is Reese's last fight before he goes pro, and he's got the goods. Former NCAA wrestling champ, getting better at striking, for the most part fearless. He actually has a shot at making it to the UFC in a year or two, which is why Jensen doesn't want to cancel. That's why I went so hard with you today. I wanted to know if you were ready to take him on."

"I'm not good enough for Reese."

"You had me on the defensive more than a few times today. Trust me, you're ready."

"I'll lose."

"Probably," Daly admitted. "But it'll be the best fight of his life to this point because you're better than you think you are." He twisted sweat from the bottom of his shirt. "I know I'm asking you to take a risk here, but it would help us out. You too. Jensen's the kind of guy who never forgets a favor. And you'd be helping us get some good publicity for my gym."

Colin wiped his face again before deciding, *Why the hell not?*

"Okay," he said. When he left the gym, his mind was on Johnny Reese. Yet he found himself strangely unexcited, and by the time he'd driven halfway home, he wasn't thinking about the upcoming fight at all. The only things on his mind were the man who had sent the roses and how someone other than Ken could have known Maria had thrown them away.

"That's quite the day," Evan commented. They were on the porch, Colin drinking water and Evan nursing a beer. "Reese, huh? He's pretty good."

"Thanks for avoiding the obvious."

"Oh, you mean about Maria and her stalker? That's what you want to talk about?" Evan paused before going on. "All right. Have you considered the idea that Ken might have hired the guy to buy and deliver the roses?"

"Then why get them from someplace an hour away?"

"Maybe the guy he hired is from there."

Colin took a long drink from his glass of water. "Maybe. But I don't think so."

"Why not?"

"Because I don't think Ken has anything to do with this."

Evan picked at the label on his bottle. "If it's any consolation, I think you're right. It isn't her boss. But on the plus side, all your private-investigator, stake-out-the-roof, and photography activities paid off in the end. Which means you're not a total idiot. Even if you're no closer to learning who it actually is."

"I learned something else, too."

"What's that?"

"I'll bet whoever it was watched Maria from that same spot on the roof where I took the picture."

"Why on earth would you think that?"

"Because the gravel had been smoothed out where I was, and there were gum wrappers littered around that hadn't blown away. Meaning that someone had been there recently. And from that vantage point, I could see directly into Maria's office. Same thing with her car and the Dumpster. Whoever it was could have spied on her for hours. I didn't put the pieces together until right before I talked to you."

For the first time, Evan was quiet. "Huh," he finally said.

"That's it?"

"Maybe you're right or maybe you're wrong. I don't have the answer for you."

"And now, I've got this fight next weekend."

"So?"

"I'm having second thoughts."

"Why?"

"Because of everything that's been going on with Maria."

"You train to fight. You like to fight. You've been offered a fight. What does any of that have to do with Maria?"

Colin opened his mouth to respond, but nothing came out.

"You know what? You give me crap all the time about how Lily has me wrapped around her little finger, but it's pretty clear that I have my relationship a lot more figured out than you do. Because right now, you're trying to live your life based on what might happen or whether you can solve her problem, even when she's told you she doesn't want you to. Do you know how messed up that is? You told me she wanted to watch you fight, right? Ask her to come, take her out for dinner afterwards, and call it a date. Boom. Problem solved."

Colin offered a partial smile. "I think you want me to fight because you're pretty sure I'm going to lose."

"And? Fine, I'll admit it—you're such an endless pain in the ass that it might be fun watching someone smack you around." When Colin laughed, Evan went on. "Good. So that's settled. On another note, are you excited about tonight?"

"Tonight?"

"You and Maria? With Lily and me? We had plans, remember? I made reservations at Caprice Bistro at seven thirty, and afterwards, we're hitting a club that's playing eighties music."

"Eighties music?"

"Is there an echo in here? Yes, eighties music. Lily's a closet Madonna fan. A leftover from her supposedly rebellious teenage years, she says. So we're doing this? As long as Maria's still game, I mean."

"Why wouldn't she be?"

"Maybe because you ruined her mood with what you learned?"

"I haven't told her yet."

"Mr. Honesty? I'm shocked."

"I was planning on telling her tonight."

"If you do that, make sure you don't make too big a deal about it. I don't need you putting a damper on the evening. For all you know, it was a one-time thing and it's over."

"Or maybe," Colin said, "it isn't."

CHAPTER 16

———— ❧ ————

Maria

Colin had been quiet since he'd picked her up, which made Maria nervous, given what he'd been up to for most of the day. Though he volunteered nothing, she knew he was thinking about the flowers. As she watched him respond to her small talk with a distracted air, she felt a pit growing in her stomach. By the time they pulled into the restaurant's parking lot, she couldn't contain herself any longer.

"Who sent the roses?"

He shut off the engine and told her what he'd learned.

She frowned, thinking about it. "If it wasn't Ken, and you don't think Ken hired him, then who is it?"

"I don't know."

She turned toward the passenger window. Beyond the glass, she watched an older couple walking into the restaurant, all smiles. *Without a care in the world.*

"I saw Ken again yesterday when I was meeting with Barney," she said in a wavering voice. "Other than the fact that he was acting a little distracted, he was completely professional. In fact, he barely seemed to notice me at all. It almost makes me think..."

That it's not Ken. She could tell by Colin's silence that he'd been able to complete her thought.

"Let's try not to worry about it tonight, okay?" he said.

She nodded, feeling the tension in her shoulders. "I'll try. It's hard not to."

"I know," he said. "But you should probably take a moment to prepare yourself for Lily. I adore her, but she does take some getting used to."

Maria forced a smile. "That's a backhanded compliment, you know."

"Guess who I learned it from?"

It took Maria only a second after entering the restaurant to identify Lily. Almost as soon as she and Colin had stepped through the door, a perfectly coiffed, ravishing blonde with eyes the color of turquoise glided toward them. She wore a stylish midlength dress and a strand of pearls. Practically every man in the restaurant turned to watch her pass. Evan, who was dressed preppy stylish and could have passed for someone still in college, trailed in her wake. Maria noticed his air of breezy confidence; he was clearly comfortable allowing Lily the limelight.

Lily's smile never faltered, and as soon as she got close, she took Maria's hands in her own. They were remarkably soft, like a silky baby blanket. "It is an absolute delight for me to have the pleasure of your company this evening! Colin has said so many wonderful things about you." By then, Evan had reached her side. "And oh, dear! Where are my manners? I'm Lily, and this handsome man beside me is my fiancé, Evan. It's so wonderful to meet you, Maria!"

"Hi there," Evan said with genuine warmth. "And please don't be offended if Lily doesn't let me get a word in the rest of the evening."

"Hush now, Evan," Lily scolded. "There's no reason to give our new friend the wrong impression about me." She returned her gaze to Maria. "Please try to forgive him. He's as sweet as can be and more intelligent than he lets on, but he went to *State* and he was in a *fraternity*. You know what that means."

"At least my university was coed," Evan countered.

"And as I've assured him repeatedly," she responded, nudging Maria, "I will never hold that flaw against him."

Despite herself, Maria smiled. "It's nice to meet you both."

Still holding Maria's hands, Lily turned to Colin. "Colin, you must admit that you weren't being fair to Maria at all when you told me about her! She's absolutely breathtaking!" Then back to Maria: "It's no wonder that you've been all that Colin has been able to think about lately. You must know that you've been the topic of discussion every time we've spoken in recent weeks, and I can certainly understand why." Letting go of Maria's hands, she kissed Colin on the cheek. "You're very handsome this evening. Did I buy you that shirt?"

"Thank you," Colin said. "And yes, you did."

"And that's a good thing, don't you agree? If I wasn't around, you'd probably be wearing one of those awful T-shirts with slogans on them."

"I like those shirts."

She patted his arm. "I know you do, bless your heart. Now, shall we head to the table? I've been on pins and needles all day and I want to know absolutely everything about the woman who already has you wrapped around her little finger."

"I'm not sure that's quite true," Maria protested.

"As true as due north. Colin—despite his stoic demeanor— is actually quite expressive in his emotions once you're familiar with them. Now, shall we?"

When she turned for the table, Colin shrugged at Maria, as if to say *I told you so.* While Maria had become acquainted with the Southern belle debutante phenomenon among the sorority girls at Chapel Hill, Colin was right: Lily took it to a whole new level. Maria initially assumed it to be partially an act, but as they settled into wide-ranging conversation over dinner, she gradually changed her mind. What was interesting was that as much as Lily could talk—and the girl could talk about *anything*—she could also draw out information simply by the way she *listened*. She had a way of leaning forward slightly and nodding when appropriate; making noises of empathy or sympathy, followed by probing questions. Maria never once had the sense that Lily was trying to think of the next thing she wanted to say while Maria was still talking, and to her surprise she even found herself telling Lily and Evan about the delivery of the roses and its aftermath. At that, the table went quiet, and Lily impulsively covered Maria's hand with her own.

Later, while the two women were freshening up in the restroom after dinner, Maria caught Lily's reflection in the mirror.

"I feel like I did most of the talking," Maria said. "I'm sorry about that."

"There is absolutely no reason to apologize. You have a lot going on in your life right now, and I'm flattered by your trust in us."

Maria added some lipstick before her voice softened. "You weren't surprised by what Colin did, were you? With the photo and tracking down where the roses came from?"

"No," Lily answered. "That's who he is. When he loves someone, he'll do anything for them."

"It feels like half the time, I'm still trying to figure him out."

"I'm not surprised," Lily said. "At the same time, since you were so honest with Evan and me, you must know that prior to dinner, my loyalties lay completely with Colin. I wanted to meet you so I could make sure that you were everything he said you were."

"You really care about him."

"I love him like a brother," Lily admitted. "He's very important to me. And I know what you're probably thinking. We couldn't be more different, and I didn't understand what Evan saw in him at first, either. All those tattoos and muscles and all the violence in his past..." Lily shook her head. "I must have visited Evan four or five times before I ever said a word to Colin, and when I finally did, the first thing that came out of my mouth was that I thought he should find a new place to live. And do you know what Colin said to me?"

"'Okay'?" Maria mimicked, and Lily laughed.

"He does that with you, too? Bless his heart. I have been trying to break that habit to no avail, but lately I've come to admit that it suits him. At the time, I do remember being offended. I complained to Evan and he promised to talk to Colin, but only on the condition that I talk to him first. Which of course I refused to do on principle."

"So who ended up breaking the ice? You or him?"

"Colin did. I'd purchased Evan a television for his birthday around that time, and it was in the trunk. Colin happened to come across me struggling with the box. He immediately offered to help. He brought it in and asked if I wanted to have it mounted or left in the box. Which was something I hadn't thought about. I told him that Evan would do it, but he sort of laughed and said that Evan wouldn't know how to do such a thing. The next thing I knew, he was on his way to the hardware store, and twenty minutes later, he was mounting it on the wall. He'd also picked up a big ribbon and bow, and it was that, more than anything, that made me wonder whether there was something about him that was worth getting to know. So we talked. It took about thirty seconds of asking him questions before I realized that he wasn't like anyone I'd ever met before."

"Colin said you recommended that he go back to college. And that you helped him with his studies."

"Someone had to. The poor man hadn't cracked a book in years. But he made it easy, because once he'd decided to go back, he was determined to do his best. And he's intelligent. Despite having moved from school to school, he must have picked up something along the way."

"And he's Evan's best man?"

Lily pulled a tissue from her purse and dabbed at her lipstick as she nodded. "Yes. Of course, my parents are absolutely aghast at the idea. As far as they know, he's Evan's friend, not mine, and they continually hint that I should keep my distance. The first time my daddy saw Colin, he actually flinched, and my mama has gone so far as to suggest that he shouldn't even be invited to the wedding, let alone be the best man. Even when I tell them that he's my friend, too, they pretend they didn't hear me say it. They are rooted in their ways and I will always be their precious child, bless their hearts."

"My mom and dad weren't too thrilled with Colin, either."

"It's understandable. But unlike my parents, I'll bet yours will give him a chance and eventually change their minds. I did, after all. Even now, I sometimes have trouble understanding it. In all candor, Colin and I don't have much in common."

"I'd have to agree."

Lily smiled, straightening her pearls before turning to Maria. "Still, there's something about that heartfelt honesty of his, coupled with not giving a damn about what other people think about him, that just gets to me."

Maria couldn't help smiling in agreement.

"You must believe me when I tell you," Lily added, "that he's much less rough around the edges than when I first met him. It's been an extraordinary effort on my part." She winked. "But there's no reason to thank me. You ready? I'm sure the lads are already pining for us."

"I don't think Colin pines."

"He's pining," she said. "He might not admit it, but he is."

"I wasn't pining," Colin said on the way to his car. Up ahead, Lily was walking with Evan toward his Prius. "I was talking to Evan about my fight."

"The one in Myrtle Beach?"

"No. The one next weekend."

"What fight?"

Colin filled her in, then added, "Evan will be coming. You should come, too."

"Will Lily come?"

"No," Colin said. "Fighting's not really Lily's thing."

"I'm surprised it's Evan's thing."

"He always goes to my fights. He enjoys them."

"Really? He doesn't seem the type."

"And what type is that?"

"People who resemble you," Maria teased. "Big muscles and tattoos, but mainly people who don't look like they'll faint at the first sign of blood."

He smiled. "Do you want to come?"

"Sure. But the same rule applies. You can't get too beat up or it'll bring back memories of the first night we met."

"Okay."

"You say that now, but the way you talked about Johnny Reese, you might not be able to guarantee it."

"No guarantees," he conceded. "What did you and Lily talk about when you were in the bathroom?"

"Mainly we talked about you."

"Okay."

"No follow-up questions?"

"No."

"How can you not be interested in what we said?"

"Because that was between you and Lily. It's not my business. And besides, it couldn't have been too bad, or you wouldn't still be holding my hand."

"So what kind of club are we going to?"

"All I know is that it plays eighties music. That's one of Lily's quirks. Evan told me that listening to Madonna was the way she rebelled when she was a teenager."

"Huh. Not much of a rebellion..."

"Not to you or me. But to Lily's parents? I'm sure they wrung their hands for years. They don't like me much."

"Maybe you should invite them to a fight," she said. "That'll probably change their minds." She heard him laugh as he opened her door, the sound continuing as he rounded the car to the driver's side.

Despite the blaring sound of REO Speedwagon, the scene at the club wasn't at all what she expected. Instead of divorced women and balding men in their forties trying to relive their youth, the club was populated primarily by students from the university; Maria half expected to spot Serena with her friends. Groups of college girls were dancing in clusters, singing or lip-syncing to the music.

Colin leaned closer to her ear. "What do you think?"

"I feel old," she admitted. "But I like the music."

Evan pointed toward the bar, and Colin nodded before reaching for her hand, maneuvering her around tables and groups of people to the thronged bar area. When they were finally able to get the bartender's attention, Colin ordered water—no surprise there—Evan ordered a beer, and both Maria and Lily ordered sea breezes. Halfway through their drinks, a song by Madonna started to play and a delighted Lily clapped before leading Evan to the floor. Suddenly thinking, *Oh, what the hell?*, Maria grabbed Colin's hand and they followed.

The evening sped by as they danced to sets of three or four songs in a row, stopping only for the occasional break. Maria ordered a second sea breeze, and though she hadn't finished the first, she felt giddy and flushed. For the first time in a week, she'd actually been able to enjoy herself.

At half past eleven, they were able to commandeer a small table for the first time. They were taking a break and debating how much longer to stay when a young cocktail waitress appeared holding a tray of drinks. She placed another sea breeze in front of Maria.

Maria waved it off. "I didn't order this."

"Your friend ordered it," the waitress explained, straining to be heard above the music.

Maria shot Colin a quizzical look. "You ordered another drink?"

When he shook his head, she turned to Evan, who seemed as surprised as Colin. Lily also appeared confused.

"Who ordered it?" Maria asked.

"Your friend from the bar," the waitress said, turning her head in that direction. "The one in the baseball cap." She leaned in. "He told me to tell you that he was upset that you didn't like the roses he sent you."

Maria gasped; a split second later, she saw a sudden movement as Colin jumped up from the table, causing his chair to tip over. In the moments that followed, Maria was only able to register a series of images, like snapshots caught in a strobe light:

Colin taking two steps toward the waitress, his jaw beginning to clench . . . closing in so quickly that she dropped the tray of cocktails . . .

Evan and Lily getting up from the table, their drinks sloshing over them . . .

Bar patrons turning their way at the commotion . . .

Colin demanding that the cocktail waitress tell him exactly who it was at the bar, ferociously angry, repeating the question . . .

The waitress backing away, terrified . . .

Bouncers beginning to move toward them . . .

Evan taking a step toward Colin, his hands raised . . .

Maria was frozen, rooted to her seat, the waitress's words ringing in her ear. *Baseball cap . . . He was upset you didn't like the roses . . .*

He was here. He'd followed her. He'd been following her all along . . .

It was hard for her to breathe, a waterfall of images, the world collapsing inward.

Bouncers pushing through the crowd, moving with frightening speed . . .

*Colin shouting, demanding to know more about the man who'd
ordered the drink . . .*

The waitress backing away, beginning to cry . . .

Bystanders beginning to surround them . . .

Evan pushing forward and grabbing Colin's arm . . .

Lily moving toward Maria . . .

Maria felt someone place both hands on her shoulders and
begin helping her from her seat. She didn't have the energy to
resist, and all at once, she realized that Lily had been the one
to whisk her to her feet. She could hear Colin shouting, even as
Evan continued to tug hard at Colin's arm, the waitress crying
out in terror, strangers circling, with bouncers close behind.

Stranger in blue shirt: "What the hell's going on?"

Colin, to the waitress: "What did he look like?"

Stranger with spiked hair: "Chill out! Leave her alone!"

*Waitress, through her tears: "I told you that I don't know! He was
wearing a hat! I don't know!"*

Stranger with tattoos: "What the hell's wrong with you?"

Evan: "We gotta go!"

Colin: "Was he young or old?"

Waitress: "I don't know! Twenties or thirties? I don't know!"

Evan: "Now, Colin! Come on!"

By then, Lily was leading Maria quickly from the table, and
out of the corner of her eye, Maria saw Evan jerk Colin off balance. Colin reacted instinctively, twisting free immediately and
quickly regaining his equilibrium, his hands ducking into fighting position. His face was red and tense, the muscles in his neck
taut; for an instant, he seemed not to recognize Evan.

"Colin! No!" Lily screamed. Evan took a step backward, and
as quickly as it had erupted, Colin's rage began to dissipate.

By then, the bouncers had reached them, and as Maria
watched, Colin slipped his hands behind his back, clasping
his left wrist with his right hand. A bouncer grabbed both his

arms, looking as angry and adrenaline-filled as Colin had been a moment earlier.

"I'll go with you," Colin said. "I'll go." Then, to the waitress, who was still crying, he said, "I apologize. I didn't mean to scare you."

But neither the waitress nor the bouncers cared; Colin was dragged outside and it was only a few minutes later that a squad car arrived, blue lights flashing. Shortly thereafter, a dark sedan pulled up.

"Who's that?" Maria asked, standing with Evan out front, arms crossed. Lily had gone back into the club a few minutes earlier. In the parking lot, Colin stood with two officers, one of the bouncers, and a man in a well-used sport coat who was chewing on a toothpick.

Evan's tone betrayed his concern. "Detective Margolis. He's been waiting for Colin to screw up again."

"Why?"

"Because he thinks Colin should be in prison."

"Is that going to happen?"

"I don't know," Evan said.

"But he didn't do anything," Maria protested. "He didn't even touch her."

"Thank God, or he'd be cuffed by now. And he still might be, unless Lily can work her magic."

"What's she doing?"

"Solving the problem," Evan answered. "That's what Lily does."

In time, Lily emerged through the front doors, stopping to shake hands with one of the bouncers who had dragged Colin out. She smiled ingenuously as she approached the officers.

Maria watched as Margolis caught sight of her and held up his hand to stop her. Lily ignored him, pressing on until she was close enough to be heard, and for an interminable few minutes, both Evan and Maria watched, wondering what Lily could possibly be saying to him. Eventually, one of the officers followed the bouncer back inside the club while Margolis and the other officer remained with Colin. Margolis was obviously furious, but still no move was made to cuff Colin. The events of the last half hour caused Maria's thoughts to ping-pong, wreaking havoc on her emotions. She'd been followed to the bar, which meant she'd been followed from the restaurant, which meant she'd been followed from home.

He knew where she lived and he'd followed her here.

Her breath caught, and she distantly registered Evan's voice.

"Are you okay?"

She squeezed her upper arms. She wanted Colin to hold her, yet she was angry that he'd lost control. Or was she afraid for him? She wasn't sure.

He knew where she lived and he'd followed her here.

"No," she admitted, realizing that she was shaking. "I'm not."

She felt Evan slip an arm around her.

"It's pretty messed up, that's for sure. If I were you, I'd be a wreck."

"What's going to happen to Colin?"

"He'll be all right."

"How do you know?"

"Because Lily looks calm and Margolis looks pissed."

Maria studied the two of them, realizing that Evan was right. But everything had gone wrong tonight.

A minute later, the officer who'd gone into the club returned to Margolis's side. They spoke for a couple of minutes before both officers reluctantly headed back to their squad car. By then, Lily was hurrying toward Evan and Maria. Evan let go of Maria to encircle Lily in his arms.

"No charges," she said. "They're letting him go."

"What did you do?" Maria asked.

"I spoke to the waitress and the manager, and I simply told them the truth," Lily replied. "That you were being stalked, and that Colin overreacted because you've been frightened, and Colin thought you might be in danger. They were surprisingly sympathetic. Especially once I gave the waitress an extra-large tip, paid for the drinks that were spilled, and offered the manager a little extra for his trouble."

Maria stared at her. "You bribed them?"

"I did no such thing. I merely did my best to rectify the situation in a way that satisfied everyone involved. By the time the officer came to speak with them, they were both adamant that no charges be filed. Still, I will admit there was a moment when I wasn't sure it was going to work again."

"Again?"

"It isn't the first time this has happened," Evan said.

Margolis dogged Colin's footsteps as Colin approached their group. To others, Colin probably appeared as controlled as he always did, but she noticed something in his expression that hinted at an understanding of how close he'd come to losing it all. He moved to her side as Margolis studied each of their faces. Colin stared back, unfazed, as did Evan and Lily.

"The dynamic duo strikes again," Margolis sneered. "How much did it cost you this time?"

"I don't have any idea what you're talking about," Lily lied sweetly, her accent as sultry as ever.

"Of course you don't," Margolis said. "I wonder what the manager and the waitress would say if I put them under oath." He let the comment hang, with all its implications, before finally going on. "But there's no reason for that, is there? Now that you've rescued your good friend Colin again."

"There was no need to rescue him," Lily drawled. "He did nothing wrong."

"That's funny. Because I recall something like this happening on at least two other occasions when you two were there."

Lily feigned confusion. "Are you speaking of those other occasions when Colin happened to be out with us and, again, did nothing wrong?"

"Keep telling yourself that. You're just postponing the inevitable. Colin knows who he is. Just ask him. He'll tell you." He turned toward Colin. "Isn't that right, Colin? Since you like to convince everyone you're as honest as the day is long?...Even though you're always on the verge of exploding."

Maria saw Colin's eyes narrow as Margolis jerked his head at Evan. "You need to thank Evan here for pulling you away when he did. Had even one of those guys around you touched you, you and I both know that we would suddenly be spending a lot of time together, with you back in the cage and me telling the DA to throw away the key."

"Colin didn't touch anyone," Evan interjected.

Margolis shifted the toothpick to the other side of his mouth. "I was thinking more along the lines of assault. I was told the waitress was terrified by the fact that Colin was screaming at her, and I've got a dozen witnesses in there who could vouch for that."

"He just wanted to know who sent over the drink," Maria protested.

As soon as Margolis's eyes met hers, she felt herself flinch. "Oh, that's right. Because of the so-called stalker, right? I'll make sure to review the report for you." Maria said nothing, regretting she'd chimed in.

"Oh, wait. You haven't filed a report? Have you even talked to a lawyer?"

"She is a lawyer," Lily said.

"Then it's even stranger, don't you think? All lawyers do is file reports." He turned toward Maria. "I'll tell you what, though; if you ever do get around to it, ask for me, okay?"

"Leave her out of this," Colin growled.

"Are you telling me what to do?" Margolis demanded.

"Yes," Colin said.

"Or what? Are you going to hit me?"

Colin continued to stare at him before reaching for Maria's hand. "Let's go," he said, beginning to walk away, Evan and Lily close behind.

"Go ahead," Margolis called out from behind them. "I'll be around."

"How much do I owe you?" Colin said.

"Let's worry about that later, okay?" Lily answered.

They'd followed Evan and Lily back to Evan's place, the four of them congregating on the front porch. It had been a quiet ride, Maria's thoughts too fragmented for conversation, and Colin in no mood to break the silence. Even now, Maria felt like an observer to her own life.

"What the hell were you doing tonight?" Evan demanded. "We've talked about this! And Margolis is right! What would have happened if Lily and I hadn't been there?"

"I don't know," Colin answered.

"You damn well know exactly what would have happened!" Evan ran a hand through his hair. "Why the hell do you keep doing this? You've got to learn to control this thing."

"Okay."

"Don't say okay!" Evan shouted. "Like Lily, I'm sick of you saying that all the time, because it's a cop-out! I thought we'd gotten past this last year, after that guy accidentally spilled his drink on Lily."

"You're right," Colin said evenly. "I made a mistake. I lost control."

"Gee, *really?*" Evan spat out. He turned, starting for the front door. "Whatever. You two deal with him for now. I'm done." The door slammed behind him, leaving the three of them on the porch.

"You know that Evan's right, Colin," Lily said.

"I wasn't going to hurt her."

"That doesn't matter," she said, her voice soft. "You're big and strong, and when you're angry, people can sense the innate violence within you. The poor waitress was cowering and crying and you wouldn't let up until Evan put everything he had into pulling you away. And then, I was almost certain you were going to hit him."

Colin's gaze dropped to the ground before slowly coming up again, and for a moment, his confidence was gone. In its place Maria saw shame and remorse, maybe even a flash of hopelessness.

"It won't happen again."

"Maybe," Lily said, kissing him on the cheek. "You said that the last time, too."

She turned toward Maria and offered a hug. "And I'm absolutely certain that all of this must feel both overwhelming and terrifying to you. If someone was stalking and taunting me, I would have already been off to Charleston by now to hide out with my parents, and knowing them, they'd send me out of the country. I'm just so sorry for what you're going through."

"Thank you," Maria said. Suddenly exhausted, she barely recognized the sound of her own voice.

"Would you like to come inside?" Lily asked when she pulled back. "I'm sure Evan is calmer by now, and we can work through some options or ideas...or we can just sit and listen if you feel like you need to talk."

"I wouldn't even know what to say," she said.

Lily understood, and with a gentle click of the door as it closed behind her, Maria and Colin were alone on the front porch.

"I'm sorry, Maria," he mumbled.

"I know."

"Would you like me to bring you home?"

In either direction, most of the houses were already dark.

"I don't want to go home," she said in a small voice. "He knows where I live."

Colin stretched out his hand. "C'mon," he said. "You can stay with me."

Leaving the porch, they walked around the side of the house, toward the downstairs entrance. Once inside, Colin turned on the lights as he led the way. Hoping for any distraction from the lingering knot in her stomach, she took in the room. Average sized, with a kitchen off to the right and a small hallway directly ahead that no doubt led to the bedroom and bath. Surprisingly neat, without clutter piled on the coffee table or on the counters. Neutral color scheme for the furniture, with no photographs or personal items, like no one lived here at all.

"This is your place?"

He nodded. "For now. Can I get you something to drink?"

"Just water," she said.

Colin filled two glasses in the kitchen, bringing one of them to her. She took a sip, suddenly remembering that she was being followed and seeing again Colin's anger as he'd demanded answers from the waitress, his muscles tense. She remembered the split second after Evan had jerked him off balance and the utter wildness and uncontrollable fury in his expression.

"How are you feeling?" he finally asked.

She tried to force the image away and realized that she couldn't. "Not good," she said. "Not good at all."

Neither of them seemed to know what to say to the other in the living room, nor later, when they were in bed together. Instead, simply needing to be held, Maria rolled over, resting her head on Colin's chest, conscious of the lingering tension in his body.

She'd hoped that by staying here, with Colin beside her, she'd feel safe.

But she didn't feel safe. Not anymore. And as she lay awake, staring into the darkness, she was beginning to wonder whether she ever would again.

In the morning, Colin drove Maria home and waited in the living room while she showered and changed, but he didn't join her for brunch at her parents'. He understood that right now, she needed to be alone with her family, a haven of stability and predictability amid a life that suddenly felt wildly off course. He walked her to her car and while they embraced, she found herself holding back slightly.

At the house, her parents were oblivious, but Serena figured out something was bothering Maria as soon as she stepped inside, something Maria didn't want to share with her parents. Serena played along perfectly, maintaining a stream of commentary as they cooked and ate, filling any silences with the sound of her voice and keeping the conversation from drifting toward anything serious.

Afterwards, Maria and Serena went for a walk. As soon as they reached a safe distance from the house, Serena turned and said, "Spill it." On a bench beneath an elm tree with leaves that had begun to turn gold, Maria told Serena everything that had happened, reliving the terror of the past several days, and when she started to cry, Serena began to cry as well. Like Maria, Serena was upset and scared; like Maria, she had more questions than answers. Questions at which Maria could only shake her head.

After lunch, Serena and her parents headed off to Maria's uncle's house, an informal family get-together like countless others, but Maria begged off, claiming she had a headache and wanted to take a nap. While her dad accepted the explanation without question, Maria's mother was dubious, though she knew enough not to press her. On the way out the door, she hugged Maria longer than usual and asked how things were going with Colin. The sound of his name brought a sudden wellspring of tears, and on her way to the car, Maria thought, *I've officially become a basket case.*

Even concentrating enough to drive was strangely difficult. Despite the traffic, all she could think was that someone was watching her, waiting for her to return . . . or maybe he was even following her now. Impulsively, she changed lanes and made a quick turn onto a side street, her eyes glued to the rearview mirror. She turned again, then once more before finally pulling over. And though she wanted to be strong—pleaded with God to help her be strong—she found herself bent over the steering wheel, sobbing.

Who was he and what did he want? The nameless, faceless man in the baseball cap—why hadn't she looked for him? All she remembered were shadows and fragments, nothing at all . . .

But there was more, too, something that kept her anxious and on the verge of tears. Without thinking, she put the car in gear and started driving, eventually making her way to a quiet stretch of Carolina Beach.

The day was cool and the breeze held the nip of the coming winter as she walked the sand. Clouds had rolled in, white and gray, and it felt like impending rain. The waves rolled in calming rhythm, and as she walked, she finally felt her thoughts beginning to settle long enough for a bit of clarity to emerge.

She wasn't on edge simply because she was being followed. Nor was she merely reliving the fears she'd felt *for* Colin as he'd stood with the police officers with the rest of his life hanging in the balance. She saw now that she was also afraid *of* Colin, and as sick as the thought made her feel, she couldn't push the feeling away.

Knowing that she needed to talk to Colin, Maria drove to Evan's. When Colin opened the door to his apartment, she saw that he had been studying at the small kitchen table. Though he invited her in, she declined, the interior of his place appearing suddenly claustrophobic. Instead, they went to Evan's porch, each taking a seat in a rocking chair as the rain began to fall.

Colin perched on the edge of his seat, forearms resting on his legs. He looked tired, the last twenty-four hours obviously taking a toll. He did nothing to break the silence, and for a moment, Maria wasn't even sure where to begin.

"I've been on edge ever since last night," she ventured, "so if I'm not making much sense, it's probably because my thoughts are still jumbled." She drew a breath. "I mean, I know you were just trying to help me. But Lily was right. Even though I believe you when you say that you weren't going to hurt the waitress, the way you were acting told a different story."

"I almost lost control."

"No," she said. "You *did* lose control."

"I can't control my emotions. The only thing I can control is my behavior, and I didn't touch her."

"Don't try to minimize what happened."

"I'm not trying to minimize it."

"What if you get angry with me?"

"I would never hurt you."

"And like the waitress, I might end up terrified and in tears anyway. If you'd acted like that toward me, I'd never want to talk to you again. And then, with Evan..."

"I didn't do anything to Evan."

"But had it been anyone else who grabbed you—a guy you didn't know—you wouldn't have been able to stop, and you know it. Just like Margolis said." She made sure to hold his gaze. "Or are you going to lie to me for the first time and say I'm wrong?"

"I was scared for you. Because the guy was there."

"But what you did didn't make it better."

"I just wanted to find out what he looked like."

"And you don't think I do?" she said, raising her voice. "But tell me this—what if he'd still been there? Just sitting at the bar? What would you have done then? Do you honestly believe that you were capable of having a reasonable conversation with him? No. You would have overreacted, and right now, you'd be in prison."

"I'm sorry."

"You already apologized." She hesitated. "As much as we've discussed your past and as much as I thought I knew you, I realize that I don't. Last night, you weren't the guy I fell in love with, or even a guy I would have dated. Instead, I saw someone that—in my past—I would have gladly put away."

"What are you trying to say?"

"I don't know," she said. "All I know is that I don't have the energy to start worrying that you'll do something dumb and throw your life away, or that you'll end up frightening me because something inside you suddenly switches on."

"It's not your job to worry about me."

At his comment, she flushed, all her fears and anxieties and anger rising to the surface like an air bubble moving through water.

"Don't be a hypocrite! What the hell do you think all that was about last night? Or the past week, for that matter? You hid out on a roof for hours to take pictures of my boss, called every florist in the city, and drove two hours to show a stranger a photograph! You did that because *you* were worried about *me*. And now you're saying that *I'm* not allowed to worry about *you*? Why is it okay for you to worry, but not for me—"

"Maria—"

"Let me finish!" she demanded. "I told you that what was happening to me wasn't your problem! I told you to let it go! But you were dead set on doing whatever the hell you wanted...And okay, maybe you did talk me into letting you take the photos. Because you made it sound like you knew what you were doing—like you could handle it. But based on last night, you obviously can't! You were almost arrested! And then what would have happened? Do you have any idea what that would have done to me? How I would have felt?"

She pressed her fingers to her eyelids and was trying to organize her thoughts when she heard her cell phone ring. Pulling it from her pocket, she recognized Serena's number and wondered why she was calling. Hadn't she said something about going on a date?

She answered and instantly heard the panic in Serena's voice, the words spilling out in rapid Spanish.

"Come home now!" Serena sobbed before Maria could say a single word.

Maria felt her chest constrict. "What's wrong? Is Dad okay? What happened?"

"It's Mom *and* Dad! Because of Copo! She's dead!"

CHAPTER 17

Colin

Colin worried that Maria was too shaky to get behind the wheel, so he drove her car to her parents' house, trying to read her mood as she stared out the rain-splattered window. Between her sobs, Serena hadn't been able to tell Maria much—no one really knew anything other than that Copo was dead. As soon as they pulled into the driveway, Maria rushed into the house, Colin trailing behind. Her parents sat holding each other on the sofa, haggard and red-eyed. Serena stood near the kitchen, wiping at her tears.

Felix stood from the couch as soon as Maria entered, and they both began weeping. Soon the whole family was standing with their arms around each other, crying while Colin stood quietly in the doorway.

When their tears abated, they all collapsed on the couch, Maria continuing to hold her father's hand. They were speaking in Spanish, so he couldn't follow much of the story, but he heard more than enough to let him know that the dog's death had made no sense at all.

Later, he sat with Maria on the back porch and she caught him up on what she'd learned, which wasn't much. Her parents and Serena had gone to their relatives' after brunch, and while normally they'd bring the dog, there were going to be a lot of kids there, and they'd been worried that Copo might get overwhelmed, or worse, accidentally hurt. Serena had returned to the house an hour later because she'd left her cell phone charging on the kitchen counter. When Serena saw Copo lying near the back slider—which had been left open—she assumed the dog was sleeping. But when the dog hadn't moved by the time she was about to leave, Serena called out to her. Copo didn't respond, so Serena went to check on her, only to realize that the dog had died. She called her parents, who drove straight home, and then Maria.

"Copo was fine before they left. She'd eaten and wasn't acting sick. There was nothing for her to have choked on, and my dad didn't find anything in her throat. There wasn't any blood or vomit..." She drew a shaky breath. "It's like she died for no reason, and my dad...I've never seen him cry before. He brought her everywhere; they hardly ever left her alone. You can't understand how much he loved that little dog."

"I can only imagine," he said.

"Maybe," she said. "But still...you have to understand that in the village my parents came from, dogs work or herd or spend time with you in the field, but they aren't regarded as pets. My father never understood the American love affair with dogs. Both Serena and I begged for a dog when we were younger, but he was adamantly opposed. And then, when Serena and I left home, there was suddenly a gigantic void in his life...At some point someone suggested they get a dog, and this time, it was like a light suddenly went on for him. Copo was like his child, but more obedient and devoted." She shook her head, quiet for a moment. "She's not even four years old. I mean...can a dog just...die? Have you ever heard of that happening before?"

"No."

She'd expected the answer, but it didn't help, and her thoughts

circled back to the reason she'd needed to talk to him. "Colin...
About what we were talking about earlier..."

"You were right. About everything."

She sighed. "I care about you, Colin. I love you and want nothing more than to be with you, but..."

The word *but* hung heavy in the air. "I'm not who you thought
I was."

"No," she said. "You're exactly who I thought you were, and
you warned me right up front. And I thought I could handle it,
but last night, I realized that I don't think I can."

"What does that mean?"

She tucked a strand of hair behind her ear. "I think that for
right now, it might be best to slow things down a bit. Between
us, I mean. With all that's going on..." She didn't finish. But she
didn't have to.

"What are you going to do about the guy following you?"

"I don't know. It's hard for me to even think straight right now."

"That's what he wants. He wants you worried and afraid, constantly on edge."

She pushed her hands into her hair, kneading her temples.
When she spoke, her voice was ragged. "Right now, I feel like I'm
stuck in this awful dream and all I want to do is wake up...And
on top of everything else, I have to support my parents. My dad
wants to bury Copo tonight, and that's only going to make him
even more emotional. My mom, too. And this rain...Of all the
weekends for Copo to die, why this one?"

Colin peered out at the backyard. "How about I help get things
ready?"

Maria brought him a shovel from the garage, and after a little
back-and-forth between Maria and Felix, Colin started digging a
hole in the shade of an oak tree, rain soaking through his shirt.
He remembered doing the same thing for his own dog, Penny, a

long-haired miniature dachshund. The dog had slept with him in bed when he'd still been living at home, and while at school he'd missed her more than his family.

He remembered how hard it had been to dig the grave the summer after his sophomore year; it was one of the few times he could recall crying since the first year he'd been sent away. With every shovelful of dirt, he'd had a memory of Penny—running through the grass or nipping at a butterfly—and he wanted to spare Felix that.

The task also got him away from Maria. He understood her need for space right now, even if he didn't like thinking about the reason. He knew he'd screwed up royally, and right now, she was probably trying to figure out whether Colin was worth the risk.

When Colin finished digging the pit under the tree, the family buried Copo. Again, all four of them cried and exchanged hugs. And after they went back inside, Colin began to shovel the dirt back in place, his thoughts returning to the stalker and the fact that Maria was being followed. He wondered what the stalker's next move might be. And he decided then and there that whether Maria wanted him in her life or not, he would be there if she ever needed him.

"Are you sure?" Maria asked him, standing with him on the front porch. "I'd be happy to drive you home." Inside, Carmen and Serena were making dinner. Felix, as far as Colin knew, was still on the back porch, sitting alone and holding Copo's collar.

"I'll be okay. I need to run anyway."

"But it's still raining."

"I'm already wet."

"Isn't it kind of far? Like five or six miles?"

"You need to stay here with your family," he said, and for a moment, neither of them said anything. "Can I call you?" he finally asked.

Her gaze flickered toward the house before returning to him. "Why don't I call you?"

He nodded before taking a step backward, and without another word, he turned and began to run.

Maria didn't call for the rest of the week, and it was the first time in his life that he cared enough about a girl for that to actually matter to him. Or enough for him to even think about it in unexpected moments, or whenever the phone rang—which wasn't often.

He wasn't going to call her. He wanted to; more than once, he'd actually reached for his phone before reminding himself she'd asked him not to. Whether she eventually called or not was her choice.

To keep from dwelling on it, he tried to stay busy. He added an extra shift at work, and after his classes and before his shifts, he spent time at the gym, working with Daly and Moore.

They were more excited about the upcoming fight than he was. While fighting someone like Reese was a rare opportunity to measure his own skill level, win or lose, it wouldn't mean much for him in the long run. For Daly and Moore, a good match might mean a minor windfall for the gym. No wonder they spent the first two hours on Monday reviewing films of Reese's former fights with Colin, studying his tendencies and evaluating strengths and weaknesses.

"He's good, but he's not unbeatable," Daly continued to insist, Moore in agreement. Colin listened while trying to tune out comments that he regarded as too wishful or optimistic—basically, anything that had the words *Reese* and *ground* in the same sentence. Reese would eat him alive on the ground.

On the plus side, the films showed that Colin's skills were slightly better than Reese's when it came to striking. Especially kicks; to that point in his career, not a single fighter had gone after Reese with kicks to the knees, despite Reese offering numerous opportunities. Reese also left himself open to shots at the ribs after any combination, which was useful to know when planning a strategy. The problem was that when the fight actually started, strategies often went right out the window, but that's where— according to Daly and Moore—Colin had the biggest advantage.

"Reese hasn't ever fought anyone with more than six or seven fights under his belt, which meant his opponents have been both outclassed and intimidated. You won't be intimidated, and that will rattle him more than anything."

Daly and Moore were right. Fighting—whether in bars, the street, or even the ring—wasn't only about skill but confidence and control as well. It was all about waiting for the right moment and then taking advantage of it; it was about experience when adrenaline was pumping, and Colin had had more *fights* than Reese. Reese had been an athlete, someone who shook hands with his opponent after a match; Colin was the kind of guy who struck first and broke beer bottles over people's heads at the end, the sole intent to cause as much damage as quickly as possible.

With that said, Reese was undefeated for a reason. On his best day, Colin figured he had only a one-in-four chance of winning, and that was only if he was able to make it through the first couple of rounds. The kicks to the knees and rib shots, the coaches continued to assure him, would wear Reese down the longer the fight went on.

"The third round will be yours," they promised.

On Tuesday, Wednesday, and Thursday, they got to work, with an hour and fifteen minutes each day devoted to specific strikes. Daly got in the ring wearing sturdy knee braces and a vest, demanding that Colin make kicks to the knees, offering openings and then taking them away. Simultaneously, Moore instructed Colin to keep his distance and concentrate on the ribs after every combination Daly threw, their exhortations heated and demanding. In the last forty-five minutes, Colin focused on ground work, honing defensive techniques. They were all fully aware that Reese had a significant advantage in this area, and the best that Colin could hope for was to survive.

He'd never trained for a specific opponent, and it proved frustrating. He missed with kicks and was too slow with strikes to the ribs; all too often, he allowed himself to get tied up, which was exactly what Reese would want. It wasn't until Thursday that the lightbulb flickered on, albeit dimly, and when he walked out of the gym, he wished he had another couple of weeks to get ready.

Friday was a rest day, the first day that Colin hadn't worked out in over a year, and he needed the break. Everything hurt. With no classes, he spent the morning and afternoon completing two papers. Later, at work, with cooler temperatures setting in, hardly any customers showed up on the rooftop, even during the dinner rush. By nine, there were no patrons at all, and Colin had the place to himself. Tips had been almost nonexistent, but it gave him time to reflect on the previous weekend. Or, more specifically, the question Maria had asked that had been plaguing him on and off ever since.

Of all the weekends for Copo to die, why this one?

There was nothing to suggest that the guy who was following Maria was responsible for Copo's death, but there wasn't anything that rendered the idea implausible, either. If the guy knew where Maria lived, it was more than conceivable he also knew where her parents lived. The back slider had been left open. Copo had been fine when they left, and three hours later the dog was dead for no apparent reason. Colin knew it wouldn't have taken much to have snapped Copo's neck or choked the dog to death.

Or, on the other hand, the dog could have died a natural, if unexplained, death.

He wondered whether the same terrible thoughts had occurred to Maria; if so, she would also suspect that the stalking had escalated to a new level, and he wondered whether she would call him. If not as her lover, then as a friend who'd promised to be there for her.

Colin checked his phone.

She hadn't called.

Colin spent Saturday morning trying to get ahead in his reading, though by noon, he wasn't sure why he'd even bothered. Nerves kept him from recalling anything of substance. He wasn't hungry, either; it had been all he could do to force down a couple of protein smoothies.

The feeling of nerves was new to him. He reminded himself that he didn't care about winning, but at the same time, he also admitted he was lying to himself. If he didn't care how he did in the ring, why watch everything he ate or drank? Why train two or three times a day? And would he have agreed to spend all week preparing for Johnny Reese?

Fact was, he hadn't yet walked into the cage thinking he'd lose a fight. Amateurs were *amateurs*. But Reese was different. Reese could give him a beat-down if Colin made a single wrong move; Reese was just plain better.

Unless my strategy pays off . . .

He felt a sudden, unexpected surge of adrenaline. Not good. Too early. He'd be wasted before the fight even started, and he had to get his mind off it. Best way to do that was to go for a run to clear his mind, even if his coaches would want him to conserve his energy.

Too bad. He ran anyway. It was only partly successful.

Hours later, Colin sat alone in the makeshift dressing room. He'd been weighed, as had his gloves. Daly made sure that the amount of athletic tape on his hands met regulations. Colin opted to wear a cup, and his shoes were inspected by officials. Tons of rules, even at the amateur level. There were only ten minutes before his fight began, and he'd asked Daly and Moore to leave him, even though he knew they wanted to stay.

Their attitude pissed him off. In the minutes leading up to any fight, pretty much everything and everyone pissed him off, which was just what he wanted. He thought about knee and rib strikes; he thought about keeping Reese rattled and owning the third round. Already the adrenaline was making every muscle taut, his senses heightened. Beyond the walls, he heard the roar of the crowd, then heard as it became even louder. No doubt a fighter was exerting his will over another, the match clearly coming to an end, an opponent getting pummeled . . .

Colin drew a long breath.

Showtime.

The next thing he knew, he was face-to-face with Reese at the center of the cage, each of them sizing the other up while the referee went over the rules: no biting, no kicks to the nuts, et cetera. As they stared at each other the world began to shrink, sounds diminishing, and then the fighters were released to their corners. Daly and Moore shouted encouragement, but Colin only vaguely registered their voices. The bell sounded, and he stepped forward.

Colin landed a kick to Reese's knee within the first twenty seconds, then another two quickly after that. All three shots seemed to catch Reese off guard, and when Colin hit the knee a fourth time, he saw Reese's first flash of anger. A fifth kick to the knee came next, and Reese began keeping his distance, already having deciphered part of Colin's plan. They traded blows for the next couple of minutes, with Colin landing three quality shots to the ribs and one more hard kick to the knee. Reese's boxing skills were about what Colin had expected, but his punches were harder, and when Reese landed a shot to Colin's temple, Colin saw stars and ended up on his back. Reese was clearly in control, but Colin was able to hold his own defensively until the bell sounded. Both fighters were breathing hard.

According to Daly, the round could go either way, though he thought Colin had the advantage.

The second round followed roughly the same pattern: Colin landed three more kicks to the knee, with Reese noticeably wincing after the final shot; Colin hammered on Reese's ribs whenever the opportunity presented itself. Two-thirds of the way through, they were on the ground again, with Reese landing a couple of strong blows while Colin did everything he could to defend himself. In the final twenty seconds, Reese's elbow connected with the bridge of Colin's nose and opened up a gash. Blood seeped into his eye, he lost concentration, and Reese took advantage, twisting his leg until Colin nearly had to tap. Colin knew as he returned to his corner that while he hadn't been completely dominated, he'd lost the round.

He also noticed that Reese was limping badly as he made his way back to his corner.

Colin attacked the knee again to open the third round, then jabbed and feinted a couple of rushes, returning to the knee repeatedly. On the final kick, Reese winced hard and instinctively bent over; Colin moved in and went hard to the ribs. Out of position, Reese tried to lock up Colin, but Colin brought up his knee, felt it connect with Reese's forehead, and for the first time in the match had Reese on his back and seriously in trouble.

Colin went as hard as he could, striking with his fists and elbows. Reese hadn't been in this position very often, and Colin could sense him begin to panic. Colin continued to strike, landing more blows with as much force as possible. Reese took a hard shot to the jaw and his body went slack; Colin landed three more shots that left Reese stunned. Colin pressed his advantage, and as the round ticked toward its close, Reese made a tactical mistake. Colin was nearly able to end the fight with an arm bar, only to have Reese somehow wiggle free. Precious seconds ticked by before Colin maneuvered Reese into position for another arm bar. Just as Colin began to apply pressure, the bell sounded, the referee jumped in, and the fight was over.

Colin reluctantly rose, only to see Daly and Moore pumping their fists; in their minds, it was clear who'd won the fight. Reese's, too; as he rose, he avoided Colin's eyes.

The judges, however, didn't score it that way. When Reese's arm was raised in victory by a plainly skeptical referee, Colin knew that he'd just been handed his first defeat. Colin shook Reese's hand and Daly and Moore charged into the ring. The crowd began to boo and catcall.

Colin tuned it all out; he was spent. He left the cage and headed toward the locker room alone, only mildly disappointed and not terribly surprised.

"If it's any consolation, you don't look nearly as bad as you did after your last fight," Evan noted. As was becoming a custom after Colin's fights, they were at a sketchy roadside diner, Evan watching Colin eat. "Just that little cut on the bridge of your nose, but other than that, you're good. Which is definitely an improvement. Last time, you could have passed for Rocky after the fight with Apollo Creed. And that guy sucked."

"He head-butted me."

"He might have cheated in the fight, but unlike tonight, the decision in that one was fair. You know you kicked his ass, right? It wasn't even close. The crowd knew it, and so did the referee. Did you see his face when they announced Reese?"

"No."

"He couldn't believe it. Even Reese's coach was shocked."

Colin used his fork to slice into his pancakes and stabbed a mouthful. "Okay."

"If it had gone on another twenty seconds, Reese would have tapped out. Maybe ten. There was no way he was stopping that last arm bar because he was toast by then. The guy could barely do anything at that point."

"I know."

"Then why aren't you more upset? Your coaches are pissed as hell. You should be pissed, too."

"Because it's over," Colin answered. "There's nothing I can do now."

"You could register a protest."

"No."

"Then at the very least, you should have clocked Reese when he started doing that stupid dance after the announcement. Did you see that?"

"No."

"The fight had to be rigged. They wanted Reese to finish his amateur career undefeated."

"Who's 'they'?"

"I don't know. The judges, the promoter, whoever. My point is, the fix was in."

"The fix was in? You sound like a character in a gangster movie."

"I'm just saying that no matter what you did, short of knocking him out or having him tap out, Reese was going to win that fight."

Colin shrugged. "Reese is heading to the pros. I was a last-minute fill-in. It's better for everyone if he finished undefeated as an amateur."

"You're kidding. That stuff matters?"

"Not officially. But produce a fighter from this area that gets to the UFC and it's good for everyone."

"You make it sound like a business, not a sport."

"It's the truth."

Evan shook his head. "Fine. Be philosophical about it or whatever. Do you think you won?"

Colin took a forkful of eggs. "Yes."

After a moment, Evan shook his head. "I still think you should have clocked him when he started doing that dance. Hell, I wanted to clock him."

"Okay."

Evan leaned back in his seat. "All right, then. Since you're fine with it, I'm glad I got to watch you get your ass kicked. Especially after the fiasco last weekend."

"Okay."

"And there's something else, too."

"Yeah?"

"Maria was there tonight."

Colin lifted his chin, instantly alert.

"She was with another girl who could have been her twin," Evan added. "Well, not exactly like her, but close enough. You know what I mean. They were on the opposite side of the ring, way in the back. But it was her, without a doubt."

"Okay."

"What's going on with the two of you, anyway?"

Colin forked a piece of sausage. "I don't know."

CHAPTER 18

———— ❧ ————

Maria

Thanks again for coming," Maria said to Serena on the drive back to Wilmington. The rain blew in soft sheets, making the oncoming headlights shimmer.

"It was fun," Serena said from the passenger seat, a soda wedged between her legs. "It was also one of the more interesting Saturday nights I've had in a long time. I think I actually know one of the fighters."

"Duh," Maria said. "You were the one who set us up."

"I'm not talking about Colin. I'm talking about one of the other fighters—I think I've seen him on campus. Of course, from where we were standing, it's not as though I could be certain. Tell me again why we didn't try to get closer?"

"Because I didn't want Colin to know I was there."

"And again . . . why is that?"

"Because we haven't talked since last weekend," Maria said. "I already told you all of this."

"I know, I know. He yelled at the waitress and the police came and you got all freaked out. Blah, blah, blah."

"I appreciate your sympathy."

"I'm sympathetic. I just think you're making a mistake."

"You didn't say that last Sunday."

"Well, I've had a chance to think about it. And on that

note, thanks for keeping me in the dark about the stalker until then."

Her voice dripped sarcasm, but Maria couldn't really blame her. "I didn't know for sure until then."

"And when you did find out? Colin was right there, trying to get answers."

"He was doing way more than that."

"Would you rather date the kind of guy who does nothing? Who would sit there like a log? Or would you have wanted him to take charge of the situation? Hell, if I'd been there, I would probably have yelled at that dingbat waitress, too. Who can't remember what someone looks like a few minutes after they've ordered a drink?"

"I saw a side of Colin that I didn't like."

"So what? Do you think that Mom hasn't seen a side of Dad that she doesn't like? Or vice versa? I've seen a side of you that I don't like, but I didn't shut you out of my life."

"What side?"

"Does it matter?"

"Yes."

"Fine. You always think you're right. It bugs me."

"No, I don't."

"You're making my point."

"And you're beginning to irritate me."

"Someone's got to keep you in line and tell you when you're wrong. And on that note, you're wrong about Colin, too. You should call him. He's good for you."

"I'm not so sure of that."

"Then why did you insist that we come watch him fight tonight?"

Why *had* she wanted to come tonight? She'd waffled, telling Serena that she'd promised Colin that she would, but Serena had merely scoffed.

"Just admit that you still like him," she'd said.

Last weekend, it had been clear that she needed some space to think. Her whipsawing emotions—about the stalker, about Colin—had left her feeling wildly off-kilter, a feeling that only grew worse as the week wore on.

Even the atmosphere at work felt odd to her. Ken had been in and out of Barney's office most of the week, looking distracted and worried, though he didn't so much as mumble a single word to her. Barney was equally tense; both he and Ken weren't in the offices at all on Thursday, and when Lynn didn't show up for work on either Thursday or Friday, she'd expected Barney to raise hell as soon as he returned, if only because Lynn hadn't so much as called to say she wouldn't be coming in. However, Barney had simply added Lynn's work to Maria's plate without explanation or comment.

Strange.

Her parents, too, were a concern. Still grieving over Copo, her dad was depressed to the point that he'd stopped going in to the restaurant, and her mom was worried about him. Maria had dinner with them on Tuesday and Thursday evenings, Serena on Monday and Wednesday, and on the way to Colin's fight, they'd both agreed that something needed to be done, even if they weren't quite sure if there was anything they could do.

The fight was supposed to be a distraction, or at least that's what she'd tried to tell herself. Serena, too. But as soon as Colin had stepped into the cage, she'd felt an almost nauseating wave of butterflies coupled with an acute sense of regret.

All of which meant... what?

With her parents grieving, the idea of begging off their usual Sunday brunch was out of the question, even if she didn't feel as though she was in the right frame of mind to support anyone.

Which was why the sight of Serena on the front porch, almost vibrating with expectant energy, caught Maria off guard. As soon as Maria pulled into the drive, Serena skipped over.

"What's going on?"

"I know what we have to do," Serena said. "And I have no idea why it took this long to figure it out, other than that I'm an idiot! On the plus side, you and I are going to get our lives back...I mean, I love Mom and Dad, but I can't keep coming over here for dinner a couple of times a week and having brunch on Sunday. I already have to spend time with them at the restaurant, and I need at least a little space, you know?"

"What are you talking about?"

"I've thought of something to help Mom and Dad."

Maria stepped out of the car. "How are they?"

"Not great."

"This should be interesting."

"Like I said, I have a plan."

It took some coaxing, but despite their reservations, Maria's parents weren't the kind to say no to their kids, especially when the girls were united in their pleas.

Climbing into their dad's SUV, they drove to the Humane Society. When they reached the parking lot of the low-slung, nondescript building, Maria couldn't help noticing how her parents dragged their feet, reluctance written in their every step. "It's too soon," their mother had protested when Serena first introduced the idea.

"We'll just see what's available," Serena had reassured them. "No pressure." Now they trailed behind their daughters, moving slowly toward the doors.

"I'm not so sure this is a good idea," Maria hissed, leaning closer to Serena. "What if they don't have a dog here that he likes?"

"Remember how I told you that Steve volunteers here? Well, after I told him about Copo, Steve mentioned that there's one dog that just might be perfect," Serena whispered back. "He even agreed to meet us here."

"Did you ever consider getting him another shih tzu? From the same breeder where they got Copo?"

"Of course I did," Serena said. "But I didn't want them to think we were trying to replace Copo."

"Isn't that exactly what we're doing?"

"Not if it's a different kind of dog."

Maria wasn't as confident in Serena's logic as her sister obviously was, but she said nothing. Steve, looking visibly nervous, greeted them as soon as they entered. After Serena offered him a hug, she introduced him to her parents. Steve eagerly led them into the back, toward the kennels.

Dogs immediately began to bark, the sound echoing off the walls. They walked slowly past the first few kennels—there was a Lab mix, a pit bull mix, and some sort of terrier—and she noted her parents' apathy.

Ahead of them, Serena and Steve stopped at one of the smaller kennels. "How about this one?" Serena called out. Felix and Carmen headed over to her, moving reluctantly, like they'd rather be anywhere else. Maria trailed in their wake.

"What do you think?" Serena pressed.

In the kennel, Maria saw a small black-and-brown dog with a face like a teddy bear's, sitting on its haunches, making no noise at all. Maria had to admit that it was just about the cutest thing she'd ever seen.

"He's a shorkie tzu," Steve offered. "It's a mix between a shih tzu and a Yorkshire terrier. He's very sweet and between two and three years old."

Steve opened the kennel; reaching in, he picked up the dog and offered it to Felix. "Would you mind carrying him outside? He'd probably love some fresh air."

With a trace of lingering reluctance, Felix cradled the dog; Carmen leaned in curiously. Maria watched as the little dog licked her father's fingers before yawning with a squeak.

Within minutes, Felix was in love, as was Carmen. Serena stood by watching them, holding Steve's hand, clearly pleased with herself.

Not that Maria could blame her.

No wonder she'd been short-listed for the scholarship; Serena was sometimes absolutely brilliant.

When Maria returned to work on Monday, the tension in the office was palpable. Everyone was on edge, paralegals whispering to each other over the partitions of their cubicles, growing silent whenever any of the attorneys approached; meanwhile, Maria learned that all the partners had been closeted in the conference room since the very early morning, which could only signify that something major was brewing.

Lynn was absent for the third consecutive workday, and with no idea what she was supposed to do—Barney had neglected to leave her any instructions—Maria poked her head into Jill's office.

Before she could get a word out, Jill began shaking her head and talking loudly enough to be heard in the hallway.

"Of course we're still on for lunch," Jill announced. "I can't wait to hear about your weekend! It sounds amazing!"

The partners were *still* behind closed doors when Maria finally took a seat across the table from Jill at a nearby restaurant.

"What in the world is going on today? It's like some sort of twilight zone back there! And what are the partners talking about? No one seems to know anything."

Jill expelled a long breath. "It's all very hush-hush right now... but I'm sure you've noticed the absence of your paralegal?"

"Does she have something to do with what's going on?"

"You could say that," Jill muttered, trailing off when the waiter approached to take their drink orders. She waited until the waiter had walked away before speaking again. "We'll get to that," she said. "And I'll answer what I can. Mainly, I wanted to have lunch with you because I wanted to run something by you in confidence."

"Yeah, of course..." Maria said.

"Are you happy working at the firm?"

"I'm doing okay. Why?"

"Because I was wondering if you'd ever consider leaving and coming to work with me at my own firm."

Maria was too stunned to formulate an answer.

Jill nodded. "I know it's a big decision, and you don't need to give me an answer right now. But I want you to think about it. Especially now, given what's going on."

"I still don't know what's going on. And wait... You're leaving?"

"We've been working on our plans since before you started here."

"We?"

"I'll be working with Leslie Shaw. She's an employment attorney with Scanton, Dilly and Marsden, and we went to law school together. She's terrific, sharp as a tack, and shrewd when it comes to labor law. I'd like you to meet her if you're open to the idea of maybe coming to work with us. You'd have to like her, of course... but if you have no desire to leave, then I hope you'll forget I said anything at all. For now, we're trying to keep this as quiet as possible."

"I won't say anything," Maria promised, the shock still reverberating. "And of course I'd be willing to meet her, but... why are you thinking about leaving?"

"Because our firm is in trouble. Like, *Titanic*-hitting-the-iceberg trouble, and the next few months aren't going to be pretty."

"What do you mean?"

"Our managing partner, Ken, is about to get sued by Lynn for sexual harassment. And I'm guessing that two, maybe even three other paralegals are also going to sue. That's what the partners have been meeting about all day. Because it's going to make the news and it's going to be ugly. From what I heard, the private mediation didn't go well last week."

"What mediation?"

"Last Thursday."

"Which explains why Lynn, Barney, and Ken were absent... Why haven't I heard anything about this?"

"Because Lynn hasn't filed with the EEOC yet."

"Then why was there a mediation at all?"

"Because Ken was warned about it a couple weeks back and has been doing everything he can to head it off. You've noticed, I'm sure, that he's been on his best behavior since then. He's terrified. I'm sure he expects the firm to negotiate a settlement, and I'm sure the other partners are balking at that. They want Ken to make it go away, but he doesn't have the money."

"How can he not have the money?"

"Two ex-wives? And this isn't the first time it's happened. Ken has settled before. That's why I used to ask you about him. Because you're young and attractive and you work in the office, which is all it takes, as far as Ken is concerned. The guy does all his thinking from below the waist. And, of course, Lynn will claim that the partners were all in cahoots with him, since they knew exactly what kind of guy he was and never did anything about it. The firm could be staring at a multimillion-dollar payout... and let's just say that a lot of clients aren't going to want to be associated with a firm known for rampant sexual harassment. Which brings me back to my original question: Are you open to the idea of joining Leslie and me at a new firm?"

Maria was overwhelmed. "I don't have employment law experience..."

"I understand, but I'm not worried. You're smart and driven, and you'll pick up on it faster than you probably imagine. The one caveat is that we're probably not going to be able to match your salary from the get-go, but you'll have more flexible hours, and just by joining on day one you'd be on the fast track to becoming a partner."

"When are you thinking of leaving?"

"Four weeks from Friday," she said. "We've already leased and furnished an office a few blocks from here; all the paperwork is filed."

"I'm sure there are others out there who are much more qualified. So why me?"

"Why not you?" Jill smiled. "We're friends, and if I've learned one thing in this profession, it's that work is a lot more enjoyable when you like the people you spend your days with. I've had enough of Ken and Barney to last a lifetime, thank you very much."

"I'm . . . flattered."

"So you'll think about it? Assuming you and Leslie hit it off?"

"I don't see why I wouldn't. What's Leslie like?"

The partners finally filed out of the conference room around three p.m., all of them looking grim. Barney immediately holed up in his office, clearly in no mood to talk. The same went for the other partners; one by one, office doors were closed. Like most of the employees, Maria decided to leave a few minutes early, and on her way out she noted that the remaining staff members acted both nervous and scared.

Jill had called her again after speaking with Leslie and confirmed plans for the three of them to have lunch on Wednesday. Jill's enthusiasm was infectious, but the upheaval was also causing Maria some trepidation. Changing jobs, changing her practice area (again), and joining a start-up still felt risky to her, even if staying here suddenly seemed even riskier.

What she really wanted, she realized, was to talk to someone other than Serena or her parents. Climbing into her car, she found herself driving past Evan's house and the gym, searching for Colin's car before winding her way to Wrightsville Beach.

The bar at Crabby Pete's was mostly empty. She was climbing onto a stool before Colin finally noticed her, and she watched his surprise slowly give way to something more reserved.

"Hi, Colin," she said quietly. "It's good to see you."

"I'm surprised you're here."

Staring at him standing behind the bar, she thought to herself that he was one of the handsomest men she'd ever met, and felt the same pang of regret she had on Saturday night.

She sighed. "I'm not."

The bar was a good place to talk; the physical barrier between them and the fact that Colin was working kept the conversation from becoming too serious too quickly. Colin briefed her on the fight with Reese and Evan's insistence that the whole thing had been rigged. Maria told him about the dog they'd helped their parents adopt, along with the crisis at the firm and her new career opportunity with Jill.

As was typical, he listened without interruption; as always, she had to draw out his explanations and thoughts; but when the time came for her to leave, he asked a waiter to cover for him for a few minutes so he could walk her to her car.

He didn't try to kiss her, and when she realized he wasn't going to, she leaned in and kissed him. As she tasted the familiar warmth of his mouth, she found herself wondering why she'd felt it necessary to take a break from him in the first place.

At home, the exhaustion of the day finally taking its toll, she fell asleep quickly. She woke to a text from Colin that thanked her for coming by and told her that he'd missed her.

Tuesday, the mood at the office was worse than it had been on Monday. While the partners seemed determined to act in a business-as-usual kind of way, the withholding of information was wearing on everyone else. There was little question that most of the office had begun to imagine the worst, and rumors began to fly. Maria heard whispers about layoffs—many of the employees had families and mortgages, which meant that their lives might just become a lot more complicated.

Maria did her best to keep her head down and concentrate on work; Barney remained quiet and distracted. The necessity for focus made the hours pass quickly, and when she finally left the office, she realized she hadn't thought about the stalker at all.

She wondered whether that was good or bad.

On Wednesday, the lunch with Leslie and Jill went even better than Maria could have hoped. Leslie was in many respects a perfect complement to her best friend in the office—just as lively and irreverent, but also nurturing and thoughtful. The idea of working side by side with them began to seem too good to be true. After lunch, when Jill popped over to report that Leslie had been equally enthusiastic about the meeting, Maria felt a wave of relief. Jill also walked her through their basic offer, including her salary, which was significantly lower, but at this point Maria didn't care. She would adjust her lifestyle accordingly.

"I'm excited," she told Jill. She wondered what—if anything— she should reveal about her stalker or the fact that she and Colin were tentatively back together, and then she realized that she hadn't even mentioned the fact that they'd been broken up.

Too much happening all at once.

Meanwhile, at Martenson, Hertzberg & Holdman, the black cloud that had descended on the office grew steadily darker, and as she and Jill approached her office, Jill leaned toward her.

"Don't be surprised if you hear something major tomorrow," she warned.

Indeed, on Thursday morning, word raced through the office that Lynn had filed with the EEOC. Ken again was a no-show. Though the report was supposed to be confidential, in an office of high-powered attorneys with favors to call in, it was soon on virtually everyone's computer. Joining the crowd, Maria read through the EEOC charges, which spelled out all the lurid details. The report recounted in blunt and highly specific, often sexual language Ken's numerous and unwanted advances, including his promises of career advancement and a higher salary in exchange for specific sexual favors. Employees, their worst fears now confirmed, were moving around in a daze.

Maria and Jill escaped the office, heading to lunch at their usual time, and discussed when to announce that they'd be leaving the firm. Maria leaned toward the idea of letting Barney know sooner rather than later so he wouldn't be caught in a bind—maybe within a few days.

"He's demanding, but he's also been fair and I've learned a lot from him," Maria said. "And I have no desire to make things even worse for him."

"That's a valid point—and it's thoughtful—but it might backfire. I'm wondering if we should let the dust settle first."

"Why?"

"Because once you and I announce that we're leaving, it might set off an exodus of other attorneys, which could lead to a death spiral. We announce, then others do, then clients leave, and the next thing you know, even people who were willing to stick around might find themselves out of work."

"I'm sure a lot of people are already considering their options."

"I'm sure. I would. But that's not the same as actually resigning."

In the end, they compromised on two weeks from Friday, leaving Barney with a short window to find a replacement. From there, the conversation moved on to the kind of firm they wanted to create—the kinds of cases they'd take on, how they'd grow their client base, which of their clients might follow them, how much support staff they'd initially need.

On Friday, another bomb went off in the office when word raced through the hallways that Heather, Ken's paralegal, and Gwen, the receptionist, had also filed complaints with the

EEOC, their statements as damaging as Lynn's had been. Once again, the partners closeted themselves behind closed doors, no doubt sending death stares in Ken's direction.

One by one, associates and staff began leaving the office—some at three, others at four. Exhausted from the week, Maria decided to join them. After all, she was planning to meet Colin later, and needed time to unwind first.

"I can't imagine how surreal it must have been all week," Colin remarked.

"It's been...awful. A lot of people are angry and scared and practically all of them feel blindsided. They had no idea something like this was coming." They were at the Pilot House again, and though they'd spoken on the phone a couple of times—both of them trying to inch their way back to normal—this was the first time Maria had seen Colin since her visit to Crabby Pete's. In his jeans and white button-down shirt with the sleeves rolled to his elbows, he looked, impossibly, even better than he had on Monday. Funny, she thought, what even a little time apart could do.

"And Jill?"

"A total lifesaver. Without her offer, I don't know what I would have done. It's not as though firms are hiring these days, and I probably would have been a basket case. And Jill's right. With three employees filing with the EEOC, it's pretty certain that even if the firm does find a way to survive, all the partners are going to be on the hook financially and it's going to be grim for the next few years."

"Which probably means they're upset."

"Try furious. I'm pretty sure that they'd all like nothing better than to strangle Ken."

"Doesn't the firm have insurance for things like this?"

"They're not sure it'll cover this. He was clearly breaking the law, and according to the complaints, there are recordings, e-mails, texts, and one of the paralegals supposedly even has a video."

"Not good."

"No," Maria agreed. "There are a lot of innocent people who are going to get hurt by this. I can't tell you how fortunate I am."

"Okay."

"Don't start saying that."

Colin smiled. "Okay."

They spent the night rediscovering each other, falling asleep with their limbs intertwined. In the morning, Maria had no regrets and was surprised to catch herself picturing something long-term between them. The thought was strangely thrilling. After they spent Saturday together flying kites at the beach, the feeling only continued to grow.

On Saturday night, she had dinner with Jill and Leslie while Colin worked; after his shift ended, they met at his place. Evan and Lily were there, and the four of them talked until past three in the morning. Unable to stay awake a minute longer, Colin and Maria didn't make love until the following morning.

Though she invited him to brunch, Colin begged off with his apologies, citing a number of upcoming exams he had to study for before working another shift that evening. When she arrived at her parents' home, she was pleased to learn that Smokey—the name her parents had chosen for the dog—now had his own rhinestone collar, bed, and various toys strewn throughout the living room, but he seemed most content when snuggled against her father. In the kitchen, Carmen couldn't stop humming. For her part, Serena talked more about Steve than she ever had before. "Okay, maybe it's getting a little serious," she admitted, eventually submitting to her mother's grilling.

At the table, it was Felix's turn to ask about Steve, and all Maria could do was smile. Between her career, her family, and now Colin, things were on the way up. As they cleared the table, Maria realized again that she was no longer obsessing about the man in the baseball hat, partly because of everything else going on, but also because there'd been no sign of him lately.

She wanted to think he'd given up—that he'd finished rattling her cage. But as much as she'd enjoyed the temporary reprieve, she wasn't yet ready to believe it was completely over.

Before a rainbow, after all, there's usually a storm.

The weather was too cool to paddleboard, and since Colin was occupied, Maria spent the rest of the afternoon and evening trying to catch up on office work. With Lynn absent and Barney operating at less than full capacity, the fact that she'd be leaving in three weeks made her feel a bit guilty. Not guilty enough to change her mind, but enough to keep her at the MacBook until her documents became a blur and writing became pointless.

When she awoke the next morning, Maria found herself wondering about the coming week—how much worse the mood at the office was going to be—and whether anyone else had made the decision to leave. Most of the partners were as distracted as Barney and Ken, which meant work was probably backlogged in every department, and making new hires was going to be tough once word of the firm's troubles leaked out. No doubt it already had.

For now, she resolved to make her own departure as painless for Barney as possible. Hitching her purse over her shoulder, she grabbed her briefcase and headed out the door, her eyes flashing to the doormat.

It took a moment to process what she was seeing before her breath caught in her throat.

A wilted rose, with petals turning black, along with a note.

You will know how it feels.

Almost like she was dreaming, her feet remained rooted to the doorstep, because she knew there would be more. On the railing near the steps was another rotting rose that drooped under the weight of another card. Willing her feet to move forward, she stepped over the flower on her doormat and moved closer to read:

Why did you hate her?

The parking lot outside her door was deserted, the sidewalk empty; no cars she didn't recognize. Her mouth was dry as she locked the door behind her and lifted the rose from the mat. Grabbing the flower that had been threaded through the railing, she forced herself to walk down the steps, her eyes scanning her car.

As she'd feared, her tires had been slashed. On the windshield, an envelope was tucked beneath the wiper.

Later, she'd be amazed at how calmly she'd handled the discoveries, at the clarity of her thoughts. When she reached for the envelope, she thought about fingerprints and how best to read the letter without damaging any evidence and held the envelope at the creases. In that moment, she felt no panic; rather, she was overcome with a slow, sinking sensation, a recognition of inevitability. Somehow, some way, she'd known this was coming.

The letter, computer generated, was printed on a single sheet of unlined printer paper, the kind that could be purchased at any office supply store. The final line, however, had been handwritten in boxy, almost childlike lettering.

You don't think I know what you did? You DON'T THINK I KNOW WHO WAS BEHIND ALL OF IT? You don't THINK I can SEE INTO YOUR MIND and know what YOU DID! You have taken THE BLOOD OF THE INNOCENT

Your HEART IS FILLED WITH POISON and you are THE DESTROYER! You POISON and you WILL NOT GET AWAY WITH IT You will know how it feels, because I am IN CONTROL NOW

I am the living INNOCENT ONE

SEE ME just as I see you!

When she finished the letter, Maria read it a second time, feeling physically ill. The disintegrating rose was still on the windshield and she reached for it, grouping it with the others in a gruesome bouquet.

Turning away from her car, she started back toward her condo, her limbs heavy with dread. The signs, she realized, had been obvious, and she'd willfully ignored them. All at once, memories sparked like blinding visions before her: Gerald Laws being interviewed by the police, with his neatly parted hair and white teeth; Cassie Manning, her young face distorted with fear; Cassie's father, Avery, frighteningly certain of Laws's intentions and possessed of a burning intensity himself; Cassie's mother, Eleanor, mousy and silent and above all, frightened. And finally Lester, the nail-chewing, nervous brother who'd sent her so many terrible notes after Cassie's death.

Those awful notes, reflecting his gradually escalating anger. *Like Laws's letters to Cassie while he was in prison.*

The first step in a *pattern* . . .

On the way up the stairs to her door, Maria's cell phone rang. Serena. She ignored the call, needing to talk to Colin. She needed him to make her feel safe; here and now, she felt exposed. With shaking hands, she dialed him, wondering how soon he'd be able to make it to her place.

A *pattern* . . .

Margolis had told her to come to him with the report, and she wanted Colin there for that as well. She had to tell Margolis about Gerald Laws and Cassie Manning, the woman whom Laws had killed. She wanted to tell him about the Manning family and everything that had happened to her recently. But mostly she wanted to tell him that she knew exactly who was stalking her, and what his endgame was going to be.

CHAPTER 19

— ❧ —

Colin

Since he'd started college, Colin had never missed a single class, let alone a whole day's worth. Only once had he come close—a day when his car hadn't started, and he'd hiked to school carrying a backpack loaded with textbooks, arriving just minutes before class had begun.

Therefore, today was a first. As soon as Maria had called, he'd raced to her place; he'd read the note, and while Maria had called Margolis, he'd called a tow truck with a flatbed, since her car was essentially resting on its rims. While they waited for the tow truck to arrive, Colin made Maria a cup of tea, but she was only able to take a couple of sips before pushing the cup away.

The tow truck came; once it was gone, Colin drove her to the police station. Maria offered her name to the officer at the front counter and she and Colin took a seat in the small lobby, noting the steady but unhurried rhythm of the station. Maria took the opportunity to leave a message for Barney, informing him that she wouldn't be in for a while. Margolis, no doubt, was already somewhere in the station, probably buried in paperwork from weekend incidents. As a detective, he dealt with significant crimes, and he was probably regretting the fact that he'd challenged Maria to call him if she ever wanted to make a simple report. Stalking—if what was happening to Maria officially rose to that level—was below his pay grade, and the fact that Colin was with Maria no doubt made the whole thing even more irritating for him. He made them wait nearly ninety minutes before finally showing up carrying a manila file. While he shook Maria's hand, he didn't offer his to Colin, and Colin wouldn't have shaken it if he had. No reason to pretend they liked each other.

Margolis asked to speak with Maria alone; Maria insisted that Colin be present. Radiating disapproval, Margolis nodded and led the three of them to one of the interrogation rooms. Having spent time in a number of police stations over the years, Colin knew that on a busy morning, the interrogation room was one of the few places with any privacy whatsoever. *Nice of him, even if he is generally an ass*, Colin thought. After closing the door and seating them at the table, Margolis set aside the file he'd been holding, asked a series of general questions—Maria's name, age, address, and the like—and began filling in the report. After that, Maria—in a shaky but surprisingly linear fashion—went through the same story she'd told Colin on the beach about Cassie Manning and Gerald Laws, as well as what had been happening to her recently. She sketched out the parallels before finally handing Margolis the letter she had found on the windshield.

Margolis read the letter slowly, saying nothing, before finally asking if he could make a copy. When she agreed, he rose from his seat and left the room, returning with a copy.

"We'll keep the original letter in the file, if that's okay," he said, his face displaying little of what he was thinking. Taking his seat again, he read the letter a third time before going on. "And you're sure that Lester Manning wrote this?"

"Yes," Maria answered. "He's also the guy who's been following me."

"That's Cassie Manning's brother?"

"Younger brother."

"Why do you think it's him?"

"Because some of what's in the letter I heard him say before."

"When?"

"After Cassie died. He also wrote the same types of things in the notes he sent me."

"Like what, specifically?"

"The blood of the innocent. My heart being filled with poison."

Margolis nodded and made another note. "Was this in the first batch of notes, or the second batch?"

"Excuse me?"

"You said the notes changed when they started to arrive again. That they were more threatening and scary."

"Second group."

"And how do you know he sent the notes?"

"Who else could it be?"

Margolis scanned his notes. "Avery Manning said that it may have been Cassie's boyfriend."

"It wasn't him."

"How do you know?"

"According to the police, he wasn't a credible suspect. He was devastated by Cassie's murder, but he didn't blame me. He denied even knowing who I was."

"Did you ever speak with him?"

"No."

Margolis made another note. "Do you remember his name? Or how he met Cassie?"

Maria pursed her lips. "I think it was Mike or Matt or Mark . . . something like that. And no, I don't know how he met Cassie. But why are we even talking about him? Lester is the one who's been stalking me! Just like he wrote those notes in Charlotte!"

"Didn't you tell me that Lester denied writing the notes when the police talked to him?"

"Of course he denied writing them."

"And it never crossed your mind that it could have been this... Michael? The boyfriend?"

"Why would he? He didn't even know me. He told the police he didn't do it."

"So did Lester."

"Have you been listening to me? Lester's crazy. The notes are crazy. It doesn't take much to put two and two together."

"Do you still have any of the original notes?"

Maria shook her head, her frustration surfacing. "I threw them away when I moved here. I didn't want anything to do with them. The Charlotte police might still have a couple of them, but I can't be certain about that."

"When you say notes, what do you mean?"

"Just a sentence or two."

"So... not like this one."

"No. But again, he used the same words and phrases. And there were two short notes that *do* fit the pattern."

"In other words, this letter is different."

"Obviously."

Margolis tapped his pen on the report in front of him. "Okay. Let's say it is Lester. When you say his notes were threatening, what do you mean? Did he say he was going to hurt you in any way? Or harm you?"

"No, but it was clear that he blamed me for his sister's death. Actually, his whole family blamed me in the end."

"What was the family like?"

"They were just... odd," she said. "Their whole dynamic, I mean."

"How so?"

Colin turned toward her, realizing that he hadn't heard Maria talk about them in much detail.

"Avery Manning—the father—was a psychiatrist, and from the very first meeting, he considered himself an expert when it came to criminal behavior. He never let Cassie meet with me alone. He was always there, and he dominated the conversations. Even in the hospital, when I was trying to get the story from Cassie, he would answer for her. It got to the point where I had to ask him to step out of the room, but he refused—the most he would do was retreat to the corner, promising to remain silent while she talked. Even then, I had the sense that Cassie was very careful with her words, like she was trying to say things exactly the way that he wanted. Almost like they'd rehearsed. I think that's why she...embellished her stories at times."

"Embellished?"

"Cassie told me that Laws had hit her before. If true, that would have been important, because we might have been able to make a more serious charge stick. Cassie told me that Laws struck her in a parking lot, and that Lester had witnessed it. Both Cassie's and Lester's stories were identical, almost word for word, but when we investigated, we learned that Laws was in another state on the date and time in question, which meant they both were lying. When we talked to Cassie about it, she wouldn't back down. That only made the plea bargain even more necessary. Laws's attorney would have had a field day with her if she had to testify."

"And the mom?"

"Eleanor. I only met her twice, and she was completely under Avery's thumb. I'm not sure she ever said anything. Just wept the whole time."

Margolis continued to jot notes as she talked. "Now let's talk about Lester. What was he like?"

"Again, I only met him twice, and he was like two entirely different people. In the first meeting, I didn't notice anything out of the ordinary. The most normal of the bunch, in fact. But when I met him the second time, after I informed them of the charges against Laws, he changed. Almost like...he was afraid of me. He'd mutter that he shouldn't be here, that no one in the family should be near me because I was dangerous. His father kept telling him to be quiet, and then he'd just sit there, fidgeting and staring at me like I was in league with the devil."

"Do you know the name of the psychiatric hospital where he was committed?"

"No."

"But the notes eventually stopped?"

"After I moved. But now he's doing it again."

Margolis twirled the pen before reaching for the file he'd originally brought into the room. "After you called, I had the Charlotte police e-mail the report about Cassie Manning's death; I'm still waiting on the report on Laws's initial arrest. I haven't really had the chance to dig through it all in detail, but from what I did read, it's clear that Gerald Laws killed Cassie Manning. Furthermore, you didn't make the decision that allowed him to plead to a misdemeanor in the first place. It was your boss—am I correct?"

"Yes."

"Then why do you think the Manning family blamed you? Or, in Lester's case, viewed you as 'dangerous'?"

"Because I was the one they were dealing with. They were counting on me to convince the DA to go for the more serious conviction. And in Lester's case, he's obviously ill...like I said, he ended up in a psychiatric hospital."

Margolis nodded. "Okay. Let's say you're right about all of this, and that Lester Manning is indeed responsible for everything that's been happening to you." He leaned back in his chair. "Even then, I'm not sure that there's anything I can do."

"Why not?"

"You haven't seen him. No one else has seen him. You don't know who bought the roses, other than that it wasn't your boss. No one saw Lester put the roses into your car. All you know about the guy who ordered you a drink was that it was a young man wearing a baseball hat. Nor did you recognize the guy who delivered the roses as Lester. In other words, you have no proof that it actually *is* Lester."

"I told you that the note used some of the same phrases!"

"You mean when compared to the notes you don't have any-more? Again, I'm not saying that you're wrong. In fact, I think there's a good probability that you're right. But as a former pros-ecutor, you know what the phrase 'beyond a reasonable doubt' means. And right now, there's not enough for an indictment under the stalking statutes."

"He's been following me, watching me, and monitoring my actions. That meets the course of conduct required in the law. He wrote a note that terrifies me. He slashed my tires. That con-stitutes harassment. His actions have caused substantial emo-tional distress, which is why I'm here. He's clearly stalking me and that's a crime."

Margolis raised an eyebrow. "All right, Miss Former Prosecutor. But if he denied writing the notes once, he'll just deny it again. And then what?"

"What about the pattern? Notes, flowers, following me around, dead flowers. He's mimicking what Laws did to Cassie."

"The pattern is *similar*, but not the *same*. Laws sent letters and identified himself. You received short, unsigned notes. Laws spied on Cassie at dinner and made sure she knew he was there. Some-one bought you a drink at a club, anonymously. Cassie knew that Laws had sent her flowers. You don't even really know for sure who sent you the roses."

"It's close enough."

"To you, maybe. But in a court of law, it's different."

"In other words, because he's been careful, he's going to get away with it? You're not even going to talk to him?"

"Don't get me wrong. I'll try to talk to him."

"Try?"

"You're assuming that he's still in town and that I can find him. On the other hand, if he's in Charlotte or another city, I'll probably have to turn it over to a detective there."

"And what would you say to him if you were able to find him?"

"I'll let him know that I know what he's up to, and that it's in his own best interest to stop, or the authorities will intervene." When it became clear that Maria hadn't expected him to say what he had, Margolis went on. "In other words, I believe you. With that said, I can't arrest him because you *think* he bought you roses. Or because you *think* he bought you a drink. Or because you *think* he put a note on your car. You and I both know that's not going to fly. And, in the end, he might make things even worse for you."

"Excuse me?" she asked.

Margolis shrugged. "You made an accusation before and the father threatened to sue you and the police. Now you're accusing him again. It's possible that he could make a claim for harassment against you."

"That's ridiculous!"

"But it's possible."

"What am I supposed to do, then? If you're not going to do anything to help me?"

Margolis leaned forward, folding his hands on the table. "I've taken your statement and the report will now be on file. I told you I would talk to him, assuming I can find him, or that someone else will. I'll review the files on Laws's arrest and Cassie's death. And I'll find out what I can learn about Lester Manning. I'll talk with the Charlotte police and have them check whether the old notes are in a file somewhere. Considering you've offered me nothing whatsoever in the way of proof that you've been threatened at all—and taking into account your questionable judgment in choosing a boyfriend—I'd say that's more than enough, wouldn't you?"

Maria's face was a mask. "What about a restraining order?"

"Anything is possible, but you and I both know it's not automatic, for all the same reasons we've discussed. But let's say that by some miracle, a judge does grant one. The law says that it's not valid unless Lester Manning can actually be served. Which, again, may or may not be possible."

"In other words, you're telling me to pretend it isn't happening."

"No. I'm telling you to let me do my job." He reached for the file. "I'll let you know what I find out."

"I don't know why I went to him in the first place," Maria said on her way back to the car, her face tight. "And you know what really pisses me off?" She didn't need an answer. "He's right. About all of it. And I know he's right. If a detective had brought me a case like this, I would have turned him away. There's nothing in the way of proof. Even if I *know* it's him."

"Margolis will check into it."

"So what?"

"Margolis may be an ass, but he's smart. He'll get Lester to say something incriminating."

"And then what? You think Margolis will convince him to stop? I thought it was over when I moved here, but even that didn't end it. He knows where I live, and for all I know, Lester killed Copo. He might have been inside my parents' house!"

It was the first time that Colin had heard her link Copo's death to everything else that had occurred, and her obvious fear made something coil inside him.

This was going to stop. Let Margolis do whatever he was going to do, but right now, that wasn't good enough for Colin. It was time, he thought, for someone to find out just what Lester was up to these days.

After he dropped Maria off at work, Colin popped in his earbuds, put on some music, and perched himself in front of the computer at his desk.

Lester Manning.

Proof or not, having a name helped to focus his thoughts, and he wanted to find out as much as he could about the man.

The only problem was that without easy access to government

databases or official records, there wasn't much he could do. There were no listings in the white pages for anyone named Lester Manning in North Carolina, nor could he find a cell number. There were two Lester Mannings on Facebook; one was listed as living in Aurora, Colorado, and the other in Madison, Wisconsin; the first a teenager, the second a man in his forties. Instagram, Twitter, and Snapchat turned up nothing, nor did a general Google search using the name and the city of Charlotte in various permutations.

There were a few sites that held out the promise of more information—phone number, most recent address, and the like—for a fee, and after debating, he typed in his credit card number and gave it a whirl. Thankfully, an address popped up in Charlotte.

There was a little more on Avery Manning, including a phone number in Charlotte listing an Avery Manning, MD, along with the same address he'd found for Lester.

Father and son living together?

Or outdated information?

There were also a few short articles on the father. The most recent one confirmed Maria's recollection that Manning had had his license suspended for eighteen months, apparently for improper care of a number of patients. The most prominent case involved a young man who'd committed suicide. According to the article, Manning failed to properly diagnose the patient's attention-deficit disorder and monitor his use of Adderall. Other patients claimed that they simply got worse under his care. If the date of the suspension was accurate, then Avery Manning still wasn't able to practice.

Interesting.

There was a photograph, too: a man in his midfifties, with thin blond hair and light blue eyes staring out of an angular, almost bony face; to Colin, he could have passed for a washed-out grave-digger. Colin couldn't imagine sitting across from the guy for an hour, spilling his guts and hoping for empathy.

Another article mentioned Manning's work with prison inmates. The article quoted Manning as saying that many prisoners were sociopaths and beyond practical rehabilitation. Humane incarceration, he said, was the most pragmatic solution to criminal pathology. Other than commenting that Manning considered himself an expert on criminal behavior, Maria hadn't mentioned his work in prisons, and he wondered whether she had even known about it.

A little more research eventually brought up the obituary for Eleanor Manning, which said nothing about suicide, but that wasn't surprising. Most people didn't want that fact made public. It also noted that she'd been a mother of three, and was survived by her husband and son. Cassie he'd heard about, but there was another sibling?

He reviewed half a dozen articles on Avery Manning before finding the answer; in an interview on the subject of depression, Avery noted that his wife had battled depression ever since their son Alexander Charles Manning had died in an automobile accident when he was six.

Alex. Cassie. Eleanor.

So much tragedy for one family. And Lester blamed Maria for one, maybe even two of the deaths.

Enough to make Lester torment and terrify her?

Yes. The original notes made that plain. As did the pattern.

Chronologically or not, Maria was experiencing the same fears that Cassie had. And like Maria, Colin knew how the rest of Cassie's story unfolded.

After he got out of prison, Laws met Cassie face-to-face.

Cassie filed a restraining order.

The police couldn't find Laws.

In the end, Cassie was abducted and murdered.

Was that part of Lester's plan as well?

It was a massive jump to go from what had happened to Maria so far to the final step. Tormenting was one thing, murder was another, and he didn't know enough about Lester to try to guess what he might do. That didn't mean, however, that Maria should take any chances.

He spent another hour without learning anything more. So much for the easy part—information that anyone could find—and he wondered about his next step.

What did he *know* about Lester? And what could he *assume*?

Lester had a car. Or had use of a car.

Not a big assumption, of course, but he wondered what kind of information he could find if he had a license plate number. A few keywords into the search engine turned up a couple of companies with access to all kinds of public records, including car registrations and license plate numbers. It was a bit expensive, but it just might be helpful, and he made note of the websites in case the need arose.

Anything else?

Yes, he thought. If he was correct in his assumption, Lester had hidden on the roof across the street when Maria was at work. As for her condo, it would have been easy for Lester to watch her as she came and went, if only because her schedule was predictable. He wouldn't have had to camp out for hours; he could have observed her from the coffee shop across the street or from a parked car. Following her to the restaurant and the nightclub would have been a piece of cake.

And?

Based on the meeting with Margolis, Colin needed proof that Lester was stalking Maria, and he wondered if he should drive to Charlotte in the hopes of putting a face to a name. Maybe even get a photograph, assuming he could find Lester. But then again, even that might not be enough. The florist had admitted he hadn't gotten a good look at the guy, and Colin doubted the waitress would recognize him. Even Maria hadn't recognized him up close.

And finally, there was Copo. The dog's death also fit with the pattern, and the more he thought about it, the more probable it seemed that Lester had killed Copo to hurt Maria and her family. Because he'd been following Maria, he'd know where her parents lived. But more than that, it also meant that he'd watched the family regularly. How else would he have known that Copo had been left behind at the house? Maria had said that Felix brought Copo everywhere, even to the restaurant. That her parents rarely left the dog at home.

But how?

The Sanchez backyard had a privacy fence, and in a tight-knit suburb, a lurking stranger would have been noticed.

How indeed.

Twenty minutes later, he was driving through the Sanchez neighborhood, trying to piece it together.

Her parents' house was quiet, apparently no one at home. There were, however, others out and about. A woman jogging on the sidewalk; an elderly man pruning the bushes in his front yard. A man pulling out of his driveway, heading somewhere.

Colin turned at the corner, then turned again, heading down the street that ran parallel to the Sanchezes' street, backyards bumping up against each other.

The neighborhood was bustling, the kind of community where people probably watched out for each other.

Lester definitely would have been noticed.

Unless...

He slowed the car as he approached the houses that backed up to the Sanchez place, and the answer became clear.

The house directly behind Maria's parents' home was for sale.

More than that, it appeared to be vacant.

Maria was reserved when he picked her up from work that evening, and their conversation was desultory. It was clear that she wanted to avoid talking about Lester or Margolis.

She wanted to spend the night at her parents', so he drove her home and waited outside while she packed an overnight bag. Next, he drove her to pick up her car at the tire shop, waiting until Maria was on her way before finally exiting the parking lot. He'd wanted to follow her, but thinking it would only make her more nervous, he asked her instead to text him when she reached her parents' place. Fifteen minutes later, she let him know that she'd arrived.

Though she said nothing, he guessed she'd spent the drive to her parents' house repeatedly glancing in the rearview mirror, wondering if Lester was following her.

Colin waited until after midnight to return to the neighborhood, his mind on Lester Manning.

Dressed in black, he'd parked a few blocks away and approached the vacant house. In his backpack he carried a small flashlight, a couple of screwdrivers, and a small crowbar. Still, if Lester had been inside the house multiple times—and unless he was an expert in picking locks or had a key—then Colin guessed he'd be able to get in through the same window or door that Lester had used. The entry point might still be unlocked; unless the Realtor had noticed it, there would have been no way for Lester to relock it once he'd left.

Colin just had to find it.

And if Lester happened to be there tonight, having realized that Maria wasn't at her condo?

As much as Colin itched to exact punishment, he'd call Margolis. Maybe they could charge Lester with trespassing, maybe even breaking and entering, in addition to stalking.

The street was quiet and empty. On either side of him, through gaps in the curtains of the nearby houses, he saw the occasional television flickering, but he suspected most people had turned in for the night.

He reached the vacant house and a quick check of the front door showed a lockbox on the doorknob, courtesy of the Realtor. There were no partially open windows on the porch, nor any pry marks. He went around to the side of the house and noiselessly hoisted himself over the fence, into the backyard. With the flashlight, he inspected the windows one by one, hunting for a small gap or pry marks.

It wasn't until he reached the opposite side of the house that he found it.

A bedroom window, five feet up, nearly but not fully closed. Pry marks on the frame, no doubt used to take off the screen. Easy for Colin to climb through, despite the distance from the ground, but for Lester? He scanned the yard and spotted an old plastic picnic table set, made for children. Based on four imprints of flattened, yellowing grass, the table from the set had been moved recently.

Bingo.

Using the screwdriver, he popped the screen off, then wedged the window open a bit farther before pushing it wide with his hands.

With a quick jump and climb, he was inside.

He walked through the darkened house, observing that the floor plan was similar to Maria's parents' house, with windows in the kitchen and a family room offering an unobstructed view of the Sanchezes' back porch. But the view was almost too perfect, facing both ways, and Colin knew that Lester wouldn't have wanted to be spotted.

Which left only one possibility.

Colin traversed the short hallway, turning into the only bedroom on the rear side of the house. Unlike the ones in the kitchen and family room, the window that offered a view of the Sanchezes' back porch had curtains. Turning his flashlight on, he scanned the pile carpet.

Indentations near the window. Footprints.

Lester Manning had been here.

And there was also the chance that he might return.

It wasn't until he was driving home that Colin realized he'd overlooked something important.

Where had Lester parked?

It struck him as unlikely that he would have parked in the driveway of the vacant house, or on the street in front of someone's home. It was too noticeable, especially since many people wanted to park their own cars in front of their houses. At the same time, Lester probably wouldn't have wanted to park too far away.

Turning around, Colin drove back through the neighborhood, not sure what he hoped to find, until he came upon a park that included a grassy field, a jungle gym, and benches stationed beneath oak trees. On the opposite side of the street, ten or twelve cars were lined up; adjacent to the park were seven more. The lateness of the hour suggested that they belonged to the people who lived across the street, owners with multiple cars and nowhere else to park.

However, another car here would be more likely to go unnoticed—ideal for Lester—and he was sure he was right. Pulling his phone from his pocket, he snapped photos of the cars, along with their license plates. He wanted to know which ones belonged. And as he did, his thoughts began to coalesce.

He wanted to know what Lester looked like.

He wanted to find Lester's car and license plate.

He wanted to know whether Lester was staying in the area, and if so, where.

Then, after that, he wanted to spend a few days watching and learning everything he could about the man.

"To what end?" Evan asked, squinting at him across the kitchen table; Lily was already asleep in the bedroom.

"Margolis said that he needs proof. I'll get him proof."

"You're sure you're not doing this because you want to beat the crap out of him?"

"Yes."

"Yes, you want to beat the crap out of him, or yes, you're not going to beat the crap out of him, even though you want to?"

"I don't intend to go anywhere near him."

"Good idea. Because you have serious issues."

"Yes."

"And how exactly do you intend to find him? Are you just going to hang out at the park and watch for strange cars?"

"Probably."

"Because you think that Lester might one day park there again?"

"Yes."

"And how are you going to know which cars belong and don't belong?"

"Persistence."

Evan was quiet for a moment. "I still think it would be a better idea if you just let Margolis do his job."

Colin nodded. "Okay."

After a few hours of sleep, Colin was back in the Sanchezes' neighborhood with a notebook the following day. He'd parked a few blocks away and headed to the park, exercising on a floor mat he'd brought from home while he waited.

It was early, the sun not yet up, and all the cars he'd seen a few hours earlier were still there.

It was more than an hour before the first person emerged from one of the houses, hopped into a car, and drove off. Colin jotted the make, model, and color in the notebook. There was a flurry of activity at half past seven, and another flurry forty-five minutes later. Two more people claimed their cars as Colin was getting ready to leave for class, leaving only a single red car—a two-door

Hyundai—adjacent to the park, and another two on the opposite side of the street.

Probably nothing, but he nonetheless noted the information.

On his way out, he detoured down the street with the vacant house. The street was empty, and he decided to risk it. Pulling over a few houses down, he headed for the house before cutting toward the fence.

Peeking over, he saw that the plastic picnic table was exactly where it had been hours earlier; the window, too, appeared to be untouched. If Lester wasn't here, then the three remaining cars weren't likely his. Call it 99 percent certain.

In class, he found himself only mildly interested in what the professors were saying and struggled to take proper notes. Instead, he wondered whether he should head to Lester Manning's last known address in Charlotte or continue to stake out the vacant house. Or, if Maria slept at her place, whether he should watch for Lester there.

All good options, but it was impossible to be in three places at once.

What if he chose wrong?

His mind continued to circle the problem.

After leaving campus, he returned to the Sanchezes' neighborhood. The red Hyundai parked adjacent to the park was still there, while the two others across the street were gone.

The lonely car seemed out of place. Again, on his way out, he stopped at the vacant house and peeked over the fence. No change.

Lester wasn't in the vacant house. Which made sense. Neither Maria nor her family were home.

He decided to stay as close as possible to Maria for the next few days. If Lester was still determined to exact his revenge, he would eventually find her, wherever she was. And wherever she planned to be, that's where Colin needed to be as well.

He called and invited her to dinner; on the phone, she was a little better than she had been the day before, but still tense. He picked her up at her place after work and drove her to a bistro near the beach, where they could hear the soothing sound of the waves.

Again, she avoided any talk of Lester or Margolis; instead, she focused on her and Jill's plans for the new firm. Talking about the new venture, along with a couple of glasses of wine, was enough of a distraction to raise her spirits.

Returning to Colin's place, they chatted with Evan and Lily before Maria finally reached for Colin's hand. Despite her relative calm, it had been clear to him all evening that Maria had no desire to return to her condo.

Colin checked the vacant house on Wednesday morning, making sure to swing by the park and continuing to note the comings and goings of parked cars. Just as he was beginning to think that Lester had either abandoned the viewing post of the house or parked his car elsewhere, Wednesday evening brought a change in that the red Hyundai adjacent to the park was gone.

Perhaps it was nothing, but it was time, he thought, to check the license plate, which ended up being a waste of time.

Like the others, it belonged to one of the homeowners.

On Thursday morning, Colin and Maria were having a breakfast of egg whites, oatmeal, and fruit at his place. She told him she was having dinner with Jill and Leslie and then planned to spend the night at her parents' house.

"They're worried about me," she explained, but Colin knew she still wasn't ready to return to her condo alone, especially since Colin had to work. "I think they're also worried about Serena."

"Why?"

"Because I told them I've been staying with her the last few nights. We're not married and they have old-school values. I know you disapprove of lying, but I can't handle my mother's disappointment on top of everything else right now."

"I didn't say anything."

"I know. But I could hear you thinking that I should be honest with them."

He smiled. "Okay. Have you heard from Margolis?"

She shook her head. "Not yet. And I'm not sure if that's good news or bad news."

"It might be no news."

"That would fall into the bad category," she said. "He didn't exactly inspire a lot of confidence in his determination to attack the problem. For all I know, he hasn't done anything yet."

Colin nodded, acknowledging that he'd been thinking the same thing. It wasn't what she wanted to hear, however, so he switched topics. "Tomorrow's the big day."

"For what?"

"Aren't you offering your two weeks' notice?"

"Oh yeah." She smiled. "And yes, it's tomorrow, but it's strange, because I barely think about it unless I'm with Jill. It's just so surreal. A few weeks ago, I could never have imagined that I'd be getting ready to join a start-up."

"What do your parents think?"

"My mom's excited, but my dad's nervous. He knows how hard it is to start a business. He also liked telling people that I worked for Martenson, Hertzberg and Holdman."

"For now."

"Yes." She flashed a wry smile. "For now."

"How's the mood at the office?"

She shrugged. "Hard to say. It's not as bad as it was last week, but it's still gloomy. Work is piling up, and I'm hearing whispers that more people are thinking about leaving. It's one rumor after another. Yesterday, there was a rumor that the firm was close to settling the whole thing—with all the plaintiffs—but that's probably just wishful thinking. If you read the EEOC complaints, Ken was a lot worse than even I thought he was."

"Did you ever tell your parents about him?"

"Not a chance. If my dad had known, he would have gone berserk. Latino blood can run as hot as yours sometimes."

"Then you probably did the right thing by not telling him."

"Maybe. But you didn't do anything."

"You're not my daughter."

She laughed. "He's still not so sure about you. Because of your past, I mean."

"Okay."

"And also because of your present persona."

"Okay."

"He even has this crazy idea that you were the one who was stalking me."

"Why would he think that?"

"Because he thinks he saw your car in the neighborhood when he was out walking the dog yesterday morning. I know he's worried about me, but sometimes he can get a little carried away."

As can I.

CHAPTER 20

————— 🌸 —————

Maria

Maria kissed Colin good-bye on his doorstep; though he'd offered to follow her to the office as he had all week, she told him that she'd be fine and to go on and head to his classes. In the instant she'd said it, she'd believed it, but as she drove to work she nonetheless found herself wondering whether Lester might be following her. For the first time since she'd moved from Charlotte, she felt her heart beginning to race for no reason whatsoever. Within seconds, it became harder to breathe and her vision began to narrow.

Instinct took over and she was somehow able to pull the car to the side of the road, feeling her body suddenly go haywire.

Tightness in her chest.

Oh my God . . .

This wasn't normal.

She couldn't breathe.

Her vision continued to narrow and her thoughts began to slip.

She was having a heart attack and needed an ambulance.

She was going to die on the side of the road.

Her phone began to ring, but she only vaguely heard it sound half a dozen times before it went silent. It dinged a moment later, someone texting.

The muscles in her chest tightened.

She couldn't get enough air.

Her heart continued to pound and terror set in, feeding on the knowledge that she was going to die.

She rested her head against the steering wheel, waiting for the end.

But it didn't come.

Instead, she simply continued to die little by little over the next few minutes, until she was no longer dying at all.

In time, she was able to lift her head from the steering wheel. Her breathing eased and her peripheral vision was returning. Her heart still pounded, but it felt less intense.

A few minutes later, she began to feel better. Still shaky, but better, and though it seemed impossible, she understood that she hadn't been having a heart attack.

Instead, she knew her panic attacks had returned.

It was another half hour before she felt completely normal, and by then she was already in her office. Barney wasn't around, but he'd left a new matter for her—the regional hospital was being sued by a family over an infection called *pseudomonas* that had eventually led to a patient's death—along with a hastily scrawled note asking her to get started on finding the appropriate legal decisions necessary to bolster their defense.

She was pondering the entry point for her research when her cell phone rang. She glanced at it, then looked closer, making sure she hadn't been mistaken. Serena?

She pressed the button, connecting the call. "Hey," she said, "what's up?"

"Are you okay?"

"Why?"

"I called earlier but you didn't answer," Serena chirped.

"Sorry," Maria said, thinking back on the panic attack. "I was in the car." The truth, even if it wasn't the whole truth. She wondered what Colin would think about that.

"How goes it with the investigation?"

"Nothing yet."

"Have you called Margolis?"

"If I don't hear from him today, I will."

"I probably would have called already."

"I'm sure. So... what's up?"

"What do you mean?"

"You never call me this early. And why aren't you in class?"

"It starts in a few minutes, but I just had to tell someone. I got an e-mail last night, and it turns out that I'm one of the three finalists for the scholarship. I guess the dinner at Mom and Dad's must have had a positive influence... Though the e-mail didn't exactly say it directly, I think I might actually be in the pole position."

"Pole position?"

"Yeah. You know, when they restart a race following a wreck or whatever, that's the car in the first position."

"I know what it is. I'm just curious how *you* know what it is."

"Steve watches a lot of NASCAR. He makes me watch it, too."

"So it's really a relationship now?"

"I don't know... there's this really cute guy in one of my classes. He's a little older though, and he's dating my sister, so that might be a problem."

"That is a problem."

"I'm just glad you put your ego aside and went to talk to him."

"It had nothing to do with my ego."

"Ego, close encounter at a bar fight, same thing."

"You're insane, do you know that?"

"Sometimes," Serena admitted. "But it's worked out so far."

Maria laughed. "That's great news," she said. "About the scholarship, I mean."

"I don't want to get too excited just yet. Don't tell Mom or Dad."

"I wasn't the one who told them last time."

"I know," she said. "Do they still think you've been staying in the dorm with me?"

"Yes. And it's my turn to say don't tell them."

Serena laughed. "I won't say anything. But I'm pretty sure Mom knows that you've been staying with Colin. Of course, she's operating under the don't-ask-don't-tell policy, which means it probably won't come up tonight."

"Tonight?"

"Yeah, tonight."

"What's tonight?"

"You're kidding, right? Mom's birthday? Family dinner? Don't tell me you forgot."

Oops. "Uh..."

"Seriously? Do you never check out my posts? Or my tweets? I know you've got a lot going on, but how could you forget Mom's birthday?"

She'd have to cancel dinner with Jill and Leslie, but they'd understand, right? "I'll be there."

"Are you going to bring Colin?"

"He's working. Why?"

"Because I was wondering whether to invite Steve."

"What does one have to do with the other?"

"It's simple. I figure that if Dad is busy glaring at Colin, he won't be able to grill Steve, and they'll think he's great in comparison."

Maria scowled. "That's not funny."

Serena laughed. "It's a little funny."

"I'm hanging up now."

"See you tonight!"

❧

After hanging up with Serena, Maria realized she felt strangely nervous as she made her way to Jill's office. She didn't think Leslie would be offended—it was an honest mistake—nor did she want Leslie to question Jill's recommendation. But when she said as much to Jill, her friend laughed aloud.

"Are you kidding? Leslie doesn't care about that kind of stuff."

"Are you sure?"

"Of course I'm sure. It's your mom's birthday. What are you supposed to do?"

"I could have remembered in the first place."

"There is that," Jill noted, and Maria grimaced. Surprising her, her cell phone rang again. Thinking it was probably Serena again, she was going to ignore it before realizing that she didn't recognize the number.

"Who is it?" Jill asked.

"I'm not sure," Maria said. After debating for a few seconds, she took the call, praying to God that it wasn't Lester.

"Hello?"

It wasn't Lester. Thank God. She listened to the voice on the other end. "Yes," Maria finally said. "I'll be there."

She disconnected the call but continued to hold the phone, thinking about it. Jill must have seen her expression.

"Bad news?" Jill asked.

"I'm not sure," Maria offered, thinking it was finally time to tell her friend about her history with Lester Manning...not to mention the drama of the past couple of weeks, including the ups and downs and ups with Colin. The thought of telling every-thing to Jill wouldn't have bothered her in the past, but volun-teering such personal information to her future boss felt...*risky*, even if Jill was likely to find out anyway.

"Who was it?"

"A cop—Detective Margolis. He asked to meet me."

"The police? What's going on?"

"It's kind of a long story."

Jill stared at her before getting up from her desk and crossing the room. She closed the door and turned around.

"What's going on?" she said.

In the end, confiding in Jill was easier than she'd imagined it would be. Future boss or not, Jill was her friend first and foremost, and more than once, she gripped Maria's hand, clearly concerned. When Maria assured her that it wouldn't affect her ability to help with the start-up, Jill merely shook her head.

"Right now, you have more important things to worry about," she said. "Leslie and I can handle whatever we still have left. You need to do whatever and take whatever time you need, so that you can find a way to put this behind you for good. It's not as though we're going to have clients lining up in the first couple of months anyway."

"It better not take that long. I don't think I'd be able to handle it. I had a panic attack this morning."

Jill was quiet for a moment. "I'll help you any way I can. Just tell me what you need."

Leaving Jill's office, Maria realized again that lower salary or not, leaving to work with Jill not only had been the best option available, but already seemed to be the best career choice she'd made to that point in her life.

What it didn't do, however, was help the rest of the morning pass more quickly. Nor did her workload; wondering what Margolis was going to say made it difficult to concentrate, which only prevented her from gaining traction on her research for the hospital suit. With her frustration beginning to rise, she set her work aside and texted Colin.

Yes, he texted back, he'd meet her at the station at a quarter past noon.

She peeked at the clock.

Then back at the claim, knowing she needed to review it closely.

Two hours until she met with Margolis.

Time inched by.

When she pulled into the lot, Colin was waiting outside the station, wearing sunglasses, shorts, and a T-shirt. She waved as she got out of her car, hoping it would hide how nervous she was but suspecting that Colin would know anyway.

He gave her a quick kiss before pulling open the door for her. Maria felt a sense of déjà vu as she glanced around. Unlike their first visit, however, Margolis didn't keep them waiting long. They'd barely taken their seats before she saw him striding toward them from the rear of the building. Again, he was holding a file, and he used it to motion them forward.

"Come on," he said. "We'll talk where we did before."

Maria smoothed her skirt as she stood and walked beside Colin, past the others working at their desks, past the group of people collected around the coffeemaker.

Margolis opened the door and pointed to the same chairs they'd used before. She and Colin took their seats as Margolis moved to the far side of the table.

"Should I be worried?" Maria blurted out.

"No. Long story short, I don't think Lester's going to be a problem."

"What does that mean?" she pressed.

Margolis tapped his pen against the folder before flicking a thumb at Colin. "It seems you're still spending time with this particular problem child. And I don't know why you keep insisting he come with you when we discuss your case. There's no reason for him to be here."

"I want him here," she said. "And yes, we're still spending time together. Happily, I might add."

"Why?"

"I like his body and he's fantastic in bed," she answered, knowing it wasn't any of his business and not bothering to hide her sarcasm.

Margolis smirked, but there was no humor behind it. "Before we begin, let me set the ground rules. For starters, the fact that you're here at all is simply because I told you I'd look into your allegations, and because I told you I'd be in contact. Because your tires were slashed in addition to possible stalking violations, this is a potential *criminal* investigation, and in such an instance, ongoing investigations are generally not discussed. Still, because there's also the potential for a *civil* no-contact order—the Fifty-C—I'm choosing to meet with you and keep you as informed as I think appropriate. Also, keep in mind that because Lester Manning has *not* been served a Fifty-C, he has—like everyone else—certain and expected rights to privacy. In other words, I'll tell you what I think is important, but I won't necessarily tell you everything I know. I also want to add that most of what I've done has been via the telephone. I've had to rely on a detective friend of mine in Charlotte for a few things, and frankly, I'm not sure how much more I'm going to be able to ask of him. He's already gone out of his way, and like me, he's got cases that are higher priority. Do you understand?"

"Yes."

"Good," he said. "First I'll walk you through the approach I took, then a bit of what I learned." Opening the folder, he pulled out his notes. "My first step was to familiarize myself with all the background information, so I perused the relevant police files. That included everything having to do with the first assault on Cassie Manning, the arrest and conviction of Gerald Laws, court documents, and finally, information regarding the murder of Cassie Manning. After that, I reviewed your first stalking report—the one you made after you received the notes in Charlotte—and I spoke to the officer in charge of that particular case. It wasn't until late Tuesday evening that I felt like I had a pretty good grasp of everything.

"Now, with regard to Lester Manning, I'm comfortable telling you what you could probably learn on your own with a simple public records search." He glanced down again. "He's twenty-five years old and unmarried. High school graduate. He doesn't own any real property and there are no cars registered in his name. He lists his phone number and address as the same as his father's. With that said, I'm not sure how much time he actually spends there."

Maria was about to ask a question, but Margolis held up his hand to stop her.

"Let me finish, okay? You'll understand why I say that in just a couple of minutes. Now, I can share the next bit of information because I think it's important to the Fifty-C, but I'm not going to go into heavy details because those may or may not be important to any future criminal case, all right?" He didn't wait for an answer. "Since Cassie's death, Lester has had some problems with the law. He's been arrested four times, but not for anything violent or dangerous. It's all minor stuff—trespassing, vandalism, resisting arrest. Things like that. It turns out that Lester has a fondness for squatting in vacant houses. In each case, the charges were eventually dropped. I haven't looked into the reasons, but in cases like these, it's usually because there was little actual damage."

Beside her, Maria saw Colin shift in his seat.

"Other than that, I wasn't able to learn much, so I called Dr. Manning, Lester's father. I left a message, and surprising me, I got a call back within a few minutes. I identified myself and told Dr. Manning that I was hoping to speak to his son, and I will say that he was entirely cooperative and more forthcoming than I expected. Among other things, toward the end of our second conversation, he gave me permission to disclose the full nature of my call with him to you. Does that surprise you?"

Maria opened her mouth, then closed it again, not sure what to say. "Should I be surprised?" she finally asked.

"I was," Margolis said, "especially given the way you described him to me. But anyway, when I asked him if he knew where I might be able to find Lester, he asked me the reason, and I told him that it was regarding a police matter. To which he responded, and I quote, 'Does this have anything to do with Maria Sanchez?'"

Margolis let the words hang before going on. "When I asked him why he brought up your name, he said that it's not the first time you accused Lester of stalking. He said that after his daughter was murdered, you made the same accusation regarding some disturbing notes that had been sent to you. He insisted that his son, Lester, was not responsible then, and that he sincerely doubted that he was responsible for anything you were claiming now. He also said to tell you that while he does feel that you made a mistake by opting for the lesser charges, he's well aware that Gerald Laws was responsible for Cassie's death, and neither he nor his son blames you for what happened."

"He's lying."

Margolis ignored her comment. "He told me that he's not taking patients at the present time, and explained that he's currently working in Tennessee for the state prison system. He said that he hasn't spoken to Lester in weeks, but that Lester has a key to the house and occasionally stays in the apartment above the garage. He said that I'd probably be able to find Lester there. When I asked what he meant by 'occasionally,' Dr. Manning was quiet for a beat, and when he spoke again, I got the sense that I'd touched a nerve. He told me that 'Lester is a bit of a nomad' and there are times when he has no idea where Lester sleeps. I think he was referring to Lester's habit of staying in vacant houses. When I pressed him, he added that he and his son are somewhat estranged these days, and for the first time, he sounded almost... apologetic. He reminded me that Lester was an adult and made his own decisions and there was only so much he could do as a father. He also added that if Lester wasn't in the apartment at the house, my best bet was to try to find him at work. A place called Ajax Cleaners. It's a janitorial service with a lot of commercial clients. He didn't have the number offhand, but it was easy enough to find, and so my next step was to talk to the owner, a guy named Joe Henderson."

Margolis looked up from his notes. "Are you following me so far?"

When Maria nodded, Margolis went on.

"When I spoke with Mr. Henderson, he said that Lester wasn't a full-time or even part-time employee. He worked as an on-call employee—someone who could cover shifts when they were short-staffed or whatever."

"How could they call him if he doesn't have a phone?"

"I asked that very same question. The way it works there is they post open shifts on the employee section of their website— Henderson said it was easier to get a list of people and have them check than always scrambling to get the shifts covered. I had the sense there's quite a few people who check the list regularly. Anyway, Lester sometimes worked two or three nights a week, but in the last couple of weeks, he hasn't worked at all. Nor has Mr. Henderson heard from him. I found that interesting, so I called the house a couple of times, and no one answered. In the end, I sent my friend over there, and as far as he could tell, no one had been in the house or the apartment for at least a week. There were flyers in the mailbox, newspapers on the porch, that kind of thing. So I reached out to Dr. Manning a second time. And this is where things get kind of interesting."

"Because you couldn't reach him?"

"On the contrary," he said. "Again, I left a message, and again, I got a call back within minutes. When I told Dr. Manning that Lester hadn't been at work and that it didn't appear that anyone had been at the house or apartment, his surprise gave way to concern. He asked again about the police matter—I hadn't yet told him what it was—and I mentioned that I was looking into a case of slashed tires. He insisted that Lester wouldn't do such a thing. He said his son isn't violent; if anything, he's terrified of conflict of any sort. He also admitted that he hadn't been as forthcoming about Lester in the previous call as he could have been. When I asked what he meant, he told me that Lester…" Margolis reached for a page in the file. "Suffers from a delusional disorder, more specifically, *'persecutory delusions of the nonbizarre type.'* While his son can generally function normally for extended periods, there are times when the disorder enters a more acute phase, sometimes lasting more than a month. In Lester's case, it has its roots in the occasional usage of illegal drugs."

Margolis looked up. "The doctor went into a bit more about the specifics of Lester's disorder—way more than I needed to know, in fact—but essentially, it can be boiled down to this: When Lester is in an acute phase—when the disorder moves from simple paranoia to actual delusions—Lester ceases to function entirely normally. In these moments, Lester strongly believes that the police are out to get him and that they'll stop at nothing to put him in prison for the rest of his life. He's convinced they want to hurt him, and he's convinced they will set other prisoners against him. He also has the same delusions about you."

"That's ridiculous. Lester's been stalking me!"

"I'm just telling you what the doctor told me. He also told me that Lester had been arrested a few times. It was always during an acute phase, which was why he would resist arrest. The police would generally use Tasers to subdue him, and Dr. Manning added that on two separate occasions, Lester was beaten by other prisoners while he was locked up. That, by the way, goes to what I said earlier about my suspicion as to why the charges were dropped. I'm guessing that Lester wasn't coherent and it didn't take all that long for everyone to figure it out."

Margolis let out a sigh. "But back to Dr. Manning. Like I told you, he sounded worried and he said that if Lester wasn't at the house or working regularly, then he was likely in an acute phase. Which also meant he'd likely be in one of two places: either hiding out in a vacant house somewhere, or at Plainview, which is a psychiatric hospital. Lester's checked himself in there numerous times in the past, more frequently since his mother died. In her will, she left a trust fund large enough to cover the cost of his treatment there. It's expensive, by the way. I couldn't get any answers on the phone, so I called my friend again and asked if he could head over to Plainview in person. He did that this morning, about an hour before I called you. And sure enough, Lester Manning is currently a patient there. He admitted himself voluntarily, but that's about all the detective could really tell me. As soon as Lester learned that a detective wanted to talk to him about Maria Sanchez, he just... freaked out. My friend could hear him screaming from down the hall and the next thing he knew, a couple of orderlies were rushing in that direction. Like I said, interesting, don't you think?"

Maria wasn't sure what to say. In the silence, she heard Colin's voice.

"When was he admitted to the hospital?"

She watched as Margolis's eyes shifted toward Colin.

"I don't know. My friend couldn't find out. Medical records are confidential and that kind of information can't be released without the patient's permission. That clearly wasn't going to happen. At least, not right then. But my friend knows what he's doing, and so he asked one of the other patients, and the guy said that he thought Lester had been there for five or six days. Of course, considering the source, you'd have to take that information with a grain of salt."

"In other words, it's possible that Lester slashed the tires and left the notes."

"Or he might have been in the hospital. And if he was in the hospital, then obviously it isn't Lester."

"It has to be him," Maria insisted. "I don't know who else it could be."

"How about Mark Atkinson?"

"Who?"

"Cassie's boyfriend. Because I looked into him, too. It turns out that he may or may not be missing."

"What does that mean?"

"I'm still doing some preliminary work on that, but here's what I can tell you. Mark Atkinson's mother filed a missing persons report on her son about a month ago. But after I talked to the detective and right before I called you, I spoke with her to get more information, and I'm still not sure what to make of it. She told me that in August, he sent her an e-mail saying that he'd met someone online and that he was quitting his job and going to Toronto to meet her in person. She had no idea what to make of that, but in the e-mail, he told her not to worry. He said he'd prepaid his rent and that other bills were being paid online. The mother says she received a couple of printed letters from him saying that he was on a road trip with the woman, one of them postmarked from Michigan and another from Kentucky, but according to her, they were—and I quote—'vague and strange and impersonal, and not what my son would write.' Other than that, there's been no contact with him, and she insists that he's missing. She says he would have called or texted her, and the fact that he hasn't done those things means that something has happened to him."

The new information left Maria's head spinning, and it was all she could do to stay seated. Even Colin seemed at a loss for words.

Margolis looked from one to the other. "So that's where I am right now. If you're wondering what my plan is, moving forward, I'm going to give the good doctor another call and see if he can grease the wheels and find out when Lester was admitted. Or better yet, have his son give the physicians at Plainview permission to tell me. Depending on what I learn there, I may or may not check into the Mark Atkinson thing. But frankly, that's a lot of legwork, and again, I don't know how much more time I can commit to this."

"It's not Atkinson," Maria repeated. "It's Lester."

"If that's the case, then for now, I wouldn't worry."

"Why do you say that?"

"Because," he said simply, "as I just told you, Lester is in the hospital."

"It doesn't make any sense," Maria said to Colin. They were in the parking lot, the sun inching out from behind thin strands of clouds. "I've never met Mark Atkinson. I've never talked to him. As far as I know, I've never even seen him. Why would he be stalking me? He wasn't even dating Cassie when Laws went to jail. He didn't come into the picture until later. It doesn't make any sense."

"I know."

"And why the hell would Lester think I'm out to get him?"

"It's a delusion."

She glanced away, her voice becoming quieter. "I hate this. I mean, I feel like I know even less than I did before I came here today. And now I have no idea what I'm supposed to do, or even what I'm supposed to think about all this."

"I'm not sure what to make of it, either."

She shook her head. "Oh, one thing I forgot to tell you. I had to cancel with Jill and Leslie tonight because it's my mom's birthday. I'll be at my parents' place tonight while you're at work."

"Do you want me to come by after my shift?"

"No. Dinner will be over by then. My dad makes the meal—it's the one time a year that he actually cooks—but it's not a big deal. It'll be just the four of us."

"Are you going to stay there overnight? Or head back to your condo?"

"I'm thinking of going home. It's probably time, don't you think?"

Colin was quiet for a moment. "How about I meet you there? Just hang at your parents' and I'll call you when my shift is done."

"Would you mind?"

"Not at all."

She let out a sigh. "I'm sorry that as soon as things started clicking between us, all this had to happen. I hate that you're having to deal with it."

He kissed her. "I wouldn't have it any other way."

CHAPTER 21

———— ❦ ————

Colin

When he got home, Colin pulled the computer from his book bag and set it on the kitchen table. He was as confused about the whole situation as Maria was, and his instinct was to try to learn as much as possible.

The first step was to understand the mind-set of Lester Manning. Or rather, *persecutory delusions of the nonbizarre type*. He'd wanted to ask Margolis more about it when it came up, but it wasn't his place to ask, and Maria had let it go. Fortunately, there were dozens of web pages on the topic, and he spent the next hour and a half learning as much as he could.

He'd been under the impression that the disorder was similar to schizophrenia, but while certain symptoms like hallucinations and delusions were common in both types of patients, a patient was diagnosed with either schizophrenia or a delusional disorder. Schizophrenia often also included disorganized speech or delusions of the bizarre type. Bizarre meant impossible—the belief that the patient could fly, or read the minds of other people, or hear voices that could control their actions. Nonbizarre delusions—the kind that Lester suffered from—were at least plausible, but untrue.

In Lester's case, assuming he suffered from a delusional disorder, it made some sense that he might believe the police were out to get him. According to Avery Manning, the police had used Tasers on him and put him in jail; while there, he had been beaten by other prisoners. And in the end, the charges had been dropped, which might underscore Lester's belief that he never should have gone to jail at all.

His paranoia regarding Maria also made sense, Colin admitted, if plausibility was the sole criteria. Not only had Maria failed to protect Cassie, but if Lester hadn't written the notes—as Dr. Manning maintained—then Maria had sent the police after him for no reason. Not just once, but twice now...

Margolis had also been right in that a person with the disorder could, as a general rule, function normally, depending on the severity of the disorder. The spectrum of delusions could run from something as simple as overvalued ideas to near psychosis; another couple of the articles stated—just as Avery Manning had told Margolis—that delusions weren't rigidly fixed. They could fluctuate in intensity and could be aggravated by the use of certain drugs.

Still, as much as everything he read made sense, and while he understood that Lester truly believed his delusions...there were aspects of the disorder that didn't line up for him. If Lester was terrified of Maria, would he have delivered roses to her? Would he have sent over a drink? And if those were meant to be peace offerings of sorts, why would he have included the messages he had? Why taunt if what you wanted was to be left alone? And why come to Wilmington to do it? Wouldn't he have wanted to keep as much distance between them as he could?

Initially, Colin had wondered why Margolis had bothered looking into Mark Atkinson, but Margolis was smart enough to recognize the same inconsistencies and wonder how to reconcile them. Hence, he'd called Atkinson's mother, and from there the story got even more confusing.

He may or may not be missing?

As vague as it was, Margolis was accurate in his description.

A quick search brought up a photograph of a missing persons poster on Pinterest, no doubt created by Atkinson's mother. Other than that, there was nothing at all. He supposed he could do the same kind of search he'd done for Lester Manning, but what would be the point? According to Margolis, any information that might be helpful was inaccurate as of the date Mark Atkinson left for Toronto. Or went missing.

Or if not missing, was he in hiding?

Colin had the sense that Margolis considered it a possibility. The timing was too coincidental for it *not* to be a possibility. But Maria's point was also valid. Why would he target her? According to her, she'd never even met the man.

Closing the computer, Colin continued to ponder the questions before coming to the conclusion that he needed to clear his mind, and he knew only one way to do that.

He ran the six miles to the gym and spent an hour lifting weights, finishing with half an hour of striking on the heavy bag. Without classes in session, the gym was relatively quiet. Daly spotted him when necessary and held the bag for a few minutes, but otherwise spent most of his time in the office.

He ran home, showered, and changed into his work clothes and drove to work. Behind the wheel, he pondered the same questions he had earlier. Perhaps his defensive instincts were on high alert, but for some reason, he couldn't shake the feeling that something bad was about to happen.

CHAPTER 22

❧

Maria

After the meeting with Margolis, Maria headed back to the office, her head swimming with all she had learned. She stopped to visit with Jill and update her on the latest, but Jill wasn't back from lunch. It reminded Maria that she hadn't eaten, but then again, she couldn't even fathom the thought of eating.

Stress. If it continued, she was going to have to buy a new wardrobe in a smaller size or have everything altered; her clothes were already getting loose.

Barney was finally back in the office, though he spent the next three hours behind closed doors, meeting with one paralegal after another. She assumed he was interviewing for Lynn's replacement—who couldn't come soon enough, in Maria's opinion—and though she had a few questions for him about the hospital case, she knew better than to disturb him. Instead, she started organizing her questions, making notes in the margin of the complaint, until eventually she heard a knock at her door. Glancing up, she saw Barney standing in her doorway.

"Hi, Maria. Would you mind coming to my office?" he asked.

"Oh, hey, Barney," she said, gathering her pages and placing them back in the file, feeling a surge of relief. "Thank goodness. I was hoping to talk to you about the complaint. I've been thinking that there are a few different angles we can take, and I wanted to make sure I was clear on what you were planning to do before I really started to dig in."

"You can leave that for now," he said. "We'll go over the case later. Will you join me? There's something we need to discuss in my office."

Despite Barney's outwardly pleasant demeanor, there was something in his tone that made her cautious as she rose from her desk. Whatever he wanted to talk about, she suddenly thought, it wasn't going to be good.

Barney trailed half a step behind her, avoiding even small talk, and it wasn't until they got to his door that he reached her side. Always the gentleman—even when about to lower the boom, no doubt—he opened the door and motioned toward the high-backed chair farthest from the window that faced his desk. It wasn't until she'd moved closer to the chairs that she saw who was already seated in one of them. She came to a sudden halt.

Ken.

By then, Barney was already moving around his desk. She continued to stand in place even as Barney began pouring three glasses of water from a pitcher on his desk.

"Please," he said, urging her to take a seat. "There's nothing to worry about. We're just here for a friendly discussion."

I should simply tell him, no, thank you, and walk out the door, she suddenly thought. What were they going to do? Fire her? And yet, the old habits began kicking in—the ones about respecting her elders and obeying the boss—and she found herself almost on autopilot as she took her seat.

"Would you like a glass?" Barney asked. From the corner of her eye, she could see him studying her.

"No, thank you," she said. She could still walk out, she told herself, but...

"I appreciate you joining us, Maria," Barney said, his drawl just a bit heavier than usual, his cadence a beat slower. It was the same way he spoke when in the courtroom. "And I'm sure you might be wondering why we asked you to join us. Now..."

"You said there was something *we* needed to discuss," she interrupted. "As in the two of us."

Barney flinched ever so slightly, his surprise at being cut off evident but only for an instant. He smiled. "Excuse me?"

"You said 'we,' as in you and I. You didn't say that anyone else would be here."

"Of course," he said, his voice smoothing once more. "You're correct. I originally asked you to join *me*. My apologies for misspeaking."

He offered an opening for her to respond—no doubt expecting her to dismiss the error—but Colin probably wouldn't have said anything, so she didn't, either. *I'm learning*, she thought.

Barney opened his hands. "I suppose we should just get to it, then, so as not to waste your time with preliminaries. The last thing I would want is for this meeting to extend your workday."

"Okay." Inwardly, she smiled to herself.

Again, it wasn't what he expected her to say, but Barney was a master of recovery. He cleared his throat. "I'm sure you've heard the rumors in the office concerning potential allegations by various employees against Ken Martenson. Allegations, by the way, that have no factual basis."

He waited, but this time she said nothing at all.

"Am I correct?" he finally asked.

She glanced over at Ken, then back to Barney. "I'm not sure."

"You're not sure if you've heard the rumors?"

"Oh, I've heard the rumors," she said.

"Then what aren't you sure about?"

"I'm not sure whether the allegations have a factual basis or not."

"I can assure you, Maria, that they do not."

She waited a couple of beats. "Okay." Colin, she thought, would be proud of her right now. More than that, she began to understand how the use of the word *okay* shifted the power dynamic in the room. Or at the very least, set the tone she wanted, even if Barney didn't like it. He didn't, but he was professional enough to hide it, the drawl and slower cadence continuing in his courtroom rhythm.

"Because Mr. Martenson is our managing director, the firm intends to vigorously contest these allegations in whatever manner the firm deems best. That includes litigation. Of course, as you know well, when reputations are at stake, cases like this are usually settled to avoid lengthy, expensive, and distracting legal proceedings. In this particular instance, any potential settlement would not reflect on the veracity of the claims, but rather the time, money, and inconvenience that contesting the charges would bring. Obviously, any settlement—if there is a settlement—would be sealed and confidential."

Maria nodded, thinking, *Just get to the point. Why did you ask me here?*

"I'm sure I don't need to review Mr. Martenson's stellar reputation with you. Those who know him best—people like you and me—know that he has always kept the best interest of the firm at the forefront of his thoughts and actions. He has made tremendous sacrifices, and it's simply not possible that he would have done anything to put either the firm or his own personal reputation at risk. The allegations, I might add, are preposterous. In his nearly three-decade career as an attorney in our community, no claims of sexual harassment have ever so much as seen the light of day in any courtroom. Three decades of hard work, now at risk because there are people in the world who are simply greedy."

Claims that never reached the light of day because they were settled, Maria thought.

"Unfortunately, whenever there is a pot of money, there are those who believe themselves to be entitled to it. In some cases, these people may lie outright; in other instances, they distort the truth with a story that fits their agenda. Other times, people simply misinterpret behavior that nearly everyone else would find inoffensive. It's my belief that a bit of all three is what is happening here, and that has led to—in colloquial terms—a feeding frenzy. Some people—these greedy sharks—now sense blood in the water and want to make sure they get their *fair share* because they believe it is owed them by birthright. But our fair Constitution does not say that you're allowed to take someone else's property because you believe that *it should have been yours all along.* Greed. It's an awful, awful thing, and too many times, I've seen good people hurt by it, even my own kin. My neighbors—fine, churchgoing folk, mind you—were ruined by greedy people. But in these twilight years, I usually feel less anger than simple pity for them. Their lives are empty and they believe they can fill that emptiness with the coins from other people's pockets. Still, Mr. Martenson's reputation is at stake, as is the good name of our firm, and I feel a responsibility—even a *duty*—to ensure that both Mr. Martenson and the firm receive the most vigorous defense possible."

He was good, Maria thought, even when distorting the truth himself. She could understand why juries liked him.

"Of course, I am certain that you feel just as strongly about integrity and maintaining the high-quality reputation of our firm. But I do have to tell you that I'm frightened, Maria. I'm frightened for the other people here. Your coworkers. Your friends. The young families with mortgages and heating bills. Their babies and their children. I feel an obligation to them to use all the skills the good Lord has given me in the hopes that right and fair and good can prevail over wrong and greedy. But then again, I'm an old man and out of touch with the way things work these days, so what do I know?"

When Barney trailed off after playing the "deeply troubled" card, Maria almost felt like applauding. Instead, she kept a poker face. In time, Barney sighed and went on.

"I know you, Maria. And I know you share my concerns. You're too good of a person not to be scared for all your friends and coworkers here. And I know you'll want to help them because you don't desire a perversion of justice any more than I do. Our firm—all of us—need to stand united as one against these... these *greed-mongers* who have deluded themselves into believing that they're entitled to *your* hard-earned money, even though they themselves did nothing to earn it."

He shook his head.

"We just want the truth to come out, Maria. That's all. Just the simple, God's honest truth. And that's why you're here. Because I need your help."

Here it comes, Maria thought.

"All we're asking of you is the same thing we're asking of all our employees. We want you to sign an affidavit that simply states the truth: that you have the greatest respect for Mr. Martenson's character, and that in your tenure at the firm, you have never witnessed, or even heard about, Mr. Martenson engaging in anything that could be construed in any way as sexually offensive to *any* employee. In your case, and for our female employees, we're also asking that they confirm that they never felt sexually harassed, in any fashion, at any time."

For an instant, all Maria could do was stare at him. Ken, she noticed, had sunk lower in his seat, and before she could respond, Barney went on.

"Of course, you don't have to do this. In the end, whatever you choose to do is completely up to you. There is no reason whatsoever to take into account the livelihoods of anyone else in this firm. All I truly want is for you to do the *right* thing."

Barney finished; by then his eyes were downcast, his body humbly positioned. Barney: a bearer of righteousness in a world he no longer understood, shouldering a burden that had to be borne by someone. No wonder he was so successful.

But Maria could think of nothing to say. As persuasive as Barney was...he was *lying*, and he knew it. She also knew that Barney knew that she knew he was lying, which meant all of this was a game. No doubt he wanted Ken in the room as a form of punishment: *Do you understand the level to which I've sunk by defending you?* For his part, Ken hadn't so much as mumbled a single word.

And yet...

Was it fair for the rest of the office—all of whom were innocent—to be penalized? Because of a single idiot? And how much money did the women want? Ken had harassed her, and she'd survived. In another couple of weeks, she would likely put it behind her entirely. In time, it might even become the subject of jokes. Ken was a jerk, but it wasn't as though he'd exposed himself or tried to grope Maria in the hallway when they'd been at the conference. He was too insecure—too pathetic—to go that far. With her, anyway. But what about the others he'd harassed?

She wasn't sure, and feeling the need to stall, she drew a deep breath. "Let me think about it."

"Of course," Barney said. "I appreciate your consideration. And remember, everyone at the firm, your coworkers and friends, just want you to do the *right* thing."

At her desk, Maria forced herself to stare at the claim that had been filed against the hospital, but every few minutes she found herself replaying the conversation and thinking of ways she could have responded better. She found herself wondering what Colin would have done...

"There you are."

Lost in thought, Maria looked up and saw Jill in the doorway. "Oh, hey..."

"Where were you?" Jill asked. "I came by a little while ago, but you weren't in your office."

"Barney wanted to talk to me," she said.

"Figures," Jill said, closing the door behind her. "How did the meeting with the detective go?"

Maria proceeded to update Jill on the things Margolis had told her. Like Maria, Jill wasn't sure quite what to think. She asked the same questions that Maria had and was left with the same sense of confusion.

"I don't know whether it's good news or bad news," Jill finally said. "It's more confusing now than it was this morning."

That's not my only problem, Maria thought.

"What are you thinking about now?"

"What do you mean?"

"Your expression just changed."

"Uh... just thinking back on my meeting with Barney."

"And?"

"Ken was there."

Jill nodded. "Because of the lawsuit?"

"Of course."

"And let me guess. Barney did all the talking... and he poured on the Southern charm and started talking about 'doing the right thing'?"

"You know him well."

"Sadly, I do. So... did you learn anything?"

"They want to present 'a united front.'"

"Okaaay... but what exactly does that mean?"

"They want me to sign an affidavit that would essentially say that I never saw Ken do anything wrong, that he's always professional, and that he never harassed me."

"Did Barney ask that you sign? Or insist that you sign?"

"He asked. In fact, he made it perfectly clear that he wanted it to be my decision."

"That's good."

"I guess."

"You guess?"

When Maria didn't answer, Jill looked at her. "Don't tell me there's even *more*," she prodded. "Something you didn't tell me this morning?"

"Well..."

"Let me guess. Ken has been harassing you for a while?"

Maria looked up. "How did you know?"

"Don't you remember our lunch? After you'd gone paddle-boarding with Colin, when I kept asking whether things at work were going okay? I knew you'd gone to the conference with Ken, and I've been around here long enough to know exactly what he might have tried to do. Even while you were swearing that everything was fine, I had my suspicions."

"Why didn't you say anything?"

Jill offered the kind of shrug that asked, *Do you really need me to answer that?* "Office politics suck. That's why Leslie and I have already outlawed them. Back then, I didn't want to put the idea in your head if it hadn't happened, but I remember thinking that I was correct in my suspicions. Which is terrible, of course. But I was kind of happy, too, and I know how awful that is for a friend to say."

"What do you mean, you were kind of happy?"

"If you loved it here, you might not have been so eager to throw your lot in with us. Of course, at the time, I didn't know about the potential lawsuits."

"I'm glad you're so concerned with my well-being."

"You're a strong woman, Maria. And frankly, I think you're smarter than Ken. I knew you'd figure out a way to keep him at bay."

"I did tell him my boyfriend, the MMA fighter, was the jealous type."

Jill laughed. "Like I said. Way smarter than Ken. Okay, but back to the meeting you had with Barney and Ken, our illustrious leader. So Barney asked you to sign and you essentially told him that you'd think about it."

Maria's jaw dropped. "How could you know what I said?"

"Because I know Barney. He's a master at masking the obvious, showing how his side is the righteous one, and then mixing in a dollop of guilt, in case you're still wavering. It's important for you to put all that aside and think about what actually happened. And by the way, what did happen?"

Maria then offered a recap of the conference—to which Jill didn't raise an eyebrow—but when she told her about the subsequent encounters, Jill went stony.

"Hold on," she said. "It's one thing to offer the 'my wife doesn't understand me' tale, but you're saying he actually touched your chest?"

"Well, my collarbone... or maybe just below. He didn't—"

"But his intent was obvious to you? And he wanted to have lunch and discuss being more of a 'team player'?"

"Yes. But I stopped it from going any further... He didn't—"

"Come with me," Jill said, reaching for the doorknob.

"Where are we going?"

"To see Barney and Ken."

"Let's just let it go... I'm leaving anyway. And he didn't actually touch my breast or anything..."

"Well, Barney doesn't know the details. And I'm sure that the meeting wasn't only about trying to protect the firm; it was also intended to keep you from joining the other women and filing with the EEOC."

Maria shook her head. "I'm not going to file."

"Are you sure you don't want to?"

Maria thought about Barney and the other employees of the firm. Ken's attentions had been awful and had caused her stress, but to her mind, simply putting it all behind her and moving on was a far more appealing option than pursuing the matter further.

"Yes, I'm sure. I'm leaving anyway."

"But don't you think Ken should be held accountable? At least a little? For all the stress he caused you?"

"I guess. But like I said, I don't want to go to the EEOC."

Jill smiled. "They don't know that."

"What are you going to say?"

"Exactly what should be said. And whatever you do, let me do all the talking. Don't say a word."

Before she even realized what was happening, Jill was marching toward Barney's office, Maria racing just to keep up with her. Barney's door was closed, but that didn't deter Jill in the slightest.

Barney and Ken, occupying the same seats they'd been in only minutes earlier, were startled by Jill's sudden appearance.

"What's going on? We're in a meeting—" Barney began, but Jill strode into the office, Maria right behind her.

"Would you mind closing the door, Maria?" Jill's voice was steady and professional, but determined. Maria realized she'd never heard her like this.

"Did you hear me, Jill?" Barney asked.

"I think you need to hear *me*."

"We're supposed to interview another paralegal in five minutes."

"Tell her that she's going to have to wait. You'll want to hear what I have to say. It's about the lawsuit and it concerns both of you."

Ken remained silent and Maria watched as he paled. Barney stared at her before finally reaching for his phone; Maria listened as he did as Jill instructed. After hanging up the phone, he stood from his seat. "Let me bring over the chair from the window—" he began, but Jill shook her head sharply.

"We'll stand," she said.

If Ken didn't understand what that meant, there was no question in Maria's mind that Barney did. She saw an ever-so-slight lifting of his eyebrows and assumed he was doing some rapid mental calculations. Most people would likely have taken their seat again, but Barney understood the value of maintaining eye level, even if Ken did not. He stood straighter.

"You said this matter concerns the firm?"

"Actually, I said that it concerns the both of you. But yes, in the end, it concerns the firm as well."

"I'm glad you came by, then," he said, the drawl and syrupy cadence returning. "We just had a discussion with Maria about the false allegations, as I'm sure you're aware, and I'm confident that Maria will do what's right for all involved."

"You shouldn't be quite so confident," Jill countered. "I wanted you two to be the first to know that Maria just informed me that Ken Martenson has been engaging in conduct that any jury would construe as sexual harassment and that she is strongly considering filing a report with the EEOC as a preliminary to filing her own lawsuit."

"That's not true!" Ken erupted, the first words Maria had heard him speak all day.

Jill turned toward him, her tone as even as before. "You told her she should try harder to be a team player. That having you in her corner could help her when she came up for partner. And then you groped her."

"I did no such thing!"

"You touched her inappropriately, on her neck and chest."

"I . . . I only touched her shoulder."

"So you admit to touching her? And keeping your hands on her even though she clearly found it offensive?"

With her words, Ken realized it was probably better to shut his mouth, and he turned toward Barney. If Barney was angered by what Jill had said, he didn't show it.

"Maria made no claim of sexual harassment in our meeting today, nor in fact has she ever said anything to me in all the months she's been working here."

"Why would she? She knew you'd cover for him. Just like before, when the other sexual harassment cases were settled."

Barney drew a long breath. "I'm sure there's been some sort of misunderstanding and we'll be able to work this out amicably. There is no reason to resort to threats."

"I haven't resorted to threats. In fact, if anything, you should be thankful that we're here so you aren't surprised."

"I am," he agreed. "I do think we could discuss the matter more civilly if we take our seats. I would like to hear what Maria has to say."

"I'm sure you would. We'll let you read her statement in detail as soon as it's filed. For now, I'll speak for her."

Ken's eyes went wide, but Barney simply looked at Jill.

"You do understand that you can't represent Maria for obvious conflict-of-interest reasons?"

"I'm here as her friend."

"I'm not sure that makes a difference."

"Then let's start with this: Both Maria and I will be leaving the firm. We had no intention of informing you of that today, but considering that Maria can additionally make a case for retaliation, I thought it best to get it over with now."

For the first time, even Barney wasn't sure what to say. He looked from Jill to Maria and back to Jill. "Did you say you're both leaving the firm?"

"Yes."

"Where will you be working?"

"That's not the issue we're discussing. Right now, we're talking about the lawsuit Maria intends to file. We all know that the allegations being made by Lynn and the others are serious, and can you imagine how much more heft their cases will have when Maria comes forward as well?"

"But I didn't do anything," Ken mumbled. Barney merely glared at him.

"Do you think anyone will believe that? After everything the others say in court? But of course, it won't get that far. Everyone in this room knows that you're going to settle. These cases are almost always settled. I'm not sure I can say the same for Maria. She was pretty upset when she spoke with me. Though I won't be her counsel on this case, my suspicion is that she may elect to take this as far as it can go."

Barney straightened his jacket. "I'm assuming that you're here not simply to inform us in advance that you're going to file or that you're leaving. I assume you're here because you would like to resolve this matter."

"Why would you think that?"

"There is nothing to be gained by telling us in advance that you intend to make a report with the EEOC."

"Maybe I just felt a remaining bit of loyalty to the firm."

"Perhaps."

"Or maybe I just wanted Ken to know that in addition to ruining the firm and having his savings wiped out, he's probably going to have to sell that ridiculous car of his by the time Maria is through with him."

Ken moaned ever so slightly. Barney ignored it.

"How can we resolve this?"

"For starters, Maria wants six weeks of vacation this year."

"Why would she want six weeks' vacation when she's planning on leaving?"

"Because it's on her bucket list. Because Ken is an ass. Because yesterday, she saw a rainbow when she was walking by a yard with the sprinklers on. Because Maria had to work evenings and weekends because of you and so she hasn't had a day off since she's been here. My point is, it doesn't matter why she wants it. She does, and that's that."

"First-year employees are only entitled to a week."

"Then make an exception. Paid vacation, mind you, which will be added to her final check."

Ken was about to say something, but Barney held up his hand to stop him. "Anything else?"

"Yes. As far as a two-week notice goes? That's out. Today is Maria's last day and she won't be coming back. She gets paid for these two weeks as well."

Barney looked like he had eaten something unpleasant. "Is that all? Two months' salary?"

"Not quite. For her mental suffering, she needs a bonus. Let's make it...three additional months' salary on top of those two months."

Barney was quiet. "And in exchange for that?"

"I'll have to talk it over with her, but I'm fairly certain you'll never hear anything from her about any of Ken's deviant behavior. No reports, no lawsuits. Just over and done and we'll go our own separate ways."

Barney was quiet, probably debating how serious Maria might be about all of this. Jill, however, knew exactly what he was thinking.

"She's not bluffing, Barney. You know how Ken is. You know what he's done to others and you also know that he sexually harassed Maria. More than that, you know we're not talking about a lot of money here. Essentially, she's offering you a gift because as much as she despises Ken, she has great respect for you."

"And the affidavit?"

"Don't even go there," Jill warned. "Maria is not going to lie. However, she won't sign an affidavit as to what actually happened. It'll just be forgotten."

"And if she's deposed by the other litigants?"

"She'll be on the planet Jupiter by then, so there's no reason to worry."

"Excuse me?"

"Oh." She smiled. "Sorry. I thought we'd detoured into fantasy land."

"Fantasy?"

"You and I both know she won't get deposed because you're not going to let it get that far. You'll end up settling. You have to, or it's going to cost you a fortune, even if you win."

Barney glanced at Ken, then back to Jill. "May I ask what your demands are? Since you'll be leaving the firm as well?"

"Only one, and it's not about money," Jill answered. "In exchange, I'll finish out the next couple of weeks here just as I planned to do, work with the partners to make sure any of my clients barely notice the transition, and after that, I'll move on."

"What's the one demand?"

"I'd like you to throw me a small going-away party here at the office. Nothing fancy—just a cake at lunch or whatever—but I'd like the chance to say good-bye to everyone in one fell swoop. Obviously, until then, I think we all know it would be best to keep our departure as quiet as possible. The other partners have to know, but I don't want to start a stampede of employees racing for the exits. Believe it or not, I hope you get this settled and are able to put it behind you as quickly and quietly as possible. There are a lot of good people here."

While Barney may have appreciated Jill's sentiment, Maria saw him twitch as he brought a hand to his chin. "Five months paid for Maria is a bit high. I'm sure the partners will balk at that. Now, three months I could probably swing..."

"Don't misinterpret my high hopes for others here as a chance to negotiate, because we aren't negotiating. This is a one-time, take-it-or-leave-it offer. Which ends the moment that Maria and I walk out the door and she starts on the EEOC paperwork. Frankly, she's asking for far less than what you're going to have to shell out to the others. So right now, you should be thanking her, not trying to lowball."

Barney took his time before answering. "I'd still have to talk to the other partners," he finally said. "I can't make this kind of decision on my own."

"Sure you can. We both know the partners will follow your lead, so let's stop playing games, all right? Are you in or out?"

※

"Five months' salary?" Maria exclaimed. They were standing in the parking lot near Maria's car. A few minutes earlier, Maria had stashed the few personal items she'd had in the office— primarily photographs of her family and a few she'd taken while paddleboarding—into a small box and had carried it outside, placing it in the trunk. At Barney's request, she hadn't said good-bye to anyone, nor had anyone seemed to notice anything out of the ordinary regarding her departure. Jill had been waiting for her.

Jill smiled. "Pretty good, huh?"

Truthfully, she was reeling. No more Ken; no more weekends trying to keep up with Barney's demands, and *five* months' salary, straight into her savings account. She'd never, ever had anything close to that; what had just happened was akin to buying a winning scratch-off lottery ticket. "I'm still in shock."

"I probably could have gotten you more."

"That's more than enough. I feel guilty for getting that much."

"Don't feel bad. Because, believe it or not, you were sexually harassed. It may not have been as obvious to you as it was to others, but you were. You deserve this. And believe me when I say that Barney is breathing a massive sigh of relief right now, or we wouldn't be standing here doing a mini-celebration."

"Thank you so much."

"You don't have to thank me. If our positions were reversed, you would have done it for me."

"I'm nowhere near as good as you are. You took on Barney. And you won."

Jill offered a sheepish grin. "And you want to know the crazy thing?"

"What's that?"

"Leslie is way, way better than me."

The thought made Maria's head spin. "Thank you again for taking a chance on me."

"You're welcome. But I know exactly what I'm getting."

Maria motioned toward the building. "It's strange to think that I'm not going to work tomorrow. And most likely, I will never walk through those doors again. It happened so . . . fast."

"Like what they say about bankruptcy? It happened slow at first and then all at once?"

Maria nodded. "I guess. As much as I dislike what Barney was trying to do just now, I still hope he'll be okay."

"Barney's the one attorney you never have to worry about. He'll be fine, no matter what. And between you and me? It wouldn't surprise me if he leaves the firm, too."

"Why would he leave?"

"Because he can. And would you want to keep working with Ken?"

Maria didn't answer, but then again she didn't have to. Jill was right, and while Maria was still trying to process her day, she suddenly found herself thinking about Lester Manning and the things Margolis had told her. She crossed her arms.

"What would you do if you were me? About Lester, I mean?" Maria asked.

"I don't think you know enough yet to reach any conclusions. I know that probably doesn't help you, but..."

She trailed off, and Maria couldn't blame her, since even to her, the pieces simply didn't fit.

Maria drove through heavy traffic to Mayfaire, an upscale shopping complex. As she drove, she tried to process the fact that she wouldn't be heading in to work tomorrow, or even on Monday. The last time that had happened had been after she'd quit her job in Charlotte...

She shook her head, forcing the thought away. She knew exactly where it would lead, and the last thing she wanted was to think about Lester or the boyfriend or anything Margolis had told her, since it would lead exactly nowhere. Unless confusion was a place.

No more Ken, she marveled. No more weekends that Barney could ruin. In two weeks, she'd be working with Jill. And five months' salary. On the career front, she doubted it was possible for things to get any better, and that called for a celebration of sorts, maybe even a splurge. She could trade in her car and get something sportier—as long as it wasn't a red Corvette—but as quickly as the thought entered her mind, she knew it was just a fantasy. She was too frugal and she had no intention of trying to explain to her dad why she'd bought a car instead of paying down some of the student debt she owed from law school or opening an investment account. Or simply saving the money, since she'd probably need to buy into the partnership in a few years.

Lost in the events of today was the idea that she could actually be a partner at a law firm someday—in her early thirties, even. Whoever could have predicted that?

By the time she reached Mayfaire, dusk had settled in. She texted Serena that she'd get to the house a few minutes before seven, but not to hold up dinner on her account.

Seconds later, her phone dinged with Serena's response. *I'll just get there late, too. I'd hate for you to miss any of the scintillating conversation!*

Maria smiled. She texted her parents and let them know when she'd arrive, then headed toward Williams-Sonoma. It was always a bit challenging to get her mom something special—Carmen always fretted about money spent on her, especially by her *children*—but since a new car was out of the question, Maria figured she could splurge a bit on some new pots and pans. Despite the restaurant and her own love of cooking, her mom had never considered buying new cookware. What she did have had been around since Maria was in elementary school. Or maybe even longer than that.

The shopping expedition ended up being more of a splurge than she'd planned. High-quality cookware was expensive, but Maria felt good about it. Her parents had paid for private schooling, a used car at sixteen that lasted until she got the one she owned now, four years of college, and half of law school, and never once had she done something like this. She knew her mom might fret—her dad would say nothing—but she deserved it.

She loaded the gifts in the trunk, next to the box of personal effects. Thankfully, the traffic had mostly cleared out. Before starting the car, she texted Serena that she was fifteen minutes away, and then realized she hadn't yet told Colin what had happened at the office. She still felt the need to celebrate and with whom better than him? Later, at his place or hers... Who knew that money could be an aphrodisiac?

Knowing he was probably behind the bar already, she texted him and asked that he call when he had the chance. He'd probably work until around ten or eleven, and that would give her enough time after leaving her parents' to head back home, light a couple of candles, maybe even have a glass of wine. She knew it would end up being a late night, but he didn't have class in the morning and she didn't have to go to work, so why did it matter?

She set the phone on the passenger seat and headed toward her parents' house. After turning into the neighborhood, she found herself wondering how many times in her life she'd made that exact turn. Tens of thousands, probably, she thought, which amazed her, as did the neighborhood itself. While people had moved in and moved out, the houses seemed largely unaffected by the passage of time, and every corner brought with it memories: lemonade stands or roller-skating, driveway fireworks on the Fourth of July. Trick-or-treating. Walking home with friends. Her phone began to ring, disrupting the flow of images. Glancing over, she saw Colin's name and answered with a smile.

"Hey," she said. "I didn't think you were allowed to make calls while at work."

"I'm not supposed to, but I saw your text. I asked the other bartender to cover for me for a few minutes. Are you okay?"

"Yeah, I'm fine," she said. "I'm almost at Mom and Dad's."

"I thought you were supposed to be there already."

"I had to buy my mom a gift first and that took forever," she said. "But hey—you'll never guess what happened today."

"Did Margolis call again?"

"No. It's about work," she said, and as she approached her parents' home, she told Colin what had transpired. "Which means I'm kinda rich right now."

"Sounds like it."

"I bought my mom some fabulous cookware."

"I'll bet she's going to love it."

"Once she gets over the guilt, she will. But the real reason I'm calling is that I've decided that I'd like you to come over tonight. To my place."

"Didn't we already agree that I'd come over? And that I'd call when I got off?"

"Yes, but when we decided that, I wasn't in the mood to celebrate. Now I am, and I wanted to warn you in advance."

"Warn me about what?"

"Well, now that I'm sorta rich, I might make a few demands on you this evening. Physical ones, I mean."

He laughed, and she could tell he liked what she was suggesting. "Okay."

Up ahead, she saw Serena's car parked in front of her parents' house; on either side of the street, the sidewalks were deserted. Up and down the block, houses were lit from the inside, lamps on and televisions flickering, families relaxing at the end of a long day. "Whatever you do, don't let the anticipation ruin your concentration at work. I'd hate for you to get in trouble with your boss."

"I'll do my best."

She pulled in behind Serena's car and shut down the engine. "And one more thing. Remember what I told Margolis? When he asked why I was still with you?"

"Yes."

She got out and rounded the car to the trunk. "I just want you to know that I meant every word," she said.

He laughed again. "Okay."

She opened the trunk. "Unfortunately, I'm going to have to cut this call a little short. I'm going to need both hands to carry everything."

"I get it. I've got to get back to work anyway."

"Oh, before you go—"

As she eyed the boxes, she registered movement in her peripheral vision and she turned. A man was crossing the street toward her, moving fast. There was a split second when she wasn't sure how to react. This was a safe place; in this neighborhood, she'd never so much as heard of a burglary or a domestic dispute that had gotten out of hand, and she'd never been afraid. She was only yards from her parents' front door, on a street so safe she used to camp out in the backyard on warm summer nights. And yet, the stranger's purposeful gait made the hairs on the back of her neck suddenly rise because she knew instinctively that whoever it was didn't belong here.

Darkness made clear recognition impossible, but in that instant the man's shadowed face was suddenly illuminated by the lights that spilled from her parents' living room. She saw a glint of metal in his hand and with the sight of the gun, fear took hold. She couldn't move and could barely breathe; only vaguely did she hear Colin say her name on the phone.

Colin repeated her name a second and third time, his mounting concern enough to finally bring her back.

"He's here," she finally whispered.

"Who's there?" Colin demanded. "What's going on?"

"He has a gun," she said.

"Who has a gun?"

"Lester Manning," she said. "He's here at the house."

CHAPTER 23

———— ❧ ————

Colin

The shock of hearing Maria say Lester's name gave way to a surge of adrenaline, the fight-or-flight reflex kicking in. Colin vaguely heard Lester shout something and the call was disconnected.

Lester.

By then, Colin was already on the move, bursting from the back room and rushing past the bar. He wove around tables and guests even as he hit the redial button.

The phone went straight to voice mail.

Redial.

Voice mail again.

Maria is in trouble.

Behind him, he heard the bartender call his name; waitresses looked over in confusion, and as Colin exploded out the entrance, the manager demanded to know where he was going.

Lester has a gun.

Colin raced around the corner of the building, his feet slipping on the lightly sanded sidewalk. Regaining his footing, he sprinted up the street, already calculating the most direct route to Maria's parents' place.

Hoping the roads were clear.

Hoping his car would start.

Please, let it start.

He'd call the police from the car.

He swerved around an elderly couple and rocketed into the street, his car in sight.

Precious seconds ticking away.

Lester could have already shoved her into his car and driven off, just like Gerald Laws did to Cassie...

It was twenty minutes to her parents'.

He would make it in ten. Or fewer.

Maria might already be gone...

At the car now. Jumping in, jamming his keys in the ignition, careful not to flood the engine even as he turned the key hard, and the old Camaro roared to life. Colin peeled away from the curb, his eyes already on the cars ahead.

Closing the gap between his car and those ahead of him, he glanced toward his phone. With one hand he frantically dialed 911 and heard the operator ask the nature of the emergency.

A man with a gun, threatening a woman, he said. Maria Sanchez. A guy named Lester Manning had been stalking her, and he'd surprised her at her parents'...

He couldn't remember the address offhand, but told the operator Maria's parents' names, as well as the street and cross street. Identifying himself, he stated that he was on the way. When the operator urged him to let the police handle the situation without interference, he hung up.

By then he was speeding along, the nose of his car practically on the bumper of the car in front of him. With the next lane blocked by a black Range Rover coasting along at the speed limit, Colin cut across the breakdown lane and zoomed past a cluster of cars before veering back onto the road. He hit the accelerator hard and within a few seconds came up on a pickup truck and a white minivan driving side by side. He passed them in the breakdown lane, too, this time barely slowing.

Reaching the turnoff to the bridge, he jerked the wheel hard, tires squealing.

Racing past more cars in the breakdown lane, he finally made it to a long stretch of road with less traffic and jammed the accelerator to the floor. Adrenaline sharpened his instincts behind the wheel, his body responding in perfect sync with the car.

He hit eighty, ninety, and then a hundred miles an hour and saw a red light ahead, brake lights glowing as cars slowed. Unwilling to slow down, he gunned into a bike lane.

Bursting through a gap at the intersection, still he pressed on, zigzagging around cars and using the bike lane when necessary. Making a turn, he accelerated toward a long line of cars, and with nowhere to go, he cut through a gas station parking lot at close to thirty miles an hour, making people jump out of the way.

The police were on their way... but it still might not be soon enough.

His mind raced frantically, wondering whether Lester had already forced Maria into a car, where he might have taken her...

Or if he had already shot her.

Another turn, this time to the left, and for the first time, he was forced to come to a complete stop at a crowded intersection. He pounded the steering wheel, then held his breath as he plunged into multiple lanes of traffic. He watched as another driver slammed on his brakes, missing him by only inches.

Speeding through a residential neighborhood at sixty miles per hour, he scanned for children or other pedestrians or pets, houses passing in a blur.

Another turn. Tires screeched and the rear of the Camaro fishtailed left and then right, Colin struggling for control. On this block, cars were parked on either side of the street, limiting visibility, and Colin reluctantly slowed the car. Just ahead, he could make out a couple pushing a stroller on the sidewalk; a kid playing catch with his dad on the opposite side of the street; a guy walking his dog with a long retractable leash...

Another turn and a clear road with better visibility; Colin sped up again, finally recognizing the Sanchez neighborhood.

It had taken him nine minutes.

He began to bank into the final turn at top speed... and almost hit a blue Camry that was approaching fast in the middle of the road. Colin swerved automatically to the right, as did the other car, the Camaro fishtailing again, tires screeching. Colin felt another sudden adrenaline surge as his heart hammered. He briefly glimpsed two men in the front seat with startled expressions, their eyes wide as the cars slid past within inches of each other, too close. Way too close, and he gripped the wheel hard, regaining control. Barely.

He was almost there, the Sanchezes' street up ahead. A single turn to go, and he didn't hit the brakes until he was almost there.

Fear taking over now.

Praying he wasn't too late.

Shearing into the turn, he heard a siren behind him. In the rearview mirror, he saw the flashing lights on top of the squad car as it barreled around the same turn he'd just made. Colin slowed only slightly, but the squad car was closing fast and Colin heard a squawk from the loudspeaker.

"Pull over!"

Not a chance, Colin thought. *No matter what happens to me.*

CHAPTER 24

❧

Maria

Maria couldn't take her eyes from the gun...or the person holding it.

Lester Manning.

Margolis had been wrong. Lester wasn't in the hospital.

He had been waiting for her here. The knowledge paralyzed her, and she watched as he snatched the phone from her hand. His face contorted into something she barely recognized.

"No calls!" he shouted, making her jump. The tone was off-key, on edge. "No police!"

As he backed away, her senses heightened and she saw it all: the unkempt hair and ratty canvas jacket, faded red shirt, and torn jeans; the dark holes of his pupils and the rapid rise and fall of his chest. In her head, the words ran together: *delusional disorder; acute phase; persecutory delusions.*

And the gun. He was holding a gun.

Her mom and dad were inside, as was Serena. Her family was in danger and it was dark and no one in the neighborhood was out...

She should have run as soon as she saw him coming, sprinted for the front door and locked him out, but she'd stood there like her legs belonged to another person...

"I know what YOU DID!" he hissed.

The words came out fast and almost unintelligible. As he continued to back away, she saw the phone light up and heard it ring. *Colin.* Lester startled, staring at the phone in his hand. She watched Lester end the call with the press of a button. Saw the phone light up and ring again. Lester frowned as he ended the second call, talking at the phone as though it were alive. "I said no calls!" he called out. "No police!" Then mumbling: "Think straight. It's not real." His hands were shaking as he muted the phone and shoved it into his jacket pocket. "They're not coming."

Please God, let Colin have already called the police, she thought. *The police are coming and will be here soon. I'll just ride it out until they get here. I will not be like Cassie. If he so much as touches me, I'm going to scream and fight like crazy.*

But...

Margolis had said that Lester could function normally sometimes; he'd been able to work a part-time job. And when she'd met him, he was...odd, but not psychotic, even when clearly struggling. Maybe she could talk to him...She just needed to stay calm.

"Hi, Lester," she began, trying to keep her voice steady and pleasant.

His eyes flashed up, his pupils huge.

No, not huge. Dilated. On drugs?

"'Hi, Lester'? That's all you can say?"

"I want you to know I'm sorry about Cassie—"

"No, no, *no!*" he said, raising his voice. "You don't get to say *her name.* She died because of you!"

She raised her hands instinctively, expecting him to lunge at her, but Lester instead moved yet another step farther away. As she waited for him to go on, she realized that he sounded less angry than...afraid?

Or paranoid. And the last thing I want is to set him off.

She lowered her eyes, her heart hammering. She could hear Lester's labored breathing as long seconds passed. The silence stretched out until she heard him sniff and then say, "No," in a softer voice. She could hear his breathing finally begin to slow, and when he spoke again, his voice was shaky but subdued.

"They're safe," he said, nodding at the house. "Your family. I saw them through the windows. I watched your sister go inside. What happens next is up to you."

She flinched at his words but held her silence. His breath continued to slow in what seemed like a conscious effort, his gaze never wavering.

"I came to talk. You need to hear what I have to say. You'll listen to me this time, won't you, Maria?"

"Yes."

"The doctors tell me it isn't real," he explained. "I tell myself it's not real. But then I remember the truth. About Cassie and my mom. The police. And what they did. And I know you're the one who started it. The doctors can tell me it's not real and that I'm making it up, but I know the truth. So tell me: You've been talking about me, haven't you?"

When she didn't answer, she watched the muscles begin to tighten in his neck.

"Don't bother lying. Remember that I already know the answer."

"Yes," she whispered.

"You've talked to the police about me again."

"Yes," she said again.

"That's why the detective came this morning."

Where is Colin? she wondered. *And the police?* She wasn't sure how long she could keep Lester calm—

"Yes."

He turned away, wincing. "When we first met you, I wanted to believe you when you said you were doing your best, and that Cassie would be safe. I came to understand that to you, Cassie was no one. Just another name, another nobody. But she wasn't a nobody. She was my sister, and it was your job to protect her. But you didn't. And then . . ."

He squeezed his eyes closed. "Cassie used to take care of me when my mom was too sick to get out of bed...She used to make me chicken noodle soup and we'd watch television and she'd read me books. Did you know that? She wasn't a nobody." He wiped at his nose with the back of his hand, and when he went on, his voice was almost childlike. "We tried to warn you what was going to happen, but you didn't listen. When Cassie died, my mom couldn't stand living anymore. Because of you, she killed herself. Did you know that? Tell the truth."

"Yes," she admitted.

"You know all about us, don't you, Maria? You know all about me."

"Yes."

"And you sent the police after me after Cassie died."

Because you sent the notes. Because you were threatening me. "Yes."

"And your boyfriend...He is your boyfriend, right? The big guy at the club? I saw how angry he got after I sent over the drink. He wanted to hurt me, didn't he?"

"Yes."

"And then, this morning, you sent the police again."

Because you slashed my tires! Because you're stalking me! "Yes."

He stood a bit straighter. "That's what I told the doctors. All of this. But they don't believe me, of course. No one ever believes me, but at least you're being honest. I *knew*, but now I *really* know...and I can feel the difference in my whole body. You understand, don't you, Maria?"

No. "Yes."

"It takes over—fear, I mean. No matter how hard you try to fight it, it takes over, crushing the life out of you. Like right now. I know you're afraid of me. Maybe like Cassie was afraid after you failed her?" He looked at her for confirmation, waiting.

"Yes."

She watched him tap the gun against the side of his leg. "Can you imagine how it feels? To lose your sister? And your mom? And watch people like you go after my dad? And then me?"

"I can't imagine how awful that was."

"No, you CAN'T!" he shouted suddenly, and in that moment, she heard the faint sound of a police siren in the distance.

Lester snapped to attention, recognition dawning as the sirens grew louder. He refocused on Maria.

"I said no police. I said NO POLICE!" His voice cracked, whipsawing between anger and disbelief as he took a step toward her. "I'm NOT going BACK! Do you HEAR me? I'm NOT going BACK!"

Maria retreated, holding up her hands. "Okay..."

"They HURT ME!" he cried, taking a step in her direction. His cheeks grew mottled as he thrust his face toward her. "They SHOT ELECTRICITY INTO ME! And they put me in the cage with ANIMALS who beat me and they didn't DO ANYTHING! They ALL laughed at me and to them it was just a game! AND YOU DON'T THINK I *KNOW* WHO PUT THEM UP TO IT?"

Oh, God . . . He's losing it . . .

"*YOU DID!*" he screamed, vibrating with rage.

Maria retreated, trying to maintain the distance between them. Her gaze kept flicking to the gun, then back to Lester again. He continued to advance as she backed away, her back almost to the garage door now.

"YOU called the POLICE! You keep coming back, but this time I'm NOT going to let you GET AWAY WITH IT!"

Serena had to have heard him that time, she thought. *Or my parents. They'll open the front door any second now and Lester will turn and fire . . .*

Through the static of her racing thoughts, Maria realized that the first siren had now been joined by another, more distant one, both of them drawing closer. Lester's jaw clenched and his eyes burned with the anguish of betrayal. His finger began inching toward the gun's trigger and a single impulse flashed through her body.

Go, go, GO!

She turned and rounded the car, sprinting toward the house, through the yard. She heard Lester shout her name in surprise, heard a grunt as he started after her, clipping the car.

GO!

Ten yards. Maybe five.

The front door began to open and a slash of light fell across the porch. Maria was sure she could hear him behind her now.

Run!

She strained forward, surging toward the light. She could feel Lester reaching for her. In what seemed to be slow motion, she watched Serena step out onto the porch.

He's going to kill us both . . .

Standing in a pool of light in front of the open door, Serena didn't understand what was happening. She stared at Maria in confusion as Maria hurtled toward the porch.

Are those his fingers skimming the back of my shirt?

She willed herself to move even faster, sprinting with everything she had.

"Maria?" Serena called out.

Only later would Maria realize that Serena had shouted her name. *Almost there . . .*

And then, she made it.

Grabbing Serena, she pushed the two of them through the still open door, slamming it shut behind them.

"What are you doing?" Serena cried, bewildered.

Maria locked the door and grabbed Serena's wrist, jerking hard. "Get away from the door!" Maria screamed. "He's got a gun!"

Serena stumbled as Maria pulled, almost falling.

"Who has a gun?"

"Lester!"

Dragging Serena to the kitchen, she spotted her mom standing near the stove, clearly startled by the commotion. But no Dad...Maria turned from side to side...

Oh, God.

Where's Dad?

"Wait—Lester? Lester's here?" Serena demanded from behind her.

"He's outside!" Maria shouted, her gaze suddenly swinging to the sliding glass doors, hoping her dad was on the porch. "Lester Manning! The guy who was chasing me!"

He'll burst through the door any second...

He'll kill me and them, and then kill himself...

Just like Gerald Laws and Cassie...

With a surge of relief, she spotted her dad at the porch table, Smokey in his lap.

Serena was babbling; her mom had started asking questions as well, but Maria registered none of it.

"Just be quiet!" she shouted. "Both of you!" She slid open the back door. "Get in here!" she hissed at her father, motioning him inside. He responded instantly, leaping to his feet with the dog tucked under his arm.

Both Serena and her mom went quiet. Maria listened intently—for the door, for the sound of a window smashing.

Silence.

Serena stared at her, fear written on her face. Both of her parents watched her openmouthed.

Still nothing.

What if Lester was coming around from the back?

In the silence, Maria registered the sounds of the sirens again. Loud enough now to be heard from inside the house.

"I don't understand," Serena finally said, her voice trembling with tears. "Where was Lester chasing you?"

"In the yard," Maria said. "You saw him. He almost grabbed me."

But Serena only shook her head in confusion. "I saw you running but no one was behind you," she said. "I saw someone else running down the street..."

"He had a gun and he was chasing me!"

"No," Serena insisted. "He wasn't."

Before Maria could process her words, the sound of the sirens filled the house and the walls were flashing red and blue in steady rhythm.

The police, she thought. *Thank God.*

At that moment, the front door crashed open.

Maria screamed.

CHAPTER 25

—— ❀ ——

Colin

All things considered, Colin decided he was okay with what he'd done. Though as the adrenaline drained from his system, leaving him feeling both exhausted and shaky, it was hard to ignore the fact that he was on his stomach with his hands cuffed behind his back, guarded by two glowering officers and most likely staring at a long prison term.

Maybe he should have pulled over for the officers who'd been following him.

And maybe he shouldn't have come to a screeching halt behind the squad car that was already at the Sanchez place while those officers had been approaching the door. And maybe he shouldn't have ignored them when they'd demanded that he stop his charge to the front door and simply let them handle it. If he'd made different decisions, the officers probably wouldn't have drawn their weapons, nor would he have faced a situation in which he'd wondered whether they might actually fire them.

On the plus side, he hadn't actually touched any of the officers after he'd kicked the door in, but none of them were in any mood to listen when he'd tried to tell them about the vacant house or the park, places that Lester may have run off to. All four were too pissed for that. They had him on speeding, reckless driving, and ignoring lawful directions, and they weren't going to settle for writing a couple of tickets and be done with it. They'd placed him under arrest, which meant his deal was going to be revoked.

His lawyers would fight it; no question about that, but more than likely, the original judge would be informed. That judge—as evidenced by his decision in the first place—was fair and reasonable, but he'd also been crystal clear in his expectations, and the court would know about it. Add in the fact that Margolis would be arguing on the other side for permanent placement among the dangerous and violent, and the writing was on the wall.

Prison.

He wasn't afraid of being locked up. As a general rule, he did well in places with rules and structure, even without freedom. He knew how to keep to himself and mind his own business and look the other way when necessary and keep his mouth shut, and after a while, the whole thing would likely become routine. He'd survive and eventually get released and he'd start over again. But...

Maria wouldn't wait for him, and he wouldn't be able to become a teacher.

He didn't want to think about those things. Given the same situation, he'd do it all again. Maria's stalker shows up with a gun? Had to try to save her. Simple as that. How could he have known that Lester would have been gone by the time he arrived?

Had they listened to him, Colin figured that the police could have found Lester already. But precious minutes had ticked by while they put on the handcuffs and read Colin his rights, and it wasn't until the officers had calmed their nerves that they were finally able to listen first to Maria's story, which came out in fits and starts, and then to Felix, who'd said that he didn't intend to press charges for the broken door and splintered frame. Both Serena and Carmen were crying throughout. Way too late, he'd finally watched two of the four officers leave in one of the squad cars in search of Lester. After that, surprising him, Maria asked the remaining officers to call Detective Margolis when her pleas to have Colin released were met with indifference.

Colin closed his eyes, hoping that the detective would be otherwise occupied.

A moment later, one of the officers announced that Margolis was on his way.

Margolis was going to *love* this. No doubt he'd put on one of his self-satisfied smirks while he gave Colin the whole *I warned you all along that this would be coming* speech that he was surely already rehearsing as he made his way here.

But again, no regrets. Maria and her family were safe, and that was all that mattered. That, and stopping Lester from showing up again...Maria had told the officers that Lester had become enraged as soon as he'd heard the sirens. Until that point, however, Maria had been able to keep him calm by talking to him. Or, rather, by letting Lester voice whatever was going through his deranged brain and simply agreeing with him. But what about the next time? Would Lester be so easily placated? Or would he just grab her and take her someplace where the police wouldn't find them?

The thought made him sick, and he wanted to kick himself for failing to check out the hospital himself. How had Lester gotten out? If he'd become delusional when the detective arrived this morning, why hadn't he been restrained? Or did they even do that anymore?

And there was another thing that was bothering him: How had Lester known Maria would be here? Maybe he went by the office and then her condo and saw that she wasn't around, but...

His thoughts were interrupted first by headlights, then by the sound of a slowing car. He heard it pull over and come to a stop, listening as a car door opened and closed with a thud a few seconds later.

Margolis.

❦

"Do you ever get that feeling like Christmas has come early?" Margolis said, squatting down next to him. Approaching Maria, he'd done a double take at the sight of Colin on the ground in cuffs and practically skipped over to him instead. "Because I think it just came early for me."

Colin said nothing. Anything he said would just get thrown back in his face.

"I mean, here I am, just heading out to get a quick bite not more than ten minutes away, and I get a call urgently requesting my presence over here. And who do I find but my old pal Colin? I must say that I haven't seen you looking this good in a long time." Colin noted the reflection of Margolis's grin in his highly polished shoes. "What did you do? Get in an argument with your girlfriend here? Maybe pushed Mom or Dad when they tried to intervene? Or did you go after one of the officers after they showed up and tried to calm you down?" He spat out his toothpick, letting it fall dangerously close to Colin's face in the grass. "You might as well drop the silent act and tell me. I'm going to find out in a minute anyway."

Colin let out a breath. "Traffic violations," he said.

Margolis cocked his head in surprise. "No kidding?" When Colin didn't respond, the detective shook his head, smirking. "I gotta admit that I never saw that one coming. But hey—I'll take it any way I can get it. So let me talk to your girlfriend over there—if you still call her your girlfriend, I mean. Even if you didn't so much as lay a finger on her, she doesn't strike me as the visit-prison-every-weekend-to-support-her-man type, and I've always been a pretty good judge of character."

Colin watched him stand. When Margolis turned and started toward Maria, Colin cleared his throat.

"Can I get up now?"

Margolis looked over his shoulder for a couple of seconds, then shrugged. "I don't know. Can you?"

Using his head to brace himself, Colin lifted his hips and shot his knees forward in a single flowing motion, landing on his feet.

Margolis waved off one of the officers, who had taken a step toward Colin. He smirked again. "With moves like that, I'm sure all the guys in prison will want to dance with you. But tell you what—why don't you wait right there while I figure out what's going on here."

Margolis signaled to the two officers to approach and Colin watched as they conferred in low tones. One of them thumbed toward Maria a couple of times; the other nodded in Colin's direction. By then, a number of the neighbors had come outside and were standing on their lawns or in the street, craning their necks for a better view. He wasn't the only one who'd noticed: Margolis did as well, and after a brief discussion with the family, everyone except Colin began to head inside. Surprising Colin, Margolis motioned for him to join them.

In the living room, Maria again went through the story from the top, including a description of what Lester had been wearing, only this time in a more linear fashion. Her family stood behind her, looking more upset than she did, while the two officers who'd arrested Colin flanked the front door. Colin watched as Margolis took notes, Serena occasionally interjecting. It wasn't until Maria was finished that Margolis asked his first question.

"Did he ever directly threaten you with the gun?" Margolis asked.

"He was holding it in his hand."

"But he didn't raise it? Or point it at you?"

"Why does that make a difference?" Maria demanded. "He showed up at the house with a gun. You need to arrest him."

Margolis held up his hands. "Don't get me wrong. I'm on your side. With his admission that he sent the roses to the office and had the drink delivered and now this, there's not a doubt that you'd be able to get the Fifty-C. I can't imagine that any judge would turn down the request, and I'll put a call in to find out if I can get it expedited. I was asking because I was trying to determine whether he additionally violated any gun laws."

"He's mentally ill. That makes it illegal for him to own a firearm in this state."

"Maybe."

Maria's eyes flashed. "He was in a psychiatric hospital this morning. Or so you told me."

"I have no reason to believe that he wasn't there, and trust me—I'll make absolutely sure the detective was correct about that. But when I was talking about mental illness, I meant *legally*. To this point, I haven't had access to his medical records, and in those instances when he was arrested, the cases were dismissed. I'm not sure his mental status has actually been adjudicated. There's also a difference between entering a hospital voluntarily and being committed involuntarily."

"You're splitting hairs," Maria said, her frustration becoming evident. "I told you how he was acting. He was talking *to the phone*, for God's sake. He's delusional and he threatened me with a gun!"

"Are you sure?"

"Did you listen to a single thing I said?"

Margolis stood straighter, defensiveness on display. "To be clear, nothing you said indicated that he raised the gun or compelled you to do anything. And when you retreated to your house, he ran in the opposite direction."

For a second, Maria said nothing, but Colin noted a flash of uncertainty in her eyes.

"What about the fact that he slashed my tires and stole my phone?"

"He told you he slashed your tires?"

"No, but..." Maria looked up at him. "Why are you doing this? Making excuses for him. It's like you're looking for any reason not to arrest him."

"On the contrary. I'm trying to find something that will stick. There's no reason to arrest him if I can't hold him."

"He had a gun! Doesn't that mean anything?"

"It would if he tried to conceal it. Or threatened you. But according to you, he didn't do either."

"That's . . . insane."

"That's the law. Of course, if he doesn't have a permit for the weapon, that's something I can use. But that won't be enough to hold him for long. Nor will the fact that he took your phone."

"What about slashing my tires?"

"Did he admit to that?" Margolis asked again.

"No, but . . ."

Margolis sighed. "I know this is frustrating for you, but I really am trying to help you here. I'm looking for something that might give rise to an actual arrest, on charges serious enough to keep him locked away."

"Okay, then. I was mistaken earlier. I remember now that he did aim the gun at me. Pointed it at me the whole time."

Margolis lifted an eyebrow. "You're changing your story?"

"I'm correcting it," she said.

"All right." He nodded. "But before we go that route, you should also realize that this entire situation may be more complex than you think."

"What does that mean?"

"I'm not at liberty to say. It's still early in the investigation. For now, all you really need to know is that I'm exploring a lot of different angles."

Different angles? Colin thought.

Maria shot him a questioning look, then turned back to Margolis just as a knock sounded at the door. One of the officers who'd been searching for Lester poked his head in. Margolis excused himself and stepped outside for a minute, then returned to Maria and the family. The other two officers joined him inside, remaining near the door.

"The officers said they couldn't find him. They went through the neighborhood a couple of times, talked with a few people who were out, and no one had seen him."

Colin opened his mouth, then closed it again. Margolis noticed.

"Something to say?"

"I was wondering if they checked the park," he said. "And the house on the next block that backs up to this one."

Margolis stared at him. "Why?"

Colin told them what he'd learned, as well as his suspicions about the vacant house and Lester's spying activities. He also mentioned where he suspected Lester had been parking his car. At Margolis's prodding, Colin admitted he'd been visiting the neighborhood late at night and early in the morning, and had spent time researching license plates. Maria's parents looked sick at the revelations; meanwhile, Margolis's stony gaze never swerved from him.

"You're just telling me this now? That you've been playing private investigator all this time?"

Colin nodded toward the officers. "I told the cops when they were arresting me where Lester might have gone. They didn't want to listen."

It was quiet for a moment. One of the officers shifted his weight from one foot to the other.

"But he wasn't running toward the park," Serena ventured softly. "Or for the house."

"Excuse me?" Margolis said.

"The park is a few streets over that way," Serena said, pointing in the direction of the kitchen. "And unless he wanted to take the long way around the block, he wasn't running toward the vacant house, either. He ran the other way, in the opposite direction."

Margolis absorbed this before excusing himself to huddle with the officers, two of whom subsequently departed. *About half an hour too late*, Colin thought.

Margolis returned to Maria. "Assuming Lester drove here, and since there are no cars registered in his name, they'll find out if any of the cars have been stolen or if we can link them to Lester in another way. Of course, Lester may have doubled back and taken the car or he may have simply run off, but the important thing for now is that I'm confident that you're safe. Are you planning to return to your place?"

"She'll be staying with us," Felix announced. "Serena too."

Margolis thumbed over his shoulder. "Your front door is broken."

"I have some two-by-fours in the garage. I'll brace it, and then tomorrow, I'll have it repaired."

"Do you have an alarm?"

"Yes," he said. "But we don't use it much."

"Use it tonight, even though you'll have to bypass the front door. And brace the door and keep the shades drawn as a precaution."

"What about police protection?" Serena asked. "Having someone at the house?"

"I won't be able to swing that," Margolis answered. "Pick your reason: budget cuts, not enough manpower, limits on overtime, or even that the Fifty-C hasn't been filed. But I'll call the commander, and I'm pretty sure I can arrange for a patrol car to swing by every few hours."

"What if Lester comes back?"

"I don't think that's likely."

"Why would you say that?"

"Because he's afraid of the police, and for all he knows, there *will* be an officer here."

"Unless he's crazy and doesn't care."

"He ran off earlier," Margolis said, but realizing how cavalier it probably sounded, he went on. "I know you're frightened and upset, Ms. Sanchez. I get it. I'll make sure a couple of the officers cruise the neighborhood for an hour or so. And who knows, maybe they'll get lucky and pick him up. If they do, they'll bring him in and I'll stick him in the interrogation room and see what I can do. And tomorrow, either way, you file for the Fifty-C, and the next time he comes anywhere near you, he'll be arrested. And that arrest will stick."

Colin noted the conflicting emotions playing out across Maria's features. She glanced at the officers near the door before drawing a long breath.

"May I talk to you alone?"

Margolis debated before finally nodding. He motioned for the other officers to leave and they quietly exited through the front door. At the same time, Serena and her parents wandered toward the kitchen, and once they were gone, Maria sighed.

"What about Colin?"

Margolis looked over at him. "What about him?"

"I was hoping you'd talk to the officer who arrested him. Maybe convince him to let Colin off with some speeding tickets or whatever. Instead of arresting him."

Margolis's expression verged on disbelief. "Why would I do that? From what they told me, he was doing sixty in a residential neighborhood. He nearly crashed head-on with someone a couple of blocks from here, and he refused to pull over." He shook his head. "Then once he got here, he defied the officers' instructions to stand down and instead made a volatile situation that much worse."

"I was in danger. You would have done the same thing if you thought someone you loved might be harmed."

"He should have just let the police handle it. Meanwhile, with the way he was driving, he was endangering other people's lives."

"Lester had a gun, for God's sake!"

"Yet another reason to let the police handle it."

"It's not fair and you know it!" Maria cried, her composure cracking. "I mean, sending him to prison? For *speeding?*"

I did a lot more than that, Colin thought. *The officers only saw me during the last two minutes of the drive.*

"He made his choices," Margolis said. "Don't forget that the officers had to draw their weapons. You could have been hurt. Your family could have been hurt."

"And once he knew I was safe, he deferred to them and submitted willingly. He didn't raise his voice, didn't resist at all. You really want to ruin the rest of his life? Because he was racing to my rescue?"

"It's not my call." Margolis shrugged.

"No. But I have the sense they'll listen to you." She put her hands on her hips, willing Margolis to meet her gaze. "I know that you don't trust Colin, and that you believe he belongs in prison. And if he'd struggled with the officers or resisted arrest or done anything else stupid, I wouldn't be asking you to intervene. But those things didn't happen, and you don't strike me as being unreasonable or needlessly vindictive." She hesitated. "I'd like to think that my impressions of you are correct. Please..."

For an impossibly long moment, Margolis stared back at her, unmoving. Then, without a word, he started for the door.

Five minutes later, Colin was standing near the couch, absently rubbing his wrists where the cuffs had cut into them.

"Thanks for coming to my aid," he said.

"You're welcome."

"I still can't believe he listened to you."

"I can. He knew it was the right thing to do. And the arresting officer wasn't upset. After he heard the whole story, I don't think his heart was in it, either."

Colin gestured at the door. "I'm sorry about that. I'll be glad to pay for it."

"My dad doesn't care. Honestly, he's too angry at the thought that Lester has been spying on the family to worry about a door."

"How about I help close it up for the night?"

When she nodded, he followed her to the garage, returning with the two-by-fours and a hammer and nails. Maria helped hold the boards in place, and when they were finally secure, she stepped toward Colin. Wrapping her arms around him, she held him for a long time before finally pulling back.

"What are you going to do now?"

"I'm going to call my boss," he said. "Let her know where I am and find out whether I've been fired. And then, I figure I'll keep watch outside for the rest of the night. I want to be here if Lester shows up."

She nodded. "What do you think Margolis meant when he said he was exploring different angles? Lester admitted to almost everything..."

Colin shrugged. "I have no idea. Something about Cassie's boyfriend Mark, maybe? Since he's gone off the grid?" Colin filled Maria in on the little that he'd learned earlier.

Behind them, Felix walked into the living room, accompanied by Carmen. Carmen handed a glass of ice water to Colin while Felix inspected the work Colin had done to brace the door.

"I'm sorry about that," Colin said, slightly abashed. "I told Maria I'd pay for it."

Felix nodded. "This is good work. Sturdy." He took a step toward Colin, meeting his gaze, his expression softening. "I wanted to thank you for rushing here when you thought Maria was in trouble. And for calling the police."

"You're welcome."

Carmen slipped back to his side as Felix went on. Behind them, Colin could just make out Serena in the kitchen, clearly listening in. "When we first met, I believe I may have misjudged you," he said. "Maria told me she felt safe with you. Now, I can understand why."

At his words, Maria slipped her hand into Colin's.

"I heard you tell Maria that you'll want to keep watch tonight. Outside. In case Lester comes back."

"Yes."

"I have a problem with that."

Colin looked at him, saying nothing.

"You should be inside the house, not outside. As our guest."

He felt Maria squeeze his hand, and despite everything, he couldn't help smiling.

"Okay."

Colin paced the living room, alternately peeking through the curtains on the front window and then doing the same through the kitchen windows.

No sign of Lester.

Margolis had been good to his word; a patrol car passed by the house four times, twice while the rest of the family was still awake and twice after everyone else had gone to bed. Maria had stayed awake the longest, sitting with Colin until a little after one. Before turning in, Felix had told Colin that he'd be up at four to take over the watch and allow Colin to get some sleep.

The time to himself felt like a blessing to Colin, allowing him to process everything that had happened that evening. He still had more questions than answers, since nothing made sense. If, for instance, Lester was delusional to the point that he believed that Maria was out to get him, then his fear should have kept him *away* from Maria, instead of drawing him to her repeatedly.

But hadn't Lester essentially admitted he'd been stalking Maria all along?

And why had Margolis told Maria that he was exploring "different angles"?

Other questions plagued him, too—why had Lester admitted to sending the flowers and the drink, but not to slashing the tires? Had Lester actually driven, and if so, where did he get the car? If he'd left his car at the park but ran in the opposite direction, where was he going and why couldn't the police find him? And, again, how had Lester known that Maria would be at the house when Maria herself had forgotten about her mom's birthday?

The more he learned, the more confused he felt.

"You're making me nervous," Maria said. "And I'm sure you've worn a groove into the floor."

Colin looked over and saw her in the hallway, dressed in her pajamas.

"Did I wake you?"

"No. I slept for a little while."

"What time is it?"

"A little after three," Maria said. She walked to the couch and patted the cushion beside her. When Colin sat, she leaned her head on his shoulder while he slipped his arm around her. "You should probably try to get some sleep."

"I only have another hour until your dad is up."

"I don't think he's sleeping. He's probably tossing and turning like I did." She kissed him on the cheek. "I'm glad you're here, but my parents are, too. Right before they went to bed, they apologized to me for the way they treated you earlier."

"There was no reason to apologize. They've been very gracious. Especially about me kicking in their door."

She shrugged. "To be honest, it was pretty impressive. Doors generally keep people out, but this one didn't even slow you down. They feel better knowing that you're here."

He nodded. Moonlight spilled in through a crack in the drapes, washing the living room with a silvery glow. "I wanted to tell you that the way you dealt with Lester was amazing. Not everyone would have been able to stay calm in that situation."

"I wasn't calm. I was terrified. Every time I closed my eyes tonight, I kept seeing his face. And it was just so . . . weird. I kept getting the feeling that he was more afraid of me than I was of him, even though he was the one with the gun."

"I don't understand it, either."

"I wish the police had found him. I hate knowing that he's still out there . . . following and watching and planning and hiding. What good will a restraining order do if they can't serve him? And what if he shows up again before they do? I thought about leaving town, but what if he follows me? Or tracks me somehow. I mean, even I didn't know I was going to be here tonight, so how did he know? And how did he know I'd be at the bar?"

"I've been wondering about those things, too."

"And? What am I supposed to do? I just want to feel...*safe*."

"I have an idea. It might be a bit over the top, but..."

"What is it?"

He told her.

CHAPTER 26

Maria

Maria was sleeping on the couch when she felt Colin kiss her good-bye and whisper that he'd be back by eight o'clock. She was dimly aware of him slipping out the garage door. Surprising herself, she was able to get a few more hours of sleep before the sounds of the household roused her.

Over coffee, she shared Colin's plans with her family. They listened with surprise. Her parents would have preferred that she stay where they could keep an eye on her, but they understood Colin's reasoning and accepted her decision, asking only that she stay in touch.

Colin showed up at her parents' house around eight with a disposable cell phone and followed Maria back to her condo. There, she showered, changed into jeans and a white T-shirt and black pumps, and packed an overnight bag. By nine, they were at the courthouse, where Maria completed and filed the necessary paperwork for the 50C. Margolis had been good to his word again; the clerk said that they'd get it before the judge to sign before the court convened for the day.

Using the disposable phone, Maria texted Margolis her number and asked that he keep her informed as to any progress regarding Lester Manning.

To her surprise, Margolis called less than half an hour later and asked to meet with her at a coffee shop. "It's a couple of blocks from the courthouse, and we'll be able to talk in private," he said cryptically. She felt good about the fact that she'd filed the paperwork and decided to go with Colin's idea. For the first time since all this had started, she'd acted instead of reacted. While there was no guarantee that they'd be able to serve Lester with the court order, taking the initiative made her feel as though she had some semblance of control.

At the coffee shop, she and Colin sat in a corner booth where they could watch for Margolis's arrival.

When he finally walked through the door half an hour late, it took only a second for him to spot them. As he wove his way between tables, Maria noticed the way the fabric of his ill-fitting blazer tightened around his biceps. Like Colin, Margolis seemed to spend a lot of time in the gym.

He paused near the register to order a cup of coffee and then slid into the booth across from Maria and Colin. When he glanced at Colin, she thought she detected a trace less of his usual animosity.

Or then again, maybe she was just imagining it.

"Any problems with the Fifty-C this morning?"

"No," Maria said. "And thank you for your help. It's clear they were expecting me."

He nodded. "Judge Carson will be in court today. I left word with his clerk, so there shouldn't be any holdup. If you don't hear from them, let me know."

"Sure," she said.

The waiter came by, dropping off the cup of coffee. Margolis waited until he left before speaking again.

"How did you hold up last night?" he asked Maria.

"I didn't sleep well, if that's what you're asking. But at least Lester didn't come back."

He nodded. "I checked this morning and he wasn't spotted on any of the patrols, either. But he'll turn up. A guy like that tends to stand out and make people nervous, which means that calls come in. I'm confident someone will let us know when he shows up."

"If he's still in town," she said. "For all we know, he could be back in Charlotte by now. Or God knows where else."

"If he is, he's not in the hospital. I checked this morning. No sign of him. You should also know that I had my friend drive past the Manning place this morning. No sign of him there, either in the garage apartment or the house."

She nodded.

"On another note," he went on, "I spoke with the sheriff's department, and they're okay with me serving Lester when we do find him. That's actually good news. It's not always that easy. But I'd hate for Lester to be located and then not get served because there are no sheriffs readily available and he disappears again before they can."

"So that's the plan?" Maria asked. "To wait until he shows himself?"

"I'm not sure there's another option. I'm just trying to make the best out of a bad situation."

"Is that why you wanted to meet with me this morning? To tell me you couldn't find him?"

"No," Margolis said. "A couple of interesting bits of information turned up and I wanted to get your take on them."

"I thought you weren't at liberty to talk about the investigation."

"You're right," he said. "Which means I'll have to limit some of what I tell you. Still, I wanted to talk to you because I need your help."

"Why?"

"Because the more I look into this situation, the less it seems to add up. I'm hoping that you can help me put the pieces together."

Welcome to my world, Maria thought.

Margolis went on. "Regarding the situation last night. I told you I was looking into possible weapons violations. But like everything else in this case, what seemed obvious isn't. So let's start with this: Lester does *not* have a gun permit. Nor has he legally purchased a weapon, which I thought was great news for you. However, it turns out that Avery Manning, the father, does have a permit for a handgun purchased about a year ago."

"And?"

"The problem is that Lester and Avery, father and son, live at the same address. It's not illegal to borrow someone's gun if the weapon is properly permitted. So I can't make a case on that, unless Avery Manning didn't give permission. But there are even more complications."

"Such as?"

"Avery Manning came to see me this morning." He let those words hang before continuing. "That's why I was late getting here, by the way. I figured it was better to meet with him before I talked to you. The story took yet another twist."

"What?"

"The gun may not have been real."

"Excuse me?"

Margolis picked up his spoon and stirred his coffee as he went on. "Let me start from the beginning, okay? We sit down and the first thing I think is that Dr. Manning looks like crap, which made sense as soon as he told me he'd just driven in from Tennessee. He was clearly upset. He must have mowed through an entire pack of gum while we were sitting there, chewing and spitting out one piece after another. Although he didn't attempt to control the conversation, which surprised me based on the way you'd described him. But anyway, I ask him what I can do for him, and he immediately says that Lester has left Plainview, and that he was worried Lester might come to see you. He begged me to warn you and to tell you that if he showed up you should call the police. He went on to say that Lester was in an acute delusional phase, and that he'd been struggling with this disorder for years, yada yada yada...pretty much all the same things he'd told me before."

"But yesterday, he wasn't even sure if his son was in the hospital."

Margolis took a sip of his coffee. "He said the hospital called him as soon as the staff realized that Lester was missing, as he's the emergency contact. Apparently, when Lester didn't show up for his appointment with the social worker, the staff spent a couple of hours searching the hospital before they realized he must have left the grounds. That's when they called Dr. Manning."

"How is that even possible? It's a psychiatric hospital. Don't they watch their patients?"

"According to Dr. Manning, Lester's been there regularly enough to understand the routines and he's familiar with the staff. The administrator also emphasized that there was no reason not to trust Lester. Lester had entered the hospital voluntarily and he'd never run off before. So free time comes along and they're guessing that Lester just...slipped away. After that, he either has use of someone's car, or someone picked him up, and he made his way to Wilmington. And he obviously had a gun stashed somewhere along the way." Margolis shrugged. "What can I say, he's paranoid."

"If he wanted to warn me, why didn't Dr. Manning call you as soon as he found out?"

"He did," Margolis said, his expression letting her know he was just as surprised as she was. "He left me a voice mail last night, but unfortunately, I didn't get around to listening to it until this morning, after I'd already met with him. Even then, I'm not sure how much good it would have done. The call came in after Lester had already been at your place."

Maria nodded.

"Anyway, after we went over those things, I told Dr. Manning that Lester had not only shown up at your parents' last night and confronted you, but that he had a gun. At that point, Dr. Manning became even more upset. Then, after he'd seemed to calm down, he insisted to me that Lester's gun couldn't have been real."

"Of course he'd say that."

"That's what I thought, too. I asked him how he could be so sure. He said that he owned only two guns: an old shotgun he's had since he was a kid that he said might not even work, and the handgun I told you about, which he keeps in a locked case in the trunk of his car. He added that there was no way he'd ever leave it at the house where Lester could get his hands on it."

"I know what I saw!"

"I don't doubt that, but let me finish," Margolis said. "Dr. Manning told me that while Lester didn't have a *real* gun, he owned a pellet gun. He said he bought it for Lester when he was a teenager, and he'd assumed that it was in one of the boxes in the attic with Lester's other things. It's possible, he said, that his son may have retrieved it at some point in the past. So my question to you is whether it's possible that Lester may have been holding a pellet gun."

Maria tried to recall the gun but couldn't conjure up the necessary detail. "I don't know," she admitted. "It looked real to me."

"That's not surprising. Same color, same size, it was dark out, and you were terrified. Who knows? But it might explain why Lester never raised it. Because he thought you may have noticed that the muzzle was too small."

Maria thought about it before finally shaking her head. "It still doesn't mean that Lester's gun wasn't real. He could have bought it at a gun show. Or bought it on the street. It's not impossible."

"True enough," Margolis conceded. "As of now, I'm not ruling anything out."

"And how do you know that Dr. Manning was telling the truth about his gun in the first place?"

"Because he showed it to me after the interview, when he was leaving. And yes, it was in a locked case in his trunk." When Maria didn't respond, Margolis went on. "There's something else you should know."

"What's that?"

Margolis reached into the file and pulled out an admission form from Plainview Psychiatric Hospital. He slid it across the table to Maria.

"Lester Manning was in the hospital the night your tires were slashed. I received this fax from Plainview this morning. You can see the date he entered the hospital."

Even as Maria stared at the document in front of her, she didn't quite believe it.

"Are you sure this is real?"

"Yes. Dr. Manning made the request while I was there, and the fax arrived a few minutes later, directly from the hospital."

"Couldn't Lester have sneaked out? Like he did yesterday?"

"Not that night. According to their records, he was in his room all night. Staff checked on him every thirty minutes." Maria said nothing. In the silence, Margolis took a sip of his coffee. "Which is part of the reason I wanted to meet with you. If someone else slashed your tires, who could it be? When I posed that question to Dr. Manning, he told me to look into Mark Atkinson."

"Why?"

"Because Atkinson might be trying to frame Lester."

"That doesn't make any sense."

"Maybe...unless Atkinson knew Lester and had a possible reason. And it just so happens that it might be the case. Lester was the one who introduced Cassie to Atkinson in the first place."

It took a few beats for Maria to absorb this. "Lester and Atkinson knew each other?"

"They both work for the same janitorial company. Or used to, anyway. According to Dr. Manning, after Cassie died, Lester and Atkinson had a falling-out. Lester confronted Atkinson about failing to protect Cassie when Laws showed up, called him a coward, and they got into a fight. There's no record of it, but that doesn't mean anything. Most of the time, in situations like this, the police are never called. Long story short, according to Dr. Manning, Atkinson was pissed."

"And you know that for certain?"

"Not about the fight. But it's true that Lester and Atkinson worked together. After we talked yesterday, I spoke to Atkinson's mother again, and then a supervisor at the janitorial company. That's what I meant, by the way, when I said that I was looking into different angles. Because something about the way Atkinson just up and left town bothered me as soon as I learned about it. I can *kind of* accept the idea that he ran off to meet the woman of his dreams or whatever—guys can be stupid like that—but no contact with his mom except for a couple of letters? That had been printed from a computer? No calls or texts to his mom or his friends? When all this with you just happens to be going on? It didn't sit right with me."

"I still don't understand why Atkinson would come after me, though. Like I told you, I've never met the man."

"Is it possible that he's angry for the same reason you think Lester is? Because Laws got out of prison and killed Cassie? And he blames you?"

"Maybe," she said slowly. "But . . . Lester's been the one following me. He sent the flowers and sent over the drink. Lester's the one who showed up at my house last night . . ."

"Exactly," Margolis agreed. "And all of this has made me wonder whether Dr. Manning was wrong about the relationship between Lester and Atkinson. If he's right, and Atkinson *is* trying to frame Lester, then how did he get Lester to play along so perfectly? Especially when you take last night into account? If you throw that idea out, however, it leaves us with a couple of other possibilities. The first is that Lester somehow knew that Atkinson was going to go after you, and he decided to join in. Of course, that raises the question as to how Lester would know what Atkinson was planning, which opens a whole new can of worms. If we put aside that idea, too, however, there's also a third possibility."

Maria looked across the table at Margolis, almost afraid to hear what he was going to say next.

"What if," he finally offered, "Lester and Atkinson are working together? And they're providing alibis for each other?"

Maria, trying to absorb Margolis's questions, said nothing.

"I know what you're thinking," Margolis said. "And it sounds crazy to me, too, but of the three explanations, it's the only one that seems to make any sense at all."

"I'm still not sure why you think Atkinson might be involved in the first place. Maybe Lester had some homeless guy or kid slash my tires and leave the note because he knew he'd have the perfect alibi. Because everything else points to the fact that Lester's probably working alone."

"Not everything," Margolis said. "See, the thing is, I ran the registrations on the cars near the park, just like Colin suggested. And one of them brought up a serious red flag."

"Why?"

"Because the car in question is registered to Mark Atkinson."

"Does that make sense to you?" Maria asked Colin after Margolis had left. "About Lester and Atkinson working together?"

"I don't know," Colin admitted.

She shook her head. "It's Lester. Alone. It has to be." Even to her ears, it sounded like she was trying to convince herself. "And if they are working together, why is Atkinson's car at the park? How did they get away? Lester doesn't have a car."

"Like Margolis suggested last night, maybe he stole one."

She shook her head. "It's just so confusing. This whole thing is like one of those Russian nesting dolls. Open up one doll, and there's another one inside, and on and on. And what am I supposed to do now? What if the detective finds something that implicates Atkinson? Am I supposed to get a Fifty-C on Atkinson, too?"

"It might come to that."

"And what if they can't find Atkinson, either? Even his mother can't find him. What good would a Fifty-C do if they can't serve it right away?"

Colin didn't answer, but he sensed that Maria didn't need him to. Her thoughts continued to spin, words tumbling out. "God only knows where Lester is, but it's the same situation. What good can the Fifty-C do if they can't find him, either?"

"They will."

"How?"

Instead of answering, Colin reached for her hand. "For now, I think our best bet is to stick with the plan, especially since there might be two of them."

"Because you think it's easier for two people to follow me?"

"Yes. And because until we really know what's going on, keeping you safe is the only thing we can do."

After dropping off Maria's car at her place, Colin and Maria drove to Independence Mall in the Camaro, taking a circuitous route that included side roads and sudden turns. Though neither of them saw anyone in the rearview mirrors, they took no chances.

At the mall, they spent forty minutes walking through different stores, holding hands and examining various things. They backtracked every now and then, studying the faces of those who'd been behind them, but Maria wasn't certain how much good it was actually doing. While she knew what Lester looked like, Atkinson was a mystery. Colin had logged into her computer with her password that morning and pulled up Pinterest, and she'd found herself scrutinizing Atkinson's missing persons photo, wondering how accurate it was. He had an unremarkable face, the kind that naturally blended into a crowd, and for all she knew, he could have changed his hair color. Or grown a mustache, or shaved his head. Through it all, Margolis's theories continued to chase each other through her brain.

Atkinson trying to frame Lester. Lester trying to frame Atkinson. Lester and Atkinson working together. Or was Lester working alone while Atkinson ran off with a girl, and in that case, was the car just a coincidence?

Who knew? Every possibility, when followed logically, broke down somewhere along the way.

Eventually, and according to plan, they made their way to a women's apparel store. There, Maria pulled a few blouses from the racks, not really caring how they looked but pretending to. Colin stood beside her and casually commented on the items. At noon exactly, she told Colin that she wanted to try the outfits on and walked toward the dressing rooms.

"I'll be out in a few minutes, Colin," she called out. As soon as she entered the bank of changing rooms, Lily peeked out from one of the stalls. Maria scooted into the same stall, noting Lily's outfit: red pumps, jeans, red blouse, and a carnation in her hair. In her hand were a pair of oversized sunglasses and a set of keys; on the floor was a navy-blue tote and a department store bag.

"Oh, sugar. Bless your heart," Lily said, reaching for her hands. "I know this is a terribly stressful situation for you and I can't imagine how you're able to keep your wits about you, let alone remain as gorgeous as you were the first time I saw you. Why, if it was me, my skin would already be breaking out."

I doubt that, Maria thought. Lily was the kind of girl who'd probably never had a pimple in her life. But it was a sweet thing to say.

"Thank you," Maria said. "And I know that I'm asking a lot..."

"You're doing no such thing," Lily said, "and I do not want

to hear another word about it. I'm your friend, and this is what friends do for each other, especially in a situation as frightening as this."

"I didn't see Evan," Maria commented.

"He went to the food court a couple of minutes ago. Probably eating something absolutely unhealthy, but considering he's been a sweetheart about all of this, I have vowed to say nothing at all to him about his dietary habits."

"Do you think it will work?"

"Of course it will work," Lily said. "People usually see what they expect to see. I learned that in my drama class. I had the most marvelous teacher, by the way. But we'll talk about that later. Let's get started, okay? Colin and Evan are watching the clock as we speak." She handed Maria the tote bag, along with the sunglasses and keys to her car. "Your wig and outfit are in here," she said. "I'm sure what I got will fit perfectly. I suspect that we're the same size."

Not quite, but close enough, Maria thought. "Where did you get the wigs so quickly?"

"From a wig shop. Where else? And though they're not perfect— such a thing would be impossible on such short notice—they'll both be more than adequate for our purposes."

Maria sorted through the tote bag. "I can pay you back for all of this..."

"No, you most certainly will not. And though what I'm about to say will likely sound awful, all the cloak-and-dagger activity this morning has been a tiny bit exciting. It reminds me of the masquerade ball at my parents' country club. Now let's get started...and don't forget the carnation. That's the kind of detail that people focus on. I'm going to text Evan, and he'll be here in just a few minutes."

Maria left Lily's dressing room, slipping into the adjoining one. In the tote bag was an outfit that matched the one Lily had been wearing, along with a blond wig and a red carnation. Maria put the outfit on along with the wig and spent a minute adjusting it to her liking. She tucked the carnation into the wig in approximately the same spot Lily had been wearing hers, then put on the sunglasses.

Up close, she still looked nothing like Lily. But from a distance, maybe...

She slid on the red pumps and at exactly a quarter past twelve left the dressing room. Evan strode toward her. "Hey, Lily," he said as he approached. "Did you find anything you liked?" In the corner, she saw Colin feigning interest in whatever was on his phone.

Maria shook her head. Evan leaned in and kissed her on the cheek before reaching for her hand. They exited the store at a leisurely pace, then cut into a department store, making for the exit doors.

Lily's car was two spaces in. Maria pressed the button on Lily's key chain, unlocking the doors, and got behind the wheel while Evan got in beside her. She checked her watch.

In the apparel store, Maria knew that Lily would exit in two more minutes, dressed as Maria had been, wearing a dark wig. Colin would take her hand and lead her to another store and dressing room, where Lily would change back into her original outfit. Lily would eventually exit the mall with Evan. Colin, meanwhile, would head to his car alone, as if Maria had never been at the mall at all.

All of which was probably unnecessary, Maria thought. But the key word, she knew, was *probably*. With two people possibly following her, neither she nor Colin wanted to take any chances, and both of them wanted her someplace where no one would ever think to look for her, someplace she'd never been before.

Lily's house.

Maria started the car and pulled out. No one exited the store behind her, nor did any other cars pull out. She circled the mall, following Evan's directions, and then pulled over as Evan hopped out at another entrance to the mall.

"Thanks," she said.

"Glad to do it," Evan said. "And remember, you'll be absolutely safe. Lily and I will be there in a bit with your things, okay?"

She nodded, still feeling on edge. Exiting the mall lot a minute later, she turned onto the main road. As she'd done way too frequently lately, she made a few random turns and continually glanced into her rearview mirror, feeling her nervousness finally begin to subside.

No one could have possibly followed her. She was certain about it.

Well, mostly certain.

Lately, nothing had seemed certain at all.

Lily's condo was less than a mile from Crabby Pete's, with private gated parking and living room windows that showcased a spectacular ocean view. It was tastefully decorated in whites, yellows, and blues—no surprise there—and felt both welcoming and comfortable. Maria spent a few minutes staring out over the beach without going outside and finally drew the shades before making her way to the couch.

She stretched out with a sigh, thinking a short nap was just what she needed. At that moment, the phone that Colin had given her rang, and answering it, she recognized Margolis's voice on the other end.

"A couple of things. I called my detective friend in Charlotte and left a message for him to see what he can scrounge up on Atkinson, either with his mom or at Atkinson's place, so that part is now in motion. More importantly, I also wanted to let you know the Fifty-C was granted. I'm waiting for the paperwork now."

"Thank you," she said, leaving the obvious unspoken; that

they still needed to find Lester to serve it. And maybe get a second one for Atkinson. When she hung up, she called Colin to tell him, then updated her parents as well. It took a few minutes to get her worried mother off the phone, and when she finally hung up, she realized again how worn out she felt. Like she'd been running nonstop for days, which, in a way, she realized, she had been.

She closed her eyes again, but sleep didn't come right away. The call with Margolis, as short as it was, had triggered another round of questions. In the end, though, exhaustion eventually won out and she felt herself finally, thankfully, drifting off.

CHAPTER 27

———— 🦋 ————

Colin

After hanging up with Maria, Colin grabbed her bags from the car, slid in his earbuds, and got some music going while he brought her computer to the dining room table. There was something he wanted to check, and while he could have mentioned the idea to Maria or Margolis while they'd been having coffee, he'd decided against it. It was a long shot, but now that the 50C was in place, he figured there was no harm in checking it out. And whether or not Atkinson was involved was beside the point; right now, finding Lester was a priority.

It had come to him that morning. He'd kissed Maria good-bye and on the way to his car, he'd tried to make sense of the facts at hand: that the court order would do no good unless they could find Lester; that time was of the essence; that Lester was dangerous; that he'd shown up with a gun and left Maria terrified; and, of course, that he'd taken her phone . . .

Her phone . . .

And with that, a memory clicked into place, a memory that took him back to the night he'd first met Maria. When it had been storming and he'd pulled over . . . she'd been skittish because of the way he'd looked after the fight . . . and she'd asked to borrow his phone because she'd misplaced hers. She'd been rambling a bit, but what had she said?

He'd paused at his car, trying to remember.

"*I didn't* lose *lose it . . . It's either at the office or I left it at my parents', but I won't know for sure until I get to my MacBook . . . I use that Find My iPhone thing . . . I can track my phone because it's synced with the computer.*"

Which meant, of course, he could track the phone, too.

It surprised him that Margolis hadn't thought of it. Or maybe Margolis had and he'd already checked, and it had amounted to nothing because Lester had either discarded the phone or turned it off, or the battery had gone dead. Or maybe that constituted information Margolis wasn't allowed to share. At the same time, there'd been so much else going on, it wasn't completely out of the question that the idea had been temporarily overlooked.

Colin didn't want to get his hopes up—the odds were slim that it would work and he knew it—but a couple of clicks of the cursor later, his heart hammered hard when he understood what he was seeing. The phone was still on and the battery had enough juice to let him know that it was located at a house on Robins Lane in Shallotte, a small town southwest of Wilmington, near Holden Beach. Shallotte was a good forty-five minutes away, and Colin stared at the location, watching to see whether the phone was still on the move.

It wasn't. The site allowed him to track the phone's previous movements as well, and a couple of clicks later, he learned that the phone had been carried from the Sanchez home to the house on Robins Lane without any detours.

Interesting. Definitely interesting, but still not proof. Maybe Lester had known the phone could be tracked, and he'd tossed it into someone's car or into the bed of a pickup as he was fleeing. Or maybe he'd dropped it and someone had happened to find it.

Or maybe Lester was too delusional to even think along those lines.

No way to know for sure, but worth checking out . . .

He debated whether to call Margolis before thinking that it

would probably be better to be certain before he did. Shallotte wasn't even in the same county, and he didn't want to waste Margolis's time if it would amount to nothing...

He felt a tap on his shoulder and flinched automatically. When he turned, Evan was standing behind him. Colin pulled out the earbuds.

"You're not planning to do what I think you are, are you?" Evan asked.

"What are you doing here? I didn't hear you come in."

"I knocked, but you didn't answer. Peeked in. Saw you with Maria's computer. Wondered if you were planning to do something stupid. Figured I would ask, just in case you were."

"It wasn't stupid. I was tracking Maria's phone," he said.

"I know," Evan said, motioning to the computer. "I can see the screen. When did you figure out to do that?"

"This morning. When I left Maria's parents' house."

"Pretty slick," Evan said. "Have you called Margolis yet?"

"No."

"Why not?"

"Because you walked in. I haven't had the chance."

"So call him now," Evan said. When Colin didn't reach for his phone, Evan let out a breath. "That's what I meant when I wondered if you were planning to do something stupid. Because you weren't planning to call him, were you? You were going to check it out yourself, before you call him."

"It might not be Lester."

"So? Let Margolis check it out. At the very least, Maria's phone is there and he'd get it back. And do I need to remind you again that this is police business? You need to let Margolis do his job. You need to call him."

"I will. When I know one way or the other."

"You know what I think?" Evan asked. "You're lying."

"I don't lie."

"Maybe not to me. But right now, I think you're lying to yourself.

This has nothing to do with wasting Margolis's time. The truth is, I think you want to be front and center in this whole thing. I think you want to see Lester and put a face to a name. I think you're pissed off and you've gotten used to handling things your own way. And I think you want to be the hero, like taking pictures from the roof or last night when you kicked through Maria's parents' door, even though the police were already there."

Colin admitted to himself that Evan might be right. "And?"

"You're making a mistake."

"If I find out it's Lester, I'll call Margolis."

"And how are you going to do that? Are you going to knock on the door and ask if Lester's home? Sneak up and try to peek through the windows? Hope he comes out to wash his car? Slip a note under the door?"

"I'll figure it out when I get there."

"Oh, that's a good plan," Evan snapped. "Because when you wing things, it *always* turns out for the best, huh? Did you happen to remember that Lester has a *gun*? And that you might get sucked into some sort of situation you could have avoided? Or that you might make things even worse? And what if Lester spots you? He might sneak out the back and then it'll be even harder to find him in the future."

"Or maybe he's planning to run already, and I'll be able to follow him."

Evan put his hands on the back of Colin's chair. "I'm not going to talk you out of this, am I?"

"No."

"Then wait until I bring Lily home and I'll go with you."

"No."

"Why not?"

"Because there's no reason for you to come."

Evan let go of the chair, standing straight again. "Don't do it," he finally said. "For your own good, call Margolis." No doubt trying to emphasize the point, he reached for Maria's computer, and near the door he stuffed it back into her bag. He grabbed Maria's other things and left Colin's apartment, slamming the door behind him.

Colin watched him go without a word.

In the car fifteen minutes later on his way to Shallotte, Colin thought about the things Evan had said.

Why was he going alone? Why hadn't he called Margolis? What did he hope to achieve?

Because, as Evan had implied, the situation had become personal. He wanted to finally put a face to a name; he wanted to see with his own eyes what the guy was like. He wanted to watch Lester get served by Margolis, and then, in the aftermath, find a way to keep an eye on him, even if he didn't tell Margolis about that, either. It was time, he thought, for Lester to begin looking over his shoulder, instead of the other way around.

If it even was Lester, of course...

And yet, Evan had reminded Colin of the risks if the hunch turned out to be correct. Evan was good for things like that, and Colin knew he had to be careful. He was a single mistake away from heading to prison, and he promised himself that all he was going to do was watch. Even if Lester strolled by the car, he wasn't going to so much as touch him. And yet Colin still felt on edge, the adrenaline already beginning to flow.

He forced himself to take long, steady breaths.

He navigated through Wilmington, hitting one red light after another and eventually reaching Highway 17. He had punched the Robins Lane address into his phone, and he watched as the directions appeared. He followed the verbal commands, and at a little after two in the afternoon, he was making the final turns, through a quiet blue-collar neighborhood that on the surface reminded him of the one where Maria's parents lived. But only on the surface. The homes were smaller and not as well kept; more than a few had overgrown lawns, and here and there, he saw FOR RENT signs, making the area feel transient. The kind of neighborhood where people kept to themselves and didn't stay long.

Or wanted to hide?

Maybe.

He parked in front of a small bungalow two doors down from the address he was looking for, one of the rentals, behind an old station wagon that had seen better days. There was a small porch out front and he could see the door and one side of the house, where a window with curtains drawn faced a neighboring house. Peeking out from the far side of the house, he could see the nose of a blue car but couldn't make out the type.

Someone home?

Had to be. Atkinson's car was at the park. Or, at least according to Margolis, it had been a few hours ago.

He wished he'd somehow been able to keep Maria's computer with him. It would have been helpful to make sure the phone was still here. He wondered whether he should call Evan and ask, but Evan would use the opportunity to lecture him again, and he wasn't in the mood for that. Besides, more than likely, Evan and Lily were already headed to Lily's condo with Maria's things. Which meant that all he could do was watch with the hope that Lester would eventually venture outside.

Then again, as Evan had reminded him, Colin still wasn't sure what Lester even looked like.

Glancing at his phone, Colin saw it was coming up on three o'clock now. He'd been watching for an hour. There'd been no signs of movement beyond the curtains of the bungalow; no one had come outside. The blue car remained in place.

On the plus side, none of the neighbors had seemed to notice him, and the street itself had been quiet. A couple of people had walked past his car; a few kids had run by kicking a soccer ball. The mailman had come by and Colin had temporarily gotten his hopes up—he could, perhaps, catch the name of whoever lived in the house by checking the mailbox—but the mailman passed the house, making no deliveries at all.

That was odd. He'd stopped at every other home on the block. It might mean nothing at all.

Or it might mean that whoever was living at the house didn't generally receive mail, because their mail was sent elsewhere.

It made him wonder.

He stayed in the car, taking long, slow breaths, and was startled when his phone dinged. Evan.

Time continued to tick by. Four o'clock now, and Colin was getting antsy. He wrestled with the urge to do...*something*. He wondered again whether to call Margolis. Wondered whether to risk a knock at the door. He trusted himself not to overreact. Or mostly did, anyway.

He stayed in the car, taking long, slow breaths, and was startled when his phone dinged. Evan.

What are you doing?

Colin texted back, *Nothing.*

Another hour passed. Five o'clock, with the sun beginning to sink lower, still bright but predicting the gradual onset of dusk. Colin wondered when, or if, the lights would go on inside; since he'd been there, it had become easier to imagine that no one was inside the bungalow at all.

His phone dinged again. Evan. Again.

I'll be there in a minute, the text read. *I'm almost at your car.*

Colin furrowed his brow, then looked over his shoulder and saw Evan approaching from behind. Evan hopped in and closed the door, then rolled up the window. Colin did the same.

"I knew you'd be here. As soon as I left you, I knew exactly what you intended to do. And then you lie to me in your text? About doing nothing?"

"I wasn't lying. I'm not doing anything."

"You came here. You're watching the house. You're watching for Lester. That's something."

"Not if I haven't seen him."

"So what's the plan now?"

"I'm still working on it," Colin answered. "How's Maria?"

"She was asleep on the couch when we got there, but as soon as she woke up, Lily started talking to her about our wedding plans. I figured I might as well check on you, since Lily can talk for hours on that subject..."

At that moment, Colin caught the flash of movement at the front of the bungalow. The door opening. A man beginning to step onto the porch, holding a can of something.

"Get down," Colin hissed as he quickly lowered himself as well. "And stay down."

Evan automatically did as he was told. "Why?"

Colin slowly poked his head up without answering, needing a closer look. The man had moved onto the porch, the front door open behind him. Colin peered closer, conjuring up Atkinson's image. Definitely not him, he decided, and he tried to remember what Maria had said about Lester's clothing last night. *Faded red shirt and torn jeans?*

Yes, Colin thought. *Same thing the man was wearing now.*

Lester?

Had to be, and Colin felt another surge of adrenaline. Lester was at the bungalow. Hadn't even changed his clothes...

A few seconds later, Lester turned around and walked back inside, the front door closing behind him.

"Is it him?" Evan whispered.

"Yeah," Colin said. "It's him."

"And you'll call Margolis now, right? Like you said you would?"

"Okay," Colin said.

❦

On the phone, after cursing Colin roundly for withholding information, Margolis snapped that he was on his way and would be there as soon as he could. No, he'd told them, do not follow Lester, or anyone else for that matter, if they leave the house. Let him handle it, Margolis demanded, and if Colin so much as got out of the car, he'd find a reason to put him in cuffs because he was getting sick and tired of Colin pretending he knew what the hell he was doing. There were a few more choice words as well, and when Colin disconnected the call, Evan looked over at him.

"I warned you that he wasn't going to be happy," Evan commented.

"Okay."

"And you don't care?"

"Why should I?"

"Because he can make your life even more miserable."

"Only if I do something that gets me in trouble."

"Like interfering in police business?"

"I'm sitting in my car. I called him with information he needed. I'm not interfering. I'm a potential witness. He told me what to do, and I'll do it."

Evan shifted. "Can I sit up again? I'm getting a cramp."

"I don't know why you're still hunkered down in the first place."

❦

Forty minutes later, Margolis rolled up to Colin's car and pulled to a stop, his sedan idling in the road, the passenger window rolled down.

"I thought I told you to get the hell out of here," Margolis said.

"No," Colin said, "you didn't. You told me not to get out of the car or follow him."

"Are you purposely trying to be a smart-ass?"

"No."

"Because you sound like a smart-ass. I go out of my way to prevent you from getting arrested last night, and then you 'forget' to mention this idea of yours this morning? So you can play Mr. Law Enforcement again?"

"Maria told you that Lester had taken her iPhone. They're easy to track. I figured that you'd probably looked into it already."

The expression on Margolis's face revealed that he'd overlooked the obvious.

Recovering, he snapped, "Believe it or not, my world doesn't revolve around you and your girlfriend. I have other cases. Big cases. I was getting to it."

Sure you were, Colin thought. "Will you get Maria's phone?"

"If he has it. I have no proof that he does, other than your word."

"As of a couple of hours ago, it was still there," Evan interjected. "I checked before I came out here."

Margolis stared at Evan, his irritation evident, before finally shaking his head.

"I'll get her phone," Margolis said. "Now get going. Both of you. I don't need you here, and I don't want you here. I'll take care of it."

He rolled up the window, released the brake, and let the car drift forward before finally pulling to a stop directly in front of the bungalow. Colin watched as Margolis stepped out and took a moment to survey the place before finally rounding the car and heading up the walkway.

As he climbed the steps to the porch, he turned toward Colin and jerked his thumb, reminding Colin it was time to go.

Fair enough, Colin thought. The key was still in the ignition and he cranked it, only to hear silence, the engine completely dead. Not even a click. Colin tried again with the same result. Dead.

"Let me guess," Evan said. "Your car sucks."

"Today, maybe."

"Margolis isn't going to be happy."

"There's nothing I can do."

He was talking to Evan while keeping his attention focused on Margolis, who'd yet to knock at the door. Instead, the detective was at the far end of the porch, peering at the car parked in the drive. When he turned, Colin thought he saw a look of confusion on Margolis's face as Margolis finally moved to the door. He hesitated before knocking; after a long pause, Margolis reached for the doorknob and turned it, cracking the door slightly.

Someone calling out, saying come in and that the door was open?

Margolis spoke through the crack, then pulled out his badge as he pushed through the already open door, vanishing from sight…

"Let's go to my car," Evan said. "We can be gone by the time Margolis gets out. I know he hates you, but I don't want him to hate you any more than he already does. Or me, for that matter. He looks mean."

Colin said nothing. Instead, he was thinking about the expression he'd seen on Margolis's face right before he'd knocked at the door. Margolis had seen something, something that…didn't make sense? Surprised him? Something he hadn't expected?

And why would Lester have invited him in if he was paranoid and afraid of the police?

"Something's wrong," Colin said, the thought coming automatically, even before he realized he'd said it.

Evan looked over at him. "What are you talking about?" he asked, and in that instant, Colin heard the distinctive pop of gunfire, loud and explosive, two shots in quick succession.

Colin was already reaching for the door when Margolis flew back out of the doorway, his jacket and shirt soaked in blood, his hand on his neck. He stumbled off the porch, falling backward onto the steps and sliding down onto the walkway.

By then, Colin was already out of the car...operating on instinct...running toward Margolis...accelerating with every step...watching Margolis as he writhed on the ground.

Lester stepped onto the porch, screaming incoherently, holding a gun. He raised it, pointing it at Margolis. Lester's face held both fear and anger, his hand on the gun shaking. Lester screamed again and lowered the gun before raising it once more...

Colin continued his sprint toward the bungalow, cutting across the neighbor's lawn, hurdling a small bush, closing in on the porch. On *Lester*. Zeroing in. A few more seconds.

Lester continued to aim the gun at Margolis without pulling the trigger. His face was red, his eyes bloodshot. *Out of control.* Screaming at Margolis: *It's not my fault!* and *I didn't do anything!* and *I'm not going back to jail!* and *I know what Maria is doing!*

Lester approached the porch steps, closing the gap between him and Margolis as he continued to aim the gun, his hand shaking. Taunting. Lester, aware of a blur out of the corner of his eye, suddenly turned, swiveling the gun in Colin's direction...

Too late.

Colin launched himself over the porch railing, arms wide as he collided hard with Lester. The gun went flying, wheeling end over end and landing on the porch.

Colin outweighed Lester by forty pounds, and he felt Lester's ribs crack as they hit the ground. Lester screamed in agony, momentarily paralyzed.

Colin moved fast, shifting off of Lester's body, his arm immediately wrapping around Lester's throat, then he locked the arm down with the opposite hand. Lester began to thrash and squirm, neck sandwiched between Colin's biceps and forearm. Colin applied hard pressure to the carotid arteries in a classic choke hold as Lester tried frantically to escape.

Within seconds, Lester's eyes began to roll back, going white, and all at once he stopped moving.

Colin kept applying the pressure, enough to keep Lester out for more than a few seconds. Then, scrambling to his feet, he rushed to Margolis.

Margolis was still breathing but no longer moving, his face a chalky white, and Colin tried to figure out what he was seeing. He'd been shot twice, in the stomach and the neck, and was losing blood fast.

Colin whipped off his shirt and tore it in half as Evan came running up, looking terrified.

"Holy crap! What do we do?"

"Call 911!" Colin shouted, trying to will his own sense of panic away, knowing that more than ever, he needed to think clearly. "Get an ambulance! Now!"

Colin knew nothing about gunshot wounds, but if Margolis kept losing blood, he had no chance at all. Because the neck wound looked worse, Colin started by applying pressure to Margolis's neck. Blood began to seep through the torn shirt immediately; he did the same for the stomach wound, where blood was still pulsing, forming a growing puddle beneath the detective.

Margolis's face began to turn a sickly gray.

He could hear Evan shouting into the phone that a cop had been shot, that they needed an ambulance, now.

"Hurry up, Evan!" Colin shouted. "I need your help!"

Evan disconnected the call, staring at Margolis as though he might pass out. From the corner of his eye, Colin saw Lester roll his head to the side. Already waking.

"Grab the cuffs!" he said. "Make sure Lester can't get away!"

Evan, still staring at Margolis, seemed frozen in place. Colin could feel the blood continuing to soak through the remnants of his shirt; he could feel the warmth in his hand, his fingers red and slick.

"Evan!" Colin shouted. "Cuffs! On Margolis's belt! Now!"

Evan shook his head and began fumbling with the cuffs.

"And then get back here as fast as you can!" Colin shouted. "I need your help!"

Evan hurried over to Lester and slapped one cuff on Lester's wrist and then dragged Lester's body closer to the rail, slapping the other cuff around a post. Lester moaned, coming to as Evan rushed back. Evan fell to his knees near Margolis, his eyes wide.

"What do I do?"

"Take over the stomach wound…where my hand is. And press hard!"

Though the blood loss was definitely slowing, Margolis's breathing had grown shallower…

Evan did as he was told and Colin used both hands on the neck wound, and seconds later, Colin heard the first of the sirens. Then a growing chorus of them, and while he willed them to get here faster, all he could think was *Don't die on me. Whatever you do, don't die…*

On the porch, Lester moaned again and his eyes finally blinked open, unfocused.

A sheriff's deputy was the first to arrive, followed quickly by an officer from the Shallotte police department, both coming to screeching halts in the middle of the street, lights flashing. Both men jumped out of their cars and rushed toward them, guns drawn, uncertain what to do.

"Detective Margolis has been shot!" Colin shouted as they approached. "The guy cuffed to the railing was the one who shot him!" Both the deputy and the officer looked toward the porch and Colin forced a steadiness in his tone. "The gun's still up there. We can't let these wounds go. And make sure the ambulance is coming—he's lost a lot of blood and I'm not sure how much longer he can hold on!"

The officer approached the porch while the deputy ran back to his car and shouted into the radio that an officer was down, demanding that the ambulance hurry. Both Colin and Evan kept their focus on the wounds; Evan had recovered enough for some color to have returned to his cheeks.

Minutes later, the ambulance arrived and a couple of paramedics hopped out and grabbed the stretcher. More sheriff's deputies had arrived by then, along with additional police officers, the street out front now crowded with vehicles.

When the paramedics finally took over for Colin and Evan, Margolis was looking even worse. He was nonresponsive and barely breathing by the time he was placed on the stretcher. The paramedics were moving quickly; the stretcher was loaded into the back and one of the paramedics hopped behind the wheel while the other stayed with Margolis. By the time it was rolling forward, the ambulance had a police and sheriff escort, sirens blaring, and only then did the world start slowly coming back into focus.

Colin could feel the shakiness in his limbs, the nerves beginning to subside. His hands and wrists were coated with the syrupy feel of drying blood; Evan's shirt looked as though it had been partially dipped in a vat of red dye. Evan wandered off, bent over, and vomited.

One of the deputies went to his trunk, returning with a couple of plain white T-shirts, and handed one to Colin, the other to Evan. Even before Colin gave his statement, he was already reaching for his phone to call Maria and tell her what had happened.

But as he spoke, all he could think about was Margolis.

Over the next hour, as the sky dimmed and finally went black, an even larger crowd of police officers and sheriff's deputies had descended on the bungalow, as well as a detective from Wilmington and the county sheriff.

Lester was delusional and argumentative, screaming gibberish and resisting arrest before finally being secured in the back of a squad car and sent on his way to jail.

Colin offered a statement to the sheriff, a police officer from Shallotte, and Detective Wright from Wilmington, all three asking questions at various times, then Evan did the same. Both admitted that they had no idea what had happened once Margolis had entered the house, only that he hadn't been in there long before the gunfire sounded. Colin also told them that Lester could have finished off Margolis, but hadn't.

Later, after he and Evan had been cleared to leave, Colin called Maria to tell her that he was heading home to change but wanted Lily to drive her to the hospital so Maria could meet him there. As he was talking to her, he overheard a nearby officer tell Detective Wright and the sheriff that the house was otherwise empty, and that Lester appeared to have been living alone.

After ending the call with Maria, Colin stared at the bungalow, wondering where Atkinson had been staying. And why, again, if Lester was so paranoid, he'd let Margolis into the house in the first place.

"You ready to go?" Evan asked, interrupting his thoughts. "I need to shower and change and just get the hell out of here."

"Yeah," Colin said, "okay."

"What do you want to do about your car?"

Colin looked over at it. "Let's deal with it later. Right now, I don't have the energy to care."

Evan must have seen something in his expression. "Are you sure that going to the hospital is such a good idea?"

For Colin, it felt like less of a choice than a requirement. "I want to know if Margolis is going to be all right."

CHAPTER 28

— ❧ —

Maria

Since Colin's phone call, Maria's mind had been racing, trying to piece together everything that had happened.

Colin tracking down Lester. Lester shooting Margolis. Lester aiming the gun at Colin. Colin taking Lester down. Colin and Evan trying to save the detective's life. Margolis being loaded into the ambulance. Lester resisting arrest, screaming that he knew what Maria had done.

Lester.

She'd known all along that it was Lester, that he was the one to worry about, and she kept reminding herself that he was behind bars now. This time, he hadn't vanished or simply run off; this time, they'd caught him, and he'd shot a cop and there was no way he could get to her.

What about Atkinson? a voice inside her asked.

She didn't want to think about that. Still wasn't sure what to make of it. It still didn't seem to fit...

Too much. What had just happened was overwhelming enough; the fact that Colin and Evan had been in the middle was nearly too much to process.

Lily, Maria thought, was experiencing the same wild flow of emotions; since they'd arrived at the hospital a few minutes earlier, she'd barely spoken and continually scanned the parking lot, watching for Evan's car. Maria had the sense that Lily needed to

see and touch and hold her fiancé, as if to prove to herself that
Evan was really and truly okay.

And Colin...

Of course he'd found Lester on his own; of course he'd rushed
toward Lester while the gun was pointed in his direction; of
course he'd taken Lester down without getting hurt in the process. And now, of course, Lester was locked away, and while she
felt relief, there was anger in the feeling as well. Worry, too, for
Margolis, and she had trouble understanding how Lester had gotten the better of him. She'd told Margolis that Lester was dangerous; she'd told him he had a gun. So why hadn't Margolis listened
to her? Why hadn't he been more cautious? How could he have
gotten shot? Maria didn't know, nor did Colin. When they had
spoken earlier, Colin had said that he wasn't sure Margolis would
survive the ride to the hospital. But Margolis must have survived,
she thought. While she'd been waiting with Lily, half a dozen
officers had entered the hospital and none had come out, which
meant he was still alive, right?

She was too afraid to ask.

By the time Evan's car finally pulled into the lot, Maria could
barely keep her thoughts straight. She followed Lily toward the
car, and as soon as Colin stepped out she put her arms around
him and held him close.

The four of them made their way into the hospital, got directions, and took the elevator to the second floor. They were
directed down the corridor to the surgical waiting area, which
was crowded with law enforcement personnel as well as a few
people who looked to be friends or family. Somber and grim faces
momentarily turned their way.

Evan stepped closer to Colin. "Maybe we shouldn't be here,"
he suggested.

Colin's face showed nothing. "He wouldn't have been shot if I
hadn't called him."

"It's not your fault," Evan said.

"He's right, Colin," Lily added. "Lester did this, not you."

Despite their words, Maria knew that Colin was still trying to convince himself of the same thing, but couldn't quite bring himself to believe it.

"Fine," Evan said. "Do you see anyone we can ask about Margolis's condition? I don't see a nurse..."

"Over there," Colin said, nodding toward a man in his forties with cropped gray hair. The man saw them as well and headed their way.

"Who's that?" Maria whispered.

"Detective Wright," Colin said. "He was one of the people who took my statement earlier. Evan's, too."

When Wright approached, he offered his hand and both Colin and Evan shook it. "I didn't expect to see you here," Wright offered.

"I had to know how he's doing," Colin said.

"I just got here a few minutes ago, but so far, there haven't been any updates from the surgeon yet, other than that he's still hanging in there. As you know, he was in pretty bad shape when he arrived." When Colin nodded, Wright motioned toward another area of the room. "I know that you've been through a lot already," Wright went on, "but I was wondering if you'd stick around for a few minutes. Someone's been asking for you. She wants to talk to you."

"Who?" Colin asked.

"Pete's wife, Rachel."

Maria watched as Colin's expression went neutral. "I'm not sure that's a good idea."

"Please," Wright said. "It's clearly important to her."

It took Colin a moment to answer. "Okay," he said.

Wright turned, heading toward the far side of the room, stopping when he reached an attractive brown-haired woman who was surrounded by half a dozen people. He nodded toward Colin and Evan. Rachel Margolis immediately excused herself from the group and started toward them. As she approached, it was clear to Maria that the woman had been crying. Her eyes were bloodshot, her mascara slightly smeared; she seemed to be barely holding it together.

Wright made the introductions and Rachel offered a brief smile that held nothing but sadness.

"Larry told me that you helped save my husband's life," Rachel said.

"I'm really sorry for what happened to him," Colin said.

"Me too," she said. "Thank you. And I...um..." She sniffed before dabbing at her eyes. "I just wanted to offer my thanks to both of you. For thinking clearly, not panicking, calling the ambulance. Putting pressure on the wounds. The paramedics told me that if you hadn't done what you did, Pete wouldn't have had a chance. If you hadn't been there..." She was on the verge of tears, the words so heartfelt that Maria felt a tightness in her throat. "Again...I..." She drew a ragged breath, trying to hold it together. "And I want you to know he's tough, so he's going to be all right. One of the toughest ever..."

"He is," Colin agreed, but Maria had the sense that Rachel Margolis barely heard him, because she'd really been talking to herself.

The evening rolled on. Maria sat beside Colin as they waited for news. Evan and Lily had gone to the cafeteria a few minutes earlier, and Maria listened as the conversations gradually gave way to murmurs of worry. People in the waiting room came and went.

Colin remained quieter than usual. Every now and then, an officer or detective would come by to thank him and shake his hand; though he was polite in his responses, Maria knew it made Colin uncomfortable because he still blamed himself for what had happened, even if no one else seemed to.

And yet, the depth of his guilt surprised her. It had been clear all along that Colin and Margolis held nothing but disdain for each other. It was a paradox of sorts, and though she wanted to draw Colin out and get him to talk about his feelings, she knew he wanted to work through them alone. She finally leaned toward him.

"Will you be all right if I step out to the hallway? I want to call my parents. Serena, too. I'm sure they're wondering what's going on."

When Colin nodded, she kissed him on the cheek, then left the waiting area, heading down the corridor to a quieter spot where she had a modicum of privacy. On the phone, her parents sounded as worried as everyone in the waiting room and had dozens of questions; toward the end, her mom said that she'd make dinner, and asked that Maria come by the house with Colin, along with Evan and Lily. Her mom asked in a way that made it hard to say no, but that was okay. After all that had happened, she wanted to see her family, too.

Back in the waiting area, Colin was in the same spot where she'd left him. He still wasn't talking much, but as soon as she sat beside him, he reached for her hand, holding tight. Lily and Evan returned from the cafeteria, and soon after that, the surgeon finally entered.

From where she was sitting, Maria watched as Rachel Margolis walked toward him, Detective Wright by her side. The room went quiet, everyone worried, everyone needing to know, and it was impossible not to hear the doctor, even from a distance.

"He's survived the surgery," the doctor announced, "but the damage was even more extensive than we expected. The procedure was also complicated by significant blood loss, and for a while, it was touch and go. But right now, his vitals are stable. On the low side, but stable."

"When can I see him?" Rachel Margolis asked.

"I want to keep an eye on him for another couple of hours," the surgeon hedged. "If things keep on like I hope they will, I may be able to let you in for a few minutes later tonight."

"And he's going to be okay, right?"

That's the million-dollar question, Maria thought. The surgeon seemed to have expected it and continued in the same professional tone.

"As I said, he's stabilized for now, but you need to understand that your husband's still in critical condition. The next few hours are going to tell us quite a bit, and I'm hoping to give you a more definitive answer tomorrow."

Rachel Margolis swallowed. "I just want to know what I should tell our boys when I go back home."

Boys? Maria thought. *Margolis has children?*

The surgeon's voice softened. "Tell them the truth. That their father survived surgery and that you'll know soon." He kept his focus on her. "Please understand, Mrs. Margolis...there was severe trauma to the trachea and your husband is currently on a ventilator..."

Maria couldn't watch any longer as the surgeon began to go into the details of Margolis's injuries. Glancing away, she heard Colin's voice.

"Come on," he whispered, no doubt thinking the same thing she was. "The details aren't our business. Let's let them have some privacy."

Maria and Colin stood; Evan and Lily followed suit, and they left the room. When they were outside, Maria stopped and told all of them about the call with her parents and what they'd asked.

"I know you're all probably exhausted and that you two were just in the cafeteria, but my mom made us dinner, and—"

"Okay," Colin said. "I still need to get back to my car tonight, but that can wait for a bit."

"You don't need to explain," Evan tossed in. "We get it."

Maria rode with Colin in Evan's car; Evan and Lily followed in Lily's car, and as they pulled to a stop in front of the family's house, Serena was waiting for them out front, along with her parents. As soon as Maria got out, Serena enveloped her in a hug.

"Mom and Dad have been crazy worried about you all night, you know. Mom hasn't left the kitchen for hours, and Dad keeps checking the windows and doors. Are you holding up all right?"

"Barely," Maria admitted.

"I'm thinking that you're going to need a seriously long vacation after this."

Despite everything, Maria laughed. "Probably."

After Serena, Maria hugged her parents, then introduced Evan and Lily. Surprising Maria—as well as her parents and Serena—Lily spoke Spanish, albeit with a Southern accent. Because the front door was still boarded up, they went through the garage and into the kitchen before taking their seats at a table that was soon covered with dishes of food.

As they ate, Maria told her family about their earlier meeting with Margolis, and Colin walked them through all that had happened after that. He paused every couple of sentences so Maria could translate for her mom. Evan added further details, especially when it came to the confrontation with Lester.

"And Lester is still in jail, right?" Felix asked when Colin had finished. "And he won't get out?"

"Crazy or not, he shot a cop," Evan said. "I'm not sure he's ever going to get out."

Felix nodded. "Good."

"What about Atkinson?" Serena broke in. "You said he was working with Lester?"

"I don't know. It was something Margolis was looking into. Supposedly they knew each other, but even so, it just doesn't add up," Maria answered.

"Then who slashed your tires?" Serena pressed.

"Maybe Lester paid some kid to do it because he knew the hospital would give him an alibi."

"And the car at the park?"

"Maybe Lester's borrowing it." Maria shrugged. "I don't know."

"If Atkinson is out there, what are you going to do?"

"I don't know," Maria repeated, hearing the frustration in her tone. She knew there were still too many unanswered questions, even after all this, but...

"Lester was the one I was worried about," she said. "He's the one who scared me, and whether he's working with Atkinson or not, the only thing I know for sure is that Lester can't get to me anymore, and..."

When Maria trailed off, Serena shook her head. "I'm sorry for asking so many questions. It's just that I'm still..."

"Worried," Felix finished for her.

So am I, Maria thought. *And Colin is, too, but—*

Her thoughts were interrupted by the muffled ringtone of Serena's phone. Serena pulled it out and sent the call to voice mail, her expression both hopeful and worried.

"Who was it?" Felix asked.

"Charles Alexander," Serena answered.

"It's kind of late for him to call, isn't it?" Felix asked. "Maybe it's important."

"I can try to reach him tomorrow."

"No, go ahead and call him back now," Maria said, thankful for the distraction, meaning it. "Like Dad said, it might be important." She didn't want to think about Atkinson any more than she wanted to think about Lester, nor did she have the energy to answer impossible questions right now. It was all she could do to process the last few hours...

Serena hesitated for a second, wondering whether it was really okay before hitting the call-back button. The table went quiet as she wandered to the kitchen with the phone at her ear.

"Charles Alexander? Why have I heard that name before?" Colin whispered.

"He's the director of the scholarship I told you about," Maria whispered back.

"What's going on?" Evan asked, and when Lily leaned close to hear, Maria filled them in briefly. Serena, meanwhile, had begun to nod, and when she finally turned, Maria could see her smile.

"You're serious?" Serena asked. "I won?"

Maria saw her mom suddenly reach for her dad's hand.

Meanwhile, Serena was going on, no longer able to keep her voice down. "Of course," she said. "That's no problem... Tomorrow night... seven o'clock... Thank you so much..."

When Serena ended the call, her parents were looking at their daughter expectantly.

"I guess you heard what happened, huh?"

"Congratulations!" Felix said, rising from the table. "That's terrific!" Carmen rushed over, talking about how proud she was, and for the next few minutes, as hugs went all around, the anxiety over all that had happened was replaced by something wonderful, a feeling Maria never wanted to end.

After dinner, Colin, Evan, and Lily said their good-byes and went to fetch Colin's car; Carmen and Felix were walking the dog around the block. Maria and Serena were in the kitchen doing the dishes.

"Are you nervous about the interview?" Maria asked.

Serena nodded as she dried a plate. "A little. The reporter is supposed to be bringing a photographer with him. I hate getting my picture taken."

"Are you kidding? You're the queen of selfies."

"Selfies are different. They're for me or my friends. It's not like I'm putting selfies in the newspaper."

"When's the story going to run?"

"He thinks it'll be Monday," Serena answered. "That's when it will be officially announced."

"Is there a banquet or presentation?"

"I'm not sure," Serena said. "I forgot to ask. I got a little excited there."

Maria smiled as she rinsed a plate and handed it to Serena. "When you do find out, let me know. I want to be there. I'm sure Mom and Dad will want to come, too."

Serena stacked the dried plate with the others. "Earlier, when I was asking those questions...I'm sorry for being so pushy about it. I wasn't thinking."

"It's okay," Maria said. "I wish I had all the answers, but I don't."

"Are you going to stay here for a while? You know Mom and Dad want you to."

"Yeah, I know," she said. "And yes. But I'll have to head to my place later to get some things."

"I thought you were already packed. Because you were going to stay at Lily's."

"I was only planning to stay there for one night, so I'll need some more clothes. I also want to get my car."

"Do you want me to drive you over now?"

"No, that's okay. Colin will do it when he gets back."

"When will that be?"

"I don't know. Eleven thirty, maybe? Eleven forty-five?"

"That's late. Aren't you tired?"

"Exhausted," Maria admitted.

"Then why don't I take you—" Serena began, then stopped herself. She glanced at Maria. "Oh...never mind. I get it."

"Get what?"

"I agree. You definitely need to have Colin drive you. Forget I even asked. That was dumb of me."

"What are you talking about?"

"Well, knowing that you'll be under the watchful eye of our hovering parents the next few days...and knowing that Colin not only found Lester but took him down and there's nothing sexy about that...and knowing you need to unwind from an incredibly stressful day...let's just say that I totally understand why you might want a little time alone with him."

"I told you I just needed to grab some things."

"Anything in particular you want to grab?"

Maria laughed. "Get your mind out of the gutter."

"I'm sorry," she said. "I can't help it. But admit it. I'm right, aren't I?"

Maria didn't respond, but then again, she didn't have to. They both already knew the answer.

CHAPTER 29

———— ❦ ————

Colin

While Lily headed back to her place at the beach, Colin rode with Evan first to Walmart—a place that was always open and had everything he needed—and then to Shallotte, where Evan parked behind the Camaro. Colin popped open the hood and began to loosen the battery clamps.

"Why do you think it's the battery? Your car's had trouble starting for a long time."

"I don't know what else it could be. I've changed out the ignition switch and the alternator."

"Shouldn't you have tried changing the battery first?"

"I did," Colin said. "I put a new one in a few months ago. Maybe it's a lemon."

"Just so you know, I'm not driving you back out here tomorrow if this doesn't work. I'm going to Lily's, and the two of us are going to spend all day tomorrow in bed. I want to see how well this whole me-being-a-hero thing works out. I'm thinking she'll find me even more attractive than she already does."

Colin smiled as he loosened the clamps, then slid the old battery out and popped the new one in.

"I've been meaning to ask you something," Evan continued. "And remember, this is coming from someone who's seen you do a lot of dumb things. But today? I have no idea how you were able to even get to Lester in the first place. From the lawn? Over the railings? Going airborne like you did? And meanwhile, he's aiming the gun, and just so you know, it sort of makes me question your sanity. What on earth were you thinking?"

"I wasn't thinking."

"That's what I figured. That's just one of your many problems. You really should start thinking before you act. I told you beforehand not to go in the first place."

Colin looked up. "Your point is?"

"My point is that despite your stupidity and possible insanity, I was actually kind of proud of you today. And not just because you ended up saving Margolis's life."

"Why?"

"Because you didn't kill Lester when you had the chance. You could have smashed him into pieces or choked the life out of him. But you didn't."

Colin finished tightening the clamps. "You're saying that you're proud of me because I didn't kill him?"

"That's exactly what I'm saying," Evan said. "Especially since you probably could have gotten away with it. He'd shot a cop. He was armed and dangerous. I can't see anyone bringing you up on charges if you'd gotten a little too carried away. So my question to you is why *didn't* you kill him?"

Colin thought about it before finally shaking his head. "I don't know."

"Well, when you do know, let me know. For me, the answer's obvious, since I'd never kill anyone. It's not in my nature. I wouldn't be able to do it, but you're different. And if you're curious, I also have to tell you that I respect this version of Colin a whole lot more than I did the old one."

"You've always respected me."

"I've always liked you, but I've always been a little afraid of you, too," Evan said. "There's a difference." He pointed to the battery, wanting to drop the subject. "Ready to give it a whirl?"

Colin rounded the car and climbed behind the wheel. He wasn't sure what to expect and was surprised when the Camaro fired up with the first turn of the key. At that moment he found his eyes drawn to the bungalow, noting that half the yard was circled with police tape, as was the porch.

"And there it is," Evan said. "You know it'll probably break down on your way to Maria's. Just to spite you. And try to stay out of trouble, okay? It seems to be following you around lately."

Colin didn't answer; instead he continued to stare at the bungalow, and it took him a few seconds to realize that something had changed since he'd left. Or rather, something was missing. It was possible, he thought, that the police had impounded it because it was evidence. Maybe there'd been blood splatters, or maybe one of the shots had hit it and the police needed the bullet for ballistics testing...

"Are you listening to me?" Evan asked.

"No."

"What are you staring at?"

"You know those questions that Serena was asking?" Colin said, avoiding the question. "The ones about whether Atkinson is part of this?"

"I remember. Why?"

"I think there's a strong possibility that he is."

"Because his car was near the park? And Lester couldn't have slashed her tires?"

"Not just for those reasons. I'm thinking about the car I saw earlier, the one in the bungalow driveway."

Evan turned, then took a step backward, improving his angle. "What car?" he finally asked.

"Exactly," Colin said, continuing to ponder it. "It's gone."

Colin returned to the Sanchez place a few minutes before midnight. Maria was sitting with her parents in the living room, and

Colin watched as she stood. She said something in Spanish to her mom—most likely that she'd be back soon—and walked with Colin out to the car.

"Where's Serena?"

"She went to bed."

"She's staying here, too?"

"Just for tonight. My parents told me to tell you that you're welcome to stay, too. Of course, since you'd have to sleep on the couch, I told them you'd probably rather go home."

"You could join me."

"It's tempting," she said. "But..."

"No worries," he said. When they reached his car, he opened the door for her.

"What was wrong with your car, by the way?" she asked as she slid in.

"The battery," he said.

"So I was right, huh? I guess that means you should listen to me more often."

"Okay."

As they were driving to her condo, Colin told her about the missing car.

"Maybe the police took it."

"Maybe."

"Do you think Atkinson came back for it?"

"I don't know. I figure I'll call Detective Wright tomorrow. They may not tell me, but considering that I kept Margolis alive until the ambulance came, I hope they will. Either way, they should know."

She turned toward the window as they navigated the largely empty roads. "I still can't believe that Lester shot him."

"If you were there, you'd believe it. He was out of control. Like he snapped."

"Do you think they'll get any answers from him?"

Colin considered it. "Yes. Once he's lucid again. I have no idea how long that will take, though."

"I know he can't get to me, but..."

Maria stopped short of saying Atkinson's name, but then again, she didn't have to. Colin wasn't taking any chances. He took a circuitous route back to Maria's condo, alert to any suspicious cars. Maria knew what he was doing and made no objection.

It was just after midnight when they pulled into a space reserved for visitors at her condo complex. Colin stayed alert to any movement, but all was quiet as they climbed the steps to her door.

There, however, Colin and Maria froze.

They both saw in the same instant that the doorknob had been broken off, and that the door stood partly ajar.

Her place had been trashed.

As Colin watched Maria wander around in a daze, crying nonstop and surveying the damage, his own outrage continued to grow.

Couches, chairs, and pillows slashed open. The dining room table overturned. Dining room chairs tilted on broken legs. Lamps shattered. Photographs torn. The contents of the refrigerator splattered and smeared throughout the kitchen. Her things. Her home. Violated. Shredded. Ruined.

In the bedroom, her mattress had been torn open, the bureau knocked over and drawers broken, another lamp shattered. Empty cans of red spray paint littered the floor and virtually every piece of clothing in her closet had been marked by the paint.

This, Colin thought, was what rage looked like. Whoever did this was as out of control as Lester, maybe more so, and the fury

Colin felt was getting difficult to control. He wanted to hurt the guy, kill the guy...

Beside him, Maria gasped, her sobs becoming even more hysterical, and Colin put his arms around her when he spotted the words that had been painted on the bedroom wall.

You will know how it feels.

Colin called 911, then Detective Wright. He hadn't expected an answer, but Wright answered on the second ring. After Colin told him what had happened, Wright said he'd head right over, that he wanted to see the damage for himself.

At Maria's request, Colin also called her parents, and while they insisted they would come over, Maria kept shaking her head. Colin understood. Here and now, Maria couldn't deal with their fears and worries, not on top of all this. She was barely holding it together as it was. He told her parents that she needed to talk to the police, and let them know that he'd keep her safe.

Two officers arrived within a few minutes and took Maria's statement, which wasn't much. There was more luck, though, with one of the neighbors who'd come out to see what was going on. Colin listened as the guy who lived next door said that he'd returned to his place only a couple of hours earlier, and was certain that the door hadn't been ajar. He would have seen the lights. No, he said, he hadn't heard anything, other than music, which he noted had been turned up loud. He'd considered coming over to ask that it be turned down, but it had stopped soon after that.

After Maria had regained a semblance of composure, Wright reviewed her and the neighbor's statements with the officers; he then spoke with Maria and Colin. Maria had trouble keeping her thoughts straight. Colin rehashed most of what he'd told Wright earlier in Shallotte, all the while fighting the urge to hit something.

Colin wanted to find Atkinson, even more than he'd wanted to find Lester.

And he wanted to kill him.

It was almost two a.m. when Wright said they could go, and he walked with them to Colin's car. Maria, Colin knew, wasn't in any shape to drive, and she didn't argue. When they reached the car, Wright held up his hand. He stared at Colin in much the same way Margolis did.

"Hold on," he said. "I don't know why I didn't realize it earlier, but I finally figured out who you are," he said.

"Who am I?"

"You're the guy Pete thinks should be in prison. The guy who gets in all those fights. Beats the crap out of people."

"Not anymore."

"Lester Manning might have a different opinion about that. Not that I give a crap what Lester Manning thinks."

"Do you know when the police will be done in there?" Maria asked. "And when I can get back in?"

"Aside from vandalism, it's not otherwise a crime scene," Wright answered. "But the forensics guys take their time. I'd guess that you won't be able to get back in until midmorning tomorrow at the earliest. I'll let you know for sure when you can, okay?"

Maria nodded. Colin wished there were something more he could do for her, but still...

"Do you know if they impounded the car that was at the bungalow?" he asked. "The one where Margolis was shot?"

Wright frowned. "I have no idea. Why?"

Colin told him.

Wright shrugged. "Seems likely that they would impound it. I'll see what I can find out, though." He turned toward Maria, then back to Colin. "I know you're both exhausted and I know you want to get out of here, but do you happen to know the name of the detective in Charlotte that Pete was working with?"

"No," Colin said. "He didn't mention his name."

"That's okay. I'll do some digging. It won't be hard to find the answer. One last question: Where do you intend to go tonight?"

"To my parents'," Maria answered. "Why?"

"I figured," Wright said. "That's why I wanted to ask. After something like this happens, people usually go to a friend's place, or to their family. If you want my opinion, I'm not so sure that's a good idea."

"Why not?"

"Because right now, I don't know what this guy Atkinson is capable of doing, and it makes me nervous. He's clearly got it out for you, and from what I saw inside, he's not only dangerous but angry and on the rampage. You might consider going someplace else tonight."

"Like where?"

"How about somewhere like the Hilton? I know some people there and I'm sure I can get you a room, along with police protection. Even if it's only for tonight. It's been quite a day and both of you need to try to get some rest. I'm not saying anything will happen, but best to be cautious, you know?"

Maria's voice was quiet. "Margolis said that they weren't able to offer police protection."

"I was talking about me. I'll watch your room tonight. I'm off the clock, so no big deal."

"Why would you do that?" Colin asked.

Wright turned toward Colin and said simply, "Because you saved my friend's life."

CHAPTER 30

❦

Maria

In the car, Maria called her parents with the news, then absently watched the detective's sedan out front as it led the way to the hotel, which was only a few blocks from her condo.

Wright must have made the arrangements in the short time they were driving, because the key was waiting at the front desk. He rode with them in the elevator and walked with them to the end of the corridor, where a folding chair was already positioned just outside the door. He handed them the room key.

"I'll be here as long as you are, so no worries."

It wasn't until she slipped into bed beside Colin that Maria realized how exhausted she was. A couple of hours earlier, she'd imagined making love, but she was too depleted for that and Colin seemed to be feeling exactly the same way. Instead, she rested her arm on his shoulder, curling close and feeling his warmth until all at once, everything went black.

When her eyes finally opened, sunlight was already streaming through the crack in the blinds. Rolling over, she noticed Colin wasn't beside her, and she saw him brushing his teeth in the bathroom. Glancing at the clock, she was surprised to see that it was almost eleven. She sat up with a start, thinking her parents were probably going crazy.

She reached for her phone and saw a text from Serena.

Colin called and said you were sleeping, and he told me what happened. Come to the house after you wake up. Dad's taken care of everything!

Maria furrowed her brow. "Colin?" she called out.

"Hold on," he mumbled, poking his head through the doorway, and she saw a mouth full of toothpaste, along with some on his finger. He rinsed his mouth and stepped into the main part of the room, moving toward the bed.

"Did you use your finger to brush your teeth?"

He sat beside her. "I didn't bring a toothbrush."

"You could have used mine."

"Germs," he said with a wink. "You slept late. I already called your parents."

"I know. Serena texted. What's going on?"

"I'll let you be surprised."

"I'm not sure I'm ready for any more surprises."

"You'll like this one."

"How long have you been up?"

"A couple of hours. But I didn't get out of bed until twenty minutes ago."

"What were you doing?"

"Thinking."

There was no reason to ask *About what?* She already knew the answer, and after they showered together, they dressed and packed. Stepping out the door, they saw Wright sitting in the folding chair.

"Would you two mind if we get a cup of coffee?" he asked.

※

"For starters," Wright began, "your apartment has been cleared for reentry. Forensics left earlier this morning and they're done. I figured you'd want to know in case you needed to grab anything. Clothes or toiletries or whatever."

If there's anything left that I even want, Maria thought. "Did they find anything?"

"No clear evidence was left behind, except for the paint cans, and there were no fingerprints on those. Atkinson must have worn gloves. As for hair samples, that'll take a little longer, but no guarantees. Hair sample analysis is always tricky, unless there's DNA from the root."

Maria nodded, trying to force away the images she'd seen the night before.

"I also made some other calls this morning," Wright said, stirring sugar and cream into his coffee. Maria noted the bags under his bloodshot eyes. "As of yet, no one has been able to talk to Lester. He hadn't been at the station for ten minutes before his attorney showed up, and a short while after that, his father appeared, too, and made the same demands that the attorney was making. Not that they were able to talk to him, either. By then, Lester Manning was strapped to a gurney in the infirmary, on psychiatric hold. And he's still sedated. The general consensus is that he's nuttier than an almond tree. According to the officers, as soon as he saw the cell, he went bonkers."

"How so?"

"Screaming. Fighting with the officers. Trying to bite the officers. And once they got him in there, he started kicking at the doors, banging his head on the wall. Crazy stuff. Even scared the other prisoners, so he had to be moved out. A doctor was called in, who gave him something to calm him down. It took five officers to restrain him, and that was when the attorney showed up. He's claiming all sorts of civil rights violations, but it's all on camera, so no one's worried about Lester having some sort of case that might spring him. I wanted you to know that right up front. That's not going to happen, no matter what his attorney might say. He shot a cop. Anyway, the point is, no one's been able to talk to him yet."

Maria nodded, feeling numb. "How's . . . ?"

"Pete?" Wright asked. "He made it through the night. He's still in critical condition, but he's stable for now and his vitals are improving. His wife is hopeful that he'll regain consciousness sometime today—the surgeon said it was possible—but we're still in a wait-and-see mode on that front. Rachel was able to spend some time with him this morning. Their boys, too. Of course, it was scary for them. They're only nine and eleven, and he's their hero, you know? After coffee, I'll head over there, see if I can sit with him a bit, or at the very least, sit with Rachel." When Maria didn't respond, Wright rotated his coffee cup in place. "I also looked into the car that was at the bungalow. I remember seeing it, too, and to answer the question from last night, the Shallotte police did *not* impound the vehicle. Nor did the sheriff's department. Which means that Atkinson showed up after the police had left to retrieve it."

"Maybe," Colin said.

"Maybe?" Wright asked.

"He may have been there all along. Maybe he ducked out the back when Evan and I were trying to save Margolis. He hid out for a while, then came back. That also might explain how Margolis got shot in the first place. He went in expecting one person, and then was surprised by two."

Wright studied Colin. "When Pete talked about you," he said, "I didn't get the sense he liked you very much."

"I don't like him, either."

Wright raised an eyebrow. "Then why did you save him?"

"He didn't deserve to die."

Wright turned to Maria. "Is he always like this?"

"Yes," she answered with a wry smile, then switched gears. "I still don't see how or why Lester and Atkinson are working together to target me—"

"There's more," he said, lifting his palm to stop her. "That's the other thing I wanted to talk to you about. I spoke to the detective in Charlotte that Pete was working with. His name's Tony Roberts, by the way, and when I filled him in on what happened to Pete, he told me that Pete had called him yesterday, but that he hadn't been able to check out Atkinson yet. Of course, this put the request on a whole new level, and he called Atkinson's mother, picked her up, and went to Atkinson's apartment. She was able to convince the manager to let him in. There's still a missing persons report on file, even if up until now, no one had believed her, and she's the next of kin. The point is, she was more than happy to let Roberts help find her son, and I guess that when Roberts got there, he hit the jackpot. It just wasn't in the way the mom wanted. It turns out that Atkinson's laptop was still there, and Roberts was able to access it."

"And?"

He looked at Maria. "He had files about you. Tons of information. Background information, school records, information about your family, where you live and work, your daily schedule. He even had information about Colin in there. Photographs, too."

"He had photographs?"

"Hundreds. Walking, at the store, on the paddleboard. Even while you were working. It seems he's been watching and following you for quite a long time. Spying on you. Roberts removed the laptop as evidence, over Mrs. Atkinson's sudden vehement protests. As soon as she saw what was on it, she tried to withdraw her consent to enter the place, but by then it was too late, and Roberts had it in hand. Defense lawyers would likely raise a stink, but there was a missing persons report, she gave her consent, and the evidence was in plain sight. Roberts, though, was better than that—he let me know he'd actually recorded her saying that she wanted him to access the computer. With that said, once we get Lester to talk, it'll probably be a moot point anyway. Lawyer or not, he'll end up talking. The crazy ones usually end up spilling everything, especially once they get lucid, because guilt sets in."

Maria wasn't sure that was true, but... "Why does Atkinson want to hurt me?"

"That part, I can't answer with certainty. I can tell you there was information about Cassie Manning on the laptop, too, but you're already aware of that link."

"Do you have any idea where Atkinson is now?"

"No. We have an APB out on him, but since no one seems to know where he's been, I'm not sure how much good that will do. Again, I'm hoping that Lester will be able to tell us more, but when that will be is still up in the air. It might take a day, it might take a few days, it might take a week, and then we'll still have to deal with the attorney and his father, both of whom will tell him not to answer any questions at all. Which raises the question of where you want to be for the next few days. If I were you, I'm not sure I'd hang around Wilmington."

"I'm supposed to go to my parents' today," she said. "I'm sure I'll be fine."

Wright looked dubious. "It's your call," he said. "Just be careful. From what Roberts was telling me, Atkinson is not only dangerous, he's probably just as crazy as Lester. So let me give you my phone number. I want you to call me if anything strikes you as out of the ordinary or something else comes to you, okay?"

If Wright's intent had been to scare her, it had worked. But after last night, Maria was going to be afraid no matter what, until Atkinson was finally caught.

They got in the car, and as Colin set out toward her parents' he reached for his phone.

"Who are you calling?"

"Evan," he said. "I want to see if he's busy today."

"Why?"

"Because after I drop you off at your parents', I'd like to go back to your place. Now that the police have cleared it, I want to get it cleaned up. Maybe do some painting."

"You don't have to do that."

"I know," he said. "But I want to. You don't need that kind of reminder when you go home. And I'd probably end up going stir-crazy just sitting around."

"But it'll take all day..."

"Not that long. A few hours, maybe. Your place isn't that big."

"Maybe I should go with you. It's not your responsibility."

"You don't need that kind of stress. And besides, you should be with your family."

He had a point and it was a kind thing to offer, but she was about to say no when he turned toward her.

"Please," he said. "I want to do this."

It was his tone that allowed her to reluctantly agree, and Colin made the call, putting it on speaker. She probably shouldn't have been surprised that Lily answered Evan's phone.

Colin told her what had happened the night before and asked if Evan might be able to help him carry out some of the heavier furniture. Before he even finished, Lily had cut him off.

"We'll both be there. Do not even *think* of asking us not to come. We had nothing on our agenda this afternoon anyway. We'd be thrilled to help."

In the background, Maria heard Evan's voice. "Help with what?"

"We're going to clean up Maria's apartment. And I have the cutest shorts I've been dying to wear! They're a little short and kind of tight, but this seems like the perfect opportunity."

In the background, Evan was silent for a beat. "What time are we going?"

When they hung up, Maria looked over at Colin. "I like your friends."

"They *are* pretty great," he agreed.

Two blocks before they reached her parents' neighborhood, the meaning of Serena's message became clear.

Her uncle Tito was in the park, kicking a soccer ball with her uncle Jose and a few of her nieces and nephews, and when both of her uncles waved, she knew that what they were really doing was keeping watch.

Meanwhile, Pedro, Juan, and Angelo, her cousins, were positioned in lawn chairs on the front lawn, and some of her younger cousins were in the street playing kickball. Cars she recognized lined the road on either side, all the way to the corner.

My God, she thought, *my entire extended family is here.* And though she'd been through hell in the last few days, she couldn't help but smile.

Despite Colin's reluctance, she dragged him into the house. Thirty or forty people milled around inside; there were another twenty in the backyard. Men and women, boys and girls...

Serena came rushing forward. "Crazy, huh? Dad actually closed the restaurant today! Can you believe that?"

"I don't think we needed everyone to come..."

"He didn't ask them to," she said. "Everyone just showed up when they found out you might be in trouble. I'm sure the neighbors wondered what on earth was going on, but Dad went around and explained that we were having a family reunion. After today, there will always be a family watch patrol in the neighborhood until Atkinson is behind bars, but they'll be more subtle about it. They've decided to organize shifts."

"For me?"

Serena smiled. "That's how we roll."

It took Colin almost half an hour to extract himself—everyone wanted to meet him, even if many of the greetings were in Spanish. As Maria walked him back to the car, she reflected that despite everything, she was blessed.

"I still think I should go with you," she said.

"I doubt your parents would let you leave."

"Probably not," she agreed. "I'm sure my dad is watching from the window right now. Just in case."

"Then I guess I'm not allowed to kiss you."

"You better," she said. "And make sure you bring Evan and Lily back here for dinner, okay? I want the rest of my family to meet them, too."

Colin didn't make it back to the house until half past five. Some family members had left, but most had stayed. For her part, Lily was perfectly at ease the moment she stepped out of the car, even if Colin and Evan seemed a bit uncertain.

"What a wonderful show of solidarity and love," Lily pronounced with a hug as soon as Maria walked up. "I simply can't wait to meet each and every member of your wonderful family!"

Lily's Southern-tinged Spanish delighted everyone she met, the same way it had charmed Maria, and as the relatives crowded around her and Evan, Maria pulled Colin away and stepped onto the back porch.

"How did it go?" she asked.

"I'll need to put a final coat of paint on the wall, but the primer was able to cover up the spray paint. We got rid of everything broken, and set aside the stuff that might be able to be cleaned. I'm not sure there's much we can do about your clothes, though." When she nodded, he went on. "Did you hear any updates on Margolis? Or have you heard from Atkinson?"

"No," she answered. "I've been checking my phone for messages all day."

He looked around. "Where's Serena?"

"She left a few minutes before you got here. She has that interview tonight, and she had to get ready." Maria reached for his hand. "You look tired."

"I'm okay."

"It was more work than you expected, wasn't it?"

"No," he said. "But it was hard for me to keep my anger in check."

"Yeah," she said. "For me, too."

After making the rounds with the family, Lily and Evan joined Colin and Maria at the table on the porch.

"Thanks for cleaning up my place," Maria said.

"It was no problem at all," Lily said. "And I must say, it's an absolutely charming location. Evan and I considered moving downtown as well, but Evan insisted that he couldn't imagine having no lawn to mow."

"I don't do that now," Evan said. "Colin does it. I hate mowing the lawn."

"Hush, now," she said. "I was just teasing. But you should know that physical labor can be quite attractive in a man."

"What do you think I was doing today?"

"My point exactly," she said. "You cut a very appealing figure as you were moving furniture, you know."

The door to the porch opened and Carmen came out carrying place settings for each of them, followed by several plates of food that occupied more than half the table. Not only had the kitchen been hopping all day, but most of the relatives had brought food as well.

"I hope you are hungry," Carmen said in English.

It was too much food. Just like always. While Colin seemed to have expected it, both Evan and Lily looked overwhelmed.

"This is great, Mom," Maria said, suddenly grateful for her mother's wordless demonstration of love. "I love you."

CHAPTER 31

───── ❧ ─────

Colin

After dinner, Colin wandered out to the front yard, seeking some time alone. A pair of uncles sat in lawn chairs overlooking the street, nodding at Colin's polite salute. Reflexively, he relived the destruction he'd seen at Maria's house, trying to piece together its connection to Atkinson and Lester.

Lester and Atkinson had once worked together, and Lester had introduced Atkinson to his sister. And while Maria believed that Lester had been sending messages to her, Dr. Manning suggested that Atkinson was responsible.

It was uncanny timing that Atkinson had disappeared shortly before Maria's stalking began. Presumably, Atkinson had slashed Maria's tires, but which of the two had killed Copo? Lester shot Margolis; Atkinson removed the car from the bungalow and later trashed Maria's place. Given the trove of information found on Atkinson's computer, his involvement in Maria's stalking seemed clear-cut, but certain details continued to bother Colin.

Dr. Manning had mentioned an argument between Lester and Atkinson and said they'd had a falling-out, but when had they regained each other's trust? Which one was in charge? Why had Dr. Manning insisted that Atkinson was trying to frame Lester when it seemed clear they had to be working together? And if they were working together, why drive two cars to the Sanchez house the night Lester attacked Maria?

And yet...as Colin had cleaned Maria's condo, he'd thought back on the earlier conversation with Detective Wright and realized that there was no evidence conclusively linking Atkinson to the trashing of the condo yet. There wasn't any conclusive evidence supporting the idea that he'd slashed Maria's tires, either. Despite the content found on his computer, Maria had never interacted with him or even seen him. She'd said all along that Atkinson's involvement never felt plausible to her, which meant...

What?

Suppose Atkinson really had gone off to meet a woman. And what if Lester knew that Atkinson would be out of town? Lester could have planted the information on Atkinson's computer and taken Atkinson's car while he was away. Lester could have—as Maria had pointed out the night before—easily paid someone to slash Maria's tires. Maybe even trash her condo. It would be the perfect setup...as long as you believed that Lester was capable of such intricate planning. Based on the behavior that Colin had witnessed at the bungalow and the way Wright had described Lester's actions at the station, that felt unlikely. And since Atkinson had apparently driven Lester back to Shallotte after he'd shown up at the Sanchezes', Atkinson had to have been nearby. They had to be working together, and Colin supposed that Lester must have been spooked by the sirens. Atkinson must have heard them, too, fueling his own panic, and he'd picked Lester up before racing the two of them out of the neighborhood. They would have been driving fast and possibly as recklessly as Colin had, but in the opposite direction...

Like the car Colin had almost hit just blocks from the Sanchezes' home?

Colin felt something akin to a key turning in a lock, and

strained to remember exactly what he'd seen. The car careening toward him, swerving in the last instant, the vehicles brushing past with only inches to spare. Two men in the front seat. What kind of car?

A Camry.

Blue.

Reaching for his phone, he called Detective Wright, who answered on the second ring.

"Have you heard anything about Margolis?" Colin asked.

"Improving. Or so they say. Still in critical care and still unconscious. How are things there?"

"They're okay. Maria's safe."

"And tonight?"

"She'll stay here. She's well protected."

"If you say so. What do you need?"

"I'm thinking that Atkinson might be driving a blue Camry. Relatively new."

"Why do you think that?"

Colin outlined his reasoning.

"You wouldn't have happened to have gotten a license plate, would you?"

"No."

"Okay. It's not much, but I'll get the word out. Everyone wants to find this guy, the sooner the better."

Colin disconnected, somehow sure that Lester had been in the blue Camry that night. He felt certain, even if he couldn't explain the reason, other than to assume that his subconscious mind was somehow ahead of his conscious mind in understanding that the answers were there, if only he could find them.

❦

"What are you doing out here?" Evan asked, joining Colin in the front yard.

"Thinking," Colin answered. It was half past six, and dusk

had given way to darkness, the autumn air hinting at even cooler temperatures as the evening wore on.

"I figured. I saw the smoke drifting out of your ears."

Colin smiled. "I just got off the phone with Detective Wright," he explained, recapping the conversation. "What are you doing out here?"

"As sweet as Carmen is, her food is kinda spicy. Lily asked me to get her some gum from the glove compartment to help cool down her mouth. If you ask me, Lily just wants her breath to smell minty fresh, because not having minty fresh breath isn't ladylike." He shrugged. "By the way, what do you make of all this? Maria's family, I mean?"

"I think they're great."

"It's kind of amazing, isn't it? Her entire *extended* family showing up to keep her safe?"

Colin nodded. "I doubt even my immediate family would show up."

Evan raised an eyebrow. "Don't kid yourself. When things were bad, even your family circled the wagons."

"Friends, too," Colin said. "Thanks for your help today. I know you wanted to spend the day in bed with Lily."

"You're welcome." Evan shrugged. "But it wasn't going to work out anyway. I couldn't stop thinking about Margolis, which kind of put a damper on my mood. I still can't figure out how he let Lester get the jump on him."

Colin paused. "When he was on the porch, did he look confused to you?"

"He looked pissed off," Evan said. "Because we hadn't left yet."

"How did he look before that?"

"I have no idea, dude," Evan said, shaking his head. "Everything is so jumbled, I'm not really sure what happened. I can remember hearing shots and seeing you doing your crazy thing, but after that... it's just all blood. My brain's so scrambled, I can't even remember why I came out here in the first place."

"You came out here to get Lily some gum," Colin reminded him.

"Oh yeah. That's right. Minty freshness." Evan started toward the car and then turned around to look back at Colin. "Do you want a piece?"

"No," Colin said.

But Dr. Manning probably would . . .

Colin wasn't sure why Margolis's description of Manning's compulsive gum chewing leaped to mind, but after considering it, he shook his head, deciding to head back inside with Evan and rejoin Maria's family. They were a marvel, he had to admit. Talk about circling the wagons. In times of crisis, family was sometimes all you really had. Hell, even Dr. Manning showed up for Lester. He'd spoken to Margolis, he'd shown up at the station, and he'd also immediately arranged for an attorney, since Lester had been in no condition to do so himself.

But . . . how had Dr. Manning even known of Lester's arrest? Wright had said that the attorney had shown up ten minutes after Lester had arrived at the station. Colin knew from experience that it was almost impossible to procure an attorney that quickly, especially on a Friday night after business hours. Which meant that Dr. Manning had known that Lester had been arrested well before his arrival at the station. It was almost like he was there . . .

And had parked his car in the driveway?

No, Colin thought. Margolis would have recognized the car. He'd seen Dr. Manning's car yesterday morning, when the doctor had shown Margolis the gun in the trunk. And if it *had* been Dr. Manning's car at the bungalow, Margolis probably would have acted . . .

Confused?

Colin stopped in his tracks. No. It wasn't possible. But . . .

Families circle the wagons . . . Son and father . . . Lester and Dr. Manning . . . Dr. Manning nervously mowing through a pack of gum while talking to Margolis . . .

Colin groped for the answer, a forgotten detail . . . And?

Hadn't he noticed a bunch of gum wrappers strewn on the roof of the building across from Maria's office?

Colin could barely breathe. It wasn't Atkinson and Lester. It was father and son circling the wagons, and all at once, the answers started cascading through his mind as quickly as Colin could form the questions.

Why hadn't Margolis been more cautious at the bungalow?

Because he saw that Avery Manning, the father, was already there.

And Lester's gun?

Dr. Manning had told Margolis the gun likely wasn't real.

Why had Margolis gone inside?

Because Dr. Manning called out to him, assuring Margolis that everything was okay.

It fit; it all fit, he thought, clarity finally emerging.

But Lester was arrested.

Only because Colin was there to take him down. Otherwise, Lester might have escaped.

But Lester might talk.

The attorney Dr. Manning hired would make sure he didn't.

But Dr. Manning had left a message for Margolis, urging him to warn Maria...

After the fact—too late to matter.

And Atkinson?

The man who failed to intervene when Laws abducted Cassie? Who Dr. Manning might feel deserves to be punished as well?

But Atkinson's laptop...the photos, the files...

All of which made Atkinson the perfect fall guy.

By then, Colin was already reaching for his phone, the truth so obvious that he wasn't sure how he could have missed it.

Who had the knowledge and skill necessary to manipulate Lester?

Dr. Manning, the psychiatrist.

How had Atkinson's name come up in the first place?

Dr. Manning.

And Laws's pattern of stalking Cassie?

Dr. Manning knew every detail.

Colin heard a voice on the other end of the phone. Wright, sounding busy and stressed.

"You again," Wright said. "What's up?"

"Check to see if Dr. Manning owns a blue Camry."

Wright hesitated. "Hold on. Why?"

"Have someone check it out while I talk," Colin said. "Just do it. It's important."

After he heard Wright call out the request to another officer, Colin told him everything. When he finished, Wright was quiet for a moment.

"That sounds a little far-fetched, don't you think?" Wright said. "But if you're right, Margolis will be able to clear all this up as soon as he regains consciousness. Besides..." Wright seemed to be wrestling with his own doubts.

"Yes?"

"It's not as though Dr. Manning is trying to hide. Far from it— he was at the station last night and he was at the hospital today—"

"He was there?" Colin asked, feeling a mounting sense of panic.

"He spoke with Rachel. He wanted to apologize for what his son did and asked if it might be possible to speak with Pete, so that he could apologize to him, too."

"Don't let him near Margolis!" Colin shouted, panic giving way to fear.

"Keep it down," Wright said. "Manning couldn't see him. Even I couldn't see him. Only family is allowed in the ICU—"

"Manning went there to kill him!" Colin interrupted. "He's a medical doctor... He'd know what to do to make the death look natural."

"Don't you think you're jumping to conclusions?"

"Lester didn't shoot Margolis! Dr. Manning did! Lester had Margolis squarely in his sights, but he couldn't pull the trigger. If you don't believe me, test Lester's hands for gunpowder residue."

"That won't tell us anything. It's too late. Those tests get less effective by the hour—"

"I know I'm right about this!"

Wright was silent for a long moment. "Okay...but what about Atkinson's computer?"

"Atkinson is dead," Colin said with sudden certainty. "Dr. Manning killed him. Made it look like he went on a trip, took his car, planted evidence on the computer, made him the prime suspect, and planned it all."

Wright said nothing. After a moment of silence, Colin heard the muffled sound of the detective speaking with someone else. Colin felt his frustration rising until Wright came back on the line, sounding slightly stunned.

"Dr. Manning," Wright said slowly, "owns a blue Camry, and...I gotta go...I want to verify that the Camry was at the bungalow..."

Wright hung up midsentence.

Colin raced inside to update Maria, finding her still on the back porch with Evan and Lily, her parents, and a scattering of aunts and uncles. As Colin related his discoveries, Maria listened silently. By the end, her eyes were closed, and though the revelations were clearly frightening to her, he also sensed a kind of peace in her at finally knowing the truth. Her relatives, meanwhile, remained silent, all of them waiting for her to respond.

"Okay," Maria finally said. "What's next?"

"I'm guessing Wright will put out an APB on Dr. Manning and then do whatever else it is cops do when searching for a suspect and building a case."

Maria thought about that. "But what about the pattern?" she finally ventured. "I mean, if Dr. Manning wanted me to experience everything Laws had done to Cassie, why would he have vandalized my place last night? He had to know that it would make it even more difficult to get to me. And why didn't Lester grab me when he had the chance to…"

Beat me, maybe burn me alive, and then kill himself, she didn't need to add. Colin remembered what Laws had done, but knew that Dr. Manning had never planned to kill himself. He'd wanted Atkinson's body found in the ashes, which would close the case for good, leaving Dr. Manning a free man. All Colin could do was shake his head.

"I don't know," he admitted.

Seven o'clock now, and the night was growing even darker, with just a sliver of moon above the horizon.

As the family, led by Felix, began making additional plans to keep Maria safe, Colin drifted to the kitchen and retrieved a glass from the cupboard. He was thirsty, but he also wanted to be alone while he pondered Maria's questions.

Moving to the refrigerator, he set the glass under the dispenser. Filling it with water, he downed the glass in a single long pull and began refilling it, his eyes absently scanning the refrigerator door. There were photos of Maria and Serena over the years, poems, Maria's confirmation certificate, and a drawing of a rainbow in crayon with Serena's name carefully etched in the corner. Some of the items had begun to yellow at the edges, and the only recent addition appeared to be the letter Serena had received from the Charles Alexander Foundation. It was in the upper corner, partially obscuring a postcard that displayed the Metropolitan Cathedral in Mexico City. As Colin glanced at the letterhead, he was again nagged by the thought that the name seemed oddly familiar.

Still…

Maria's questions had left him feeling unsettled. Why *had* Dr. Manning vandalized her condo? If Dr. Manning wanted Maria to experience everything Cassie had, then why deviate from the pattern now? And why paint the words *You will know how it feels* in her bedroom when doing so only made her more inaccessible? It was possible, he supposed, that Dr. Manning had panicked or lost control after Lester had been arrested. Colin wanted to believe that, tried to force himself to, but couldn't quite make that leap. Instead, he felt like he'd overlooked something. Either he was missing a piece of the puzzle, or Dr. Manning no longer cared whether he could get to Maria at all...

But why wouldn't he care?

Turning from the fridge, he took another drink, consoling himself with the notion that even without the answers, not only was Maria safe, but she'd remain safe until Dr. Manning was apprehended. Colin and her family would make sure of that. They gave *circling the wagons* a whole new meaning. Hell, all of them were here right now, standing watch...

But in that instant, he realized he was wrong. Not all of them were here. One of them was missing... and Dr. Manning no longer cared whether he could get to Maria at all...

Because Maria had never been part of Dr. Manning's endgame in the first place?

In Colin's mind, the answers began to tumble fast, clarity emerging... the name on the letterhead and why it seemed so familiar... why Maria's place had been trashed... how Lester had known about Carmen's birthday... the real meaning behind the words that had been painted in the bedroom...

You will know how it feels . . .

Dropping the glass, Colin burst from the kitchen, through the living room, and down the short hallway into Maria's bedroom. He located her bags and spotted her laptop in her tote bag. Grabbing it, he flipped up the lid, thinking, *No, no, no . . . please God, let me be wrong about this . . .*

He opened the search program and typed in the name of the foundation that had awarded Serena's scholarship... wanted to see it... prayed for it to come up...

No website displayed; just a notice saying the site had been taken down and that the domain name was available.

No, no, no . . .

He typed in Avery Manning's name and recognized the same links he'd perused after he and Maria had met with Margolis the first time. He remembered the link that had included Avery Manning's photograph, and clicked on it even as he rushed back to the living room. Looking up, he spotted Carmen, but not Felix.

"Carmen!" he shouted, hoping she'd be able to understand what he was about to say.

Relatives turned his way, alarmed. Colin ignored them. Ignored Carmen's sudden expression of fright. From the corner of his eye, he saw the back slider opening, Maria about to enter.

By then, he'd reached Carmen. He held up the computer and was pointing to the photograph.

"Do you recognize him?" Colin said, talking loud and fast. Fear now building to panic. "Is this the man who came to the house for dinner? Is this the director of the foundation?"

Carmen began shaking her head. *"No sé . . . No entiendo . . . Habla más despacio, por favor."*

"What's going on?" Maria cried. "What are you doing, Colin? You're scaring her!"

"It's him!" Colin shouted.

"Who?" Maria yelled, his fear contagious. "What's happening?" By then, Felix had come rushing through the slider, too, followed by Evan and Lily, more relatives . . .

"Look at him!" Colin said to Carmen, pointing to the photograph, lowering his voice, trying and failing to sound calm. "Look at the photo! The director! Is this him? Is this who came to your house for dinner?"

"¡Mira la foto, Mamá!" Maria translated, moving next to her. *"¿Es ésto el director de la fundación? ¿Quién vino a la casa para la cena?"*

Carmen's eyes swiveled in terror between Colin and Maria

before she leaned in to scrutinize the photo on the screen. After a moment, she began nodding quickly.

"¡Sí!" Carmen said, seemingly on the verge of tears. "Charles Alexander! *¡Él es el director! ¡Él estaba aquí en la casa!*"

"Colin!" Maria yelled, grabbing his arm. He turned, his panicked gaze on her.

"Where's Serena?" he demanded. "Where is she?"

"At the interview, you know that...What's wrong?"

"Where's the interview? Where's it taking place?"

"I don't know. I guess at the foundation's office..."

"Where's the office?" Colin shouted.

"Downtown...on the waterfront," Maria stammered. "The older commercial area, not the historic district. Tell me what's happening!"

Abandoned buildings, Colin thought. *Foreclosed* buildings. *Fire*...Thoughts falling as fast as shuffling cards...Dr. Manning no longer caring whether he could get to Maria...Maria needing to *know how it feels*...Because it wasn't only about making Maria experience Cassie's terror, it was about punishing Maria, making her feel the same way Dr. Manning and Lester felt after someone they loved had been murdered.

Oh, God...

"Call the police!" Colin shouted. "Call 911!"

"Colin!" Maria screamed. "Talk to me!"

"Avery Manning pretended to be Charles Alexander!" Colin shouted, feeling the clock was ticking and knowing there wasn't time to explain everything. "Dr. Manning had a child named Alexander Charles. There is no foundation. Or scholarship. Dr. Manning made it up," he hissed. "You weren't the target—Serena's the target. She's with him right now and I need to know exactly where she is before..."

Maria understood everything in an instant, her expression stricken as Colin grabbed her hand and pulled her along with him, racing for the door that led to the garage. He vaguely heard

Maria screaming, "¡Llame a la policía! ¡Emergencia! ¡Llame a nueve-uno-uno!" over her shoulder as they burst from the garage, racing to his car.

Maria dove in and Colin was rounding the car when he heard Evan shouting that they were coming, too.

Colin jumped behind the wheel, barking out instructions for Maria to call Detective Wright. He turned the key hard, gunning the engine, his tires screeching as he tore away from the house. In the rearview mirror, he vaguely noticed headlights turning on, Evan and Lily and various relatives trailing in his wake.

"When did Serena say she had the interview?" Colin demanded, even as Maria was waiting for Wright to answer her call.

"I can't remember... Seven, maybe?"

"What's the address?"

"I picked her up at the office once, but I don't know..."

Colin pressed the accelerator to the floor and the engine roared, the car shuddering as it rounded the first curve... Colin fighting the thought that he might already be too late... cursing himself for not figuring it out sooner. The headlights in the rearview mirror grew smaller as the speedometer nosed toward seventy, and then eighty.

He slammed on the brakes, skidding onto the main road to the screech of an oncoming car's tires. Undeterred, he sped up again, only dimly aware that Maria was screaming into the phone at Detective Wright.

Colin continued to accelerate, surging close to a hundred miles an hour, feeling déjà vu as he swerved into the bike lane and slowing but not stopping for red lights. He leaned on his horn, flashed his lights, and cut through parking lots as precious seconds ticked by.

Maria had hung up with Detective Wright and was now frantically dialing and redialing, her actions growing even more panicked.

"Serena's not answering her phone!"

"Find out when she left the dorm!" Colin shouted.

"But...how?"

"I don't know!"

Colin changed lanes, ran another red light, and checked the rearview mirror. Evan's headlights were too far behind to see anymore, and Colin squeezed the steering wheel, furious with himself for being so stupid, for missing the obvious. Thinking about Serena, telling himself that he'd get there in time to save her.

He'd get there. He had to get there.

Charles Alexander. Alexander Charles. He'd seen the name on the computer, and the connection was right there on the refrigerator, in the damn letterhead! And Serena had even said the name at dinner! It was obvious, and Colin couldn't understand why it had taken him so long to put it together. If something happened to Serena because he'd been so damn stupid...

Colin vaguely heard Maria shout the name Steve into the phone...Heard her demanding to know when Serena had left... heard her say that Serena was running late and had left at 6:40...

"What time is it?" Colin demanded, speeding so fast he was unable to take his eyes from the road for a second. "Check your phone!"

"Seven twelve..."

Serena might not have arrived yet...

Or she was there already...

Colin pressed his teeth together, his jaw muscles pulsing, thinking that if anything had happened to her...

He'd hunt Dr. Manning to the ends of the earth. The man deserved to die, and in that instant, Colin's thoughts began narrowing as he felt a visceral, almost tangible urge to kill him.

In his ever growing rage, the speedometer topped 120, and all Colin could think was *Go, go, go...*

CHAPTER 32

Maria

Colin was driving so fast that the images beyond the windows were blurry. Despite the seat belt, Maria was being flung from side to side whenever he made a turn or braked or accelerated. And yet, all she could think about was Serena and that she'd been the target all along. And he'd toyed with her...

The fake scholarship. Interviews. Slowly earning her trust...

But all the while, he'd been planning. Following Serena. Stalking. Not just in person, but on Serena's social media, too. He'd come to dinner with the family because he'd known Maria wouldn't be there...Serena had told the world that Maria had a date. He'd known Maria would celebrate their mom's birthday because Serena had posted about that, too. As the reality of what was happening sank in, Maria felt a mounting sense of panic that began to take on a life of its own. It was getting harder to catch her breath as the muscles in her chest began to compress. She tried to will the sensations away and from past experience knew she was having a panic attack, but she kept thinking about Serena. What if they were already too late? What if Dr. Manning had already abducted Serena and would do to her what had been done to Cassie?

Maria's mind flashed on the photos from Laws's crime scene and her lungs suddenly constricted even more, making breathing almost impossible. She told herself again that it was simply a panic attack, but as she tried and failed to draw a breath, she knew that she was mistaken. This wasn't a panic attack. It wasn't like this the last time. All at once, she felt a searing pain in her chest that traveled down her left arm.

Oh my God, she thought. *I'm having a heart attack . . .*

Colin hit the brakes and the momentum flung Maria hard into the shoulder harness. She was flung again moments later as he made another turn, her head banging the window. Maria barely registered the pain; all she could think about was the pressure in her chest and the fact that she couldn't breathe. She tried to scream, but no sound came out. In that instant, she was only vaguely aware that her phone had suddenly dinged and vibrated with an incoming text, the thought immediately vanishing as the world began going black at the edges.

"Maria? What's wrong?" Colin called out. "Are you okay?"

I'm having a heart attack! Maria tried to say as her eyes began to close. *I'm dying!* But the words still wouldn't come. She couldn't breathe, her heart was giving out, and though she heard Colin calling out her name, it sounded both underwater and far away, and she couldn't understand why Colin wasn't doing anything, why he wasn't helping her. He needed to call an ambulance and rush her to the hospital . . .

Her thoughts were disrupted as she was suddenly shoved upright in her seat and felt pressure on her shoulder; a moment later, her body was being shaken.

"Take control of this, Maria!" Colin commanded. "You're having a panic attack!"

It's not a panic attack! her mind screamed as she fought for every breath, frantically wondering why he wasn't helping her. *It's real this time, can't you see that?*

"Maria! Listen to me! Maria!" Colin shouted. "I need to know where Serena went! Manning is with her right now! I need your help! Serena needs your help!"

Serena . . .

Maria instinctively opened her eyes at the mention of her sister's name and latched on to the sound, focusing on it, but it was too late . . .

"Maria!"

This time, it was the sound of her own name that jolted her. She thought; *Colin is talking to me.* She thought; *Serena.* She thought; *Dr. Manning.* Somehow, she was able to hold her eyes open, though she still couldn't breathe and she was dizzy. But . . . *Serena . . . oh, God, Serena needed . . .*

Help.

Every cell in her body continued to hammer its death omen at Maria, drowning out the reality of the situation. She fought to regain clarity; she forced herself to think about Serena and knew they were going to the waterfront to save her sister, and that her phone had vibrated with a text.

It was all she could do to turn the screen faceup and focus, but she was somehow able to make out the words . . .

Sorry. Ringer off. Walking to interview now. Wish me luck!

Serena. Her sister was still alive, and they were racing to save her. Maria forced herself to draw a long, steady breath, and then another. *A panic attack, that's all,* she thought. *I can get through this . . .*

But her body was still rebelling, even if her mind had begun to clear. Her hands shook and her fingers weren't working right. She was able to hit the redial button, but the call went to voice mail. Meanwhile, Colin continued to shout at her from the driver's seat, even as he skidded through another turn . . .

"Maria! Are you okay? Tell me you're going to be okay!"

Though it took her a moment, she realized they'd reached South Front Street and were headed in the right direction.

"I'm okay," she mumbled, still catching her breath, amazed she could speak at all, realizing that breathing was no longer impossible. "Just need a minute."

Colin quickly glanced over at her before facing forward again, pressing down on the accelerator. "How much farther?" he asked. "I need to know where she is."

"I don't know," Maria answered, her voice still weak, her body struggling to recover. "A few more blocks," she huffed, feeling dizzy.

"You sure?"

Was she? She looked up the street, wanting to make sure. "Yes."

"On the left or right?"

"Left," Maria answered. Straining, she forced herself to sit higher in the seat. Her body continued to tremble.

Colin sped through the next intersection. Staring out the window, Maria vaguely noticed a half-dozen shacks and boathouses closer to the river, looking dark and shadowed. Streetlights barely cut through the darkness. The car's momentum began to decrease as Colin lifted his foot from the accelerator, and they coasted the next block and through another intersection. Here, the architecture immediately shifted; the flat-roofed buildings were now sandwiched together like row houses, some of the buildings in better condition than others. There were office lights blazing on some floors but most were blackened, and the cars on the street were separated by wider gaps. There was no traffic in either direction. As they drove through another block, the area suddenly began to feel familiar and Maria knew they were close, even as she struggled with a sudden rush of anger and guilt she felt for having a panic attack at the worst possible moment, when Serena needed her most.

She reminded herself that she'd been here before, and despite her body's continued rebellion, she forced herself to take long breaths as she scanned the buildings. It was hard to tell for sure which was the one they wanted, since she hadn't been paying that much attention the first time she'd come here. She vaguely recalled that Serena had been standing at an intersection and there'd been some construction workers staring from the opposite side of the street... She squinted, spotted scaffolding on a building at the corner, and then, on the opposite side of the street, Serena's car...

"There!" she said, pointing. "The four-story brick one on the corner!"

Colin immediately pulled over, braking hard. He jumped out of the car and took off running, not waiting for Maria as she struggled to open her door, furious that her body had gone into revolt and needed to recover. She didn't have time for that. Not now. Especially not now. Finally pushing the door open, she willed herself to stand and start moving.

By then, Colin had already reached the lobby door. She saw him struggling to open it, finding it locked, then jabbing at something beside the handle. When Maria looked up, there were seven or eight offices still illuminated on various floors, and she watched as Colin pounded the glass. She could tell from his body language that he was debating whether to smash his way in, but Maria instinctively knew that Serena wasn't in the office building. Nor was Dr. Manning. He'd been far too careful to this point to make that mistake now; he'd been far too meticulous, and there were too many people in the building, too many potential witnesses, too many things that could go wrong. She guessed that Dr. Manning had been waiting for Serena on the sidewalk in front of the building and probably had a story about a pipe that burst or whatever, so the interview would be held elsewhere. She knew that he wanted someplace private, where he knew he wouldn't be caught, a place that would burn.

"Colin!" she tried to shout. The sound came out weak. She tried to wave her arms, but the dizziness came back in a rush and she stumbled. "Colin!" she called out again, and this time he heard her voice and ran toward her.

"The door has one of those key-code locks! There's no listing for the foundation, so I just hit all the buttons, but no one's buzzing."

"Serena's not in there," Maria forced out. "Manning took her someplace else. There are too many people inside, too many people still working."

"If she got in his car..."

"She texted that she was walking to the interview."

"Then where's his car? I don't see it."

"Check around the corner," Maria wheezed, still fighting waves of dizziness. "He probably parked there. If he's looking for someplace deserted, he took her to one of the shacks or boathouses near the river. Hurry!" she said, feeling like she was about to fall over. "Just go. I'll get my phone and call the police..." *And my parents, my relatives, Lily, everyone who jumped in their cars to follow us,* she thought.

By then, Colin was already backing up toward the intersection, uncertain, wanting to trust her, but...

"How do you know that's where they'll be?"

"Because," she said, wondering when the police would arrive, remembering the lakeside cabin where Cassie had been murdered, remembering the shacks and boathouses common to this portion of the Cape Fear River, "that's where Laws would have gone."

CHAPTER 33

---- ❦ ----

Colin

Maria's instincts had been right. He found the blue Camry parked on the cross street that ran beside the building. He sprinted past it. Straight ahead was an unkempt field that stretched toward the muddy banks of the Cape Fear River, a black void ahead of him, barren of reflection on this almost moonless night.

The street gave way to a gravel road that forked to the left and right, toward the river's edge. One way led to a small, rundown marina with a rusting metal structure that was home to a hodgepodge of boats, protected by low fencing; in the other direction stood two decaying barnlike structures near the riverbank, spaced maybe fifty yards apart. Those buildings looked abandoned, with cracked planks and peeling, faded paint, overgrown weeds and kudzu surrounding them. Colin slowed, frantically trying to guess where Manning had taken Serena. In that instant, he saw a ray of light leaking out intermittently between the planks of the abandoned building on the left, vanishing and reappearing.

The beam of a flashlight?

He left the gravel, cutting through grass and weeds that were shin-high in places, willing himself to move even faster, hoping he hadn't arrived too late. Still unsure what he was going to do, or what he was going to find.

As he reached the building where he'd seen the light, he pressed himself flush to the side of the wall. Up close, he realized that the structure had once been an icehouse, probably used by fishermen to load blocks of ice into their boats to keep their catch fresh.

There was no door on this side of the building, but a boarded-over window emitted a weak and flickering light. He began inching toward the side farthest from the river, hoping to find the door, when he heard a scream rip from inside...

Serena...

The sound galvanized him. He raced around the corner, but the door on that side had been boarded over. He accelerated past it, to the third side, seeing another boarded-up window. One option left. He peeked around the corner and immediately spotted the door he'd been looking for. Reaching for the knob, he found it locked. In that instant, he heard Serena cry out again.

Stepping back, he drove his heel into the door next to the knob. It was a perfect shot, hard and fast, the frame splintering as the door cracked open. He kicked again and it swung fully open. In that split second, he saw Serena tied to a chair in the middle of a dimly lit room, Dr. Manning beside her with a flashlight in his hand. There was the shape of a body in the corner, surrounded by rusting paint cans. Serena's face was bruised and bloodied. Both Serena and Dr. Manning cried out in surprise when Colin burst into the room. A beam of light suddenly hit Colin straight in the eyes.

Blinded and disoriented, Colin barreled ahead, reaching out in the direction he'd last seen Dr. Manning. He spread his arms, but Manning had the advantage and sidestepped him. Colin felt the heavy metal flashlight crash into the back of his hand and heard the bones snap. The combination of shock and searing pain kept him from reacting quickly enough. As Serena screamed again, Colin twisted, trying to square his shoulders at Manning, but he was too late. The flashlight smashed into his temple, the sudden impact turning everything black. His body went limp and his legs buckled; he hit the floor even as his mind was still trying to process what had happened. Instinct and experience urged him to get up quickly, and after years of training, the movements should have been automatic, but his body wouldn't respond. He felt another hard blow to his skull, which shot radiant bursts of agony through his system. His mind was teetering on the edge of coherent thought; he registered nothing other than pain and confusion.

Time seemed to shatter and fragment. Above the steady ringing in his ears, he could vaguely hear the sound of someone crying and screaming... begging... a woman's voice... and a man's...

Twilight descended and pain broke over him like a wave.

The sound of whimpering dimly penetrated his stupor; when he recognized his name, he was finally able to somehow open one eye. The world appeared hazy, nothing but a fog-filled dream, but when he thought he saw Maria tied to a chair, it was enough to allow him to finally comprehend what had happened and where he was.

No, not Maria. Serena.

But he still couldn't move. Still unable to fully focus, he could distantly make out Dr. Manning as he moved along the far wall. He was holding something red and square in his hands. Colin heard Serena's continued cries and his nostrils were suddenly flooded with the odor of gasoline. It took a moment to put everything together. Dully, he watched Manning toss the gas can aside. Colin saw a flicker of light, a match, and watched it arc toward the ground. He heard the *whoop* of ignition, like lighter fluid on charcoal. He saw flames begin leaping at the walls, the old planks as dry as tinder. Heat began to rise. Smoke thickened.

He tried to move his hands, tried to move his legs, but felt only numb paralysis. His mouth tasted metallic and coppery, and he saw a blur of movement as Manning ran past him, toward the door that Colin had kicked in.

The flames were reaching toward the ceiling, Serena's cries

telegraphing pure terror. He heard her cough once, and then again. Colin willed himself to move and wondered why his body wasn't working. Finally, his left arm began to inch forward. Then his right. He slid both arms under him and tried to rise, but his broken hand bones shifted. Colin screamed and his chest hit the floor, pain twisting his anger into rage, fueling his need for violence and revenge.

He got to all fours and slowly managed to stand. He felt dizzy, his balance still off. He took a step and stumbled, his eyes stinging in the acrid smoke, tearing up. Serena's cries had turned to uncontrollable coughing; Colin felt as though he couldn't breathe at all. The flames had spread to the other walls, surrounding them. The heat was intense, the smoke becoming black, searing his lungs. Colin stumbled the couple of steps it took to reach Serena and eyed the ragged macramé jungle of rope binding her to the chair. He knew that with one hand, there was no way to untie the rope in time, and he scanned his surroundings, hoping to see a knife. An ax. Anything sharp...

Colin heard a loud crack, followed by a roar as the roof of the icehouse suddenly sagged, sending sparks in all directions. A rafter beam crashed within a few feet of them, then another fell even closer. Along three walls, flames seemed to multiply, the heat so intense that Colin felt as if his clothing had ignited. Beginning to panic, he grabbed the chair with Serena still in it and heaved, feeling a burst of pain in his broken hand. His mind flashed white, and it fueled the rage inside him. He could handle pain; he knew how to harness it, and tried to draw on it, but his hand would no longer grip.

Unable to carry Serena, he had no other option. There were five, maybe six strides to the door, and grabbing the back of her chair with his good hand, he spun it around and began dragging it toward the doorway. He needed to get there before the flames did. He tugged and dragged, every jerk sending pain through his hand and his head.

He burst through the open doorway. Smoke and heat followed them out, and he knew he needed to get Serena a safe distance away from the smoke. He couldn't drag her through the field or the mud, and spotting gravel to the right, he went that direction, toward the other building. Behind them, the icehouse was nearly engulfed in flames; the sound rose in volume, magnifying the continued ringing in his ears. He kept moving, resting only when the heat from the fire began to diminish.

Serena hadn't stopped coughing, and in the darkness, her skin looked almost blue. He knew she needed an ambulance. She needed oxygen, and he still had to get her out of the chair. He saw nothing he could use to cut the rope, and he wondered if there might be something in the other building. Just as he started toward it, he saw a figure step out from the corner and move into firing position. The barrel of a gun reflected the fire...

The shotgun Margolis had mentioned, the one Manning had said might not even work...

Colin knocked Serena and the chair over and dove to block her in the same instant he heard the explosion. The shotgun had been fired from forty yards, pushing the maximum range, and Manning's aim had been high. The second shot was slightly more accurate. Colin felt the pellets tear through his shoulder and upper back, blood spilling. He went dizzy again, fighting to remain conscious as he blearily watched Manning start running for his car.

There was no way Colin could catch him. Manning's figure receded and there was nothing Colin could do. He wondered why it was taking so long for the police to arrive and hoped they'd catch him.

His thoughts were interrupted by a roar as fire suddenly mushroomed through the roof of the icehouse, alive and screaming, the sound almost deafening. Part of the wall exploded, sending burning pieces of wood and sparks in their direction. He could barely hear Serena crying through her coughs, and he realized they were still in danger, too close to the fire. There was no way Colin could drag her farther, but he could get help, and he forced himself to rise. He needed to get to a place where someone would see him. He staggered forward a few dozen steps, losing blood, his left arm and hand now useless, his nerve endings radiating agony.

By then, Manning had reached his car and Colin saw the headlights flash on. The Camry tore away from the curb, heading directly toward him.

And toward Serena.

Colin knew he couldn't outrun the car; no way he could so much as dodge it. But Serena was even more helpless, and Manning knew exactly where she was.

Gritting his teeth, Colin staggered forward as fast as he could, creating distance between him and Serena. Hoping Manning would follow him. Hoping Manning would flee. But the head-lights remained aimed in Serena's direction. Not knowing what else to do, Colin stopped and began waving his right arm, trying to draw Manning's attention.

He flipped Manning the bird.

The Camry immediately veered away from Serena and toward Colin, accelerating and closing the distance. The icehouse con-tinued to emit an eerie high-pitched shriek as fire consumed it. Colin staggered as fast as he could away from Serena, knowing he had only a few more seconds, knowing he was about to die. The car was almost upon him when all at once, the ground in front of him was bathed in another set of headlights racing up from somewhere behind him.

He barely saw the blur of Evan's Prius as it crashed into the Camry with ear-splitting force, pushing both cars toward the fire. The Camry smashed into the corner of the icehouse, the Prius bulldozing it forward. The roof of the building began to collapse as flames leaped farther upward, toward the sky.

Colin tried to rush forward, but his legs gave out. Blood con-tinued to pulse from his wounds, and as he lay on the ground, he could feel himself growing dizzy again. He could hear sirens now, competing with the sound of the fire. He suspected they were too late, that he wouldn't survive, but that didn't matter to him. He couldn't take his eyes from the Prius, and he watched for the door to open or for the window to go down. Evan and Lily could escape the fire if they moved fast, but the chances of that happening were slim.

He had to get to them, and tried again to rise. Lifting his head nearly caused him to black out. He thought he saw swirling red and blue lights on the side streets and bright headlights moving closer. He heard panicked voices calling out for Serena and for him, and he wanted to shout at them that they should hurry, that Evan and Lily needed help, but all that came out was a raspy whisper.

He heard Maria then, heard as she screamed his name and reached his side.

"I'm here!" she cried. "Hold on! The ambulance is coming!"

Even then, Colin couldn't answer. Everything had begun to spin and images became disjointed, nothing making sense. In one instant, the Prius was swallowed whole by flames; when he blinked again, only half of the car was gone. He thought he saw the passenger door creak open, but there was too much smoke and there were no other signs of movement, and he couldn't be sure. He felt himself slipping away, darkness settling in, and in his last moment of consciousness, he prayed that the two best friends he'd ever known would somehow make it out alive.

EPILOGUE

April never ceased to surprise Maria. Though she'd grown up in the South and knew what to expect, there were always a few glorious days, perfect days, when it seemed as though anything were possible. Cloudless blue skies would greet green lawns that had been brown all winter, and everything would suddenly explode with color. Dogwoods and cherry trees and azaleas would burst into life throughout the city, while tulips sprang forth from carefully tended gardens. Mornings were cool, but the days would warm up as the sun rose bright in the sky.

Today was one of those ephemeral spring days, and as Maria stood on the carefully tended lawn, she could see Serena chatting animatedly with a group of people Maria didn't recognize, the smile on her face wide and joyful. Seeing her now, it was hard to believe that until recently, Serena had struggled to smile at all; she'd suffered nightmares about her ordeal for months, and when she'd looked in the mirror, she'd seen bruises and cuts Manning had inflicted while she'd been tied to the chair. Two of the cuts had left scars—one near her eye, the other on her jawline—but they were already beginning to fade. In another year, Maria doubted anyone would notice them at all, unless they knew exactly where to look. But that would also mean they would have to remember that horrible night, and with those memories there was always pain.

It had been two weeks before Detective Wright, along with a still recuperating Pete Margolis, had met with Maria and admitted that Colin had been right about everything. The remains of Atkinson's body were found in what was left of the burned-out icehouse. Ballistics testing eventually connected the bullet in Atkinson's head to the gun that had been in Lester's possession. The fire made it impossible to determine exactly when he'd been killed, though investigators suspected that it was around the time he'd vanished. They were able to determine that his body had been stored in a large, otherwise empty freezer in Dr. Manning's garage in Charlotte thanks to a few strands of Atkinson's hair found frozen to the sides. Research into Manning's bank accounts showed numerous cash disbursements, the numbers matching the amounts that had been transferred into Atkinson's accounts to pay his bills, and also confirmed the rental of the bungalow in Shallotte.

Lester's fingerprints had been found in Atkinson's car, and investigators had hoped that Lester would provide even more answers. It was not to be. After spending three days in the infirmary under constant supervision, he was evaluated by a psychiatrist and deemed fit to be returned to a cell, subject to frequent monitoring. Later that afternoon, Lester met with his attorney, who reported that Lester, though heavily medicated and shaken by the loss of his father, seemed fairly lucid. Lester agreed to be interviewed by detectives the following day, as long as his attorney was present. He was returned to his cell and finished the tray of food that had been brought to him. Video recordings indicated that guards checked on him every fifteen to twenty minutes, but Lester nonetheless managed to hang himself, using strips from the bedsheet that he'd tied together. By the time the guards found him, it was too late.

Maria wondered sometimes whether Lester had truly been an accomplice or was simply another victim of Dr. Manning's. Or maybe even both. Pete Margolis admitted after he woke from his coma that he was unsure who had shot him. Dr. Manning had called out, telling him to come in, but Margolis saw only a brief glimpse of a gun barrel poking through the gap in a closet door before he was hit. The only thing Maria knew for sure was that Lester and Dr. Manning were both dead, and neither would ever come for her again. But despite *what they'd done to her and to Serena, she sometimes felt flashes of grief and pity for the Manning family. A young son who died in an accident, an older sister murdered, a mother long struggling with depression who committed suicide . . . She wondered who she would have become had those things happened to her, or had Serena died that night in the icehouse.*

Glancing over her shoulder, she surveyed the crowd that had gathered on the lawn and silently counted her blessings. Her mom and dad were managing to keep their protective instincts in check, her job with Jill was hugely satisfying, and she'd used some of her severance package to refurnish her condo and buy a new wardrobe—and still had enough left over to start building a small nest egg. Last weekend, she'd even wandered into a camera shop and fallen in love with a wildly expensive UV lens. The water was warming, too, her paddle-board calling to her . . .

The wedding had been spectacular, though with Lily directing and stage-managing, Maria had expected nothing less. While Wilmington would always be home, Maria could see that Charleston definitely had its charms. Lily was ethereal in her wedding dress, a confection of floating satin, tiny seed pearls, and fragile lace. Evan had been dreamy-eyed as he stared at her during their vows at St. Michael's Church. The oldest religious structure in Charleston, it was the preferred wedding venue for the more aristocratic families of Charleston, but when Lily drawled, "Why, I simply can't imagine why anyone would want to be married anywhere else," she somehow made it sound logical and sincere rather than snobbish.

On that awful night, Lily had miraculously escaped unharmed. Evan had been less fortunate, however. He'd emerged with second-degree burns on his back and a couple of broken bones in his leg. He'd been in a cast for nearly two months and had only recently begun walking without a limp again, in part due to his new exercise regime. His workouts weren't quite up to Colin's standards, but he'd confided to Maria that he'd been putting extra work in on his arms and was hoping Lily would notice on their honeymoon to the Bahamas.

They'd both had angels on their shoulders. Maria believed that as she'd seen Lily and Evan emerge from the Prius, and though some people might laugh at the notion, she didn't care.

She knew.

Behind her, the wedding reception was in full swing, solemnity finally giving way to festivities. Lily had wanted the reception held at her parents' spacious second home on the banks of the Ashley River, and as far as Maria could tell, no expense had been spared. A palatial white tent glowed with elaborately strung lights, and guests were dancing on a parquet floor before a ten-piece band. The food had been catered by one of the finest restaurants in the city, and the spring flower arrangements were works of art. Maria knew she'd never have a wedding like this; it wasn't her style. As long as she had her friends and family—and maybe a couple of piñatas later for the younger guests—she would be happy.

Not that she was thinking of getting married in the near future. The subject had yet to come up, and Maria had no intention of asking Colin about it directly. In most ways, Colin hadn't changed at all. He'd tell her the truth, and she wasn't sure she was ready to hear the answer. She might be inclined to hint if the opportunity presented itself, but even the thought of that sometimes made her nervous.

Colin had only recently managed to resume his workout routine, but he was sometimes frustrated he wasn't able to do the things he used to do, including MMA training. He needed at least another six months, the doctors insisted. The shotgun blast had torn through part of his shoulder muscle, leaving vivid scars and a weakness that might be permanent. He'd already undergone one operation on his hand, and another was planned in a few more months. The injury that concerned the doctors most, however, had been the skull fracture, and he'd spent four days in the ICU, near Pete Margolis.

Margolis had been the first one to speak to Colin when he regained consciousness.

"They tell me you saved my life," Margolis had said to him. "But don't think this changes anything about your deal. I'm still going to keep an eye on you."

"Okay," Colin had managed to croak out.

"They also tell me that Dr. Manning beat the crap out of you, and that Evan ended up being the one who finally took him out. I find that very hard to imagine."

"Okay," Colin said again.

"My wife said you came to check on me. Said you were polite, too. And that my friend Larry apparently thinks you're pretty smart."

His throat dry, Colin merely grunted this time.

Margolis shook his head and sighed. "Do me a favor and stay out of trouble. And one more thing." He finally cracked a smile. "Thank you."

Since then, Margolis hadn't dropped by to check on Colin even once.

🌿

Maria sensed Colin's approach and then felt his arm settle around her. She leaned into him.

"There you are," he said. "I was looking for you."

"It's so beautiful by the water," she said. She turned, slipping her arms around him.

"Maria?" he whispered into her hair. "Would you do something for me?" When she pulled back and looked at him quizzically, he went on. "I'd like you to meet my parents."

Her eyes widened. "They're here? Why didn't you tell me earlier?"

"I wanted to talk to them first. See where we stand."

"And?"

"They're good people. I told them about you. They asked if they could meet you, but I said I'd have to check with you first."

"Of course I'll meet your parents. Why would you have to check with me?"

"I wasn't sure what else to say. I've never introduced them to a girl before."

"Never? Wow. That makes me feel pretty special."

"It should. You are."

"So let's go meet your parents. Since I'm so special and you're crazy about me and you probably can't imagine living without me. In fact, you just might be thinking that I'm the one, right?"

He smiled, his eyes never leaving hers. "Okay."

ACKNOWLEDGMENTS

Every novel presents its own unique set of challenges, and this novel was no different. As always, there are those whose help and support were invaluable to me as I worked my way through those challenges.

I'd like to thank:

Cathy, who remains a wonderful friend. She will always be dear to me.

Our children—**Miles, Ryan, Landon, Lexie,** and **Savannah**— for the joy they continually add to my life.

Theresa Park, my fabulous literary agent, manager, and producing partner, who is always there to listen to me and provide constructive advice when I need it most. I'm not sure where I would be without her.

Jamie Raab, my terrific editor, who works wonders with my manuscripts. We've worked together on every book, and I consider myself blessed not only because of her expertise, but because of her unwavering friendship.

Howie Sanders and **Keya Khayatian**, my film agents at UTA, who are not only exceptional at what they do, they're creative, intelligent, and fun to be around.

Scott Schwimer, my entertainment attorney, is one of the best friends I have in the world, and my life has been enriched by his presence.

Stacey Levin, who runs my television production company, is an amazingly talented individual, with great instincts and passion for her job. Thanks also to **Erika McGrath** and **Corey**

Hanley for their talents in the same areas. **Larry Salz** at UTA, my television agent, keeps the complex ship running as smoothly as possible. I appreciate all that you do.

Denise DiNovi, the producer of *Message in a Bottle*, *A Walk to Remember*, *Nights in Rodanthe*, *The Lucky One*, and *The Best of Me*, with whom I've been lucky to associate, has true-blue instincts. In working with her, I've always been the lucky one. And many thanks to **Alison Greenspan** as well, for all you've done with these memorable projects.

Marty Bowen, the producer of *The Longest Ride*, *Safe Haven*, and *Dear John*, for his excellent work, his creativity, his humor, and friendship. Our time together is always enjoyable. Thanks also to **Wyck Godfrey**, who works with Marty in everything they do.

Michael Nyman, Catherine Olim, Jill Fritzo, and **Michael Geiser** at PMK-BNC, my publicists, who are first-rate at their jobs, and have become close friends as well.

LaQuishe Wright—or Q—who handles all things social media related in my world, not only does incredible work, but is someone with whom I simply enjoy spending time. **Mollie Smith** handles my website, and without you both, it would be impossible to keep people informed as to all that's going on in my world.

Michael Pietsch, at the Hachette Book Group, deserves my gratitude for all he does to make my novels a success. I'm honored to work with you.

Peter Safran, the producer of *The Choice*, for his enthusiasm and knowledge, and for welcoming my team into your exciting world.

Elizabeth Gabler, who has unbelievable passion for what she does, and the talent and drive to make it work. *The Longest Ride* was a remarkable and beautiful film. Also, my thanks go to **Erin Siminoff** for her extraordinary commitment to making that project a success. I loved working with you both.

Tucker Tooley, whom I consider a friend. I'm honored by your endless support for my work.

Ryan Kavanaugh and **Robbie Brenner** at Relativity Media, for the numerous great films they've helped to adapt from my work. It's been fabulous working with you both.

Courtenay Valenti, at Warner Bros., for helping to launch the Hollywood side of my career. It's always fun to catch up with you whenever I'm in town with a new project.

Emily Sweet, at the Park Literary Group, is always available to lend a helping hand in whatever capacity is needed. Thanks so much for temporarily taking over the reins of my foundation, and for listening whenever I call.

Abby Koons, at the Park Literary Group, for so deftly handling my foreign rights. I am always aware of the amazing work you do. You're the best, and I'm the first to understand that.

Andrea Mai, at the Park Literary Group, for all she does with our retail partnerships. It's been an extraordinary working relationship, and I must say that I'm in awe when it comes to your enthusiasm and persistence. And many thanks also to **Alexandra Greene**, who not only peruses every contract, but has incredible creative instincts. I would not be where I am today without you both.

My gratitude also goes to **Brian McLendon**, **Amanda Pritzker**, and **Maddie Caldwell** at Grand Central Publishing—your enthusiasm and commitment mean the world to me.

Pam Pope and **Oscara Stevick**, my accountants, have been a blessing in so many ways, not only for their work, but for their friendship. You've both been terrific.

Tia Scott, my assistant, is not only a friend, but she keeps my daily life on track. I appreciate all you do.

Andrew Sommers has always been an essential sounding board, and does important work behind the scenes in my world. My life has been the better for it. Thanks also to **Hannah Mensch** for all you've done this past year.

Michael Armentrout and **Kyle Haddad-Fonda**, who do amazing work at the Nicholas Sparks Foundation. Thanks so much.

Tracey Lorentzen, who is always willing to lend a helping hand in the way that I most need it, when I most need it. I don't know what I would have done without you.

Sara Fernstrom, formerly of UTA, and **David Herrin**, my oracle at UTA, have unique talents and abilities, and I've benefited much from their expertise.

Dwight Carlblom and **David Wang**, who run the Epiphany School of Global Studies, are terrific educators. I am so appreciative.

Michael "Stick" Smith, a friend, who has always been there to listen and offer support. The next few years should be interesting and fun, don't you think?

Jeff Van Wie, who has been a friend since we roomed together in college. Thanks for always being there for me.

Micah Sparks, my brother, is the best brother a guy could have. We'll make a point to do more traveling together this year, okay?

David Buchalter, who help arranges my speeches, is consistently outstanding. Thanks for everything.

Eric Collins, who has helped in ways that I can't even express. The same goes for **Jill Compton**. Thanks.

Pete Knapp and **Danny Hertz**, who always did whatever they could to help. Thanks, guys!

Other friends, with whom I always enjoy speaking, the kind of friends who make life worthwhile: **Todd** and **Kari Wagner, David Geffen, Anjanette Schmeltzer, Chelsea Kane, Slade Smiley, Jim Tyler, Pat Armentrout, Drew** and **Brittany Brees, Scott Eastwood,** and **Britt Robertson.**

Don't Miss Nicholas Sparks's New Novel

A powerful story of unconditional love—its challenges, risks, and, most of all, its unexpected rewards.

Please see the next page for an excerpt from

TWO BY TWO

CHAPTER I

———— ✿ ————

And Baby Makes Three

Wow!" I can remember saying as soon as Vivian stepped out of the bathroom and showed me the positive result of the pregnancy test. "That's great!"

In truth, my feelings were closer to . . . Really? Already?

It was more shock than anything, with a bit of terror mixed in. We'd been married for a little more than two years, and Vivian had already told me that she intended to stay home for the first few years after we had a baby. I'd always agreed when she'd said it—I wanted the same thing—but in that moment, I also realized that our life as a couple with two incomes would soon be coming to an end. Moreover, I wasn't sure in that moment whether I was even ready to become a father, but what could I do? It wasn't as though she'd tricked me, nor had she concealed the fact that she wanted to have a baby, and she'd let me know when she stopped taking the pill. I wanted children as well, of course, but Vivian had stopped the pill only three weeks earlier. I can remember thinking that I probably had a few months at least before her body readjusted to its normal, baby-making state. For all I knew, it could be hard for her to become pregnant, which meant it might even be a year or two.

But not my Vivian. Her body had adjusted right away. My Vivian was fertile.

I slipped my arms around her, studying her to see if she was already glowing. But it was too soon for that, right? What exactly is glowing, *anyway? Is it just another way of saying someone looks hot and sweaty? How were our lives going to change? For better or for worse?*

Questions tumbled over each other in my mind. And in that moment, as I held my wife, I, Russell Green, had answers to none of them.

Months later, the big *IT* happened, though I admit much of the day remains a blur.

Looking back, I probably should have written it all down while it was still fresh in my mind. A day like the big *IT* should be remembered in vivid detail—not the fuzzy snapshots I tend to recall. The only reason I remember as much as I do is because of Vivian. Every detail seemed etched into her consciousness, but then she was the one in labor and pain has a way of sometimes sharpening the mind. Or so they say.

What I do know is this: sometimes, in recalling events of that day, she and I are of slightly differing opinions. For instance, I considered my actions completely understandable under the circumstances, whereas Vivian would declare alternately that I was selfish, or simply a complete idiot. When she told the story to friends—and she has done so many times—people inevitably laughed, or shook their heads and offered her pitying glances.

In all fairness, I don't think I was either selfish or a complete idiot; after all, it was our first child, and neither of us knew exactly what to expect when she went into labor. Does anyone really feel prepared for what's coming? Labor, I was told, is unpredictable; during her pregnancy, Vivian reminded me more than once that the process from initial contractions to actual birth could take more than a day—especially for the first child—and labors of twelve hours or more were not uncommon. Like most young fathers-to-be, I considered my wife the expert and took her at her word. After all, she was the one who'd read all the books.

It should also be noted that I wasn't entirely deficient on the morning in question. I had taken my responsibilities seriously. Both her overnight bag and the baby's bag were packed, and the contents of both had been checked and double-checked. The camera and video camera were charged and ready, and the baby's room was fully stocked with everything our child would need for at least a month, including a bunch of things I didn't even know existed. I knew the quickest route to the hospital and had planned alternate routes, if there happened to be an accident on the highway. I had also known the baby would be coming soon; in the days leading up to the actual birth, there'd been numerous false alarms, but even I knew the countdown had officially started.

In other words, I wasn't entirely surprised when my wife shook me awake at half past four on Saturday, August 16, 2008, announcing that the contractions were about four minutes apart and that it was time to go to the hospital. I didn't doubt her; she knew the difference between Braxton Hicks and the *real thing*, and yet, in that moment, I also have to admit that as much as I'd been preparing myself, my first thoughts weren't about throwing on my clothes and loading up the car; in fact, they weren't about my wife and soon-to-be-born child at all. Rather, my thoughts went something like this: *Today's the big IT, and people are going to be taking a lot of photographs. Other people will be looking at these photographs forever, and—considering it's for posterity—I should probably hop in the shower before we go, since my hair looks as though I'd spent the night in a wind tunnel.*

It's not that I'm vain; I simply thought I had *plenty of time*, so I told Vivian I'd be ready to go in a few minutes. As a general rule, I shower quickly—no more than ten minutes on a normal day, including shaving—but just after I'd applied the shaving cream, I thought heard my wife cry out from the living room. I listened again, hearing nothing, but sped up nonetheless. By the time I was rinsing off, I heard her shouting, though strangely it seemed as though she was shouting *about* me, not *at* me. I wrapped a towel around me and stepped into the darkened hallway, still dripping wet. As God is my witness, I was in the shower for less than five minutes.

Vivian cried out again and it took me a moment to process that Vivian was on all fours and shouting into her cell phone that I was *IN THE DAMN SHOWER!* and demanding *WHAT IN THE HELL CAN THAT IDIOT BE THINKING?!?!?!? Idiot,* by the way, was the nicest term she used to describe me in that same conversation; her language was actually quite a bit more colorful. What I didn't know was that the contractions that had been four minutes apart were now—in the blink of an eye—only two minutes apart, and that she also in back labor. Back labor, by the way, is excruciating, and Vivian suddenly let out a scream so powerful that it became its own living entity, one that may still be hovering above our neighborhood in Charlotte, North Carolina, an otherwise peaceful place.

Rest assured, I moved into even higher gear after that, slapping on clothes without completely toweling off, and loading the car. I supported Vivian as she continued to grimace, buckling her into the front seat and trying not to comment on the fact that she was digging her fingernails into my forearm. A moment later, I was behind the wheel, and once on the road, I called the obstetrician, who promised to meet us at the hospital.

The contractions were still a couple of minutes apart when we arrived, but Vivian's continuing anguish meant that she was taken straight to labor and delivery. I held her hand and tried to guide her through her breathing—during which she again offered various colorful sentiments about me and where I could *stick the damn breathing!*—until the anesthesiologist arrived for the epidural. Early in the pregnancy, Vivian had debated whether or not to get one before reluctantly deciding in favor, and now it appeared to be a blessing. As soon as the medication kicked in her agony vanished entirely, and I saw my wife smile for the first time since she'd shaken me awake that morning. Her obstetrician—in his sixties, with neat gray hair and a friendly face—

wandered into the room every twenty to thirty minutes to see how dilated she was, and in between those visits I called both sets of parents, as well as my sister.

Then, it was time. Nurses were summoned and they readied the equipment with calm professionalism. Then, all at once, the doctor told my wife to push.

Vivian had pushed through three contractions when the doctor announced that one more should do it. Vivian was less exhausted than I'd imagined she might be—to that point, she'd been in labor only three hours—and when she pushed, the doctor began rotating his wrists and hands like a magician pulling a rabbit from his hat. The next thing I knew, I was a father.

Just like that.

The pediatrician took our baby, and though she was slightly anemic, she had ten fingers, ten toes, a healthy heart, and a set of obviously functioning lungs. I asked about the anemia—the pediatrician said it was nothing to worry about—and after the pediatrician squirted a bunch of goop in our baby's eyes, she was cleaned and swaddled and placed in my wife's arms.

Just as I'd predicted, photos were taken all day long. But the funny thing is, when people glanced at those same photos later, no one seemed to care how I looked at all.

It's been said that babies are born looking like either Winston Churchill or Mahatma Gandhi, but because the anemia lent a grayish pallor to my daughter's skin, my first thought was that she looked a little bit like Yoda, without the ears of course. A *beautiful* Yoda, mind you, a *breathtaking* Yoda, a Yoda so *miraculous* that when she gripped my finger, my heart nearly burst. My parents arrived a few minutes later, and in my nervousness and excitement, I met them in the hallway and blurted out the first words that came to mind.

"We have a gray baby!"

My mother looked at me as though I'd gone insane while my father dug his finger into his ear as if wondering if the waxy buildup had clouded his ability to hear correctly. Ignoring my comment, they entered the room and saw Vivian cradling our daughter in her arms, her expression serene. My eyes followed theirs, and when I looked upon my wife and daughter, I thought to myself that this baby had to be the single most precious little girl in the history of the world. While I'm sure all new fathers think the same thing about their own children, the simple fact is that there can only be one child who is actually the *most precious*, and part of me marveled that others in the hospital weren't stopping by our room, simply to witness history in the making.

My mom stepped toward the bed, craning her neck to peer even closer.

"Did you decide on a name?" she asked.

"London," my wife answered, without looking up, her attention completely devoted to our child. "We've decided to name her London."

My parents eventually left, then returned later that afternoon. In between, Vivian's parents visited as well. They'd flown in from Alexandria, Virginia, where Vivian had been raised, and while Vivian was thrilled, I immediately felt the tension in the room begin to rise. I'd always sensed that they believed their daughter had *settled* when deciding to marry me, and who knows? If the future was any indication, maybe they were right. Nor did they seem to like my parents, and the feeling was mutual. While the four of them were always cordial, it was nonetheless obvious that they preferred to avoid each other's company.

My older sister, Marge, also came by with her partner, Liz, bearing gifts. Marge and Liz had been together longer than Vivian and I had—they were going on seven years at the time. Not only did I think Liz was a terrific partner for my sister, but I knew that Marge was the greatest older sibling a guy could have. With both my parents working—Dad was a plumber and Mom worked as a receptionist at a dentist's office until her retirement a few years back—Marge had not only served as a substitute parent at times, but as a sibling confidante who helped me wade through the angst of adolescence. Neither Liz nor Marge liked Vivian's parents either, by the way, a feeling that had coalesced at my wedding, when Vivian's parents refused to let Marge and Liz sit together at the main table. Granted, Marge had been in the wedding party and Liz had not—and Liz had opted to wear a tuxedo—but it was the kind of slight that neither of them had been able to forgive, since other couples, all heterosexual, had been allowed the privilege. Frankly, I don't blame Marge or Liz for being upset about it, because I was bothered, too. She and Liz get along better than most of the married couples I know.

While our visitors came and went, I stayed in the room with my wife for the rest of the day, alternately sitting in the rocking chair near the window or on the bed beside her, both of us repeatedly whispering in amazement that *we had a daughter.* I would stare at Vivian and stare at London, knowing with certainty that I belonged with these two and that the three of us would forever be connected. The feeling was overwhelming—like everything else that day—and I found myself speculating what London would look like as a teenager, or what she would dream about, or what she would do with her life. Whenever London cried, Vivian would automatically move her to her breast, and I would witness yet another miracle.

How does London know how to do that? I wondered to myself. *How on earth does she know?*

There is another moment, however, that is all mine, a precious memory and the only one I can still recall with pristine clarity.

It occurred on that first night in the hospital, long after our final visitors had left. Vivian was asleep and I was dozing in the rocking chair when I heard my daughter begin to fuss. I knew that I'd have to wake my wife in a few moments—my breasts didn't have what London needed—but I gently scooped my daughter into my arms. Before that day, I'd never actually held a newborn, and terrified that I might break her, I immediately pulled her close to my body.

I thought that London would begin to cry, and I was ready to hand her to Vivian, but instead, I saw my daughter staring up at me with unfocused eyes. She blinked twice and began to settle, finally closing her eyes again. I inched back to the rocking chair, and for the next twenty minutes, all I could do was marvel at the feelings she induced in me. That I adored her, I already knew; what I hadn't realized was that the thought of life without her seemed suddenly inconceivable, and I remember whispering to her that as her father, I would always be there for her, no matter what the future might bring. As if knowing exactly what I was saying, London pooped and squirmed and then began to cry. In the end, I handed her back to Vivian.

CHAPTER 2

———— ❧ ————

In the Beginning

I told them today," Vivian announced.

It was a little past ten on a Friday night, and for the first time in what seemed like forever, we'd been able to share some alone time. We'd sat on the couch with the television on—harkening back to the pre-London days. As Vivian thumbed through a magazine, I realized how much I'd missed these simple moments.

Later, when we were in the bedroom, Vivian had slipped into her pajamas and crawled into bed. London had been asleep for three hours; at six weeks, she was sleeping almost four hours at a stretch, giving us hope that she might hit five or six hours sooner rather than later. Vivian hadn't had a full night's sleep since the night before the birth, and though she hadn't complained, she looked tired. Beautiful, but definitely tired.

"Told who what?" I asked.

"Rob," she answered, meaning her boss at the media company where she worked. "I officially let him know that after my maternity leave was up, I wouldn't be coming back."

"Oh," I said, feeling the same pang of terror I'd felt when I'd seen the positive pregnancy result. Since that time, I'd tried my best not to think about it. Vivian earned nearly as much as I did, and I think part of me hoped that she'd change her mind, even if the other part also wanted her to stay at home.

"He said the door was always open if I changed my mind," she added. "But I told him that London was not going to be raised by strangers. Otherwise, why have a child in the first place? If you don't want to be there, I mean?"

"You don't have to convince me," I said, doing my best to hide my feelings. "I'm on your side." Well, part of me was, anyway.

"Good. Otherwise, you shouldn't have married me in the first place."

I forced a smile. "You know that means we can't go out to dinner as much and we'll have to cut back on discretionary spending, right?"

"I know."

"And you're okay with not shopping as much?"

"You say it like I waste money. I never do that."

The credit card bills sometimes seemed to indicate otherwise—as did her closet, which bulged with clothes and shoes and bags—but I could hear the irritation in her tone, and the last thing I wanted to do was argue with her. Instead, I rolled toward her, pulling her close, something else on my mind. I nuzzled and kissed her neck, and she exhaled softly.

"Now?"

"It's been a long time."

"And my poor baby feels like he's about to blow up, doesn't he?"

"Frankly, I don't want to risk it."

She laughed, and as I began to unbutton her pajama top, a noise sounded on the baby monitor. In that instant, we both froze—as if London could hear us as well—and waited. Hoped.

Nothing.

Still nothing.

And just when I thought the coast was clear and I let out a breath I didn't even know I'd been holding, the noise from the baby monitor began again, this time at higher volume. With a sigh, I rolled onto my back and Vivian slipped from the bed, as disappointed as I was. By the time London finally calmed—which took a good half hour—Vivian wasn't in the mood for a second attempt and I didn't want to push her.

In the morning, Vivian and I had more luck. So much luck, in fact, that I cheerfully volunteered to take care of London when she woke so that Vivian could go back to sleep and get some much-needed rest. London, however, must have been just as tired as Vivian; it wasn't until I'd finished my second cup of coffee that I heard various noises but no cries emanating from the baby monitor.

In her room, the mobile above the crib was rotating, and when I looked down at London, I saw a wiggly baby, full of energy, her legs shooting like pistons. I couldn't help but smile, and recognizing me, she suddenly smiled as well.

It wasn't gas; it wasn't a reflexive tic. This was a real smile, as true as the sunrise, and when she emitted an unexpected giggle, the already brilliant start to my day was suddenly a thousand times even better.

It's funny what life can teach a person, and the main thing I've learned is this: I'm not a wise man.

I'm not unintelligent, mind you. Or at least I don't like to think so. But wisdom means more than being intelligent, because it encompasses understanding, empathy, experience, inner peace, and intuition, and in retrospect, I obviously lack many of these traits.

Here's what else I've learned: age doesn't guarantee wisdom, any more than age guarantees intelligence. I know that's not a popular notion—don't we frequently regard our elders as wise partially because they're gray and wrinkled?—but lately I've come to believe that some people are born with the capacity to become wise while others aren't, and in some people, wisdom seems to be evident even at a young age.

My sister, Marge, for instance. She's wise, and she's only six years older than I am. Frankly, she's been wise as long as I've known her. My mom and dad are wise, too, and I've been thinking about it a lot these days because it's become clear to me that even though wisdom runs in the family, it bypassed me entirely.

If I were wise, after all, I would have listened to Marge ten years ago, when she drove me out to the cemetery where our grandparents were buried and asked me whether I was absolutely sure whether Vivian was right for me and if I really knew what I might be getting into.

If I were wise, I would have listened to my father when he asked me whether I was sure I should strike out on my own and start my own advertising company, when I was thirty-five years old.

If I were wise, I would have listened to my mom when she told me to spend as much time with London as I could, since children grow up so fast, and you can never get those years back.

But like I said, I'm not a wise man. And because of that, my life pretty much went into a tailspin, and even now, I wonder if I'll ever recover.

Where does one begin when trying to make sense of a story that makes little sense at all? At the beginning? And where is the beginning?

Who knows?

So let's start with this. When I was child, I grew up believing that I'd feel like an adult by the time I was eighteen, and I was right. At eighteen, I was already making plans. My family had lived paycheck to paycheck, and I had no intention of doing the same. I had dreams of starting my own business, of being my own boss, even if I wasn't sure what I was actually going to do. Figuring that college would help steer me in the proper direction, I went to NC State but gradually came to the realization that I'd been fooling myself. The longer I was there, the younger I seemed to feel, and by the time I collected my degree, I couldn't shake the feeling that I was pretty much the same guy I'd been in high school.

Nor had college helped me decide on the kind of business I'd start. I had little in the way of real-world experience and even less capital, so deferring the idea of my own business, I took a job in advertising for a man named Jesse Peters. I wore suits to the office and worked a ton of hours, and yet, more often than not, I still felt *younger* than my actual age might indicate. On weekends, I'd frequent the same bars I did in college, and I imagined that I could start over as a freshman, fitting right in with whatever fraternity I happened to join. Over the next few years there would be even more changes; I'd get married and purchase a house and drive a hybrid, but even then I didn't necessarily always feel like the adult version of me. Peters, after all, had essentially taken the place of my parents—like my parents, he could tell me what to do *or else*—which made it seem as though I was still *pretending.* In quiet moments, I'd sometimes try to convince myself: *Okay, it's official. I'm now a grown-up.*

That realization came, of course, after London was born and Vivian quit her job. I was thirty years old, destined to remain an employee and be told what to do forever. While setting aside my dream was hard, it also fostered my maturity. The pressure I felt to provide for my family over the next few years required sacrifice on a scale that even I hadn't expected, and if that isn't being a grown-up, I don't know what is. After finishing at the agency—on days when I actually made it home at a reasonable hour—I'd walk through the door and hear London call out "Daddy!" and always wish that I could spend more time with her. She'd come running and I'd crouch to let her jump in my arms. She'd start talking a mile a minute about whatever she'd been doing, whether it was coloring or feeding the fish, or the bow that Mommy had put in her hair, and I'd remind myself that all the sacrifices had been worth it, if only because of the wonderful little girl I held in my arms.

I waded through my early thirties thinking I'd finally figured it all out. In the hectic rush of life, it was easy to convince myself that the important things—my wife and daughter, my job, my family—were going okay, even if I couldn't be my own boss. In rare moments when I imagined a future, I would find myself picturing a life that wasn't all that different than the one I was currently leading, and that was okay, too. On the surface, things seemed to be running rather smoothly, and looking back, that should have been a warning sign. Trust me when I say that I had *absolutely no idea* that within a couple of years—I'm thirty-seven now—I'd wake in the mornings feeling like one of those immigrants on Ellis Island who'd arrived in America with nothing in their possession but the clothes on their back, not speaking the language, and wondering, *What am I going to do now?*

When, exactly, did it all begin to go wrong? If you ask Marge, the answer is obvious: "It started going downhill as soon as you met Vivian," she's told me more than once. Of course, being Marge, she would automatically correct herself. "I take that back," she would add. "It started way before that, when you were still in grade school and hung that poster on your wall, the one with the girl in the skimpy bikini with the big bahoonas. I always liked that poster, by the way, but it warped your thinking." Then, after further consideration, she would shake her head, speculating, "Now that I think about it, you were always kind of screwed up, and coming from the person who's always been regarded as the family screwup, that's saying something. Maybe your real problem is that you've always been too damn nice for your own good. Being *too nice* always ends up biting you in the ass."

And that's the thing. When you start trying to figure out what went wrong—or, more specifically, where *you* went wrong—it's a bit like peeling an onion. There's always another layer, another mistake in the past or a painful memory that stands out, which then leads one back even further in time, and then even further, in search of the *ultimate truth*. All I really know is that I've reached the point where I've stopped caring where or when or why my life suddenly began to feel like I'd made a series of massive wrong turns: the only thing that really matters now is learning enough to avoid making the same mistakes again.

To understand why I feel the way I do, it's important to understand me. Which isn't easy, by the way. I've been me for more than a third of a century, and half the time, I still don't understand myself. So let me start with this. As I've grown older, I've come to believe that there are two types of men in the world: the marrying type, and the bachelor type. The marrying type is the kind of guy who pretty much sizes up every girl he dates, assessing whether or not she could be The One. It's the reason that women in their thirties and forties often say things like *All the good men are taken.* By that, women mean guys who are ready, willing, and able to commit to being part of a couple.

I've always been the marrying type. And I'm good with that. Lots of men—including my father, with whom I share virtually nothing else in common—are the marrying type, and their lives are better for it. To me, being part of a couple—being committed—just feels *right.* For whatever reason, I've always been more comfortable in the presence of women than men, even in friendship, and spending time with one woman *who also happened to be madly in love with me* struck me as the best of all possible worlds.

And it can be, I suppose. But that's where things get a bit trickier, because not all marrying types are the same. There are subgroups within the marrying types, guys who may also consider themselves to be *romantic,* for instance. Sounds nice, right? The kind of guy that most women insist they want? It probably is, and I must admit that I'm a card-carrying member of this particular subgroup. In rare instances, however, this particular subtype is also wired to be a *people pleaser,* and these three traits are, according to Marge, the root of all my problems. Because when taken together, these three things made me believe that anything was possible . . . that with just a bit more effort—if only I tried a little harder—then everything would turn out fine.

Marge is probably right, but lately I've begun to wonder how that happened. What was it that made me that way? Was it simply my nature? Was I influenced by family dynamics? Or did I simply watch too many romantic movies at an impressionable age? Or all of the above?

I have no idea, but I state without hesitation that the *watching too many romantic movies* thing was entirely Marge's fault. She loved the classics, like *An Affair to Remember* and *Casablanca*, but *Ghost* and *Dirty Dancing* were up there, too, and we must have watched *Pretty Woman* at least twenty times. That movie was her all-time favorite. What I didn't know, of course, was that Marge and I enjoyed watching it because we both had massive crushes on Julia Roberts at the time, but that's beside the point. The film will probably live on forever because it *works*. The characters played by Richard Gere and Julia Roberts had...*chemistry*. They talked. They learned to trust each other, despite the odds. They fell in love. And how can one possibly forget the scene in which Richard Gere is waiting for Julia—he's planning to take her to the opera—and she emerges wearing a gown that utterly transforms her? The audience sees Richard's awestruck expression, and he eventually opens a velvet box, which holds the diamond necklace Julia will also be wearing that evening. As Julia reaches for it, Richard snaps the lid closed, and Julia's sudden joyful surprise...

It was all there, really, in just those few scenes. The romance, I mean—trust, anticipation, and joy combined with opera, dressing up, and jewelry all led to *love*. In my nine-year-old brain, it just clicked: a how-to manual of sorts to impress a girl. All I really had to do was remember that girls had to *like* the guy first and that romantic gestures would then lead to *love*. In the end, another romantic in the real world was created. I've been one ever since.

In sixth grade—after seeing *Pretty Woman* and the first year I started having serious crushes on the opposite sex—a new girl joined my class, Melissa Anderson. She'd moved from Minnesota during the previous summer, and with blond hair and blue eyes, she shared the look of her Swedish ancestors. When I saw her on the first day of school, I'm pretty sure I went slack-jawed, and I wasn't the only one. Every guy was mesmerized. There was little doubt in my mind that Melissa Anderson was far and away the prettiest girl who'd ever set foot in Mrs. Hartman's class at Arthur E. Edmonds elementary school, or any other class in any other school for that matter.

Every boy in class had a crush her at one point or another that year, including me, but the difference was that I knew exactly what to do while they did not. I was planning to win her over—what is romance for, if not exactly that?—and though I wasn't Richard Gere with private jets and diamond necklaces, I did have a bicycle and I had learned how to macramé bracelets, complete with wooden beads. Those, however, would come later. First—just like Richard and Julia—we had to get to *like* each other. I began to find reasons to sit at the same table with her at lunch. While she talked, I listened and asked questions, lots of them over the next few weeks, and when she finally told me that she thought I was nice, I knew it was time to take the next step. I wrote her a poem—about her life in Minnesota and how pretty she was—and I slipped it to her on the bus one afternoon, along with a flower. I took my seat, knowing exactly what would happen: She would realize I was different, and with that would come an even greater epiphany; she'd turn toward me and meet my gaze before offering a smile, and when we got off the bus, she'd reach for my hand and ask me to walk her home.

Except it didn't work out that way. Instead of reading the poem, she gabbed with her friend April the whole way home, and the following day, she sat next to Tommy Harmon at lunch and didn't talk to me at all. Nor did she talk to me the following day, or the day after that. When Marge found me sulking in my bedroom later, she told me that I was trying too hard and that I should just be myself.

"But that's who I am."

"Then you'd better think twice about that," Marge snorted, "because it makes you seem desperate."

Problem was, I didn't think twice. Did Richard Gere think twice? He clearly knew more than my sister, and again, here's where wisdom and I were obviously traveling in opposite directions down the highway. Because *Pretty Woman* was a movie and I was living in the real world, the pattern I established with Melissa Anderson continued, with variations, until it eventually became a habit I couldn't break. I became the king of romantic gestures—flowers, notes, cards, and the like—and in college, I was even the "secret admirer" to a girl I happened to fancy. I opened doors and paid for dates, and I listened whenever a girl wanted to talk, even if it was about how much she still loved her ex-boyfriend. Most girls sincerely liked me. I mean that. To them, I was a *friend*, the kind of guy who'd get invited to hang out with a group of girlfriends whenever they went out, but I seldom succeeded in landing the girl I'd set my sights on. I can't tell you how many times I've heard, *"You're the nicest guy I know, and I'm sure you'll meet someone special. I have two or three friends I could probably set you up with . . ."*

It wasn't easy being the guy who was *perfect for someone else*. It often left me brokenhearted, but in my obstinacy, I remained the king of romantic gestures whenever someone captured my imagination. And through it all, I tried to understand why women told me that they wanted certain traits—romance and kindness, interest and the ability to listen—while not seeming to appreciate it when they were actually offered to them.

I wasn't altogether unlucky in love, of course. In high school, I had a girlfriend named Angela for most of my sophomore year; in college, Rachel and I were together most of my junior year. And during the summer after graduation from college, less than a week after I'd taken a job with the Peters Group, I met a woman named Emily, and that's where things got interesting.

Emily still lives in the area, and over the years, I'd see her out and about, either alone or with her husband and their son. She was the first woman I ever loved, and I've come to realize that *romance* and *nostalgia* are often intertwined. I still often miss her. Emily was sweet and kind, quick to laugh, intelligent and with a passion for painting, a woman who might have been perfect for me. My parents loved her; Marge loved her. When we were together, we were comfortable even when silent. Our relationship was easy and relaxed; more than lovers, we were friends. We trusted each other and could talk about anything. She delighted in the notes I'd place under her pillow or the flowers I'd have delivered to her workplace for no reason whatsoever. Emily loved me as much as she loved romantic gestures, and after dating her for a little more than a year, I made plans to propose, even putting a deposit down on an engagement ring.

And then, I screwed it up. Don't ask me why. I could blame the booze that night—I'd been drinking with friends at a bar— or maybe there was some part of me that was afraid that I was still too young to get tied down. For whatever reason, I struck up a conversation with a woman named Carly. She was beautiful and she knew how to flirt and she'd recently broken up with a long-term boyfriend. One drink led to another, which led to more flirting, and we eventually ended up in bed together. In the morning, Carly made it clear that what had happened was simply a fling, with no strings attached, and though she kissed me goodbye, she didn't bother giving me her phone number.

There are a couple of very simple Guy Rules in this sort of situation, and Rule Number One goes like this: *Never ever tell.* And if your sweetheart ever suspects anything and asks directly, go immediately to Rule Number Two: *Deny, deny, deny.*

All guys know these rules, but the thing was, I also felt guilty. Horribly guilty. I was ashamed every time I looked at Emily, and even after a month, I couldn't put the experience behind me, nor could I seem to forgive myself. Keeping it secret seemed inconceivable; I couldn't imagine building a future with Emily knowing it was constructed, at least in part, on a lie. I talked to Marge about it, and Marge was, as always, helpful in that sisterly way of hers.

"Keep your stupid trap shut, you dimwit. You made a mistake—a whopper—and you should feel guilty. That's a crappy thing you did. But if you're never going to do it again, then don't hurt Emily's feelings, too. Something like this will crush her."

I knew Marge was right, and yet...

I wanted Emily's forgiveness, because I wasn't sure I could forgive myself without it, and so in the end, I went to Emily and said the words that even now, I wish I could take back.

"There's something I have to tell you," I began, and proceeded to spill everything.

If forgiveness was the goal, it didn't work. If trying to build a long-term relationship on a foundation of truth was another goal, that didn't work either. Through angry tears, she told me to get out and that she needed some time to think.

I left her alone for a week, waiting for her to call while moping around my apartment, but the phone never rang. The following week, I left two messages—and apologized again both times—but she still wouldn't call. It wasn't until the following week that we finally had lunch, but it was strained, and when she left the restaurant, she told me not to walk her to her car. The writing was on the wall, and a week after that, she left a message saying it was over for good. A little while later, I learned through the grapevine that she'd gone on a date with someone from work and had plans to go out with him again. I don't know whatever happened to him, but a few years later, she met the guy she eventually did marry. It was the year before I married Vivian, and I can remember feeling glum for a few weeks.

The passage of time has lessened my guilt—time always does—and I try to console myself with the idea that at least for her, my indiscretion was a blessing in disguise. I heard from a friend of a friend a couple of years after our breakup that she'd married an Australian guy, and in those rare moments I caught a glimpse of her, it looked as though life was treating her well. I'd tell myself that I was happy for her. Emily, more than anyone, deserved a wonderful life, and Marge feels exactly the same way. Even after I'd married Vivian, my sister would sometimes turn to me in quiet moments and say, "That Emily sure was something. You really messed that up, didn't you?"

I was born in Charlotte, North Carolina, and aside from a single year in another city, I've lived there all my life. Even now, it strikes me as almost impossible that Vivian and I met in the place where we did, or even that we ever met at all. After all, she, like me, was from the south; like mine, her job kept required long hours, and she seldom went out. What are the odds, then, that I'd meet Vivian at a cocktail party in Manhattan?

At the time, I was working at the agency's satellite office in midtown, which probably sounds like a bigger deal than it really was. Jesse Peters was of the opinion that pretty much anyone who showed promise in the Charlotte office had to serve at least a little time up north, if only because a number of our clients are banks, and every bank has a major presence in New York City. You've probably seen some of the commercials I've worked on; I like to think of them as thoughtful and serious, project-ing the soul of integrity. The first of those commercials, by the way, was conceived while I was living in a small studio on West 77th, between Columbus and Amsterdam, and trying to figure out whether my ATM accurately reflected my checking account, which showed a balance with just enough funds to purchase a meal deal at a nearby fast food place.

On a Saturday night in May, a CEO of the one of the banks who *loved my vision* was hosting a charity event to benefit MoMA. The CEO was seriously into art—something I knew nothing about—and even though it was an exclusive, black-tie event, I hadn't wanted to attend. But his bank was a client and Peters was my *do-what-I-tell-you-or-else* boss, so what could I do?

I remember almost nothing about the first half hour, other

than that I clearly didn't belong. Well over half the people in attendance were old enough to be my grandparents, and practically everyone was in a different stratosphere when it came to our respective levels of wealth. At one point, I found myself listening as two gray-haired gentlemen debated the merits of the G-IV when compared to the Falcon 2000. It took me a while to figure out that they were comparing their private jets.

When I turned away from the conversation, I saw on the other side of the room a familiar-looking man who was, I soon discovered, Vivian's boss. I recognized him from late night television, and Vivian would later tell me that he considered himself an art collector. She'd wrinkled her nose when she said it, implying that he had money but no taste, which didn't surprise me at all. Despite famous guests, his show's trademark humor was best described as low-brow.

Vivian was standing behind him, hidden from my line of sight at first. Like everyone else in the room, I couldn't help watching the talk show host, even though I didn't particularly like him. A minute or so later, he took a few steps forward to greet someone, and all at once I saw her. I could only stare, suddenly wondering whether she was the reason that everyone had been gazing in their direction. Her dark hair, flawless skin, and cheekbones that supermodels dream about made me sure she was the most beautiful woman I'd ever seen.

At first I thought she was his date, but the longer I watched, the more confident I was that they weren't *together*, that she instead worked for him in some capacity. Nor was she wearing a ring, another good sign...but really, what chance did I have?

Yet the romantic within me was undeterred, and when she went to the bar to get a cocktail, I sidled up to the bar as well. Up close, she was even more gorgeous, and when she happened to turn in my direction, her sultry eyes drew me in.

"It's you," I said.

"Excuse me?"

"The one the Disney artists think about when they draw the eyes of their princesses."

Not great, I'll admit. Ham-handed, maybe even cheesy, and in the awkward pause that ensued, I knew I'd blown it. But here's the thing: she laughed.

"Now there's a pickup line I've never heard before."

"It wouldn't work on just anyone," I said. I offered my hand and smiled. "I'm Russell Green."

She hesitated before taking my hand, but her eyes still showed amusement.

"I'm Vivian Hamilton," she said, and I almost gasped.

Her name was *Vivian.*

Just like Julia Roberts's character in *Pretty Woman.*

How does one actually know when another is *right* for you? What kind of signals does that entail? To meet a person and think, *this is the one with whom I want to spend the rest of my life.* For example, how could Emily seem right, and Vivian seem right, when they were as different as night and day? When the relationships were as different as night and day?

I don't know, but when I think about Vivian, it's still easy to remember the heady thrill of our first few evenings together. While Emily and I were warm and comfortable, Vivian and I burned hot, almost from the very beginning. Every interaction, every conversation seemed to amplify my growing belief that we were fated for one another.

As the marrying type, I began to fantasize about the paths our life together would take, our passionate connection burning forever. Within a couple of months, I was certain I wanted Vivian to be my wife, even if I didn't say as much. Vivian took longer to feel the same way about me, but by the time we'd been seeing each other six months, Vivian and I were a *serious item*, testing the waters on how each felt about God, money, politics, families, neighborhoods, kids, and our core values. More often than not, we were in agreement. Taking a cue from yet another romantic movie, the week before I moved back to Charlotte, I proposed on the viewing deck of the Empire State Building.

I *thought* I knew what I was getting when I dropped to one knee. But looking back, Vivian *knew* with certainty—not only that I was the kind of man she wanted, but *needed*.

And then what, you may wonder? After we made our vows?

Like every married couple, we had our ups and downs, our challenges and opportunities, successes and failures. When all the dust had settled, I came to realize that marriage, at least in theory, is wonderful.

In practice, though, I think a more accurate word is *complicated*.

Marriage, after all, is never quite what one imagines it will be, and even now I'm not exactly sure what I expected. Part of me—the romantic part—no doubt imagined the entire venture as an extended commercial for Hallmark cards with roses and candles and everything in soft focus, a dimension in which love and trust could surmount any challenge. The more practical side of me knew that remaining a couple over the long term was work, and took effort on both sides. It requires commitment and compromise, communication and cooperation, especially as life tends to throw curveballs, often when we least expect them. Ideally, the curveball slides past the couple with little damage; at other times, facing those pitches together makes the couple more committed to each other.

But sometimes, the curveballs end up smacking us in the chest and close to the heart, leaving bruises that never seem to heal.

Use the code below to get a select Nicholas Sparks
audiobook FREE at Downpour.com

20WALMART%SPARKS16

1) Go to http://www.downpour.com/SparksWalmartOffer
and browse available titles
2) Add the title to your cart
3) Enter code into promo code box and click "Apply"
4) Click the "Checkout" button to proceed
5) Create a free Downpour.com account or log in into
an existing account
6) Click the "Place Order" button to complete
the checkout process

The title can now be downloaded from your Library! Enjoy!

Customer care: 1-855-369-6768 | Expires: 12/31/2016

All of Nicholas Sparks's beloved stories are available as
audiobooks from Hachette Audio, where books and
music are sold, on CD and as digital downloads.

hachette
AUDIO